Praise for **Blackfly Season**

"Blunt's plot grabs you by the throat and won't let go until the suspense is played out on the final page. Excellent."
—*Western Daily Press* (UK)

"Stunning characterizations of the biker gangs and other criminals who move drugs in this region of fierce winters and cruel springs."
—*The New York Times*

"Blunt has been successful in creating a character, Cardinal, who should sustain our interest and sympathies for many books to come."
—*Hamilton Spectator*

"Cardinal fans, and those who haven't experienced him before, won't be disappointed by the veteran detective's latest outing, which has enough twists and turns to keep them guessing."
—*The Halifax Chronicle-Herald*

"His characters, even to the lonely guy sitting by himself at the end of the bar, are wonderfully realistic; his pacing never flags; his knowledge of police procedure is accurate without being show-offy; and he leaves the reader not so much with a story as with a glimpse into a perfectly realized world. First-rate."
—*Booklist* (starred review)

"Blunt has produced another well-structured story with sharply drawn characters."
—*The Sunday Telegraph* (UK)

"The pulsing, tightly plotted narrative again shows why Blunt should be considered among the new practitioners of crime drama's elite."
—*Publishers Weekly*

"Blunt deftly weaves various plotlines together and tells a chilling story set in a beautiful but primitive environment."
—*London Free Press*

Blackfly

Season

Blackfly Season

Giles Blunt

Seal Books

Seal Books and colophon are trademarks of
Random House of Canada Limited.

BLACKFLY SEASON
Seal Books/published by arrangement with
Random House Canada
Random House Canada edition published 2005
Seal Books edition published October 2006

ISBN-13: 978-0-7704-2933-1
ISBN-10: 0-7704-2933-5

Cover image: Greg Guirard / Getty Images
Cover design: Leah Springate

Seal Books are published by Random House of Canada Limited.
"Seal Books" and the portrayal of a seal are the property of
Random House of Canada Limited.

Visit Random House of Canada Limited's website:
www.randomhouse.ca

PRINTED AND BOUND IN THE USA

OPM 10 9 8 7 6 5 4 3 2 1

To Janna

1

ANYBODY WHO HAS SPENT any length of time in Algonquin Bay will tell you there are plenty of good reasons to live somewhere else. There is the distance from civilization, by which Canadians mean Toronto, 250 miles south. There is the gradual decay of the once-charming downtown, victim to the twin scourges of suburban malls and an unlucky series of fires. And, of course, there are the winters, which are ferocious, snowy and long. It's not unusual for winter to extend its bone-numbing grip into April, and the last snowfall often occurs in May.

Then there are the blackflies. Every year, following an all-too-brief patch of spring weather, blackflies burst from the beds of northern Ontario's numberless rivers and streams to feast on the blood of birds, livestock and the citizens of Algonquin Bay. They're well equipped for it, too. The blackfly may be less than a quarter-inch long, but up close it resembles an attack helicopter, fitted with a sucker at one end and a nasty hook at the other. Even one of these creatures can be a misery. Caught in a swarm, a person can very rapidly go mad.

The World Tavern may not have looked too crazy on this particular Friday, but Blaine Styles, the bartender, knew there would be problems. Blackfly season just doesn't bring out the best in people—those that drink, anyway. Blaine wasn't a hundred percent sure which quarter the trouble would come from, but he had his candidates.

For one, there was the trio of dorks at the bar—a guy named Regis and his two friends in baseball caps, Bob and Tony. They were drinking quietly, but they had flirted a little too long with Darla, the waitress, and there was a restlessness about them that didn't bode well for later. For another, there was the table at the back by the map of Africa. They'd been drinking Molson pretty steadily for a couple of hours now. Quiet, but steady. And then there was the girl, a redhead Blaine had never seen before who kept moving from table to table in a way that he found— professionally speaking—disturbing.

A Labatt Blue bottle flew across the room and hit the map of Canada just above Newfoundland. Blaine shot from behind the bar and waltzed the drunk who'd thrown it out the door before he could even protest. It bothered Blaine that he hadn't even seen this one coming. The jerk had been sitting with a couple of guys in leather jackets under France, and hadn't raised even a blip on the bartender's radar. The World Tavern, oldest and least respectable gin joint in Algonquin Bay, could get pretty hairy on a Friday night, especially in blackfly season, and Blaine preferred to set the limits early.

He went back behind the bar and poured a couple of pitchers for the table over by the map of Africa—getting a little louder, he noticed. Then there was an order for six continentals and a couple of frozen margaritas that kept him hopping. After that there was a slack period, and he rested his foot on a beer case, easing his back while he washed a few glasses.

There weren't too many regulars tonight; he was glad about that. Television shows would have you believe that the regulars in a bar are eccentrics with hearts of gold, but Blaine found they were mostly just hopeless dipwads with serious issues around self-esteem. The stained, shellacked maps on the walls of the World Tavern were the closest these people would ever get to leaving Algonquin Bay.

Jerry Commanda was sitting at the end of the bar nursing his usual Diet Coke with a squeeze of lemon and reading *Maclean's*. A bit of a mystery, Jerry. On the whole, Blaine liked him, despite his being a regular—respected him, anyway—even if he was an awful tipper.

Jerry used to be a serious drinker—not a complete alky, but a serious drinker. This was back when he was in high school, maybe into his early twenties. But then something had sobered him up and he'd never touched alcohol again. Didn't set foot in the World or any other bar for five, six years after that. Then, a few years ago, he'd started coming in on Friday nights, and he'd always park his skinny butt at the end of the bar. You could see everything that was going on from there.

Blaine had once asked Jerry how he'd kicked the bottle, if he'd gone the twelve-step route.

"Couldn't stand twelve-step," Jerry had said. "Couldn't stand the meetings. Everyone saying they're powerless, asking God to get them out of this pickle." Jerry used words like that now and again, even though he was only about forty. Old-fashioned words like *pickle* or *fellow* or *cantankerous.* "But it turned out to be pretty easy to quit alcohol, once I figured out what I had to do was quit thinking, not drinking."

"No one can quit thinking," Blaine had said. "Thinking's like breathing. Or sweating. It's just something you do."

Jerry then launched into some weird psychological bushwah. Said it might be true you couldn't stop the thoughts from coming, but you could change what you did with them. The secret was being able to sidestep them. Blaine remembered the words exactly because Jerry was a four-time Ontario kick-boxing champion, and when he'd said *sidestep* he'd made a nifty little manoeuvre that looked kind of, well, disciplined.

So Jerry Commanda had learned to sidestep his thoughts, and the result was him parking himself at the end of the bar every Friday night for an hour or so, with his Diet Coke and his squeeze of lemon. Blaine figured it was partly to deter some of the young guys from the reserve from drinking too much. Pretty hard for them to cut loose with the reserve's best-known cop sitting at the bar, reading a magazine and sipping his Coke. Some of them, minute they saw him, just did a 180 and walked out.

Blaine swept his wary bartender's gaze over his domain. The Africa table was definitely getting boisterous. Boisterous was okay, but it was just one level down from obnoxious. Blaine cocked his head to one side, listening for warning notes—the gruff challenge, the outraged cry that was inevitably followed by the scraping of a chair. Except for the bottle tosser, it looked to be a peaceful night. The bottle tosser, and the girl.

Blaine squinted into the far corner beyond the jukebox. A flash of red. She had masses of red curls that bounced this way and that every time she turned her head, catching the light. She was all in blue denim—good jeans, short nipped jacket—cute, but they looked like they'd been slept in. Why was she going table to table? That was the third table she'd sat at in the last hour and a half. Two women and two men, postal workers partying later than usual, and it was clear the two women didn't like this kid invading their table. The guys didn't seem to mind one bit.

"Three Blue, one Creemore, one vodka tonic."

Blaine scooped four bottles out of the ice and set them on Darla's tray.

"What's up with the redhead, Darla? What's she drinking?"

"Nothing, far as I can tell. Last table ordered a glass to share their pitcher with her, but she didn't finish it."

Blaine poured a shot of vodka and put it on her tray. Darla filled the glass with tonic from the soda gun.

"Is she high? Why's she hopping tables like that?"

"I don't know, Blaine. Maybe she's going into business for herself." Darla hoisted her tray and headed out into the zoo, as she called it.

"Barkeep!"

Blaine attended to the trio at the bar. The guy named Regis was an old high-school acquaintance, came in maybe twice a year. His friends in the baseball caps were new. Anyone calls you *barkeep*, you know they're going to end up being a burden one way or another.

"Hey, Blaine," Regis said. "When are you gonna tell us what happened to your face, guy?"

"Yeah," one of the baseball caps said. "You look Chinese, man."

"Went canoeing Sunday. Blackflies were out of control."

"Fly musta been the size of a dog, man. You look like a sumo wrestler."

People had been telling him he looked Chinese all week. Blackflies were always a problem this time of year, but Blaine had never seen them like this. Millions of them swarming in huge black clouds. He'd taken the usual measures—wore the repellent, wore a hat, kept his pants tucked into his socks—but the flies were so thick you couldn't even breathe without inhaling them. Little mothers had fallen totally in love with him, and bit all around his face. By Monday morning his eyes were swollen shut, couldn't see a thing.

He rang up the three Molsons. When he turned around again, the redhead was there.

"Hello," she said, climbing onto a stool.

"What can I get you?"

"Just some water would be nice. I don't seem to take to beer."

Blaine poured her a glass of ice water and set it down on a napkin.

"You sure are a big man, aren't you?"

"Big enough."

Blaine moved down the bar a little and stacked some glasses.

"You seem nice."

Blaine laughed. The redhead looked to be in her mid-twenties, still with a lot of freckles. She had the thickest, curliest hair he had ever seen. Didn't take care of herself any too well, though. Like Blaine, she had a lot of black-fly bites, and there were bits of leaves stuck in her hair.

"What's your name?" she said.

"Blaine."

"Blaine? That's a nice name."

"If you say so. What's yours?"

"I don't actually know. Isn't that amazing?"

Blaine felt an odd turning sensation in his stomach. The girl didn't look high; her manner was calm and pleasant. She slid off the stool and went over to Regis and his baseball-cap buddies.

"You guys look nice."

"Well, hey there," Regis said. "You don't look too bad yourself. Can we buy you a drink?"

"No, that's okay. I'm not thirsty."

"Barkeep! A Molson for the young lady here."

"Can't do that," Blaine said. "She said she didn't want one."

"Thanks a lot, Blaine. I love you too." Regis reached over the bar and grabbed one of the glasses drying on the rack. He poured beer into it and handed it to the redhead.

"Thank you. You're very nice." She took a sip and made a face.

Blaine brought her glass of water down the bar and set it in front of her.

"Oh, thanks. That's nice of you."

Nice, nice, everything's nice. Honey, have you got a lot to learn.

"I'm Regis. This is Bob, and that's Tony. What's your name?"

"I don't know it at the moment."

They laughed.

"That's fine," Regis said. "You don't have to tell us."

"We'll just call you Red," the one called Tony said.

"We'll just call you Anonymous," the one called Bob said.

"Anonymous Sex," Regis said, and they all laughed. "Like *Tyrannosaurus rex*."

He fingered her denim jacket.

"This is cute."

"Yes, I like it."

The one called Tony put his arm around her shoulder and ran a hand through her hair. He pulled out a piece of leaf.

"Man, you have got the most amazing hair I've ever seen. Leafy, but amazing."

"You guys are so friendly."

"You're pretty friendly yourself," Regis said. "Got some nasty bites on you, but I can fix that." He leaned forward and kissed her cheek.

The girl smiled and rubbed her face.

Blaine moved closer.

"Miss, don't you think it's time you went home?"

"Hey, mind your own business, Blaine." Regis smacked the bar, upsetting a dish of peanuts. "She's not drunk, she's just having a good time."

"No, you're having a good time. She doesn't know what

kind of time she's having."

The girl smiled, not looking at either of them.

"Two Creemore, three Blue, one Export!"

Blaine moved down the bar to take care of Darla. When he came back, the redhead was on Regis's lap.

"Honey, I think we're going to have to go for a ride," Regis said.

"You guys are funny."

Bob was feeling her hair now. "I think you should come for a ride with us," he said. "Get to know us better."

Regis's hand crept up her denim jacket. The girl smiled and started humming something. Regis's hand went inside the jacket.

"Leave her alone."

Regis leaned back from the girl and peered down the bar at Jerry Commanda.

"What did you say?"

"I said leave her alone."

"Why don't you mind your own business, Chingachgook?"

Jerry got down off his stool and came round the bar.

"Do you know your name?" he said to the girl.

"Hey, Tonto," Regis said. "Back off."

"Shut up. Do you know your name?"

"I don't," the girl said. "Not at the moment."

"Do you know what day it is?"

"Um, no."

Regis shifted her off his lap and stood up. "I think you and me have something to discuss outside."

Jerry ignored him. "Do you know where you are?" he said to the girl.

"Somebody told me a while ago, but I forget."

"Did you hear me?" Regis said. "I can understand why you might not want to go back to your squaw, but that doesn't give you the right to—"

Jerry didn't look at him. He just reached into his jacket, pulled out his shield and held it an inch from the guy's nose.

"Oh, hey, I'm sorry, man. I didn't realize."

"Do you have any ID?" Jerry said to the girl. "A wallet? Credit card? Something with your name on it?"

"No, I don't have anything like that."

Regis tapped Jerry on the shoulder, shifting into I'm-the-nicest-guy-in-the-world mode. "No hard feelings, okay? Do you think she's all right? I'm kinda worried about her."

"Would you come with me, miss? I want to take you someplace safe."

The girl shrugged. "Okay. Sure."

Blaine watched Regis follow them to the exit, apologizing the whole way. It was the kind of sight that did a bartender's heart good.

—

In the car, Jerry asked where she was from.

"I don't know. This is a nice car you have here."

"Where have you been staying?"

"Staying?"

"Yeah. I'm guessing you're from out of town. Who are you staying with?"

"I don't know. That's a nice building, is that a school?"

They passed École Secondaire Algonquin and headed uphill. Jerry made a left on McGowan. "You have a lot of blackfly bites on you. Were you out in the woods?"

"Is that what these are?" Her left hand rose absently and rubbed at the red blotches along her hairline. "They're itchy. I have them all over my ankles, too. They kind of hurt."

"Were you out in the woods?"

"Yes. This morning. I woke up there."

"You slept outside? Is that why you have leaves in your hair?"

"Leaves?" Again, the pale, freckled hand rose to her curls. No wedding ring, Jerry noticed.

"Red, do me a favour, will you? Could you just check your pockets and see if you have any ID on you?"

She patted her pockets, felt inside. From her jeans, she pulled out some coins and a pair of nail clippers. She offered Jerry a LifeSaver, which he declined.

"That's all I have," she said.

"No keys?"

"No keys."

Someone must have removed them, Jerry was pretty sure. People don't tend to go out with no keys. He parked in a spot near the emergency entrance to City Hospital. The lights of Algonquin and Main curved away from the hill below them.

"You know, I don't think I need a hospital. They're only insect bites."

"Let's just see if we can find out where you left your memory, okay?"

"Okay. You look nice. Are you an Indian?"

"Yes. You?"

"I'm not sure. I don't think so."

Her response was so solemn Jerry laughed. He'd never seen anyone who looked less Indian.

In the ER, a young man behind the counter handed him a clipboard with a form on it.

"We're not going to be able to answer any of these questions," Jerry said. "Young lady's got no ID and no memory."

The young man didn't blink, as if amnesia cases walked in every night. "Just fill it out for Jane Doe, and approximate the rest of the stuff. The triage nurse will be with you shortly."

The girl sat humming tunelessly while they waited. Jerry filled out the form, writing "unknown" over and over again. The room started to get busier. John Cardinal came in with a middle-aged man who looked like an assault victim. He nodded to Jerry. It was not unusual to bump into another cop in emerg; on a Friday night, you pretty much expected it. The triage nurse came over and talked to them for about three minutes, just long enough to order up a chem screen and put the girl on priority. Eventually, Dr. Michael Fortis came out of an examining room and conferred with the nurse. Jerry went over; he'd worked with Fortis a lot.

"Pretty slow for a Friday," Jerry said. "You sending them all to St. Francis?"

"You should have seen us an hour ago. We had two separate MVAs, cars got in arguments with moose up on Highway 11. The one in the four-by-four wasn't bad, but the guy in the Miata will be lucky if he ever walks again. Always happens this time of year. Blackflies drive the moose out of the woods, and *bam!*"

"I got something a little more unusual for you."

Twenty minutes later, Dr. Fortis came out of an examining room, shutting the door behind him.

"This young woman is completely disoriented in time and space. She's also showing flattened affect and a dramatic level of amnesia. She could be a schizophrenic or bipolar off her meds. Do we know anything at all about her?"

"Nothing," Jerry said. "She may be local, but I doubt it. She says she woke up in the woods."

"Yes, I saw the bites."

An attendant handed the doctor a clipboard. He flipped a page once, twice. "Her chem screen. Negative for intoxicants. First thing I want to do is call the psychiatric hospital and see if any of their patients are AWOL. If everyone's accounted for, I'll call for a psych consult, but that won't happen till morning. In the meantime, we'll take a skull X-ray. Frankly, I don't know what else to do."

He opened the examining room door and brought the girl out.

"Who are you?" she said to Jerry.

"Do you remember who I am?" Dr. Fortis said.

"Not really."

"I'm Dr. Fortis. The kind of trouble you're having with your memory just now is usually a symptom of trauma. I'm going to take you down the hall and take a picture."

Jerry went back to the waiting area. It was filling up now with the usual cursing drunks, and infants wailing from colic or fly bites. He called the city station to see if there was a missing persons report on the redhead. The duty sergeant joked around with him; Jerry was with the Ontario Provincial Police now, but he'd worked for the city before that, and the sergeant was an old friend. No missing redheads on file.

Jerry thought about what would need to be done for her. It would be a city problem, not his, but if the hospital didn't admit the girl, they'd have to find her a place to stay, maybe the Crisis Centre. And if it turned out she was the victim of an assault, it would mean going back to the bar and finding out if anybody knew her, trying to backtrack to when she came in and where she was before that. He wondered how she came to be in the woods. She wasn't dressed for camping.

He found John Cardinal signing forms, talking to the young man behind the counter. The guy was listening, nodding attentively. Cardinal had always had the knack of making people feel that what they did was important, that how they handled the details mattered. It was a knack that could mean the difference between making a case and blowing it. Jerry waited for him to finish.

"I think I got a case for you," he said. "I know you don't have enough to do."

"I told you never to call me here, Jerry."

"I know. But without you, I'm only half a cop. My life is a stony, barren place."

"Haven't seen you around lately. I suppose you've been snorkelling down in Florida or somewhere."

"I wish. Been stuck in Reed's Falls working surveillance. Came across something in town tonight, though. Bit of an anomaly." Jerry told him about the redhead.

"No drugs? Sounds like she took a knock on the head."

"Yeah. No ID, no keys, no nothing."

Dr. Fortis came back from radiology, a worried expression on his face.

"Something unexpected," he said to Jerry. "Come and take a look."

"John should probably be in on it. She'll be a city case. You know Detective Cardinal?"

"Of course. Come this way."

Cardinal followed them down the hall to an office where darkened X-rays were clamped to light boards. Dr. Fortis snapped on the light, and the gracile cranium and neck bones of the young woman glowed before them, front and side views.

"I think we've found why our red-headed friend is in such a placid mood. In fact, we're going to be sending her down to Toronto for surgery," Dr. Fortis said. "You see here?" He pointed to a bright spot in the middle of the lateral view.

"Is that what I think it is?" Cardinal said.

"I can tell you I'm feeling pretty incompetent right about now. Totally missed it on physical examination. I can only plead the thickness and colour of her hair."

"Looks like a .32," Jerry said.

"Entered through the right parietal region and partially severed the frontal lobes," Dr. Fortis said. "Hence the flattened affect."

"Will that be permanent?" Jerry said.

"I'm no expert, but people do make amazing recoveries from these sorts of things. This is really one for the medical journals, though: self-inflicted lobotomy."

"Maybe not self-inflicted," Cardinal said. "Women who want to commit suicide almost never shoot themselves. They take an overdose, they use the car exhaust. We'll get ident to do a gunshot-residue on her hand."

"Might not have to," Jerry said.

The girl was in a wheelchair at the door, still smiling, an orderly behind her.

"We've got the EEG results," the orderly said.

Dr. Fortis examined the printout.

Jerry turned to him. "You said the entry wound is on the right?"

"That's correct. The right temple."

"Hey, Red." Jerry took a pen from his pocket. "Catch."

He tossed the pen over her head. A pale hand shot up and snagged it out of the air. Her left hand.

"Well," Cardinal said, "so much for suicide."

2

ALGONQUIN BAY, WITH A POPULATION of 58,000 and only two small hospitals, cannot lay claim to any neurosurgeons of its own, which was why, forty-five minutes later, Cardinal was barrelling down Highway 11 toward Toronto, four hours south.

After Dr. Fortis had scanned the EEG results, he had ordered the redhead put into a neck brace and shot her full of antibiotics and anti-seizure medication. Then he ordered an ambulance. "She appears stable," he said, "but I'm seeing some seizure activity on her readout. They'll want to operate on her right away."

"I'm pretty sure she's not a suicide attempt," Cardinal said, "but I'll get ident to do a gunshot-residue on her before we leave."

"We?"

"I'm going to have to accompany her, be there when that bullet comes out of her head."

"Of course. Chain of evidence and all that. Have to be quick, though. The sooner she's in surgery, the better."

Using electric clippers, Dr. Fortis shaved a small patch of hair away from the girl's right temple. A placid smile played across her features, but otherwise she didn't react at all.

"Perfectly round entrance wound," Cardinal noted. "No burn, no smudge and no tattooing."

"There's no way that gun was fired within a foot of this girl," Jerry said. "I hope you find whoever pulled the trigger. Let me know if I can be any help. I'm heading home to enjoy what's left of my day off." He waved at the girl. "You take care, Red."

The girl's smile was frozen in place. The anti-seizure medication was starting to take hold.

Cardinal put in a call to Detective Sergeant Daniel Chouinard at home.

"What is it, Cardinal, I'm watching *Homicide*, here."

"I thought that was off the air."

"Not in my house. I own the entire first three seasons on DVD. There's something soothing about watching cops with problems a lot worse than mine."

Cardinal told him about the girl.

"Well, you've got to go to Toronto and see that bullet come out. Is there anything else?"

"That's it."

"Good. Now, I'm going to go back and watch how those big-city cops handle things."

Bob Collingwood from the ident section arrived a few minutes later. He was the youngest detective on the squad, and by far the quietest. He took some Polaroids of the girl's wound and gave them to Cardinal. Then he tested the girl with a GSR "dabber," a flat, sticky object not unlike a tongue depressor, pressing it over the back of both her hands and into the space between thumb and forefinger. The girl appeared not to notice; it was as if she had disappeared from the room. Collingwood slipped the dabber into a Baggie, handed it to Cardinal without a word and went on his way.

—

When Cardinal arrived home, he found his wife excited about her own trip to Toronto, although she wasn't leaving for another week. Catherine was going to be leading a three-day field trip to the big city with members of the photography class she taught at Northern University.

"I can't wait till next week," she said. "Algonquin Bay's a great place to live, but let's face it, there's not a lot of culture per square foot. I'm going to take a million photographs in Toronto, I'm going to have some wonderful meals and I'm going to spend every spare minute in the museums seeing art, art, art!"

She was checking cameras, cleaning them with blasts of canned air, and polishing lenses. Catherine never travelled with fewer than two cameras, but it looked like she had enough lenses for five. Her hair was all in a tangle, the way it tended to get when she was busy with a project. She would shower and then forget to dry it as she got involved in something else.

"I wish I could come down with you, right now," she said. "But I've got a class tomorrow, and a darkroom workshop on Thursday."

Cardinal tossed a few things into an overnight bag.

"Where will you stay?" Catherine said.

"The Best Western on Carlton. They always have a room."

"I'll call them right now and book it for you."

Cardinal was digging around in the dresser for his electric razor. The only time he used it was when he travelled, and he never remembered where he'd put it from one trip to the next.

Catherine called Toronto directory information and got the hotel's number, all the while chatting to Cardinal. The eleven o'clock news was winding down on the television, but Catherine was just revving up.

A familiar unease fluttered in Cardinal's chest. This time, his wife had managed to stay out of hospital for two years. She'd been doing well. Took her medication faithfully, kept up with her yoga, made sure she got a good night's sleep. But this was one of the worst aspects of her illness: Cardinal could never be sure if his wife was just happy and excited, or if she was entering a trajectory that would fling her into the intergalactic reaches of mania.

Should I say something? It was as if, when the psychiatrists had first diagnosed Catherine's disorder twenty years ago, they had initiated Cardinal into the brotherhood of anguished spouses with that endlessly repeated mantra: *Should I say something?*

"This trip is going to be fantastic," Catherine said. "I can feel it. We're going to shoot the waterfront. Capture some of the old industrial buildings before they get all touristy and unrecognizable."

Cardinal came over and stood behind her, put his hands on her shoulders. Catherine froze. Lens in one hand, lens tissue in the other.

"I'm all right, John." There was an edge in her voice.

"I know, hon."

"You don't have to worry."

She didn't turn to look at him. Not a good sign.

—

Bugs spattered on the windshield like rain. The occasional truck clattered along, blocking Cardinal's progress, but mostly the highway was empty. He'd left the ambulance behind somewhere around Huntsville.

Cardinal forced himself to stop fretting about Catherine and focus on the young redhead. The Baggie and the photographs were on the passenger seat beside him. He had no doubt that he was dealing with an attempted murder, but Cardinal had been a cop for more than twenty years—ten in Toronto, more than that in Algonquin Bay—and he had long ago learned never to jump to conclusions.

At the Catholic boys' school he had attended, the priests had always dourly insisted that an errant youth view his actions through the eyes of his Maker, or if he lacked that much imagination, then through the eyes of his mother. In Cardinal's mind, these inquisitors had been replaced with a defence attorney, who was always nosing around for reasonable doubt like a rat after the cheese.

"And you say you did not perform a test for gunshot residue, is that correct, Detective?"

"*That's correct.*"

"*Without such a test to prove otherwise, it's possible the victim fired the bullet into her own head, is it not?*"

"*She's left-handed, for one thing. And there was no residue on her scalp. It's highly unlikely she could have fired the bullet herself.*"

"*Just answer the question, Detective. I asked you if it was possible.*"

Cardinal put in a call to 52 Division in Toronto and requested a twenty-four-hour police guard on the girl.

—

Dr. Melanie Schaff was cool and efficient and a good two inches taller than Cardinal. She had the kind of wary brusqueness one often finds in women who have struggled to make their way in a predominantly male world; Cardinal's colleague Lise Delorme had it.

"Your Jane Doe has sustained a partial lobotomy and the bullet has lodged near the hippocampus," Dr. Schaff said. "Sometimes it can be safer to leave a bullet in than take it out, but this one is close to one of the cerebral arteries. With the seizure activity we're seeing on her EEG there's no way we can leave it in. One or two good seizures and Jane Doe could end up Jane Dead."

"What are the risks?"

"Minor, compared to leaving it in. I've explained that to her and she seems quite prepared for the surgery."

"Is she in a state to make that decision?"

"Oh, yes. It's her memory and affect that's impaired,

not her reasoning ability."

"What are the chances of a total recovery?"

"There's only a partial severing of the frontal lobe, and it's only on one side, so there's a good chance she'll exhibit the full range of emotions eventually. No guarantees, however. There's no direct damage to areas of the brain that control memory, so I expect she's just in a traumatic fog, which should pass. I'll be recommending therapy with a neuropsychologist for that. Now, what exactly do you need from me, Detective, other than the bullet?"

"Is there any chance she'll remember anything while you're operating?"

"We'll be nudging along the hippocampus. It's certainly possible she'll get random flashes. Whether they'll be dreams or memories, I can't say. But you've seen the state she's in. There won't be any context for them."

"If you could just keep in mind that it might be useful for us, and it could save her life. We don't know who's trying to kill her."

"That it?"

"I need to actually see you take the bullet out."

"All right. Let's get you gloved and gowned. We'll be working with something called a Stealth Station. It's a 3-D cat scan hooked up to the microscope I'll be using. Should give you a ringside seat."

—

Like most cops, Cardinal had witnessed his share of gore—the torn wreckage of accidents and the blood-spattered kitchens, bedrooms, basements and living rooms where men commit violence on each other or, more often, on women. A policeman's heart gets calloused, like a carpenter's thumb. What Cardinal had never got used to, however, was the operating room. For some reason he could not fathom—he hoped it was not cowardice—the gleam of surgical blades made his stomach turn in a way that burns, dismemberments and impalings did not.

Two physicians assisted Dr. Schaff, and two nurses. "Red," as Cardinal had begun to think of her, was drowsy from sedatives and anti-seizure medication, but conscious. A bigger patch had been shaved around the entrance wound, and she had been given injections of local anaesthetic from a huge hypodermic. General anaesthetic was not required, the brain being insensitive to pain.

Masked and gowned, Cardinal stood to one side near Red's feet, where he could see an overhead monitor and observe the surgeon at the same time.

"Okay, Red," Dr. Schaff said. "How you feeling?"

"My goodness, you all have such beautiful eyes."

Cardinal glanced around the O.R. What the girl said was true: Between the masks and the surgical caps, the eyes were emphasized; everyone appeared gentle and wise.

"Flattery will get you everywhere," Dr. Schaff said. She strapped on a pair of goggles that made her look like a benign alien. "Are you ready for us? It won't hurt, I promise."

"I'm ready."

Cardinal had thought he was ready too, until Dr. Schaff took a scalpel and cut a flap in Red's scalp. For a moment it formed a fine scarlet geometry, but then the red lines thickened and flowed, and Cardinal wished he were somewhere else.

Dr. Schaff asked for the bone saw. Cardinal spent a lot of his off-hours doing woodwork, and it amazed him that the instrument in her gloved hand might have been a tool in his basement. It gave off a high-pitched whine, like a dentist's drill, but once it touched bone the sound was not all that different from ripping plywood. Red didn't even blink as Dr. Schaff extracted the piece of skull and set it aside. It would be preserved and put back in place in a day or two, when any brain swelling had gone down.

First, do no damage. Of all medical endeavours, brain surgery is probably the one where physicians are most cognizant of Hippocrates' proscription. Dr. Schaff began to probe through layer after layer of tissue with unbearable gentleness. Except for the beep of the monitors and the occasional clank of metal on metal, there was utter silence. Every so often, Dr. Schaff would call for a different instrument, now a "McGill," now a "Foster," now a "Bircher."

Seeing a length of stainless steel moving millimetre by millimetre deeper into the girl's brain, Cardinal felt a distinct softness in his knees. Looking up didn't help. The monitor showed the same thing in lateral close-up. He felt as if he were slowly tumbling down an elevator shaft. Sweat gathered under his surgical cap.

Two hours went by. Three. The doctors made occasional remarks back and forth, commenting on pulse, blood pressure. There were calls for hemostats and spreaders and cautery. Dr. Schaff spoke now and again to Red as she inched further into the girl's brain.

"Are you all right, Red? You doing okay?"

"I'm fine, Doctor. I'm just fine."

To calm his stomach, Cardinal concentrated on the background sounds, the beeping monitors, the whirring ventilation, the buzzing lights. On the monitor, the instrument was a bar of bright metal several inches inside the girl's skull.

"Coming up on the hippocampus . . ."

Red began singing. "A-hunting we will go, a-hunting we will go . . ."

"Yes, we're on a hunt here, Red. And I think it's just about over."

"Heigh-ho, the dairy-o . . ."

"Okay, looks like we're there," Dr. Schaff said. "I'm going to try and grab it."

On the screen, the dark blot of the bullet was now within the angle of flat jaws. The instrument began pulling back. Cardinal had a daughter about the same age as Red, perhaps a little older. He had a strong paternal urge to reach out and protect the young woman in some way—absurd, really, since she wasn't in the slightest pain.

Red spoke up as if in mid-conversation. "The clouds were amazing."

"Really?" Dr. Schaff said. "Clouds, huh?"

The bullet was steadily rising through the tunnel on the screen. Cardinal looked from the screen to Dr. Schaff. Her gloves were slick with blood.

Then Red spoke in a different tone. "The flies," she said, hushed, even awed. "My God, the flies."

Dr. Schaff leaned over her patient. "Are you talking to us, Red?"

"Her eyes are closed," someone else said. "It's a memory. Or maybe a dream."

Cardinal tensed, waiting for the girl to say more, but her eyes opened again and she stared blandly into space.

A moment later, Dr. Schaff extracted the bullet. A nurse held out a Baggie to receive it, then handed it to Cardinal. He went out to the prep room, took off his scrubs and slipped the Baggie into his breast pocket. A moment later, he felt a tiny spot of heat there, the bullet still warm from the girl's brain.

3

CARDINAL SLEPT FOR THREE HOURS in the crisply starched sheets of the Best Western hotel. After a scalding shower that nearly removed a layer of skin, he went down to the coffee shop, where he ate a chewy omelette and read *The Globe and Mail*. Outside, the morning sunlight slanted over the banks and insurance buildings. The air was crisp, and Cardinal noticed with pleasure the absence of blackflies. He walked over to Ontario's Centre of Forensic Sciences on Grosvenor Street, where he handed in the bullet and filled out several forms. They told him to come back in an hour.

Cardinal returned to the hotel and checked out.

He was back at Forensics in forty-five minutes. The young man who had been assigned to the case in Firearms was named Cornelius Venn. He wore a white short-sleeved shirt with a blue tie and had the clean-cut, slightly dorky good looks of a senior boy scout. Cardinal suspected a sizable collection of model airplanes.

Venn took the Polaroids Cardinal had given him and

tacked them up on a bulletin board. "Nice round hole. No burn, no soot, just slight tattooing."

"Which tells you what?" Cardinal said.

"Oh, no. I'm not getting into that particular box. There's no way I'm going to do a distance determination without having a suspect weapon in my hand."

"Just give me ballpark figures. We may not need them in court."

"There is no ballpark. Not without a suspect weapon. How can I give you a ballpark when I don't know the barrel length? Even if I know the type of weapon, I don't know if it's been altered in some way that would affect the patterns."

"So you're not going to give me an estimate?"

"Just told you. I can't."

"Well, we've pretty much ruled out suicide. The victim's left-handed. And to my less-than-expert eyes, the entry wound looks like the gun was somewhere between twelve and twenty inches away."

"I have no opinion on that point, as I've indicated," Venn said. "But with a suicide you'd expect a contact wound or something close to it. Unless your Jane Doe's got arms four feet long, there's no way this wound is self-inflicted."

"A defence attorney might say it's accidental."

"Accidental? Within a distance of two feet? You hold a loaded gun to someone's head and pull the trigger? Well, I suppose *some* might say there's reasonable doubt there."

Cardinal pointed to the spectroscope obscuring a poster for a Van Damme movie that featured an exotic machine gun. "How about the GSR results? Did you get anywhere with those?"

"Didn't run them. Don't look at me like that, Detective. There's no point in running a GSR on someone who's just been shot at close range. She's going to turn out positive for powder and soot whether she fired the gun or not."

That was true. Cardinal was annoyed with himself for forgetting.

Venn pinned a piece of paper up on the corkboard; it showed a series of grey streaks of varying intensity.

"Characteristics," he said. "You've got a plain, unjacketed, lead, .32-calibre bullet. Looks to me like a .32 long. Normally, with a shot to the skull you'd expect it to flatten out completely, making it hard to read. In this case, you have a shot to the temple—much thinner bone—and the bullet is pretty much intact. I don't suppose you have any casings?"

"You've got everything we've got."

"Then none of this is going to help you much, but here goes." He pointed to the printout as he spoke; his fingernail was gnawed to the quick. "You've got six right-hand grooves with a land-groove ratio of one-to-one-plus. Grooves are zero point five-six; lands are zero point six-oh."

"Pistol?"

Venn nodded. "Pistol. And you're lucky in one way."

"Oh?"

"The rifling in the weapon has a left-hand twist. Right away that narrows it down. You're probably looking for a Colt."

Venn rolled his swivel chair over to his computer and started typing figures into the database. "From what you tell me of the injury—minimal motion inside the skull, minimal damage to tissue—I think you're dealing with rounds that are either very old or got wet at some point. Or it could be a defective weapon. If the firing pin is far enough off kilter it could result in a misfire like this. Of course we won't know that until you bring us a casing. Or, God forbid, an actual weapon."

"That's it? We may be looking for a Colt .32?"

Venn looked up at him. "In your impatience, Detective, you're not letting me finish."

Cardinal scanned Venn's face to see if he was joking. He wasn't.

"This left-hand twist, coupled with this land-groove ratio, narrows it down to two possibilities. You could be looking for a J.C. Higgins model 80. Or a Colt Police Positive."

"And I bet there's more than a few of 'em, right?"

"In Ontario? Think in hundreds."

—

Ten minutes later Cardinal was back amid the chlorine-and-bandage smells of Toronto General Hospital. Jane Doe had been moved to a semi-private room on the third floor. The police guard on the door had so many gadgets hanging from his hips he looked bottom-heavy, like a ten-pin. Cardinal showed his badge and was waved inside. The young redhead was propped up in bed in a hospital gown, reading *Chatelaine*. She smiled when he came in; there was a small bandage on her temple.

"Are you my doctor?"

"No, I'm a detective. John Cardinal. We met last night."

"Detective? You're with the police? I'm sorry. I don't remember."

"That's okay. I bet you'll get your memory back in no time."

"I hope so. Right now, I don't even know who I am."

"Dr. Schaff tells me she's pretty sure it will all come back."

"I'm not even that worried about it."

Cardinal didn't tell her that Dr. Schaff had been less certain about appropriate affect.

The girl turned to adjust her pillows. Cardinal caught a flash of pale breast and looked away.

"Red, I need your help with something."

"Of course."

"I need your permission to go through your clothes and see if there's any identification."

"Oh, sure. Be my guest."

No doubt the hospital had already done this, but Cardinal opened the closet anyway. A denim jacket hung from a wire hanger, with a pair of jeans beside it. On the shelf, a T-shirt, bra and underpants. Cardinal made notes of the brand names: Gap, Levi's, Lucky. Then he went through the jeans pockets. No keys, no ID, no receipts or ticket stubs, just a few coins and a pair of nail clippers. He felt in the side pockets of the denim jacket and pulled out a half-roll of LifeSavers. Nothing useful.

When he turned around, Red was looking blankly out the window as if he wasn't there. Between the buildings, small white clouds hung in rhomboids of blue sky. Beyond these, the concrete shaft of Toronto's landmark CN Tower.

"One more thing," Cardinal said. "Would you mind if I took your picture?"

"No, of course not."

Cardinal closed the blinds to shut out the identifiable view. Then he sat the young woman in front of them, and had her turn her head to one side so the shaved patch didn't show. He took a close-up with his Polaroid.

She had no reaction when he showed her the result.

"They'll be sending you back to Algonquin Bay tomorrow," Cardinal said. "Are you ready for that?"

"I don't know where that is," she said. "I don't even know if I'm from there."

"We have to assume you are, until we hear anything different."

A pale, freckled hand reached up absently, feeling the edges of the bandage. Cardinal was sure she was going to ask where she would stay in Algonquin Bay—a question he had been dreading—but she didn't say anything. Just that same placid smile. Fine, let Dr. Schaff tell her.

"Listen, um, Red—sorry, I have to call you Red until we know your name . . ."

"It's all right. I don't mind."

"Pretty soon there's going to be a missing persons report out on you. Young women like you don't go missing without someone noticing. Then we'll know who you are and where you're from. In the meantime, we're going to have a police guard on you at all times."

"Okay."

She doesn't protest, she doesn't ask why, Cardinal thought. She doesn't seem afraid or even curious. He felt duty bound to answer the questions she hadn't asked.

"Someone put a bullet in your head," he said. "And because of the nature of the wound, and the type of weapon used, we think it was a deliberate attempt on your life. So, you're going to have to keep a low profile until we find whoever did it. In case they decide to make another try at it."

"Okay."

"Do you understand what I'm saying? It's not going to take long before you're tired of being cooped up, but it won't be safe for you to go out."

"Oh." The pale brows met in a display of—Cardinal wasn't sure if it was worry or just confusion. She said after a moment, "Whoever I am, I think I must be quite a lazy person, because right now I don't feel like doing anything but sitting in bed."

"Well, that's fine," Cardinal said. "You take it easy and let the doctors look after you."

"I will." She gave him a smile and it was as if a lamp had been turned on. "Thank you, Doctor."

4

THE ALGONQUIN BAY POLICE DEPARTMENT is
not the kind of grunge pit one sees on television shows
about New York cops. Since the new headquarters opened
a dozen years ago, the CID has maintained the bland
decor of a small mortgage outfit. The windows on the east
side provide good light—in the morning, at least—as well
as an excellent view of the parking lot.

Cardinal was in the boardroom packing up the last of
the files from a case that had consumed all his energy for
the last six months. It had involved a third-generation,
felony-prone family who, by way of registering a noise
complaint, had sacked a neighbouring family's afternoon
barbecue. One of the patriarchs had ended up face down
in his Worcestershire sauce, dead of a heart attack.
Months of Cardinal's work had resulted in nothing more
than a finding of accidental death.

Every now and then, Cardinal's thoughts were interrupted by a feminine *tack, tack, tack* of hammer and nail.
Frances, long-time receptionist and factotum to Police

Chief Kendall, was hanging a set of newly framed photographs on the pine panelling. So far, she had hung a photo
of Chief Kendall being sworn in, and another of Ian
McLeod, fully clothed and soaking wet, after having res-
cued a mother of three from drowning in Trout Lake.

"What do you think of this one?" Frances said.

A black-and-white eight-by-ten of a much younger
Jerry Commanda, back when he was still on the city force,
dressed in baseball cap and sunglasses. He was standing in
front of a stone gate with a wrought-iron eagle perched
on top—iron talons flexed, black wings spread as if about
to take off.

"Is that Eagle Park?" Cardinal said.

"Uh-huh."

"I remember that. It was a charity ball game against the
fire department."

"Can you believe how skinny Jerry was?"

"He's still skinny. Yet another reason, if one were
needed, to find him irritating."

"Go on. Everyone loves Jerry." Frances had a saintlike
immunity to irony.

"Another reason," Cardinal said.

"Oh, you . . ."

Cardinal settled back into the quiet. The boardroom was
plush, compared to the squad room. It even had carpeting,
royal blue, with a deep pile that went some way toward
damping the noise of Frances's hammer and the general
hubbub of the booking area. It was not, however, deep
enough the dampen the noise of one Jasper Colin Crouch.

Jasper Colin Crouch was a permanently unemployed
and unemployable construction worker, built like a grizzly

but with a temper much worse. Crouch was, as the cliché has it, well known to the police, owing to his penchant for battering his wife when sober and his numerous offspring when drunk. Detective Lise Delorme had hauled him in a few days previously on a charge of criminal assault after his twelve-year-old boy had been hospitalized with a broken arm. The boy was now a temporary ward of the Children's Aid Society.

A tremendous bellow—a sort of high-volume moose-honk—made Cardinal look up. He knew exactly who it was. The bellow was followed by an equally tremendous crash.

"My goodness," Frances said, and covered her heart.

Cardinal jumped up and ran to the booking area.

The floor was flooded, Crouch having somehow top-pled the water cooler. Now he was squared off with Delorme, who was five-foot-four but looked a lot smaller facing the cathedral of fat and muscle that was Jasper Colin Crouch. Delorme was down on one knee in the water, a cut above her left eye.

Bob Collingwood had hold of Crouch from behind, but Crouch simply made a kind of operatic shrug and Collingwood went flying. Before Cardinal could inter-vene, Crouch leaned into a full-force kick at Delorme. Delorme dodged to one side, caught his heel in her left hand and half-rose.

"Mr. Crouch, you're going to stop right now or I'm going to drop you."

"Suck my dick." He jerked his leg but Delorme held on.

"That's it," she said. She propped his foot on her shoul-der and stood up. Crouch's skull connected with the tile floor and he was out, as if someone had pressed the Off button on a remote. There was a pattering of applause.

"That really needs a stitch or two," Cardinal said when Delorme came back from the washroom. Her left eyebrow was bisected by a gash about a quarter of an inch long.

"I'll live." She sat down at the cubicle next to his. "How's our Jane Doe doing?"

Cardinal had called Delorme after he'd got the ballistics report.

"Jane Doe is still a Jane Doe," he said. "Neurosurgeon thinks her memory will come back, but there's no saying when."

"Bullet in the head—me, I take it we won't be putting any ads in the paper asking *Do You Know This Woman?*"

"No. We don't want whoever shot her to know she's been found, let alone found alive. I don't suppose you dug anything up on the gun?"

"Used in recent crimes?" Delorme shook her head. "Doesn't match anything." She added in an offhand, nothing-important, probably-shouldn't-mention-it tone: "On the other hand, I did check out reports of stolen firearms. Surprise, surprise, turns out we had one three weeks ago."

"You're kidding. A .32 pistol?"

Delorme held up a scrap of paper on which she had written a name and address.

"Missing. One pistol. Thirty-two calibre. Manufacturer: Colt. Model: Police Positive."

—

Rod Milcher lived in a nicely maintained split-level in the Pinedale section of town, at one time a desirable address, but now, owing to the proliferation of drab concrete apartment buildings, an area mostly populated by the newly married. Pinedale is where you find what real estate people like to call starter homes.

Unlike Jasper Crouch, Milcher was not well known to the police. In fact, not known at all. And his house, with its neatly clipped lawn and its pretty cedar hedge, did not look the home of a felon—more like that of a dentist. The only unusual thing about the whole place was what was parked in its driveway: a plump, much-chromed motorcycle.

"Six-fifty Harley," Cardinal said before they were even out of the car. "Serious bike."

"You couldn't pay me to ride one of those things," Delorme said. "Friend of mine got killed on one at the age of twenty-six. Lost an argument with a cement truck."

"Male friend?"

"Male friend. Thought he was tough but he wasn't."

Cardinal rapped on the side door. It was just after six o'clock; they had waited until Milcher was likely to be home. The door was answered by a thirtyish woman wearing a business suit. As if to balance the boardroom look with something more homey, she was also clutching a saucepan. "I'm not interested in religion," she said through the screen door. "I get tired of telling you people."

Delorme held up her badge. "Is Rod Milcher at home? We need to ask him a few questions."

The woman turned her head to one side without moving the rest of her body and yelled, "Rod! The police are here! Better pack your toothbrush!" She opened the screen door. "Step lively. Don't want to let the bugs in."

The side door led through a small vestibule to the kitchen. Cardinal and Delorme stood beside a Formica table set for two while the woman attacked a small cairn of potatoes with a peeler.

"What seems to be the problem, Officers?"

A diminutive man in a checked shirt and khakis addressed them from the hall doorway. He didn't come near to filling it.

"Mr. Milcher, you're the registered owner of a .32 pistol, is that correct?" Cardinal said. "A Colt Police Positive?"

"Yes. Why, did you find it?"

"What can you tell us about the circumstances under which it was stolen?"

"I told you all that. I put everything in the report."

"We'd like to hear it again," Delorme said.

"My wife and I were in Toronto for the weekend. When we came back, the gun was missing. Along with some other items—the stereo and a camera."

"And why did you have a licence to carry a gun in the first place?"

"I manage the back office for Zellers. Lots of times I have to make sizable deposits at night, after the armoured truck has already gone."

"Do you still have that job?"

"Yes, I do."

"Why don't you show us where the stereo was," Cardinal said.

Milcher looked from Cardinal to Delorme and back again.

"It was in here."

They followed him into a living room that was furnished almost entirely in white: white carpet, white curtains, white leatherette sofa and matching recliner. Milcher waved a hand at a glass-fronted set of shelves, a Yamaha stereo and speakers.

Delorme went up and peered at it.

"You replaced the stereo pretty fast."

"This was an old one I had sitting in the basement."

"Doesn't look old."

"Looks like a pretty expensive stereo to just be sitting in the basement," Cardinal said.

Milcher shrugged. "I don't see what all this has to do with my gun. Did you find it or didn't you?"

"Where did you keep the gun?" Delorme said.

"In that box right there." Milcher pointed to a small oak chest on the shelf. The hasp on the lock was broken.

"Who else knew you kept it there?"

"No one. Well, my wife. No one else. Look, you still haven't told me if the gun has turned up or not. I did my duty in reporting it. I think I have a right to know."

"Your gun hasn't turned up," Cardinal said. "But we think one of your bullets did."

"I don't know what you mean."

"Did you keep the ammunition with your weapon?"

"Uh, yeah. The bullets were stolen, too. They were really old, though. I wasn't a hundred percent sure they'd even work, to tell you the truth."

"Do you know this young woman?" Cardinal said. He handed Milcher the photo of Red he had taken that morning. The bandage didn't show, and you couldn't tell it had been taken in a hospital. She looked as if she had been caught daydreaming.

"I've never seen her," Milcher said. "Why?"

"Because it looks like one of your bullets has turned up in her skull," Cardinal said.

"Oh, my God," Milcher said. "That's terrible."

"How many Colt Police Positives do you suppose there are in Algonquin Bay, Mr. Milcher?"

"I didn't have anything to do with this. Hell, I reported the thing stolen the minute I knew it was gone."

"How do we know you didn't report it stolen, knowing you were going to·use it on someone?"

"Look, I've never seen this woman. I had nothing to do with this. I reported the gun stolen, I don't have a clue who stole it, end of story."

"Oh, what is all this bullshit, Rodney?"

All three of them turned to Mrs. Milcher, who was in the doorway now with an oven mitt on one hand.

"Stay out of this, Lorraine."

Mrs. Milcher let out a theatrical sigh. "The truth is, Officers, my husband has never grown up. If you saw the two-wheeler in the driveway, you know that he fancies himself something out of *Easy Rider*. He's never quite gotten over the fantasy of riding with the big boys."

"I did used to ride with them," Milcher said. "It was over ten years ago, and I didn't get into any of their other activities. But I rode with them lots of times."

"Uh-huh. And I used to sing with the Spice Girls."

"Who are we talking about?" Delorme said. "Who are the so-called big boys?"

"The Viking Riders," Mrs. Milcher said. "I mean, doesn't

everybody think they're heroes?"

"I don't think they're heroes," Milcher said. "A couple of them are old friends, that's all."

"Grow up, Rod. One of them was over here three weeks ago, just before that stinking gun went missing." She turned to Delorme as if only another woman could understand what it was like dealing with an incompetent male. "Genius, here, decides to impress his Viking friend by pulling out his little gun."

"Lay off, Lorraine."

"You know what I'm thinking?" Delorme said to Milcher. "I'm thinking that your stereo never did get stolen. I think you just said that so it would look like you didn't have a clue who took your gun. Because if it was just the gun that was taken, that would indicate the thief knew exactly what he was looking for, and knew exactly where it was. In other words, the thief would have to be someone you knew."

"Hey, look. You don't know what those guys'll do to me if they think I ratted on them."

"Someone shot this young woman in the head, Mr. Milcher. We're going to need a name."

5

ALGONQUIN BAY, ALTHOUGH MODESTLY popu-
lated, was not so long ago the second-biggest city in
Canada (measured by area). In the late sixties, three former municipalities of no size whatsoever had come
together in a Small Bang of amalgamation to create a
city that measured some 130 square miles. Only Calgary
had been bigger.

Since then, many other cities and townships have suc-
cumbed to amalgamation fever, and Algonquin Bay can
no longer claim to be bigger than Toronto, Ottawa or
Montreal. Even so, it's possible to motor for half an hour
in certain directions from the centre of town and still find
yourself within city limits.

Walter "Wombat" Guthrie lived in the basement flat of
a former farmhouse just within the city's southern border; in other words, several miles from downtown.

"A biker named Wombat," Delorme said in the car.
"They probably imagine it's some ferocious predator.
Razor-sharp teeth. But I've seen wombats at the Toronto

Zoo. They're these cute, fuzzy little things. You want to pick them up and take them home."

"Walter Guthrie is not little and he's not cute. He's got a sheet as long as your arm including assault, armed robbery and grievous bodily harm. He's been a member of the Viking Riders practically since kindergarten, and if they had such a thing as a prenatal chapter, he'd have been a founding member of that, too."

"How come I haven't run into him?"

"Because you were working white-collar crime when the Riders had their headquarters in town, and Walter 'Wombat' Guthrie can't even spell *white collar*." Cardinal made a right onto Kennington Road. "The only reason we haven't run up against Wombat and his brethren lately is because they moved the clubhouse beyond city limits. Good news for us; headache for the OPP."

"I thought all these guys were in their sixties by now— you know, grey ponytails flying in the breeze."

"Not all of them. Some of them. But that doesn't mean they can't still cause trouble. They're the reason Algonquin Bay has a heroin problem these days. They basically dumped the stuff—sold it at a loss and as soon as people couldn't live without it, they jacked up the price."

"It's an effective business model," Delorme said. "AOL works the same way."

"Effective is right. We now have thirty or forty full-time heroin addicts. "

"Yeah, I've met a few. But it's hard to get an idea of the big picture since the hiring freeze."

Over the past year, a city budget crunch had cost them first one and then another detective. The squad was down from a force of eight to an overworked six, and they'd had to leave the drug scene pretty much to the OPP.

Cardinal drove past a mouldering Sunoco station and turned into the driveway just beyond. He parked beside a wooden house that had once been white. Plastic sheeting flapped at the windows, and an eavestrough hung from the roof like a disabled limb.

Delorme let out a low whistle.

"Yeah," Cardinal said. "Where are the arsonists when you need them?"

"No bike in the drive, I notice."

"Keep that up, Sergeant Delorme, and you'll make lieutenant in no time."

They went to a side door, a doorbell labelled Guthrie. Cardinal ignored it and pounded on the door with his fist. They waited a couple of moments, swatting away blackflies, then went round to the front door.

"Landlady," was Cardinal's one-word explanation. This time he used the bell.

It was answered by a bony woman in a bathrobe, black hair streaked with grey and still wet from the shower. Other than that, she was all nose and cigarette.

"We're looking for your tenant," Cardinal said. "Walter Guthrie."

"Join the line," the woman said. "I ain't seen him in two weeks and he owes me rent."

"You have any idea where he is?"

She shrugged and cocked her alarming nose toward the highway. "Same place he always is. The clubhouse. Lots of times he don't come home for a week, but two weeks is a little unusual."

"Do us a favour," Cardinal said, handing her a business card. "Give us a call the minute you see him."

"Oh, sure," the woman said. "And you can take me directly to the morgue after."

Cardinal started to say something, but the woman closed the door.

"That was great," Delorme said as they headed back to the car. "You have such a way with women."

With certain colourful exceptions, motorcycle gangs in northern Ontario have learned that it doesn't pay to draw a lot of attention. That's why several years ago the Viking Riders relocated their clubhouse from Trout Lake Road to a remote site off Highway 11 near Powassan. Nothing about the four-square, red-brick structure indicates its function as headquarters for travelling pandemonium. In fact, the casual passerby might judge by the faded sign on the third floor and the persistent odour of burlap that it is still home to the Bronco Bag Factory, which hasn't been in business since 1987. The building never had a lot of windows, and most of those that remain have been bricked up to little more than slits, as if the current Dark Age tenants fully intend to fire arrows at any enemy fool-ish enough to lay siege to the former factory.

While Cardinal banged on the steel door he held his shield up to an armoured security camera. So did Delorme.

The door opened, and the man who answered it didn't look anything like a biker: thirty-five, five-ten, maybe one-seventy. Short hair neatly parted and a pair of round-rimmed designer glasses gave him a collegiate air. This was Steve Lasalle, president of the local chapter of the Viking Riders; he was about twenty years younger than his colleagues, but Cardinal had done business with him before.

"What can I do for you?" Lasalle said. "I'd invite you in but the place is a mess."

"We're looking for Walter Guthrie," Delorme said. "Is he inside?"

"Sorry. Not here."

"He's not at home, either. His landlady hasn't seen him for two weeks."

"Surprise, surprise. Neither have I."

"When exactly was the last time you saw him?"

The door banged all the way open, and Lasalle looked positively frail next to the Visigoth who now loomed beside him: Harlan Calhoun, fifty years old and 250 pounds of mayhem in motion, known to his friends and associates as "Haystack." If he'd had a neck, it would have been a size 20, about the size of the snakeskin cowboy boots on his feet.

"Who the fuck are you assholes?" His tone lacked warmth.

"It's okay, Haystack," Lasalle said. "I'm dealing with it."

"I'm Detective Cardinal, and this is Detective Delorme. Algonquin Bay Police."

"News flash," Haystack said. "This ain't your jurisdiction. Now get the fuck out of here before I rip your arm off and beat you to death with it."

"Who's your fat friend?" Cardinal said to Lasalle.

Calhoun stepped out of the doorway so that his chest was an inch from Cardinal's face.

"Go back inside, Haystack," Lasalle said.

"Cardinal," Calhoun said. "That's an Indian name."

"Not today," Cardinal said. "But thanks for the compliment."

"How about I send you back to the teepee? On the end of my boot."

"Tell you what, Shitstack—why don't you go back inside and trim that goat's ass on your face? Oh, sorry— is that meant to be a beard?"

Lasalle blocked the punch an inch from Cardinal's cheekbone. His knuckles were white where he gripped Calhoun's wrist. "I said go back inside."

Cardinal held up a pair of handcuffs and jiggled them at Calhoun. "Here, boy! Walkies?"

Calhoun smiled, gold gleaming amid the unwholesome thickets of his beard.

"Next time, Cardinal. Next time."

"Count on it."

Then Calhoun was gone, and Lasalle gave them a what-can-you-do shrug.

"You haven't answered my question," Delorme said. "When was the last time you saw Walter Guthrie?"

"Is there any reason I should answer that question?"

"I can think of several." Delorme was giving him her best French-Canadian deep-freeze. "One, you've got nothing to lose by answering it. Two, there are the interests of diplomacy to consider—you can't put a price on goodwill with your local police force. And three, there's the problem with getting your building up to code."

"You see any code violations here?"

"An inspector might. Just like Natural Resources might find you have a problem with your garbage out back. Just like the health department might find you've got a problem with your septic tank. Just like the—"

Lasalle looked at Cardinal. "She always this irritable?"

"You haven't seen her irritable."

"Look, lady," Lasalle said. "I haven't seen the guy. Nobody's seen him. In fact, if you should happen to come across the Wombat in your travels, bring him here when you're done with him."

"I thought you guys were blood brothers," Cardinal said. "Don't tell me he done you wrong."

"Let's just say old Wombat has some 'splaining to do."

"Which might answer the question of why he's missing. Maybe you already made your point with him and he isn't coming back again."

"When did you see him last?" Delorme said. "You still haven't answered that."

"Believe it or not I don't keep track of his comings and goings. Last time I remember seeing him we had a few people round, we watched a video, Wombat passed out on the couch. Not unusual for him. I expected to find him here next morning but I didn't. Now he doesn't answer his cellphone and he doesn't seem to be home and I have no idea where he is. He doesn't write, he doesn't phone and we're all just worried sick."

"You want to find him," Delorme said. "You're pissed off at him."

"What are you, my therapist? You want to explore my feelings, honey, make an appointment. Don't just come banging on my door."

"Where would Wombat be most likely to go?"

"You're letting the bugs in," Lasalle said and closed the door.

Cardinal and Delorme hopped back to the car, each in a penumbra of flies.

Delorme started the engine. "That was a weird testosterone display you had with Haystack."

"Guys like that are like dogs. They need to know where they stand."

"If you say so. Anyway, me, I get the feeling the Vikings are seriously annoyed with Wombat."

"Which could mean they did away with him." Cardinal rubbed at a bite on his neck.

"Don't scratch. You'll only make it worse."

When they were back on the highway, Delorme said, "You know, that Lasalle is seriously good-looking for a biker."

"Well, we're very good-looking for cops."

They were quiet for the rest of the drive back. There was only the sound of wind and tires and the odd squawk from the radio. Cardinal was thinking about the young woman with no memory. Those green eyes looked so innocent, her whole manner was so benign, it was hard to imagine anyone wanting to kill her. Then again, who knew what her previous personality might have been? For all Cardinal knew, she could be Bitch Incarnate. The only thing he was sure of: With no home and no memory, she must be the loneliest woman on earth, and he wanted to find the person who had done that to her.

6

CATHERINE CARDINAL HAD PACKED HER cameras several times over the past few days, only to unpack them, check the lenses and batteries, and pack them again. But when the rented minivan with its load of student shutterbugs honked outside the house early that morning, she was still folding T-shirts and zipping up toiletries and searching in the closet and under the bed for extra shoes.

Cardinal answered the door. The woman on the porch was tall, maybe forty, not exactly pretty, but she looked smart, and Cardinal always found that attractive.

"I just thought I'd see if Catherine needed any help," she said.

"I think she's got everything under control. It'll just be a minute."

"My name's Christine Nadeau," the woman said, offering her hand to shake. "This is the third course I've taken with your wife. Do you have any idea what a great teacher she is?"

"I have heard that before. But thanks for telling me."

"Everybody's very excited about this trip."

"Good. So is Catherine."

Christine Nadeau went back to wait in the van, and Cardinal found Catherine zipping up her carry-on in the bedroom. Her face was flushed, and she looked short of breath. *Should I say something?*

"I'm so disorganized," Catherine said. She was shoving loose change and bills into her jeans pocket as Cardinal hauled the suitcase to the front room. "You'd think I'd learn by now."

"You're not disorganized. You were just focused on making sure your camera gear was in shape."

"I'm not going to check it again," Catherine said. "It's a supreme act of will, but I'm not going to check it again."

She put on a khaki fisherman's vest. Even on Catherine it was perfectly hideous, but it had thousands of pockets for film, flash, batteries, pens, labels and filters—the myriad doodads of the serious photographer.

"Did you pack your medication?" Cardinal said. He had to. It wasn't in him to let her leave town and not ask this.

Catherine turned her back on him and put on a light coat over the vest. A slim black coat. It had a hood with a red lining that gave off echoes of fairy tales.

"Did you hear me, sweetheart?"

"Yes, John, I heard you. Yes, I packed my medication. Thank you so much for reminding me that I can't be trusted to so much as cross the road without supervision."

"All right. I shouldn't have said anything."

"Here I am excited about a big project and you just have to rain on my parade, don't you."

"Don't overreact, honey. I'm glad you're taking the trip. You should know by now—after twenty-five years, or however long it's been—I'm a worrywart. Always have been, always will be. Have a good time, and I'll see you when you get back."

Catherine hauled her suitcase outside without another word. Cardinal watched her get into the van, an ache in his chest. *I shouldn't have said anything.*

He was in the kitchen clearing away the breakfast things when Catherine rushed back in. She stopped in the kitchen doorway and took a deep breath.

"Okay," she said. "I'm sorry. I didn't mean to be a bitch. It's just sometimes, once in a while—once in a *great* while—I actually imagine I'm normal. I actually fantasize that I can do all the things normal people do without a second thought, and why should anyone worry about it. It's hard for me to remember I have this problem. It's painful to be reminded of it."

"I'm sorry if I brought you down," Cardinal said. "Old habits . . ."

Catherine came closer, and stood on tiptoe to kiss him on the cheek.

"You worry too much."

—

A little later, Cardinal and Delorme drove up to St. Francis Hospital. It wasn't actually called St. Francis any more, but Cardinal still thought of it that way. Algonquin Bay's City Hospital consisted of two brick boxes that used to be two separate hospitals until the provincial government decided they would be better off united in holy parsimony. The smaller one, the former St. Francis, sits halfway up a hill, overlooking École Secondaire Algonquin and the grubby cinders of the CNR tracks. It is this building that houses the hospital's psychiatric ward. On any given day, the half-dozen or so patients who wander its halls consist of attempted suicides, drug overdoses or emotionally symphonic teenagers—patients not deemed crazy enough or long-term enough for residence at the local Ontario Psychiatric Hospital, where Catherine went to recover from the worst of her depressions.

Cardinal and Delorme were here to check in on Jane Doe, but Cardinal was having trouble focusing just now, the sight of a hospital having thrown his mind back upon Catherine.

Perhaps there was no cause for concern. Perhaps Catherine's excitement about her trip was just that: excitement. She hadn't flown off on any flights of fancy; she'd made no grand announcements of omnipotence, unveiled no cosmic plans for changing the nature of reality as we know it. Perhaps it really was just girlish excitement about going to the big city on a photographic project. In a normal woman, it would have been no cause for concern. But in Catherine . . .

Cardinal and Delorme took the elevator to the third floor, the psychiatric wing. They had arranged to meet a neuropsychologist who had been brought in to try to help their mysterious redhead recover her memory. City

Hospital did not have a neuropsychologist on staff. There was only one in the entire city, and he was there on loan, teaching a course at Northern University's school of nursing. Dr. Garth Paley.

If I ever need a shrink, Cardinal thought as Dr. Paley introduced himself, I want one who looks just like this guy. Paley was dressed in a tweed jacket and jeans, which gave him the look of a man who could be comfortable in the library or in the bar. Although he was not older than mid-fifties, he had grandfatherly white hair and a silvery beard. His brows were dark, shadowing his eyes in a way that gave them a perceptive, almost prehensile, look. A man who could understand and empathize before you even said anything. Some people are just perfectly suited to their jobs; Cardinal often wished he were one.

"I appreciate your letting me know you were coming up to see my Jane Doe," Dr. Paley told them. "Please sit."

The office they were in might have been anywhere. It had the usual computer, the usual metal bookshelves bolted to the wall. It was an uncomfortable place and didn't suit Dr. Paley at all.

"A couple of things you should know before you talk to her," he said. "First off, you mentioned on the phone, Detective, that you were hoping her amnesia was temporary. The short answer is, it isn't amnesia." Dr. Paley grinned at them, his cheeks suddenly rosy. Santa Claus as a youngish man.

"I don't understand," Cardinal said. "She doesn't remember who she is or where she's from . . ."

Dr. Paley raised a manicured finger. "That isn't amnesia. It's post-traumatic confusion. We don't know what the mechanism is, but basically when the brain receives a jolt it's as if all the pathways get scrambled and information doesn't flow the way it normally does. She hasn't really forgotten who she is, she just can't retrieve it."

"She will be able to, though, right?" Delorme said. "She will remember eventually?"

"Oh, yes. Dr. Schaff assures me that the actual brain damage is minimal. We can expect normal affect to return probably in a week, maybe three at the most. And by then she should have pretty much a continuous autobiography, too."

"And what about the crime itself? Getting shot?"

"That she will never remember."

"Can't blame her," Delorme muttered. "For sure, it must have been pretty horrific."

"That's not why," Dr. Paley said. "She's not repressing the memory—the information just isn't there. People make the mistake of thinking memory is like a videotape. It isn't. It's not a recording of what happened. Two sets of encoding have to occur before an event is stored in long-term memory. First, information has to be processed by the brain in a way that makes it comprehensible. Then, it varies, but in about twenty minutes, half an hour, the information gets encoded into long-term memory—different location in the brain, different recovery system. If some trauma shocks the brain before this happens, it will be as if the event itself and everything within about a half-hour on either side of it never happened."

Cardinal sagged. "So we're not going to get any info out of her?"

"Afraid not."

"Can't you use hypnosis?"

"God forbid. Hypnosis has been thoroughly and completely discredited. You remember all those child abuse witch hunts? Satanic ritual abuse? Daycare centres that were the scene of orgies? There's never been any corroborative evidence for any of it. Furthermore, the interview records show that those bits that weren't infantile fantasy on the part of the children were memories put there inadvertently by overzealous police, prosecutors and social workers. Same with sodium amytal. You'll get what a patient thinks you want to hear, you won't get the truth. Don't worry. You'll get lots out of this young woman eventually. Just not a direct memory of who shot her and where. Think of it like a computer. You know what happens if you're typing something up in your word processor and there's a power failure before you save it?"

"Yes," Delorme said. "Unfortunately."

"It's a pretty exact analogy. And I want to caution you before you talk to her. Please note my words, now. People in a confused state are extremely suggestible. If you go in there and suggest maybe her brother shot her, she'll start 'remembering' that her brother shot her. So, please—for the good of this young woman as well as for the good of your case—do not make any suggestions to her as to how she might have come to be shot, or even how she might have come to be in Algonquin Bay. If you hint that maybe she was going to school here, something like that, she'll start remembering that she was going to school here. That's why I videotape all my interactions with her; I want people to know that her memories are hers, not mine."

"False memories are the last thing we want," Cardinal said. "But we need to find out who might be after her."

"I hope you do. Just don't ask her."

"Even without suggesting an answer?"

"You'll only slow her progress. She'll try and try to remember, and it'll upset her, and that's only going to set her back."

Dr. Paley picked up a mug with a picture of a fat tabby on it. "I'm sorry," he said, "I've just made some tea. Will you have some? Or coffee? It's pretty awful stuff, I'm afraid."

Cardinal and Delorme demurred.

"You know what it's like," Dr. Paley continued, "when you're trying to remember a name or a movie title that's just on the tip of your tongue? You try and you try and you can't do it. Then half an hour later, when you're not trying, it comes to you."

"So what are you going to do for her?" Delorme said. "Just keep her in bed for three weeks?"

"No, we'll let her have the run of the ward when she wants. I go at things sort of sideways. I'll be giving our young friend cues of various sorts. Various stimuli—music, images, smells—that might provoke a response. Well, tell you what, why don't you go in and introduce yourselves? She won't remember you from the other day, Detective, but maybe you can establish some kind of rapport. Why don't you meet me in the staff lounge when you're done? It's just down the hall on the right, past her room. I'll have something to show you."

Cardinal and Delorme went down the hall. The door to the girl's room was manned by a uniformed cop named Quigley. Cardinal was going to pass by with a nod, but Quigley was clearly relieved to have some company.

"No one's come to visit," he said. "Except Dr. Paley. I think she's getting a bit better, though."

"Has she been out of her room yet?"

"Nope. But they leave the door open most of the time. I see her getting up and staring out the window. What do I do if she decides she wants to wander around, visit other patients?"

"Keep track of anyone she visits. And especially keep an eye out for visitors. No one gets in to see her without talking to me or Delorme first. You make them wait right here. Anyone hanging around in a suspicious manner, you check 'em out and let us know right away."

"Will do," Quigley said. "Seems like a nice kid."

She looked small and frail lying against the pillow. Her hair was a red blaze against the white of the bed, her skin, except for the freckles, almost matching the sheets. The bandage on her temple was a miniature pale flag. She stared at Cardinal with no sign of recognition, which was unnerving even though he had been expecting it.

"We met a few days ago," he said. "I'm Detective Cardinal. But here's someone you haven't met—my partner, Lise Delorme."

The girl smiled shyly as Delorme shook her hand.

There was a pause, during which Cardinal became aware that he was in an awkward position. If he couldn't ask her questions relating to her injury, he didn't know what he was doing there.

"How's your head, after your operation?" Delorme asked. "You must have one nasty headache."

"My head?" The girl touched her hair absently, fingers fluttering round the bandage. "It's actually not too bad." She wrinkled her nose.

"Maybe when you're doing better, I can take you to a good stylist. See what she can do with that shaved patch."

"That would be nice. What's your name again?"

"Lise."

"Lise."

The young woman looked out the window. Down the hill, a train loaded with oil tankers rolled lazily past the school.

"You know what I can't understand? I can't understand why I remember some things and not others. Why do I know what a stylist does, when I can't remember my own name? Why do I remember how to speak, how to tie my shoe, but not where I'm from? How come I can't remember any of the people I meet?"

"You'll have to ask Dr. Paley that one," Cardinal said. He noted the irritation in her voice. The rise in her emotional temperature, slight though it was, seemed a harbinger of recovery.

"I'm afraid to ask anybody anything," she said. "I'm afraid I've already asked it nine times and people will hate me."

"Don't you worry about that," Delorme said. "Dr. Paley only wants to help you. So do we."

"What I really want to do is get out of here. It's boring lying in bed all day."

"It's not safe for you to go out yet. You might be seen by the person who tried to kill you."

"Someone shot me. I keep forgetting."

Cardinal and Delorme looked at one another.

"I don't feel like I'm the kind of person people would want to shoot. Isn't it possible that it was just an accident?"

Cardinal shook his head. "You were shot from very close range. If it was an accident, why didn't anyone go for help?"

The pale fingers fluttered over the bandage. "I just can't . . ." Her voice trailed off and the green eyes filled.

"Look at it this way," Cardinal said. "You're feeling bored, bewildered by your memory problems and nervous about asking questions. A few days ago you weren't feeling anything. I'd say things are looking up."

"You're safe here," Delorme said. "There's a huge cop guarding your door, and we're going to do everything we can to catch the person that did this to you."

"Thank you."

"We'd better go," Cardinal said. "Dr. Paley wants to talk to us again."

"He seems very optimistic," Delorme said to the young woman, "so try not to worry too much."

"How can I?" the girl said, and smiled wanly. "I can't remember what I'm supposed to worry about."

—

Dr. Paley was waiting for them in the staff lounge down the hall. There was a fridge, a microwave and a few plastic chairs around a table. The blue screen of a combination TV and VCR glowed high up on a shelf. Dr. Paley slipped a videotape into it and sat down beside them with a remote in his hand. He pointed it at the screen and the VCR began to whirr.

"I won't play you the whole thing," he said. "The way I went about this, I told her I was an avid shutterbug—true, by the way—and I wanted to show her some of my favourite photographs. They're scenes from around Algonquin Bay—places any local person would recognize. I got my wife and kids to pose, so the pictures wouldn't seem so obvious as memory cues."

"How will we know which one she's looking at?"

Dr. Paley clicked the remote and froze the image that appeared. They were looking at a wide-angle shot that included both him and Red, with the angle favouring the young woman. In the upper left-hand corner was a smaller image of the doctor's daughter in a red snowsuit, standing in front of the *Gateway to the North* sign.

"I use a video set-up with picture-in-picture capability. You see what she's seeing in the little box. You'll notice she has no particular reaction to the *Gateway to the North* arch."

He clicked the remote again. Onscreen, Red made a polite comment, inquiring about the child's age.

The Gateway sign morphed into an image of the cathedral.

"Same again, you see?" Dr. Paley pointed to his patient. "She's polite. Kind-hearted, too, asking about the kids and so on. But nothing in her reaction indicates that she recognizes the church."

Onscreen, the girl smiled. The insert showed a triumphant six-year-old hoisting a fish he had just caught off the government dock, a local landmark. The white bulk of the *Chippewa Princess*, a cruise boat, loomed in the background.

"No change, right?"

"These are certainly the places you think of when you think of Algonquin Bay," Cardinal said. "But her not recognizing them doesn't mean she isn't from here, right? It may just mean her memory isn't budging for now."

"Correct," Dr. Paley said. "But watch what happens coming up." He hit fast-forward and the image smeared and leaned. They waited a couple of minutes while he kept his eye on the numbers that clicked round on the bottom of the screen. The tape halted with a clunk. "Here we are. I'm showing her my photographic vista of Beaufort Hill."

"Yes, there's the old fire tower," Delorme said. A tiny dirt road that led up to it curved away from a line of hydro pylons below, forming an elongated Y.

"She doesn't say anything, you notice, but look at the crease between her brows. She lifts her hand and starts to speak . . ."

The insert suddenly went snowy and there was a loud hiss—almost a roar—of static. The girl's eyes went as round as two zeroes, and her hand flew to her mouth.

"What is it?" Dr. Paley asked onscreen. "What's wrong?"

The girl's face went blank, the horror gone.

Dr. Paley asked her again what was wrong.

"Nothing," the young woman said. "I mean, I don't know. I felt scared all of a sudden."

"Note the return of affect," Dr. Paley said to Cardinal and Delorme. "A good sign."

"What startled her?" Delorme said.

"There was a short in the jumper cable and it caused that awful spray of static that made her jump out of her skin. But before that, I think she was about to recognize Beaufort Hill, or at least say something about it. So it's not clear whether her fright reaction is to Beaufort Hill or just to the sudden noise. As you can see, I didn't get anything else out of her."

Onscreen, Dr. Paley gently tried to get the girl to say what had scared her.

"I don't know," she said again. "I just felt this sudden . . . I don't know."

"Was it the noise that frightened you?"

She shook her head. "I'm not sure."

"Was there something about the picture? The picture of the hill? Could you look at it again?"

"I don't know . . ."

"I promise it won't make that noise this time. I'll hold the cable."

"I guess . . ."

The insert of Beaufort Hill appeared again. The girl's expression changed only slightly this time, to one of concentration. Then she shook her head. "It doesn't mean anything to me. At least, I don't think so. I don't know what made me jump like that."

Dr. Paley hit the pause button. "I wrapped it up a few minutes after that. It's probably not much use to you, but I wanted you to see it, if only to give you an idea of how gently this sort of recovery has to proceed."

"Is it possible that hill is where she got shot?" Delorme asked.

"Very unlikely. As I said, she won't remember anything about that—at least not anything that occurred within half an hour before or after. If she was held somewhere first, or if she was fleeing for a time, that may come back, but not the memory of the shooting itself."

"So it's possible something happened there," Cardinal said.

"Oh, yes. Possibly something leading up to the trauma. Possibly something when she regained consciousness. If so, we can expect it to come back to her at a later date. We just have to be patient."

7

"YOU FEEL LIKE A LITTLE HIKE?" Delorme said when they were outside. She tucked a strand of hair behind one ear; a damp breeze was blowing across the parking lot. "Take a look at that hill close up? You recognized it, right?"

"Yeah, it was taken from somewhere up behind the university," Cardinal said. "Why don't we drive over that way before it starts to rain?"

"You think she's a student at Northern?"

"We'd have heard from them by now, if she was."

"Well, if she was on Beaufort Hill, the most likely route for anyone not a student would be via the lookout off Highway 11. Why don't I drive to the lookout and I'll meet you in the middle?"

"Top of Nishinabe Creek?"

"Yeah. Where it splits 'round that little island. Figure forty-five minutes to an hour."

Algonquin Bay does not have any serious mountains, but the high-backed hills of the Precambrian Shield lumber around it like a herd of gargantuan buffalo. The terrain is unforgiving granite, luckily covered with a layer of loamy soil that supports thousands of square miles of forest. The Northern University campus is flung across the top of one of these hills, affording the students a spectacular view of the city and the blue expanse of Lake Nipissing. Not that it was blue today. A light drizzle had set in, and the sky was a depressing shade of grey from one horizon to the other.

Delorme dropped Cardinal at headquarters before they took their separate routes. On the way up to the campus, Cardinal stopped at a curve on Sackville Road, where there was a small, comma-shaped lay-by. Back when Cardinal was in high school, he used to come up here with Brenda Stewart, his sweetheart of the time, but Brenda Stewart had staunchly refused to go all the way in his parents' Impala. Now, he looked out across the rooftops of the city toward the Manitou Islands some seven miles south. Beaufort Hill lay behind the forest to the west; you couldn't quite see it from here.

Cardinal drove the rest of the way up to the university and parked in the visitors' lot. He walked across campus toward the network of trails that fanned out behind the school. A group of students spilled giggling from the main entrance and travelled in a boisterous, shifting knot toward the residence. How young they seemed—younger even than Cardinal's daughter, Kelly—and how innocent. Cardinal envied their easy camaraderie. When he had been a student in Toronto he had tried to save money by living off-campus in a smelly little room near Kensington Market. Thus he had missed the experience of living in a building full of fellow students, and it probably had ended up costing him more anyway.

There was a large gazebo among the pines, and then the trails. Cardinal took the one that led toward the top of the nearest hill, waving blackflies away from his face and hair, moving fast to keep ahead of them. About three hundred yards into the woods, the trail looped back toward a tiny man-made lake. Cardinal stepped off the trail and kept heading up the hill. The air was thick with smells of pine and loam and wet leaves. The drizzle didn't reach the forest floor; it hovered in a fine mist that clung to the skin.

The worst thing about blackflies, Cardinal thought— the truly diabolical thing—is that they are absolutely silent. They do not buzz like bees, or drone like horseflies, or even emit the high-pitched whine of mosquitoes; there's no warning, no chance of a pre-emptive smack. Cardinal felt a nip on his ankle, as if someone had stuck him with a hot pin. He bent down to tuck his pants into his socks. The only good thing you could say about blackflies is that, unlike mosquitoes, they do not bite through clothing. While he was bent over, another fly excised a piece of his neck. He slapped, and his hand came away bloody. He turned his collar up and continued toward the crest of the hill.

Ten minutes later—sweating, puffing and swearing yet again to put in more hours wrestling the many-armed Mr. Nautilus in the police gym—Cardinal climbed atop an outcropping of granite. Lake Nipissing, roughly palette-shaped, glimmered dully to the south, but off to the west he could now see Beaufort Hill. The old fire tower was just beneath the summit; the narrow dirt road that led up to it curved away from the line of hydro towers below. This was where Dr. Paley had taken his picture.

Maybe Red had stood here, too. Cardinal looked around at the clearing, swatting flies away as if he were conducting an orchestra. Signs of human activity lay everywhere—a rusted Sprite can, a wrapper from an Aero bar, the remains of a campfire. Obviously a popular spot for students, but surely not in blackfly season. Cardinal swatted at his temple.

He jumped down from the rock and, moving as fast as he could through the trees, headed west. There was no trail here, but the rocks made it the easiest route from the clearing, which was otherwise surrounded by thick brush. He kept moving, not sure what he was looking for. Bites itched on his neck and ankles.

No one in their right mind would come wandering around up here. What might have drawn a young woman like Red? Of course, if she wasn't from the north, she wouldn't have known about the flies.

Cardinal pushed his way through the trees, dogged now by a squadron of flies targeting his ears. Finally he found the trail that ran beside Nishinabe Creek. Winter had been particularly snowy this year, with blizzards into March and snowfalls to the end of April. In a normal summer, you could almost jump across the creek, but now it was bursting its banks with runoff.

Cardinal hurried up the trail, toward the pool he knew was at the next ridge. The "island"—little more than an outcropping of rock, really—where he was to meet Delorme wasn't far above that. There was a faint hiss in the air. As he approached the ridge, the hissing grew louder, until it sounded like radio static. The falls. He had forgotten about Nishinabe Falls. Cardinal stopped.

Most years, Nishinabe Creek is too small to boast anything resembling a falls. The pool is fed by a trickle of water—about what you'd get from your eavestroughs in a summer storm. But this year the heavy snows had turned it into a glassy curtain of water that tumbled over the rocks and hid the cavelike recession behind it. Cardinal gripped his collar round his neck, staring.

Had the hiss of static reminded Red of this rushing falls? Of something that had frightened her up here? The water foamed and frothed at Cardinal's feet. Further out in the pool it was black as onyx. A fly gouged his scalp, and he swatted at it, hurting his ear. He badly wanted to rush uphill, find Delorme and flee these miniature vampires, but he was stopped by the sense that Red had been here, perhaps in search of something. Perhaps against her will.

When he had been up here on a hike a couple of years back, Cardinal had crossed the creek stone by stone, but now the stones were submerged in froth. Luckily, beavers had been busy nearby and a birch tree was sprawled across the water. Cardinal stepped onto the trunk, and it crumbled under his foot. It was stronger higher up. When he had a good footing, he edged his way across the creek. A fly bit into his neck and he cuffed at it, nearly toppling.

As soon as he was near enough, he leaped to solid ground and went after the flies in a fury, slapping his neck, the side of his face, the crown of his head. Anger and frustration were aggravated by the consciousness of looking ridiculous, even though there was no one to see. He climbed a series of boulders and then he was at the edge of the pool with the falls before him. He stepped under the overhang and right away he could smell the sickly odour of rotting meat.

Cardinal edged between a rock and the falling water. He stopped again and listened. The blackflies had abandoned him now, driven back by the spray. Something else had Cardinal's attention. The granite face of the wall behind him was defaced, not with the usual graffiti, but with long columns of hieroglyphics. They looked ancient, but Cardinal knew they had not been there two years ago.

There were pictographs of arrows three or four inches long that intersected in weird patterns. Others were heaped in bunches with one longer arrow extruding, as if indicating a direction. Along the edges of the rock, there were drawings of the moon in various stages—full, half, three-quarter, new—and everywhere there were numbers, inscribed in coloured chalk.

Cardinal moved away from the rock face and stepped around a sharp corner of granite. The smell on the other side was nauseating. He pulled out his shirt-tail and covered his mouth and nose.

The thing on the floor of the cave had once been human, but there was nothing lifelike about it. The body was naked, male, with muscular arms and legs. All that working out hadn't come to much, though: a pale heap of flesh in a dark, cold cave. However this human being had lived, his death had been savage. The hands and feet were missing, as was the head. Maggots heaved on the major wounds, giving the appearance of movement.

There was a noise, and Cardinal whirled around.

Delorme was behind him, staring at the body from behind the corner of granite.

"I don't know about you," she said. "But me, I don't think the blackflies did that."

8

KEVIN TAIT PICKED UP THE FLY SWATTER and moved with great stealth to the window. The fly that had just taken a piece out of his ankle was trying repeatedly to exit through the glass. Kevin brought the fly swatter down, and the fly went to its reward. Using the swatter like a spatula, Kevin scooped up the tiny corpse and carried it to the cabin door. He opened the door just long enough to fling the dead fly outside without inviting any of its cousins to the Kevin Tait smorgasbord.

He cleaned the little smear from the windowpane with a Kleenex. Across the field, Red Bear was arriving in his black BMW. You had to hand it to Red Bear, the guy knew how to live. Dressed in white from head to toe, all six feet of him, and then he's got that glossy black hair down to his shoulders and the Wayfarers dark as outer space. He climbed out of the Beamer and two nifty-looking babes got out with him, a blond and a brunette with the kind of bodies that spoke of hours in the gym.

The three of them walked across the former baseball diamond to Red Bear's cabin, by far the nicest in this crumbling old camp. Kevin watched them from his window, the tall Indian all in white, like Elvis in his final years, an arm around each of the women. Red Bear wore so many beads and bracelets he rattled as he walked. Somehow his good looks and his aura of power overcame the vulgarity.

Kevin Tait was not the kind of young man who believed in personal power or charisma, perhaps because he sensed that he possessed none. Oh, he knew he could be charming. Women have always had a weak spot for penniless poets, and the erotic power of melancholy is well known.

Kevin flopped across the bed and opened his notebook. He pulled out the black pen Terri had given him for his twenty-first birthday. He thought he might start a poem about misery and lust, but the pen remained inert.

He flipped through the notebook, browsing through jottings he'd made over the past months—musings, observations, bits of verse.

Her first love was a captain
For whom she would become
The muse of Navigation
The smoke of opium

Just a fragment, and too Leonard Cohenish at that.

A wizard turning wisdom into wine . . .

God knows where he was going with that one. It seemed ages since he'd finished anything substantial. There had been a poem in March, but he hadn't bothered to send it out to the small magazines; it needed another polish or two. The last few months he'd been conserving his strength, lying fallow, waiting for just the right idea; he'd know it when it came along. It would go off like a Roman candle, sparks pinwheeling across the jet-black sky of his mind.

"Kevin Tait, good to have you on the show."

Kevin liked to do this thing in his head where he was being interviewed by David Letterman, even though he knew Letterman never interviewed poets. He figured he would be the first.

"Kevin Tait," Letterman said again. "Here you are, your last volume of poems sold a gazillion copies. People quote your lines to each other day in and day out. You're not just a poet any more, you're a force in the culture. And—I don't know how to put this gently—you're hanging out with scumbags. Ne'er-do-wells. Drug dealers. What are you thinking?" Letterman's fratboy grin took the sting out of the question.

"Drug dealers, Dave, provide a much-needed service to a, let's face it, underappreciated crowd. People have used drugs down through the centuries, and they always will. Look at Coleridge. Look at Rimbaud. A little disorder in the senses never hurt anybody. And not just artists. It's a long dark night out there, Dave, and everyone needs a little help getting through."

Applause. Letterman ignores it.

"But you're a *poet*. And you're hanging out with *thugs*. Doesn't that make you nervous?"

"Nervous? Not really." Kevin gave it a beat. "I'm actually terrified."

Laughter.

"So give us the big picture, here. How does this—sorry, I gotta say it—oddball behaviour fit into your grand plan?"

"My plan, Dave, is to make a lot of money by selling as much contraband as possible in as short a time as possible. Then I'm heading off to Greece for a few years to write the big one. Maybe Barcelona, Tangiers, I'm not sure."

Letterman then had him read his latest poem. There was a respectful pause after he read the last line, then a balmy wave of applause.

The plan had a flaw that Letterman didn't know about: Kevin had a weakness for the product he sold. He liked to think his personal appreciation of his wares was what made him an exceptional salesman. In any case, he was clean these days; just a little skin-popping now and again. Nobody ever came to grief by skin-popping. Besides, he knew he could quit. It was just a matter of getting back to twelve-step.

So that was his plan: keep clean and stow away a ton of cash over the next year. Then he'd hightail it to—who knew?—Greece, Tangiers, Barcelona and spend his time in creative isolation, doing nothing but drinking strong coffee and writing poems. He'd mail them back to Terri one by one, so she'd know he was doing fine. Otherwise, she was likely to chase him around the world, trying to look after him.

Terri had always had a tendency to mother him, and sometimes it just got out of hand. Just a few days ago, he'd had to tell her what was what on that score. That had sent her packing, and he hadn't heard from her since. Probably she'd gone back to Vancouver, which was perfectly fine with Kevin. He'd call her in a couple of weeks, let her know he didn't hold a grudge. For now, the important thing was to get a nest egg together, and Red Bear was just the man to help him do it.

When Red Bear had first come along, all dressed in white, talking of his contacts in the spirit world, Kevin had written him off as just another nutcase. That had been almost a year ago. Kevin and Leon had been sitting outside the Lemon Tree on Algonquin Avenue, shooting the breeze, watching the girls go by. It was likely going to be the last perfect day of summer, and all the tables were taken. Red Bear got out of a black car—someone else had been driving—and headed inside the shop. A few minutes later he reappeared with a lemonade and came right over.

"You mind if I sit here?" He said it to Leon, not Kevin.

Leon shrugged. "It's a free country."

Red Bear pulled the chair out and spun it around, then sat down facing them with his elbows on its back. The fringes of his white jacket hung nearly to the pavement.

"In exchange for your kindness, I will read your cards." Red Bear had a curiously formal way of speaking, as if he were translating from another language.

Kevin was expecting a Tarot deck, but Red Bear pulled out an ordinary pack of cards and fanned them out across the table. "Pick a card to represent yourself," he said to Leon. Leon tapped the king of hearts, nothing subtle about Leon. He sat back and rubbed his forehead with his index finger. He had a small scar there, and sometimes he rubbed at it as if he could erase it.

Red Bear gathered up all the cards except the king, shuffled them, and then began laying them out in squares and crosses. A deep groove of concentration formed between his brows. "You've recently had trouble with a relative," he said. "A difference over money."

Leon looked at Kevin. His cousin had stayed with him the past winter and had stolen two hundred dollars before hopping on a Greyhound in the middle of the night. Next day, Leon had gotten drunk and beat the hell out of some stranger in the Chinook Tavern, till Kevin had managed to pull him off. Leon had raged about his cousin for weeks afterwards.

"That's pretty right on," he said to Red Bear. "Keep going."

"There is violence in your past." Red Bear looked up from the cards, a trace of concern on his brow. "You can be a violent man."

Leon laughed. Maybe with nerves.

"Not really. I've mellowed out a lot. Well, okay. Yeah. I been known to lose my temper now and again."

Red Bear returned his gaze to the cards. "You have coming up some major opportunities for development. Perhaps a way to channel this anger."

"Okay, all right. Can we move on to another subject, please?"

"You are leaving behind a period of romantic frustration."

"I hope so," Leon said. "Women, man. I could use a little action along that line."

"You are alone right now—romantically, I mean— you've been alone for some time." Red Bear snapped a two of hearts across the king and took off his sunglasses, looked up at Leon. "That, my friend, is about to change."

It was then that Kevin realized what a handsome guy Red Bear was. Strong bones in that face, two little parentheses at the corners of his mouth when he smiled, and those eyes. When he took off his sunglasses, Red Bear's eyes were the palest blue Kevin had ever seen, paler than a husky's, almost transparent.

Red Bear had pointed out a lot of other stuff in Leon's cards that Kevin could not now remember. Leon had been impressed, excited even, but Kevin hadn't been, not then: lucky guess on the money thing, and the rest was the sort of crap you saw in astrology columns all the time.

"You're skeptical," Red Bear had said to Kevin. Those transparent eyes, those amazing cheekbones. Cherokee. The word had popped into Kevin's mind, even though he didn't know a Cherokee from a Blackfoot. The man looked every inch the Red Bear, even before he mentioned his background.

"It doesn't matter if you believe," Red Bear said. "A thing will be true whether you believe it or not." He spread the cards again. "Pick one to represent yourself."

"Naw, that's okay."

"Go ahead. Pick one."

"No, really. It's not my kind of thing."

"I'll pick one for you." Red Bear selected a jack of diamonds. Jack of all trades? Jack-off? One-eyed jack? One-eyed monster?

Red Bear shuffled the cards and snapped them off the top of the deck one by one.

"Problems with the family," he said. "Someone older than you. The two of you bump heads now and again."

Close. Very close, but Kevin didn't say anything.

"You have recently overcome a bad habit, perhaps an addiction. That shows clearly, here." He tapped the pair of threes with a seven of diamonds. Kevin felt the hair at the back of his neck lift.

The queen of hearts came up, separated from the king by another three. "You have a lady in your life," Red Bear said.

"Not me, man. Broke up with one about six months ago, and now I'm as single as they come."

"I didn't say a lover. I said you had a lady in your life. A good woman who loves you. But this habit or addiction is a problem between you."

Well, all right. That could be Terri. Once you have an addiction, a lot of stuff follows. Call it a lucky guess followed by common sense.

Snap, snap, snap. King, ace, king.

"Oh, you are easy to read, my friend. A pleasure, too."

"Why's that?"

Red Bear tapped the cards—strong finger, manicured nail. "The kings, my friend. The kings. You are going to be rich."

Kevin laughed out loud at that one.

Red Bear leaned forward, squinted at the air around him. "I'm seeing a lot of odd shapes around you. T shapes. This lady of yours, is her name Tammy? Something like that?"

"There's someone named Terri," Kevin said. "But she's not my lady."

"Really? I see a strong connection there."

Red Bear finished his lemonade and got up. Somehow he could drink a lemonade and make it seem as serious as bourbon. He signalled to the black car parked across the street. The car started up and made a U-turn, stopping right in front of the café.

"If I see you again, my friend, maybe you'll tell me how you plan to make all that money."

"You're the one who sees the future. You're going to have to tell me."

Red Bear had grinned—teeth by Paramount Pictures—and opened the car door.

Kevin rubbed the bite on his neck and stared at the rough wood of the cabin ceiling. He heard another car drive up, and a couple of shouts. That would be Leon back from town; he always made a racket when he rolled up. He'd be knocking on Kevin's door any minute, wanting to shoot the breeze. Big talker, Leon, but a little too prone to violence for Kevin's peace of mind. And his talk was getting strange since they'd taken up with Red Bear. Spooky, even.

Although Kevin didn't believe in astrology or card reading or any of that paranormal blather, Red Bear had been close enough on a couple of counts that a tiny vibration of fear had started in the pit of his stomach. And even though Red Bear treated him pretty well, that fear had never really quit; it hung on like a low-grade fever.

There had been four in Kevin's outfit back before Red Bear arrived on the scene. Kanga was ostensibly their leader—basically because he owned the only car that could be trusted to make the trip to Toronto and back to pick up the dope. Kanga was a serious pothead who smoked the stuff all day long. He'd once told Kevin that the only reason he'd started dealing was so he could afford his own habit. He tried to counterbalance the weed with a regimen of weight training, but Kevin figured he only did the weight training because it involved a lot of sitting still. Kanga was an optimist, a hopelessly amiable leader—if you could call someone who could hardly keep a toe on the earth *leader*. He was trim and fit and didn't spend a lot of time worrying about the future.

Leon Rutkowski was a reformed speed freak with an extremely unpredictable temper. Except for the incident in the Chinook, Kevin had never seen it personally, but he had heard things: one story concerning a man who ended up in hospital, another involving a baseball bat. Leon was all for making lots of money. In fact, Kanga had once said he never would have gotten into the heroin trade if Leon hadn't bugged him about it so much. They were already well into it when Kevin joined up. Leon was stringy, but with a pot belly that hung over the belt of his jeans owing to the junk food he was so fond of. Kevin wasn't sure why, but Leon had seemed a good deal calmer since Red Bear had come on the scene; healthier, too, putting more thought into what he ate. And he'd stopped complaining about not getting laid. Every now and again Red Bear would bring babes up from Toronto, hookers no doubt, and share them with Leon.

Then there was Toof. His real name was Morris Tilley, but everyone called him Toof because of the extra incisor that pushed its way to the front of his unruly dentition. That, along with his floppy hair and the droopy way he held his head, combined to give him a doglike air, which was quite appropriate because he was really more of a mascot than a serious member of the outfit. Toof talked a lot and, owing to the fact that he was a hopeless pothead, what he said did not always make sense. And he had an absolute genius for getting lost—not easy to do in a place the size of Algonquin Bay, but Toof seemed to lack the inner positioning device that allows most human beings to leave home in the morning with a reasonable expectation of finding their way back.

Red Bear had come along at the lowest point in their fortunes. The Viking Riders had become more aggressive, consolidating their grip on the whole northern territory. Suddenly they seemed to be moving tons more dope, and there was precious little Kanga and his boys could do about it. Kevin had been reduced to skulking along Oak Street, hoping that some of his old clientele would remain loyal enough to buy the odd dime of smack. A few did, but not enough. Everyone was afraid of the Viking Riders.

Kanga had decided it was time to have a "sit-down" with the bikers. See, that was the kind of blue-sky optimist Kanga was. You have a problem with bikers, you take over a bag of sensimilla and smoke a peace pipe with them. The bikers had agreed to the sit-down, but it hadn't gone well at all. The gang told Kanga, overexplicitly in his view, to cease and desist operating in their territory. Otherwise, they would introduce him to a world of pain. To emphasize the point, one of the bikers—a big mother named Wombat—had pissed on him. Literally.

First their customers, then their suppliers dried up; they didn't want Kanga's group as subcontractors. Everybody had to deal exclusively with the Riders or risk being put out of business, to use the polite term. In desperation, Kanga had ventured further afield for product, driving as far as Montreal to round up first-class narcotics.

"You're out of your mind," Kevin had told him. "There's no way we're going to be able to move that stuff without the Riders going berserk."

They were in Kanga's basement apartment. Kanga was on his back at his Universal gym, smoking a joint. He took a hit, offered it to Kevin, who declined, and set it in the ashtray.

Kanga smiled and pressed another one-fifty. He held the weight and released smoke through his teeth. "That's the beauty part," he said, his voice all gaspy from the weed. "I'm not gonna go into competition with them. I'm going to set us up as their suppliers."

"Don't do it, man. Don't even think that. They'll just rip you off. They're already moving so much dope, you're not going to be able to beat whatever price they're getting."

"Leave it to me, man. I know what I'm doing."

"You going to wear a wetsuit this time?"

"Hey, fuck you, man. That was just one goon." Kanga set down the weight and took another hit off the joint. His words emerged smokily between clenched teeth. "The other guys were actually kind of apologetic about it."

And so Kanga had set up another meeting with the Viking Riders. Kevin and Leon and Toof had never seen him again.

Without Kanga, the group had rapidly gone to hell. Kevin had made regular trips to Toronto and brought back small amounts of speed and heroin by train. But it didn't add up to a paying proposition. What with all the stress of their misfortunes, he'd found himself once again with a needle in his arm. It had taken all his strength to quit again: methadone, twelve-step, the whole pathetic cabaret. By then, he had been barely able to make the rent on his miserable little apartment.

"The thing to do," Leon had mused one day. "Instead of buying from the Viking Riders, or trying to buy around them—what we should do is take over their import business."

They were sitting in the sun on a rock cut near the railway tracks, watching the French girls heading down Front Street to the École Secondaire.

"Somehow they're bringing the stuff in from the States," Leon went on, "and now they're shipping it across the goddamn country. If we could somehow take over that end of things they'd be forced to deal with us."

"Yeah," Toof said, wheezing through a plume of pot smoke. "That sounds good. Why don't we do that?"

"Because Kanga had the same idea," Kevin said. "And Kanga never came back."

So there they had been: Leon a talker, not a leader; Kevin with no ambition whatsoever to run things; and Toof out of the question. It was onto this bleak stage that Red Bear had first strode, promising them magic and riches. How could a junkie resist?

Red Bear rapidly made Algonquin Bay his own, using little more than his good looks and a deck of cards. He could often be found at Everett's Coffee Bar on Sumner, the last of the independent coffee joints. He would sit at a corner table with his deck of cards, and after a while people just came to him. Everett's didn't mind; Red Bear brought people in. They'd buy a coffee and go over to him and he'd read their cards. They knew he was good, Kevin figured, because he charged so much: seventy-five bucks a pop, thank you very much. He also did astrology charts, which cost twice as much.

It was difficult to have a conversation with him, because people were always coming over to the table to get a reading. Kevin didn't know how much he earned doing this, but it had to be substantial, and naturally tax-free. And it gave him an in with all sorts of people: The local musicians started going to him, and once he'd got a couple of hairstylists among his clientele, they spread the word. He claimed to have done some modelling in Toronto—he was certainly handsome enough—but Kevin figured he had to have some other source of income. But whatever it was, Red Bear kept it pretty much under wraps. Certainly he never attracted any police attention.

When he wasn't reading cards, Red Bear went out of his way to befriend Kevin and Leon. He gave them samples of the best pot either of them had ever tried, he took them to the movies a couple of times and he was always buying them drinks, although he didn't drink much himself. He didn't even seem to mind Toof. Like the other two, Kevin was flattered by the attention, even if he remained a little suspicious of it.

Over the next few months, Red Bear became a major part of their lives. Eventually he revealed his other business to them, which was shipping medium-sized packets of cocaine and heroin cross-country. He did this from a location just outside Algonquin Bay. He wouldn't say where.

"You'd better watch out for the Viking Riders," Kevin warned him. "We told you what happened to Kanga."

"I am not worried about the Riders," Red Bear said. "I am protected."

"Protected?"

By way of answer, Red Bear had just pointed to the sky. One chilly spring night—it must have been late April, early May, before the flies were out—they were all down at the beach. Red Bear had constructed a beautiful fire— an altar fire, he called it—that burned slow and steady for hours. Leon and Toof were there, the sky was all Milky Way and a breeze blew in off the lake. Waves slapped quietly on the shore; from further down the beach came the noises of a party in progress, but the mood among the four had been contemplative, even solemn.

Red Bear had asked about their life stories. Leon poked thoughtfully at the treads of his hiking boots with a stick, cleaning the mud off them, while he talked about his past. He was the only child of two drunkards, one of whom had killed the other when Leon was sixteen and would probably never get out of prison. He got the scar on his forehead when his mother had thrown a toaster at him. Toof stared into the flames, firelight flickering in his eyes, as he told Red Bear he was the youngest of seven, raised by a widowed mom who worked three jobs and never knew which of her sons would end up in the nick next. Kevin didn't say too much. Parents died when he was ten years old. Fell in love with poetry. Dropped out of college after second year. Got wired to smack. Kicked it. He didn't mention that he was skin-popping again; no need to burden the others with too much information.

The three of them looked at Red Bear. So far, they knew nothing about him, other than that he came from a reserve somewhere up north.

He smiled, those perfect teeth gleaming in the firelight.

"You want to know about me? I will tell you. This, of course, is the first thing you have to know." He pulled out his wallet and snapped a card on the table.

Kevin picked it up. It was a status card issued by the Department of Indian and Northern Affairs, confirming that Raymond Red Bear was a member of the Chippewa First Nation at Red Lake, which was located beyond the northern shores of Lake Superior and boasted a climate that made Algonquin Bay look like Florida.

Firelight flickered on Red Bear's face like a stage effect. His voice was soft, all but inaudible above the lapping waves.

"Life on the reserve," he told them, "was cold. Hard. Our house never had enough heat. There was never enough food in the refrigerator. Every morning the frost formed patterns on the bedroom window."

Red Bear fell silent, staring into the fire. No one said anything for a while.

Finally Leon said, "Are you going to tell us more?"

Red Bear shook his head. "I would like to. I trust you. I trust all of you." He looked at them: Leon, Kevin and Toof, one after another. "But there are things of which I cannot speak. And other things which you are just not ready to know. There is certain knowledge only a few must have."

Kevin wanted to get out of there and get to bed and just sleep. The mood was way too weird.

Red Bear smiled. "Don't worry," he said. "In a week or two, I will make a sacrifice, and then we will know exactly how to turn our fortunes around."

"Sacrifice?" Kevin said.

"Don't say anything more just now, Kevin. You will see soon enough what I mean."

Leon flicked his cigarette into the fire. "Does this sacrifice mean I get to walk down Main Street again without worrying I'm going to get seriously fucked up by bikers?"

"Oh, yes. I guarantee it. If things go the way I expect them to, six months from now the Viking Riders will tremble when you approach."

"Righteous, man," Leon said. "Way it should be."

9

A WEEK AFTER THAT SOLEMN NIGHT on the beach, the four of them meet up at the Rosebud Diner, a greasy spoon just south of town by Reed's Falls. Red Bear, Kevin, Leon and Toof. Toof's looking shame-faced because he got lost on his way to the Rosebud—a place he has been to at least three times, by Kevin's count—and the others had to wait. Red Bear doesn't say anything, just stares at Toof with those husky's eyes of his. Then he leads them out into the woods.

First they follow the hydro lines over the hill, then they veer off into a snowmobile trail, deserted at this time of year. After a few hundred yards, they venture onto a trail that is a trail in theory but is scarcely easier to walk than the thickest of the brush surrounding it. Eventually they come to the crest of a hill, a rocky clearing.

Red Bear had them build an altar fire the way he had shown them. He pointed to the three-quarter moon, riding some low clouds. "Perfect," he said. "Just perfect." He was dressed in buckskin pants and vest, both with a fringe, the vest decorated with intricate beadwork. Hollywood Indian, Kevin thought, preposterous on any-one else, but not on Red Bear. A canteen clanked against his belt, next to a long knife sheathed in buckskin.

Red Bear waited until the fire was blazing.

"Our sacrifice is waiting on the other side of the hill. You three stay here, and do not move—no matter what you hear, do not move. You may hear nothing. When I return I will do a ceremonial dance. If this is too strange for you, if you cannot open yourself to other cultures, other customs, then I ask you to back out now. Back out now, and never return."

Nobody moved.

"If you choose to stay, you must never speak of this to anyone. Do you understand?"

Red Bear stepped up to Kevin, his face inches away, pale eyes otherworldly. "Do you understand?"

"Yeah, sure. I understand. I'll stay."

Red Bear did the same to Leon. Leon also said he would stay.

Then Toof. Runty little Toof with his turned-up nose almost like a pig's. In the firelight he looked like some nocturnal creature.

"Do you understand?" Red Bear said to Toof. "You must never speak of this to anyone."

"I won't. I promise."

"On pain of death," Red Bear said.

"Don't worry about me," Toof said. "I won't tell a soul, eh? You guys are like my brothers."

"Exactly. We are your family now."

Red Bear unsheathed his knife.

"Wait in silence. I will return in ten minutes. Do not speak during this time. Stare into the flames and empty your minds. I will ask the spirits for direction."

Red Bear pointed the knife high over his head, stretching on tiptoe as if hoping for lightning to strike. He began to speak in what Kevin figured was Ojibwa or Chippewa or some damn thing. Sounded like nothing he'd ever heard, full of clicks and gutturals, not sentences so much as a meandering flow of syllables. There were many repetitions. Then Red Bear lowered the knife and strode over the hill, beads rattling.

Kevin stared into the flames.

No sounds came from the far side of the hill, and none of the three figures around the crackling fire said a word.

Kevin's face felt scorched, but his back was uncomfortably cold. He wished they were downtown, sinking a few pints at the World Tavern.

There was a cry, and then a dark shape came over the hill. Red Bear broke into a run, cried out again and leaped into the circle between them and the fire. He was chanting now, and doing a loose-limbed shuffle around the flames, accompanied by his low singsong. His shadow, thrown by the firelight, reared and stretched across the surrounding rocks and trees.

Gradually the dance became more energetic. Red Bear leaped and spun, his arms and shoulders gleaming in the firelight. His arms were soaked in blood up to the elbows. He swung a large leather bag from hand to hand around his body, and he revolved around the fire, making a wheels-within-wheels pattern. Then he stopped, opened the bag and held it upside down over the flames. The contents crashed onto the burning wood, and sparks swirled into the sky.

The other three jerked back from the fire, coughing and brushing at their clothes. When Kevin turned back, a pig's head was sizzling in the flames, its little eyes shut tight and crinkled at the corners as if in merriment. His muzzle was wrapped with duct tape. His four trotters sizzled and blackened around him.

Red Bear stood close to the fire and stretched toward the sky, every muscle in his body straining. The veins in his neck stood out like electrical cords. His voice had gone thin and raspy and the words came streaming out of him with a terrible urgency. The words—if in fact they were words—collided with one another. Spit flew across the firelight, and at one point Red Bear sounded like he was going to choke. Kevin wondered if he was insane. Leon didn't look particularly perturbed, but Toof was open-mouthed, a kid at the circus.

Then the voice stopped, and Red Bear seemed to go slack, released from whatever had held him. He sank slowly to the ground.

Nobody spoke.

After a while, Red Bear spoke in his normal voice. "Did I say anything?"

"Yeah," Kevin said. "You said a lot. Unfortunately, not in English."

"Sometimes I don't know if I am just hearing the voices, or if I am transmitting them."

"Oh, you were transmitting loud and clear."

"Perfect," Red Bear said. "We have direction now."

"Which way do we go?" Toof said. "North?"

Leon gave him a look of pity. "Not that kind of direction, you moron." He turned to Red Bear. "How much direction? Do we know what to do next?"

"Oh, yes. I have a time and a place, an actual address." Red Bear slapped his knees and looked at the others. "You were frightened?"

"No, it was fantastic," Toof said. "Like something out of the movies, man. Cool dance."

"You?" Red Bear looked at Leon.

"Naw, I wasn't scared. Can't say it was the most comfortable I've ever been in my life."

"You?" Red Bear's gaze fell on Kevin.

"Nervous," Kevin said. "The voice thing definitely made me nervous. Also, you have a lot of blood on you."

Red Bear looked at his arms as if he had never seen them before. He opened his canteen and poured water over first one arm, then the other. It took him several minutes to get the blood off.

"Did you really kill a pig over there?" Toof said.

Red Bear ignored the question, or maybe he didn't hear it. He was concentrating on cleaning the blood off his arms. "Probably my voice changed, no?"

"Yeah," Toof said. "You went all fuzzy."

"That is not my voice. That is the spirit talking. He doesn't want to talk, so it's a difficult thing sometimes. But what he told me . . ." Red Bear dumped the rest of his canteen onto the fire. Water hissed and steamed. "If what he told me is true, we are going to have great success."

"When?" Toof wanted to know. "When does it start?"

"Three days from now. We'll take a little trip together."

"Where? Where are we going?"

"You ask too many questions. I'll tell you where when it's time to leave."

———

A few days later, Red Bear had Leon round up the other two and bring them out to the Rosebud. Leon refused to tell them what it was about; it was supposed to be a surprise. Red Bear was waiting for them at his usual table.

"I have found us the perfect home," he said, leaving a fiver on the table for his coffee.

Outside, he climbed into his BMW, and the rest of them followed in Leon's Trans Am. The place turned out to be an abandoned summer camp on the south shore of Lake Nipissing. The collection of little cabins was slated for demolition, after which a hotel was planned on the site. Red Bear had some connection in the demolition company and had arranged use of the place for the summer. There was an overgrown baseball diamond, a big stone fireplace for cooking outdoors and a collapsed ruin of a dock.

"Man, it's got a beach and everything," Toof said. "Volleyball posts, too. I wonder if there's a net anywhere."

"Why, you wanna start a team?" Leon said. "There's no net, no ball—there's no supplies of any kind. There's just the cabins."

"What's it going to cost?" Kevin said.

"Nothing at all," Red Bear said. He smiled behind glittering sunglasses. "Our only costs are water and electricity."

Within a day, all of them had moved in. Each had his own cabin and could come and go as he pleased. Cooking facilities at the camp were minimal, so they would have to eat a lot of their meals at the Rosebud, but Red Bear and Leon spent as much time at the camp as possible. Kevin and Toof, on the whole, preferred town life during the day, but you couldn't beat the rent.

—

A couple of nights after moving into the camp, Kevin had found himself in the back of a small cabin cruiser that cut across the choppy north bay of Lake Nipissing. Toof leaned over the side, trailing a hand in the water. Leon was at the wheel, and Red Bear was in the big leather seat beside him. He swivelled slowly back and forth, a small smile on his lips. He still wore his sunglasses, even though it was well past sundown.

A stiff wind was blowing in from the west, and Kevin was wishing he had brought his jacket. They had pushed off from a private dock in Shanley and now they were scooting across the vast north bay. They were so far out that the car headlights looked like fireflies. A full moon lit the silvery spire of the cathedral and the blocky apartment buildings that form Algonquin Bay's skyline. The Manitou Islands slid by on their left, the Anishinabeck reserve on their right. After that, lights on the shore became sparse. When the moon ducked behind a cloud, the lake went black as velvet.

Twenty minutes later, Red Bear pointed to a set of lighted buoys. "French River," he said, yelling over the noise of the inboard. "Nearly there." He stood up, placing a hand on Leon's shoulder. He leaned down and said something to him, pointing through the windshield. Leon turned the wheel and the boat scooped around toward the shore. Three lights glimmered among the trees, a triangular constellation.

"That is what the spirit showed me," Red Bear shouted above the noise. "That triangle."

At a signal from Red Bear, Leon cut the motor and they drifted on the black water.

"From this point on, no one speaks. Leon and I will do all the talking. There may be no one there, or maybe one person at the most. Either way, it won't be a problem. Toof, you stay in the boat."

"No, I wanna come, too. Come on, Bear. Lemme come, too."

"You stay in the boat. It's important. You must be ready to take off at any moment. Can I trust you to do that?"

"Oh, sure, eh. I'd just rather go with you guys is all."

A dock materialized before them in the dark. Red Bear leaped onto it and wrapped a rope around a cleat, then said to Kevin almost in a whisper, "Toss me that one."

Kevin tossed him the aft rope, and Red Bear pulled the stern around so that the boat was facing out toward the lake. Then he took another coil of rope from the stern and hung it over his shoulder as if he were about to climb a mountain. Toof went up front behind the wheel.

Kevin and Leon jumped onto the dock. The three of them moved silently along the sand toward the triangle of lights. Kevin followed Leon up stone steps to someone's backyard, a small bungalow all but hidden among tall bushes. He looked around and saw that Red Bear was no longer with them. There were lights on in the house, and the shifting cool glow of a television. Kevin's heart thudded against his ribs.

Leon didn't hesitate. He went right up to the door and knocked.

The TV went silent. Then a man's voice, not friendly: "Who is it?"

"Peter Northwind sent me."

There was the sound of something sliding and then a pinhole of light in the door. It dimmed, and the voice came again. "You're not Northwind."

"Well, no *duh*, asshole. That's why I said Northwind *sent* me. You Wombat?"

"Never mind who I am. You're early. Like four hours early."

"We had a tailwind. What're we supposed to do, float around your fucking lake for a couple of hours?"

"Password."

"What?"

"You heard me. What's the password?"

"There isn't one, cowboy. I got twenty pounds of passwords right here." Leon held up the suitcase.

"Stand back from the door."

Leon and Kevin stepped back a little.

"Make a move and you're dead."

"Don't worry. We're not moving."

The door opened and a human immensity with a grey ponytail filled the doorway. A gun gleamed in the moonlight.

"No one fucks with the Viking Riders and lives to tell about it," he said. "I hope for your sake you're not trying to do that."

"Hell, no," Leon said. "We're not about to mess up a great relationship."

"I got no relationship with you. I got a relationship with Northwind. Put the suitcase down and step back."

Leon put down the case, and he and Kevin moved back. Kevin had never had a gun pointed at him before and he was amazed at how effective it was. His kneecaps were doing a major shimmy and he badly needed a bathroom.

"Open it."

Leon dropped to one knee and pressed the catches of the case.

"Hang on a second, I think they're stuck." He rattled them a little, cursing.

"I don't like it," the man said. "You can go fuck yourself."

A soft thud. A blade was pressed against the man's neck. "Drop it," Red Bear said. "Or I'll cut you another mouth."

The gun stayed where it was. "You so much as give me a paper cut, your friend here dies."

"Yes, but he will die quickly. Whereas you . . ."

"How do I know you won't kill me anyway?"

"I don't need to," Red Bear said. "If you don't give me a reason to kill you, then I won't."

The man lowered the gun. Red Bear pulled it from his hand and brought it down on his head.

The man sank to his knees, struggled to rise, and Red Bear clouted him again. The man toppled and stayed down. Red Bear tossed the gun to Leon, slipped the rope off his shoulder and tied the man's hands with a complicated knot.

Leon pulled at Kevin's sleeve. "Come on."

Kevin followed Leon through the doorway into the kitchen.

"Anybody home?" Leon yelled, then giggled. "I love this thing," he said, waving the gun. "I could get used to this. Let's do a circuit. I feel like making a withdrawal."

They went from room to room, looking for the cash Red Bear had said would be there. The place had an unused look, definitely underfurnished. Kevin threw open a few closets, finding nothing.

Then Leon shouted from another room, "Found it!"

Leon was in a small bedroom, empty except for a narrow cot. He had already pulled the briefcase from the closet. It was the kind that had combination locks on the latches, but the Vikings hadn't bothered to use them. He snapped them open, and then they were looking at the most cash either of them had ever seen, stacks of it bound in tight bundles.

"Oh, boy," Kevin said. "Why do I have a desperate urge to pee?"

"'Cause you're wettin' yourself, man. We're rich."

"Now maybe you believe in magic, hey?" Red Bear had come in behind them.

"I always did," Leon said. "But now I'm a magic evangelist. I'm a magic missionary. I want to convert people to magic."

"Back to the boat," Red Bear said. "We don't want to be here when the rest of the Vikings get back."

When they were outside again, Red Bear slapped their biker hostage into partial consciousness. The man got to his knees, swayed and threw up. It took a while, and some prodding with the knife, to get him down to the dock.

Kevin didn't like seeing so much of the knife. Nothing Red Bear had said before this adventure had prepared him for violence.

Toof started the motor as they stepped into the boat. He touched the briefcase as if it were a holy relic. "Are we on top, or what?"

"We're on Mount Everest, man," Leon said.

Red Bear pushed the groggy Rider, now reeking of vomit, on board. "Keep him below. Clean him up and put this over his mouth." He tossed Leon a roll of duct tape. "But make sure he can breathe. I don't want him to die on us."

Leon shoved the biker down the steps ahead of him and disappeared below.

"What are we going to do with him?" Kevin said. A tumour of anxiety was growing in his belly.

"We'll just hold him until this little transaction is over, then we'll let him go."

"The Riders will kill us, you realize. I mean, really kill us. Kanga disappeared from the face of the earth."

Red Bear stepped so close to Kevin he could feel the heat from his face. The look in Red Bear's eyes was so tender, Kevin was suddenly afraid he was going to be kissed.

"You don't have to worry about anything any more, Kevin. I am looking after you now. And as you can see . . ." he gestured toward the shore, the sky, the lake, ". . . there are others looking after me. All you have to do is trust me."

"I'm just scared, that's all. We just ripped off a biker gang."

"I understand. But don't you trust me?"

"I trust you."

Red Bear sat in the seat beside Toof, who had cast off. He put his face right up to Toof's so that Toof drew back surprised. "Do you trust me?"

"Yeah, sure, I trust you," Toof said. "'Course I trust you. You're my Red Bear!"

Red Bear clapped a hand on his shoulder. "Good. Sit back and let me take the wheel."

"Oh, come on. Lemme drive."

"Another time."

Toof looked disappointed but he got up and moved to the back of the boat.

Red Bear steered them toward the south side of the Manitous. The lights of Algonquin Bay brightened for a few minutes, then disappeared behind the black shoulders of the islands. The temperature had dropped, and Kevin hugged himself to keep warm. His arms were stippled with goosebumps.

After a while, Red Bear cut the motor and allowed the boat to drift, waves smacking the hull.

The buzz of a small airplane became audible. Kevin scanned the horizon, but all he could see were the outlines of moonlit clouds. The buzz grew louder. The plane dipped beneath the clouds, a four-seater at most. It came up behind them with a roar and then wafted down toward the water, wings see-sawing a little.

The pontoons skimmed the surface, then plowed up twin white furrows in the black water. Red Bear started the inboard and cruised up to the plane. There were numbers and letters on its side, but Kevin had no idea what they meant. It could be a local plane or it could be fresh in from Chicago or the Caribbean, for all he knew. The tiny door opened, and Kevin caught a glimpse of a face framed by shoulder-length dark hair, but not before he saw the shotgun.

"You Red Bear?"

"That's me."

"Show me your status card."

"My what?"

"Your status card. Make it quick."

Red Bear extracted the card from his wallet and handed it up. "Don't take my word for anything," he said. "You can check with Chief Whiteflint up at—"

"Up at Red Lake. Yeah, I already did that. He says you're okay."

"Just don't ask me to speak any Ojibwa."

"Doesn't mean shit to me, either."

There were some delicate manoeuvres while Red Bear and the man in the plane exchanged briefcases. Leon opened the new briefcase, revealing stacks of six-ounce Baggies filled with white powder.

"Test it," Red Bear said.

Kevin pulled out one of the lower bags and poked a tiny hole in it. He took a deep breath and held it, trying to get his hands to stop shaking. He lifted a miniature heap of powder on the tip of his knife and dropped it on his tongue. The bitter taste of heroin filled his entire being. He opened up his "chemistry set" and tipped a speck of powder into a small flask. Then he broke an ampoule of clear liquid into it and swirled the mixture around for about thirty seconds. Traces of red and green appeared, then faded. He broke open a second ampoule, added it to the flask and swirled again for five seconds.

Red Bear aimed the beam of a large flashlight at the flask. The liquid had settled to one colour.

"Deep purple," Kevin said. "We're looking at something around eighty-percent purity. Virtually step-free."

"You finished counting?" Red Bear called up to the plane.

The face reappeared in the window.

"I just got one question."

"Go ahead," Red Bear said.

"How'd you manage to take over the Viking Riders' milk run?"

"We persuaded them that it was just better business to go along with us."

"Uh-huh. And how'd you do that?"

"Magic," Red Bear said.

A moment later, the plane took off, a shadow slipping across the moonlit clouds.

Red Bear piloted the boat across the bay and back to the private dock they had borrowed it from. Kevin had no idea if they had really borrowed it or if they had ripped off the boat as well as the money. Well, he supposed he could live with a rip-off, provided there was a little something in the spoon when you were done.

Red Bear got off the boat first. Then he turned to them and spread his hands like a priest giving a blessing. "Thank you, everyone. This little venture went like clockwork, and you will all be well paid. Tomorrow night we'll have a major celebration. Really, you behaved like professionals, and I'm very proud of you all."

"What about our Viking friend?" Kevin said.

"I can see you are still frightened, Kevin. But I have knowledge that you lack in this matter. You don't have to

worry about our Viking friend. I am going to introduce
him to the wonders of the spirit world, and the Vikings
won't cause us the slightest trouble."

"But as soon as he goes back to them he's going to tell
them everything. He'll have to. They'll kill him otherwise."

"He isn't going back to them." Red Bear smiled benev-
olently into their disbelief. "After tonight, he will be
working for us."

Red Bear led the groggy Viking to his BMW and top-
pled him into the trunk.

A couple of weeks went by, and they didn't hear anything more of Wombat Guthrie. Whether or not he was
actually working for Red Bear, Kevin had no idea. The
thing was, he was now part-owner of more grade-A
heroin than he'd ever seen in his life, and he was not
about to separate himself from it by getting too nosy.

—

Kevin smacked at a fly with the swatter. It made a big
noise, but the fly just zigzagged over to the cabin window. He wondered once again where Terri was, if she
really had gone all the way back to Vancouver. He
thought about calling her up and apologizing, but then
figured what the hell.

"She says she's just trying to help you," Letterman
pointed out, chin on hand.

"I know, I know."

"And she could be right about Red Bear. He's not
exactly the boy next door."

"I realize that, Dave. I'm not eight years old. I don't need anyone playing mommy for me. She had to be told."

Letterman leaned forward. "You said you got off the dope. Why are you still hanging around a mountain of it? You're a skier, is that it?"

"Oh, I'm definitely over the dope thing, Dave. It was just something I needed to go through, and I think I've grown tremendously. But I don't need it any more. I'm strictly in this for the money and then I'm out that door."

10

WHATEVER ELSE PEOPLE MIGHT say about Paul Arsenault and Bob Collingwood—and their colleagues said a lot—they were always prepared. The two-man ident team arrived on the scene behind Nishinabe Falls in hiking boots, khakis and bug shirts. Bug shirts come with a hood and veil too fine for flies to penetrate, and elastic at the cuffs. As they moved about the falls, now reaching up to examine a stain, now kneeling to collect minuscule objects, they looked like a pair of beekeepers.

The young coroner who worked beside them had contented himself with a can of Off. As it turned out, the flies weren't bad behind the falls.

Arsenault collected servings of maggots into several vials, labelling each one. He often thought out loud as he worked, speaking to himself or to anyone who might be interested. Collingwood rarely spoke at all.

"You know, I'm no entomologist," Arsenault said now. He had to raise his voice to be heard over the falling water. "But I got to say, there's way fewer maggots here than I'd expect with a body this old. Got to be around two weeks, anyways. You'd expect the thing to be swarming with them, but this here could be the work of maybe a dozen flies. Handful."

Collingwood was attaching a thermometer to a nearby rock, taking an ambient reading. He turned around and said, "Place is hard to get to."

It took Cardinal a second to figure out what he meant: The flies wouldn't be as likely to come across a body hidden behind a veil of water, or even catch the scent. Also, it was quite chilly amid the damp and the dark.

The coroner stepped back from the body. Arsenault made a sign to Collingwood, and they turned it over. There was a tattoo on the bicep; it had been hidden before: a helmet with horns, and underneath this a banner emblazoned VR. Viking Riders.

"I don't know if a tattoo qualifies as a positive ID," Delorme said. "But me, I'd say Walter 'Wombat' Guthrie has taken his last ride."

Cardinal nodded. "The question is, did the other Riders do this?"

"Not their usual style, is it? All this mutilation, body out in the open?"

"No, they'd be more likely to bury him in a barrel or something so we'd never find him. I'm wondering how this is connected to our Jane Doe."

"Maybe she saw something she shouldn't have."

"Could be—but what? When?"

The coroner was a physician Cardinal had never worked with before, a Dr. Rayburn, who looked like a schoolboy fairly new to shaving. He was a lot easier on the nerves than the malevolent codger they usually got. Dr. Rayburn filled out a form and tore off the top two copies, handing one to Cardinal.

"No trouble determining foul play, obviously. You can ship it straight to Grenville Street. The pathologist is going to have a field day with this one."

"Why's that?"

"Well, you no doubt noticed the extremities are missing."

"Yes, Doc. Even I managed to catch that."

"Even worse, there's a big patch of skin missing from the lower back."

"The killer tried to skin him?"

"Alive, unfortunately. I'm not a pathologist, but it's clear to me that a lot of the injuries were inflicted before death. If not all of them. You've got bleeding into the bones."

"Can you pin down a cause?"

"You mean can I tell you which wound finished him off? I can't, but a pathologist might be able to. Most likely bled to death before he was decapitated."

"Bled to death?" Delorme said. "But there's almost no blood."

Dr. Rayburn looked at the corpse and shook his head, a student giving up on a problem. "I can't explain that."

"Sometimes murderers will spread plastic over a floor," Cardinal said. "But I've never heard of it being done outside. Hey, Szelagy!"

The face of Ken Szelagy, a great wide Hungarian bear of a man, appeared around a sharp edge of granite wall.

"Make sure you do the ViCLAS booklet on this one," Cardinal said. ViCLAS was a nationwide database of violent crime. The OPP had an analysis office in Orillia.

Szelagy let out a theatrical groan. "Oh, man. Do you know how many questions those ViCLAS things expect you to answer?"

"Two hundred and sixty-two," Cardinal said. "So, the sooner, the better, right?"

"Of course. As always."

"Ask them to run it with the hieroglyphics as part of the MO, and also without. Those could be unrelated, or they could be a one-time thing."

They began filling many bags with evidence, although *evidence* is too precise a term for the ragtag items they collected. It's a problem common with outdoor crime scenes that there are many artifacts, very few of which, if any, will end up as evidence. Matchbooks, cigarette butts, soft-drink cans, footprints, hairs, fibres—and there's no way of telling which items will prove utterly unrelated to the crime and which may prove crucial in securing a conviction. So it all has to be painstakingly photographed, bagged and labelled. And it takes time.

Cardinal kept a running log in his notebook of their findings. In addition to the usual distracting junk that might later prove to be gold, there were several interesting items.

The first was a Swiss Army knife that Arsenault discovered on the far side of the corpse. It was between two boulders that formed rocky steps out from behind the falls. The knife was too small to be a murder weapon. It was attached to a key chain that held a silver locket.

Arsenault sprung the clasp with a gloved finger. Inside was a black-and-white photo of a couple who appeared to be in their mid-forties. The man was wearing a uniform, but the photo was too small to make out what kind.

"Of course, the probabilities are that it just belongs to some camper," Cardinal said, but he made a note of it anyway.

"It's in pretty good shape," Arsenault said. "Probably hasn't been here that long. For sure, not through the winter."

Collingwood found a rusty railway spike.

"What is a railway spike doing here?" Delorme said. "The train tracks have to be at least two miles from here—on the far side of a highway, the First Nations reserve and a subdivision. It didn't get here by accident."

"But we don't know the killer brought it here," Cardinal said. "And why would he, anyway? It's not sharp enough for a weapon."

The spike was bagged and labelled.

Three sticks turned up, each about an inch thick, and all about a yard long. They had been cut from a birch and stripped of bark. It was Delorme who found them, under a bush a little way down from the site. At first she had thought they had something to do with a campfire. They were exactly the sort of stick you might use to poke a fire, or even use for kindling. But all three were discoloured for about half their length.

"Could be blood," Collingwood said, pointing to the discoloration.

"An expert on edged weapons might be able to tell us if that Swiss Army knife is the blade that cut the sticks," Arsenault said. "Connect the blood to the victim, sticks to the blood, knife to the sticks, the locket to a person."

"Arsenault's already solved the case," Cardinal said. "We can all go home."

"No, it's true," Arsenault said.

"Of course," Cardinal said. "It's good thinking."

Collingwood put the sticks into a large paper bag.

Cardinal went back to the other side of the falls.

Lise Delorme was standing on a shelf of granite, a finger in one ear and her cellphone at the other. She spoke quietly into the phone. There was something sexy about her posture, but Cardinal could not have said exactly what.

She snapped her phone shut and looked up, catching Cardinal's glance. "Body Removal," she said. "They'll be here soon. Didn't sound too enthusiastic, though." She pointed her phone at the markings on the cave wall. "Do those mean anything to you?"

Cardinal stepped closer to the images, the strange drawings of arrows and moons. The numbered charts. "I don't know. I suppose we could be dealing with a Satanist of some sort."

"Don't they go in for pentagrams? I don't see anything like that here. Big on candles, too, I believe. I'm not seeing wax on any of these rocks."

"Well, there's no astrological signs, but there's a serpent down here. God knows what the crossed hammers mean."

"Of course, it's always possible these signs had nothing whatever to do with the murder. Wombat was a biker. Bikers have enemies. We'll get a list and compare times."

"Good luck pinning down a time of death from that mess," Cardinal said, jerking a thumb toward the corpse.

Arsenault got up, brushing off the knees of his pants. He held up a small vial. "These'll help us nail it."

Delorme winced at the squirming mass of maggots.

Arsenault grinned. "Witnesses."

11

LATER, CARDINAL DROVE WITH Arsenault and his vials of "witnesses" along Highway 11. Arsenault was wearing wraparound sunglasses. With his moustache and longish hair, they made him look more like a Viking Rider than a cop.

"So why the hell are we using Angus Chin?" Arsenault wanted to know.

"Because if we take it to Toronto we'll have to get in line like everybody else and it'll slow things down. Besides which, Angus Chin has three post-graduate degrees—in biology, entomology and parasitology—and he knows what the hell he's talking about."

"Yeah. But there's reasons why we've never used him before. I mean, you do know about the rumours, don't you?"

Cardinal knew about the rumours. Some individuals are born to be the subject of gossip; others ask for it. Angus Chin was both. First, there was his background— his father a Scottish merchant seaman, his mother a pharmacist from Hong Kong. In a place like Algonquin Bay, such a background was exotic, if not actually suspect.

Then there were his looks. The Scottish part of Chin's ancestry had rounded his eyes a little, and put some curl in his hair, but he insisted on wearing it in a mandarin ponytail that hung down to his coccyx. This despite the fact that the closest he'd ever got to China was the campus of UCLA.

The rumours began to fly the moment he returned to Algonquin Bay after his lengthy education in Toronto and Los Angeles: He was running from a homicidal homosexual love affair; he was working for mainland China in some malign capacity; he was a doctor who had been defrocked because of unorthodox procedures.

But these were not the rumours that made Paul Arsenault turn to Cardinal, remove his ridiculous sunglasses and squint at him.

"I'm not talking about the little rumours. I'm talking about The Rumour. Capital T, capital R."

"Ah, yes. The big one," Cardinal said.

"And you don't care about this rumour?" Arsenault poked Cardinal in the arm. "You don't think it has any bearing on the case?"

"All I know about The Rumour is that it is a rumour. It's not a fact, and we probably shouldn't be discussing it just before we meet the man."

Arsenault shrugged dramatically. He put his sunglasses back on and looked straight ahead.

The *big* rumour revolved around Angus Chin's interest in parasitology and the study of tapeworms. It was whispered around town that he kept a tapeworm as a pet.

There were, of course, the inevitable questions: *How? In God's name, where?* The answer was that Dr. Chin reportedly kept his tapeworm where tapeworms lived, in his intestine. He would change his diet or some other variable and study the worm's response. Did it grow faster or slower? Fatter or thinner? And how did he measure this response? How did he get access? He would fast for two days. On the third day, he would place a lump of sugar on his tongue. The worm, sensing the presence of nourishment, would make its way up the digestive tract and eventually up the esophagus. When the moment was right, the doctor would reach in and pull the worm from his throat—no small feat, considering the creature was said to be over five feet long.

"Have you considered what a competent defence attorney might do with this information in the event of a trial?" Arsenault didn't take off his sunglasses this time. He stared at Cardinal, and it was like being examined by a huge fly. He mimicked a defence attorney: "Dr. Chin, would you tell the court—do you have any hobbies? Do you keep any pets? A tapeworm. I see. And where do you house your pet worm? In your intestine. How quaint. And is it true you take it out for walks?"

Cardinal said, "Chin doesn't do court. You can't be at the beck and call of judges and prosecutors if you're a full-time academic."

He found a space in the parking lot and they made their way over to the science building. The last of the sun made the brick glow burnt orange. A fresh, watery breeze blew from the lake, and there was the sound of wind through the trees. The campus was intensely green just now.

A group of girls emerged from the student centre, chattering at high volume and with great urgency.

"Geez," Arsenault observed, "they get younger every year. College students actually look like children to me."

"They *are* children." Cardinal's own daughter was only a couple of years out of college.

They followed signs to the biology department and, after some trial and error, found Dr. Chin's office. Cardinal rapped on the door.

"If you're looking for Dr. Chin," a young man with very thick glasses told them, "he's in Bio Lab Three, downstairs."

Dr. Chin was supervising student projects, bending over an array of Petri dishes as he gripped a male student's arm, shaking him. "Don't rush it. Sometimes the fastest way to get your answer is to move very slowly."

"Dr. Chin?"

The doctor stood up and flipped his ponytail over his shoulder. "Who are you?"

"I'm Detective Cardinal, Algonquin Bay Police. This is Detective Arsenault from our ident section."

"Really. How pleasant."

"Can we talk someplace else?"

Chin beckoned to an older student a few desks away, a man with rubbery features that gave him an unhealthy, boneless look.

"This is Dr. Filbert," Chin said. "It won't hurt him to meet our local detectives. Dr. Filbert is a former student of mine and now my unfortunate post-doc. I keep him around solely for purposes of torture."

"You make me wash test tubes that haven't even been used yet."

"Post-docs don't wash test tubes," Chin said. "Dr. Filbert is prone to exaggeration. Nevertheless, I'll allow him to join us if he promises to behave."

"What about the students?"

"They can survive without us for a few moments, I think."

Chin led them to an adjoining lab and hung his white coat on the back of a chair. He was slender, even skinny; at five-six or -seven, he couldn't weigh much over one-twenty. Cardinal wondered about the tapeworm.

Chin sat at a desk equipped with a large magnifier. "All right. Show me what you have."

Arsenault handed the professor a vial.

Chin switched on the magnifier and held the vial under it.

"Very interesting. You have a nice collection of maggots here. Nice work," he said without looking up. "Good label."

"My partner calls me Avis," Arsenault said. "I try harder."

"Okay, you've got a body found outside. Probably in the woods. Somewhere pretty cool, right? Maybe hidden among rocks? Near water, too, I think."

Arsenault looked at Cardinal and back to Dr. Chin. "You can really tell all that?"

"Simple. You've got *Calliphora celliphoridae vomitoria.* It's common in wooded areas."

"Gotta love that name," Filbert said. "Did you know Linnaeus named it?"

"Not everyone is a fly geek, Dr. Filbert." Chin was still staring at the vial under his magnifier. "You also have *Phormia regina.* That's a blowfly that you're going to find absolutely everywhere. But you've also got *Calliphora vicina*. That tells us what, Dr. Filbert?"

"*Vicina* is another blowfly. It only goes places that are shady and cool."

"That's why Dr. Filbert gets the big grants," Dr. Chin said. "Justice Department, no less. They wouldn't give me dick, pardon my French."

"Justice loves DNA," Filbert said cryptically.

"I'm not seeing any other species here. Is that all you have?"

Arsenault handed him three more vials. Chin examined them one after another under the magnifier. "Okay, now you have *Cynomyopsis cadavarina*. Shiny bluebottle. You only get this fly in advanced stages of decay. You've also got rove beetles and staph beetles, short for *Staphylinidae*. They feed on maggots."

"Normally, you'd expect a lot more species than that at an outdoor site," Filbert said. "Especially in the late stages."

"The body was behind a waterfall," Cardinal said.

"Hah!" Chin waggled a finger. "The flies couldn't find it. Couldn't smell it. Makes perfect sense." He rolled his chair back from the magnifier.

"Can you give us anything on time of death?" Arsenault asked.

"What am I—Mr. Wizard? Obviously I have to put these under a microscope to be absolutely sure what they are. And even then, for court purposes, you're going to need them to hatch. That way you nail down the species beyond a doubt. But you've got third-instar *Cynomyopsis* and you've got rove beetles; you're looking at about fourteen days since time of death."

"Can you narrow it down any more than that?"

"Come back next week, gentlemen. I'll be able to tell you a whole lot more."

The double doors of the lab were swinging closed behind them when Arsenault suddenly stopped. "I'm sorry," he said. "I gotta ask."

Before Cardinal could prevent him, Arsenault yanked open one of the doors. "Hey, Doc. I gotta ask you something. Rumour I heard."

"Arsenault," Cardinal said. "For God's sake."

"What rumour would that be, Detective?"

Arsenault appeared to think a minute. "Is it true that blackflies always come out before Victoria Day?"

"In this region? That's not a rumour, Detective. That's a fact."

"Well, thanks for setting me straight. It was bothering me."

"Very amusing," Cardinal said once they were in the parking lot. "Really, you could sit in for Conan O'Brien sometime."

"I gotta tell Delorme," Arsenault said. "The look on your face."

12

DELORME HAD OTHER THINGS on her mind. The body removal service had come and gone (with appropriate expressions of horror and disgust), and the remains of Wombat Guthrie were now in transit to the Centre of Forensic Sciences in Toronto. That left the rest of the evidence to gather up.

With the help of Ken Szelagy and Bob Collingwood, she was collecting gum wrappers, bits of foil, cigarette packs of various ages and conditions, a rusted Dr Pepper can and countless cigarette butts. There were bits of Kleenex, the odd heel print, a handful of beads and a postcard depicting the citadel at Quebec City. This Delorme retrieved from under a rock.

On the back, written in French in a feminine hand: *Dear Robert, Quebec is a fantastic city. Wish you were here with me. I'm missing you all the time.*

"Hey, Bob," Delorme said to Collingwood. "This a letter from your girlfriend?" She held it up for him to see. Collingwood, whose sense of humour had been surgically removed at birth, shook his head.

Delorme slipped the postcard into an evidence bag and tagged it.

A few minutes later she discovered a condom underneath a bush. Even wearing latex gloves, she wasn't about to touch that one. She picked it up with a pair of ident's tongs. "Probably belongs to the same guy as the postcard," she said. Collingwood looked up for a moment, then went back to sifting dirt with a sieve.

"Collingwood, did anyone ever tell you you talk too much?" Delorme dropped the condom into an evidence bag.

Half an hour went by, then Collingwood offered up a single syllable: "Hair." He held a pair of tweezers in the air; Delorme couldn't see anything else.

"How long?"

He shrugged. "Twelve, fourteen inches. Black."

"Good. Let's hope we can eventually connect it to a person."

Another half-hour.

"So, you don't make anything out of these drawings?" Szelagy said. Ken Szelagy, the biggest man on the detective squad, was usually the most talkative. But today he was fascinated by the cave wall, and it had been keeping him uncharacteristically quiet. "You don't find something creepy about all these weird birds and snakes? Don't you think they mean something?"

"Yes, I think they mean something," Delorme said, "to whoever drew them. But personally I don't make anything out of them because I'm not into astrology or whatever they're about, and until we find someone who is, I'm not even going to hazard a guess."

"What're those things?"

Delorme was dropping some bits of shell into a Baggie. "They look like seashells to me."

"Kinda colourful ones. Makes you wonder how the hell they got out to the middle of the woods."

Delorme slapped at a fly and missed. "Well, someone brought them here. The trouble is, we've no way of knowing if it was the killer or just some innocent hiker."

"Yeah. That's the trouble with all this stuff. But about all these arrows and tomahawks the guy scratched on the wall, I'm thinking we should ask a certain person of the Indian persuasion." He jerked his chin toward the mouth of the cave.

Delorme turned around and saw Jerry Commanda standing there, hands on hips, his slim build silhouetted against the waterfall. With the quiet roar of the water, Delorme hadn't heard him approach.

"Who bought it?" he said.

"Wombat Guthrie," Delorme said. "You know him?"

Jerry nodded. "Wombat Guthrie was a noxious individual from the time he was three. It's amazing he lived as long as he did. You called me in from Reed's Falls to tell me this?"

"I didn't call you, Szelagy did. What's so hot in Reed's Falls?"

"Drugs. It's always drugs. I wish people would take up a new vice."

"You know we have your picture up in the boardroom now?"

"That must be the nude shot. I asked Kendall not to do that. Now I feel so cheap."

"Reason I called, Jerry." Szelagy indicated the cave wall. "We can't make head or tail of these hieroglyphics. Figured maybe you could help us."

Jerry stepped up to the wall and peered at the markings. He stood there for a long time, hands folded behind his back like a math teacher checking a student's work. "Interesting," he said. "Very intriguing."

Szelagy looked at Delorme and back to Jerry, waiting for more. When nothing came, he said, "What's intriguing? Why is it intriguing?"

Jerry squatted to look at some of the marks near the bottom of the wall. "Fascinating," he said. "I haven't seen petroglyphs like this since . . . well, I can't remember the last time."

"See, I knew it was some Indian thing," Szelagy said to Delorme. Then, to Jerry: "What's it say? Can you translate? This is great."

"I think so." Jerry pointed at the first three rows of arrows. "See here? This is a reference to space. And over here, he's referring to time. Yes, absolutely. It says, 'Meet me at Tim Hortons, three o'clock on Saturday.'"

"Get the hell outta here," Szelagy said. "No way it says that."

Jerry shrugged. "Could be saying Starbucks. My hieroglyphics are a little rusty."

Delorme shook her head. "Very good, Jerry. Thanks for making the trip."

"Oh," Szelagy said. "I get it. You're making a joke. You don't know what these symbols mean?"

"Haven't the foggiest," Jerry said. "I know that may shock you. I mean, since it has bows and arrows and all."

"Hey, I didn't call you just because you're Indian," Szelagy said. His face was turning red. "I called because you used to know all sorts of Aboriginal stuff. I remember you used to be always carrying big fat books about Native history and that."

"Well, those marks don't mean anything to me. I've never seen anything like them. Bows, arrows, hatchets, but other than that is there any reason to think it's even Indian in origin? I'm not saying it isn't. I'm just saying I wouldn't know. It's not Ojibwa stuff, I can tell you that. And probably not any of the central or eastern people. But if it's from out west or from somewhere in the States, I wouldn't know."

"Who *would* know?" Delorme said quietly. "If it was your case, who would you take it to?"

"You could try our behavioural sciences unit in Orillia. They keep up on all the Satanism and supernatural crap the serial killers go in for. Ask for Frank Izzard. He's a smart guy." Jerry caught a blackfly in his fist and flicked it away. Then he turned and headed back down the hill.

"One thing you can say about Jerry," Szelagy said when he was gone, "he's his own man. Real different sense of humour."

13

CARDINAL WENT HOME THAT NIGHT to an empty house. The message light was flashing on the phone, and when he hit the button it was his daughter, Kelly. She was twenty-six, a painter and lived in New York City. Her message said she was just calling to chat—to Catherine, she meant, not to Cardinal—but most likely she needed money.

He warmed up some shepherd's pie from the fridge, opened a Creemore and sat down at the kitchen table with the *Algonquin Lode*, but found he couldn't concentrate on the articles. He would read a few lines and then skip ahead to another story, another photograph.

It's funny, he thought, fifty years old you pretty much consider yourself a grown-up. Independent. In fact, a lot of the time he wished Catherine would take a trip somewhere. He liked the idea of waking up alone, eating breakfast alone, coming home alone. Solitude, in his imagination at least, always seemed so attractive. An effect of the movies, he supposed. You watch a solitary character onscreen, even just going about their daily routine, it always seems so interesting, so important. But the reality was that when Catherine was away, Cardinal felt restless and dissatisfied, anxious even. Was she looking after herself? Taking her medication? Why can't I leave it alone?

The little lakeside house with its wood stove and its angular rooms was cozy, comfortable. And the location out on Madonna Road ensured that—much of the time, at least—it was blessedly quiet. But tonight the quiet irritated him. He missed the sound of Catherine fussing with her plants, playing Bach on the stereo, chatting to him about photography, about her students, about anything at all, really. And as for Kelly—well, Kelly wouldn't have called if she'd realized her mother was away.

When he had finished his supper, Cardinal called the Delta Chelsea Hotel in Toronto. They put him through to Catherine's room but there was no answer. He had tried to get Catherine to buy a cellphone but she wanted nothing to do with them. "A cellphone?" she'd said. "No, thank you. When I'm alone I want to be alone. I don't want to be getting phone calls." He left a message saying he missed her and hung up.

She was probably out with some of the students; she had mentioned wanting to get photographs of the waterfront at night. Cardinal hoped she wasn't having a drink with her class. Alcohol did not mix well with the medication. It tended to make her a little manic, and then she'd stop taking the lithium. After that, the fragile connections that tethered his wife to reality would break loose until she came crashing to earth and a bed in the psychiatric hospital. It had happened more times than he cared to remember, but he couldn't keep her on a leash and he couldn't be her babysitter. Luckily, when she was well, Catherine was level-headed and knew what she had to avoid.

Cardinal stared at the phone. He wanted to call Kelly, but knew she didn't want to speak to him. This provoked an inner slide show of memories from when Kelly had been young and they had lived in Toronto: Kelly knee-deep in a creek in one of Toronto's many ravines, a squirming frog raised in her triumphant little fist. Kelly on the observation deck of the CN Tower, tiny arms outstretched as if she could lift the vast blue basin of Lake Ontario to the sky. Kelly inconsolable at age fourteen over the wayward heart of some youthful, athletic cad.

Catherine had been in hospital for much of Kelly's growing up, and Cardinal and his daughter had become very close. Raising a little girl mostly on his own had been fraught with difficulties, but Kelly's happiness had become the paramount object in Cardinal's life. Eventually Catherine had been lucky enough to go under the care of Dr. Carl Jonas at the Clarke Institute. He was a long-haired, pink-faced man with a salt-and-pepper beard and a pungent Hungarian accent who had the knack of finding the right balance of therapy and medication quicker than anyone else.

But there had come a time when Catherine had sunk into the worst bout of depression Cardinal had ever seen. A case of the blues had lingered too long, and then she had taken to her bed and nothing Cardinal did could raise her spirits. Soon she was unable even to speak. It was as if she had been lowered into the depths in a bathysphere, the sides threatening to crumple under the stupendous pressure of her sorrows. And Dr. Jonas had been away in Hungary for a year on a teaching assignment.

Catherine had been trundled from one clinic to another and she had got no better. On the verge of despair—and hounded by Catherine's American parents, who were possessed by a fierce love for their daughter combined with the Yankee certainty that a non-American thing was an inferior thing—Cardinal had had Catherine admitted to the renowned Tamarind Clinic in Chicago. The bills were breathtaking, so extreme that at first they had seemed a joke, then the stuff of nightmare. There was no way Cardinal could ever pay them on his salary; he and Catherine would never own a house, never get out of debt.

He had been working narcotics with the Toronto police department for several years by then. He had slammed the prison gates on dozens of cocaine and heroin dealers. Staggering sums of cash had been offered to him to look the other way; Cardinal had turned them down every time. Turned them down and locked the bad guys up. Then one night—a night he had regretted every day of his life since—his resistance had crumbled.

He and the other guys on the squad had raided the headquarters of a murderous thug named Rick Bouchard. In the barely controlled mayhem that ensued, Cardinal had come across a suitcase full of cash hidden under the floorboards of a closet. He had pocketed a few huge stacks of bills and turned the rest in as evidence. The case was made, and Bouchard was put away.

For a time, Cardinal had managed to rationalize the theft. He had paid off Catherine's medical bills and invested the rest to finance Kelly's education. Eventually she went to the finest art school in North America, taking a graduate course at Yale. But then Cardinal's conscience, which had been tormenting him for years, finally broke through his wall of denial.

He wrote a letter of confession to Catherine and to Kelly. He also wrote a letter of resignation to Algonquin Bay's police chief and gave what remained of the stolen money to a drug rehabilitation program. Delorme had intercepted that letter and talked him out of quitting the force. "You'll just be depriving us of a fine investigator," she had said. "It won't help anything." Unfortunately, Cardinal's daughter was the one who had ended up suffering for his crime: She'd had to leave Yale before completing her graduate degree.

That had been nearly two years ago. Kelly had moved from New Haven to New York and had not spoken to him since. Well, that wasn't quite true; there had been times when she couldn't avoid speaking to him: She had come back to Algonquin Bay for her grandfather's funeral. But the warmth was gone. There was a brittle tone in her voice now, as if being betrayed had somehow damaged her vocal cords.

Cardinal snatched up the phone and dialled Kelly's number. If one of her roommates answered, she would not come to the phone. There would be a pause, and then he'd get something lame like, "I'm sorry. I thought she was here. She must have gone out."

But it was Kelly who picked up.

"Hi, Kelly. It's Dad."

The pause that followed opened under Cardinal like an elevator shaft.

"Oh, hi. I actually just called to ask Mom something."

That voice. Give me back my daughter!

"Mom's away right now. She took her class down to Toronto."

"When will she be back?"

"Day after tomorrow."

"Okay, I'll call back in a couple of days."

"Hang on a second, Kelly. How are things going?"

"Fine."

"Any luck on the art front?" Cardinal immediately regretted the question.

"The Whitney hasn't exactly been banging down my door, if that's what you mean."

Cardinal hadn't a clue what the Whitney might be. "I just meant are you working well and are you enjoying it?"

"Everything's fine."

"Are you making some contacts, at least? People who can help you?"

"I have to go, Dad. We're heading out to a movie."

"Oh. What are you going to see?"

"I don't know. Some Gwyneth Paltrow thing."

"Are you okay for cash? Do you need money?"

"I have a job, Dad. I can look after myself."

"I know, but New York's expensive. If you need help, you can always—"

"I gotta go, Dad."

"Okay, Kelly. Okay."

She hung up.

Cardinal put the phone down and sat staring at the wood stove.

"Smart move," he said aloud. "Really won her over that time."

Later, in bed, Cardinal tried to read—a true crime book Delorme had recommended—but the words kept disintegrating and getting pushed off the page by thoughts of Kelly. He hated to imagine her scrounging to make the rent in an unforgiving town like New York. On the other hand, he could understand why she would loathe the idea of asking him for money, and that understanding lodged like a sharp object somewhere in his rib cage.

Gradually his thoughts turned to Jane Doe. The redhead was roughly Kelly's age, but seemed less sophisticated. Even innocent and unworldly. Of course, that could be a result of her brain injury. Who would want to kill her? A jealous lover? Some paranoid, possessive loser who couldn't stand to see those sweet green eyes look at another man? It was hard to imagine how she could have got caught up with the Viking Riders.

Two images haunted Cardinal as he fell asleep: Jane Doe with her pale skin and her blazing red hair spread out against the pillow. And the X-ray of her skull, the bullet glowing in her brain.

14

RED WAS LOUNGING IN THE sunroom in her hospital pyjamas and gown, iPod blasting in her ears. She had asked the cop guarding her door not to follow her to the sunroom, but he did anyway. She could see the bulky outline of his shoulder in the doorway.

Dr. Paley had lent her the iPod, which was crammed with music he'd downloaded from the Web. He was a kind man, Dr. Paley. You could see it in his round face and his white hair and the crinkles at the corners of his eyes. Dr. Paley was a creature who seemed to think only of others.

Red knew that his visits were attempts to coax her memory back. But the doctor was skilful enough, and friendly enough, that their times together did not seem at all clinical. It was as if a cheerful uncle had just stopped in to say hi. And the music was good. A band called Rocket Science belted out their hit "Run, Run, Run," and Red couldn't resist singing along.

Still, it was deadly being on a floor practically crawling with failed suicides. There were three teenage girls (two

overdoses, one wrist-slasher), a phalanx of the pierced
and pouting, who were constantly demanding to go outside and smoke, which was a real pain for everybody else
because they had to have a staff member with them. The
rest of the time they lay in their beds reading *Teen People*
and looking homicidally bored.

There was a boy, too, younger than the girls, and he
just cried all the time. A nurse would trundle in with
sympathy and medication, and the boy would conk out
for a few hours only to wake up in the middle of the
night and start crying again. Red had awoken the
previous night at 3 a.m., and the night before at 2, the
boy's sobs and wails wafting along the corridors like
some disembodied misery out of Edgar Allan Poe. Now,
why would I remember Edgar Allan Poe, Red said to
herself, and not my own name?

Boredom, restlessness, concern about the future—
Red's re-entry into an emotional life was proving to be
rocky. Sometimes she yearned for the return of bland
indifference the way a nervous person might yearn for
Valium. And what about happiness? Amusement? Love?
When would she get to feel some positive emotions?

Her memory still eluded her, though she had experienced some near moments. Twice, now, she had sensed
the heat of familiar identity hovering beside her the way a
blind person might sense the proximity of another
human being. It was like a world-changing truth one "dis-
covers" in a dream, only to have it vanish upon waking.

The first of these near-self experiences had occurred
when a nurse brought in a bouquet of flowers. The card
was from *your new friend, Dr. Paley*. She felt a blip of

elation when she realized that she remembered who Dr. Paley was. She was no longer forgetting people the moment they left the room. And then Red had wondered, very briefly, if the doctor was sweet on her. But, of course, he was just trying to jog her memory. The fragrance of the lilies was an undertow pulling her into the depths of some old memory. She knew it reminded her of something. But the memory would not form: no sound, no image, just that anxious tugging at her heart.

The last time Dr. Paley had come by, he had waved hello in his offhand way and plopped down in the chair beside the bed. Right away he started chatting, but his conversation was overpowered by his aftershave. A pillar of absolute certainty formed in Red's mind: She knew she had smelled it before. The aromas of citrus and wood, faintly mossy, were deeply familiar, but where had she smelled them? She must have looked electrified, because Dr. Paley broke off in mid-sentence.

"Try to relax," he said softly. "Don't try to force it. It'll come."

That lemony scent, that trace of oak and leather, where had she smelled it before? Who did it remind her of?

"It's right there," she wailed. "It's right in front of me and I can't see it. It's right there!"

"It will come," Dr. Paley said again. "Probably sooner rather than later."

Red started yelling at him, couldn't stop herself.

"I don't want to remember a month from now. Or a year from now. Or even tomorrow, Dr. Paley."

"Look, you're getting better already. Two days ago you wouldn't have felt this emotion."

"I don't want to feel like this! Do you know what it's like to not know who you are? Do you have any idea?"

"No," he said. "You're right. I can't know that."

"I don't know where I'm from or who I am or where I belong. Maybe I'm the type of person who hates hospitals. Maybe I live in some huge city like London or New York. I don't have a ring on my hand, but I don't even know if I'm married." She slapped her hands on the bed. "And this place. I don't belong here. I'm not sick. I'm half-alive; I'm a ghost, not a person. A person has a past, a history, an identity. Well, I'm as lost as you can possibly be. I'm just a lump of flesh, and nobody cares if I live or die."

"That's not true," Dr. Paley said. "I have no doubt whatsoever that when you get your memory back we will discover people who love you and will thank God you're safe and sound."

"You don't know that. You're just trying to shut me up."

"Not at all. I have no doubt about this. And in the meantime there are people here who care about you: the doctors and nurses. Me. Detective Cardinal. The first thing he did was order police protection for you."

"Everyone you mention is *paid* to care."

"That doesn't mean they don't really care." He pointed to the iPod on her nightstand. "You enjoy music. Lots of different kinds of music. Those musicians were paid to perform, paid to record. Do you think that means they didn't care?"

"Of course they cared. But who wants to be someone else's work?"

The doctor touched her forearm, and it calmed her.

"Your emotions are coming back—that's a very good sign. Your memory will come back, too. But try not to force it. Next time you feel a memory stirring, take a few slow, deep breaths. Try to relax and just let it come in its own time."

But the song was really getting to her. At first she thought it was just the song itself, the yearning chorus. But then that undertow began to tug at her once more. Her instinct was to sit up and stop everything, but she remembered Dr. Paley's advice. She was trying not to get too worked up.

It was stuffy in the sunroom. Red got up and went back to her room, the heavy step of the guard cop thudding behind her. She closed the door and flopped down on the bed. She turned on her side and closed her eyes, iPod clasped to her chest. She breathed deeply, slowly, and told her body to relax. She hit stop and then repeat.

The song started again. The first memory to come was neither image nor sound, just a sensation of weight on her chest. Just pressure on her chest, and a blur. A blur of grey and green. "Run, Run, Run" was playing. Gradually, the blur swirled into form: a highway, a highway out west and trees flashing by.

She was being driven somewhere. Somewhere sad. That pressure on her chest was a deep sorrow. She knew this was a memory, not a dream, but she could not yet say of what.

Other images crowded in. A middle-aged couple on the beach, sitting in deck chairs beside an open cooler with a Coke bottle sticking out of it. Small lake, water so deep it was almost black. Her mother sitting up and squinting into the sun, scanning the water for her children. Then the deep green of a hedgerow, the smell of burdock, a "tree-house" she had built in a giant hedge behind the house. How old had she been then—eight? Nine?

The skating rink in the backyard that her father made with the garden hose. How her feet burned and tingled when she came into the kitchen and pulled off her skates. Snow weighing down the trees, and a wild sky above the hills.

Her bicycle, her dog, her First Communion. Piano lessons with the nuns. Ballet. Girl Guides. Running away from home at the age of twelve, a fit of preadolescent pique that lasted about three hours past suppertime. The memories flashed before her, unstoppable.

"Oh, Terri," her mother had cried when she came back after running away. "Oh, Terri, thank God you're home."

And now she remembered that home. Looking out the window, now—the railroad tracks, the school, the cathedral spire glinting like platinum and the blue lake in the distance. She had been here before, lived here in Algonquin Bay; she was not just a visitor, not just a ghost. She didn't live here now, but she had lived here in the past. With her mom and dad and brother. Then in Vancouver.

Terri. My name is Terri Tait, I come from Vancouver, British Columbia, and I'm twenty-seven years old.

That highway again, the flashing trees and the pressure on her chest. She had been crying her heart out. She had just been to visit someone. Her brother. Her younger brother had been taken away to prison, and she had visited him for the first time.

"Kevin," she said aloud. "Your name is Kevin."

She remembered him, now. They were close, even though they hadn't lived in the same house for quite a while.

Oh, Kevin. You're an arrow in my heart and I'm always telling you what to do, but I love you to pieces and I can't let you destroy your life like this. I'll drag you kicking and screaming back to Vancouver if it's the last thing I do, Kevin. Kevin Tait.

And Terri Tait. My name is Terri Tait.

Tears were rolling in hot rivulets down her cheeks, but they were tears of happiness.

She pulled Dr. Paley's business card from the drawer in the nightstand and dialled his number. His voice mail answered; he was probably teaching.

"I know who I am," she blurted out. "I know who I am! I remember everything! Oh, why aren't you there when I need you? Come and see me and I'll tell you everything."

She hung up, her heart pounding. It reminded her of being onstage. Another memory: the sweet rainfall of applause gusting over her. She had played Miss Julie in the graduate production at Simon Fraser. Other parts, too. Smaller parts, after that.

A restaurant kitchen. Slamming plates, the clash of silverware and the chef shouting at everyone: "Pick up! Pick up! Pick up!"

"I know who I am," she said aloud. She wanted to tell someone, but there was no one there. The other bed in her room was empty. She got up and opened the closet. Why shouldn't she be dressed like everybody else? It wasn't as if she had cancer or something.

She slipped into the jeans and the green T-shirt she had been wearing the night she had been brought to hospital. The green of the shirt really picked up the green of her eyes. At least I had good taste, she thought, and realized that she still thought of the person she had been before the blank days as a separate being. Those days—or was it just hours?—were still blank.

Out in the hall she made a beeline for the nurses' station.

"Hey, hey," a voice called from behind. "Hold up, there."

She turned and saw the guard cop catching up to her.

"Where you off to?"

"The nurses' station. I just got my memory back."

"You did? Hey, sweetheart, that's fantastic. What's your name?"

"Terri," she said. "My name is Terri! I know who I am," she said to the nurse behind the counter. "I know my name and where I'm from and everything."

"Well, that's wonderful," the nurse said, and her face lit up. "That's just great—I probably shouldn't call you Red any more."

"My name's Terri," she said. "Terri. It sounds kind of funny to me at the moment. I know it's right, but it still sounds funny."

She called to the black man who was dry-mopping the corridor. "I know who I am! I just got my memory back!"

"That's good," he said. "Hope they're good memories."

She looked around for someone else to tell. The cop was talking into his radio.

15

THE FORMER JANE DOE WAS certainly looking a lot better, Delorme thought. There was some colour in those cheeks, now, and a lot more spark in those green eyes. She and Cardinal were sitting on a couple of uncomfortable chairs in the girl's hospital room. Terri Tait was on the bed, but only because there was no place else to sit. She was fully dressed and, except for the small white bandage on her temple, you would never know she had been injured at all, let alone shot in the head.

"I'm an actress," she told them. "An actress in Vancouver. Well, I think I'm mostly a waitress just now."

"And an artist, too, it looks like." Cardinal held up a sketch pad that showed a pretty good likeness of Dr. Paley in pencil. It caught the good humour in his eyes.

"Dr. Paley gave me that. He's always trying ways to jog my memory. He thinks I don't notice."

"My daughter's a painter," Cardinal said. "Still a starving artist at this point, much like yourself."

Terri nodded, her hair rustling audibly against the

starched sheets. "Basically you have to expect fifty rejections for every part you get. I bet half the waitresses in Vancouver are actresses."

"Where do you work?" Delorme said. She wanted some hard facts. "Do you remember the name of the restaurant?"

"Not yet, I'm afraid. But I will." She smiled broadly, but her eyes—to Delorme, at least—seemed focused somewhere else.

"And Vancouver? Can you give us an address?" Delorme asked.

Terri shook her head. "Not yet."

"What about an address for your parents?"

"I don't want you to call my parents. I'm not a child, Detective."

"Of course not. But talking to your family will help us piece together your background, sort out possible enemies."

"I left home when I was eighteen. I've looked after myself ever since. My parents moved out of the city and I only see them every couple of years, if then."

"Why is that?"

The girl shrugged. "We don't have anything in common."

"Do you have any brothers or sisters?"

"One brother. He's a few years younger than me."

"What's his name?"

"Kevin." The girl's hand flew to her mouth.

"What's wrong?" Delorme said.

"It's just, I'm not sure. I said Kevin but I'm not sure. It may be Ken or something like that. Some things are still pretty fuzzy."

"Can we contact him?"

"He's away right now."

"Away where?"

"Um, I don't know."

"You hesitated. Why is that?"

"Because I'm not sure if I just don't remember where he is or if I never knew."

"Really," Delorme said. This girl could end up being a lot less helpful than they had hoped. "Do you live in a house? An apartment?"

"A house. In a house with a bunch of people. It's downtown, I think."

"Are there any landmarks nearby? Churches? Clubs? Bridges?"

"I don't know. I don't think so. It's a rundown house somewhere downtown. I called directory assistance to see if they had a listing for me, but they don't. The phone must be in someone else's name."

"Do you remember the names of your roommates?" Delorme said.

Terri shook her head. "I don't. I can see their faces, some of them, but I don't have names yet."

Cardinal pulled out photographs of Wombat Guthrie and other members of the Viking Riders. "What about these faces? Any of them seem familiar?"

The girl peered at them for a few moments. "No. But that doesn't mean much just yet."

"Do you remember where you were staying in town here?" Delorme said.

Terri winced a little, wrinkling her nose. "Very vaguely. A motel out on a highway."

"Do you remember the name of this motel?"

"Sorry."

Delorme leaned forward in her chair. "The highway—did it have a lot of shopping malls on it? Or was it kind of empty?"

"There were malls. And motels and cottages."

Cardinal looked at Delorme. "Lakeshore," he said. "Has to be."

"Can you describe the motel?" Delorme asked.

"I don't think so."

"Anything at all would be helpful. Was it wood or brick, for example? Or if you remember the colour . . ."

"I just told you, I don't remember." Terri put a hand to the small bandage on her temple. "I'm getting a headache."

"All right," Cardinal said. "Just a couple of more questions."

"Do we have to? I was feeling so good and now I feel so lousy."

"How many days were you at the motel?" Cardinal said.

"I don't know. It could be one, it could be three, I just don't know." She sniffed, and her eyes watered a little.

It looked—to Delorme's skeptical eye, at least—a little rehearsed. She was an actress, after all. But all she said was: "What made you come to Algonquin Bay?"

"It was to see my boyfriend. Tom. His name's Tom."

"Tom what?"

"Josephson. Tom Josephson."

"He lives here, and you live in Vancouver? How does that work?"

"We split up, sort of. He came here to stay with some friends—I don't know them. I came here to talk him into coming back.They were staying at this place out on the lake. Oh, my head really hurts."

"Which lake?" Delorme said,

"I don't know. Some lake."

It could be any one of ten lakes in a fifty-mile radius.

"Anyway, he took me out there. And I spent the afternoon." Terri reached for the call button and squeezed. "God. I really need something for my head."

Cardinal touched Delorme's shoulder. "Why don't we pack it in for now," he said. "We'll come back when she's feeling better."

Delorme didn't even look at him. She kept her eyes on the girl, whose lower lip was now quivering. "What happened at the lake, Terri?"

"We had a fight. A quarrel."

"What did you fight about?"

"I don't know. Personal stuff. What's it matter?"

"Obviously it matters very much. You have a bullet wound in your head. What did you fight about?"

"I wanted him to come back to Vancouver with me and he didn't want to, all right? Where is that fucking nurse?"

Emotions would certainly appear to be coming back, Delorme noted, but there was something about the display of anger she didn't trust. Something a little stagy.

"What happened then? You fought, and then what happened?"

"Sergeant Delorme," Cardinal said.

"Tom didn't shoot me, if that's what you're thinking. He's the most harmless guy you'd ever want to meet."

"So tell me what happened."

"We had a fight. I left. I walked down this endless dirt road. It was hot as hell and there were flies everywhere. It was a long way back to town so I put my thumb out. The second car that came along stopped."

"Make? Colour?"

"Some bright colour—white or silver or something. It flashed in the sun and nearly blinded me."

"And the driver?"

"I don't know, all right? He had sunglasses on. Jesus Christ, lady, will you lay off me? Who the fuck do you think you are? I got a fucking bullet wound in my head and you're treating me like a goddamn criminal!"

She turned over on her side, jammed a pillow over her head and wept loudly.

Just like they do in the movies, Delorme thought.

The duty nurse came in. She looked at the girl quivering on the bed, then turned to the two detectives. Her glare was a vote for their immediate execution. She pointed to the door and said one word: "Out."

—

"Nice work," Cardinal said in the corridor. "You should win some kind of sensitivity award for that little effort."

"Cardinal, we need information out of that woman. I don't see why you're pussyfooting around with her."

"Miss Tait is the victim here, remember. She has a bullet wound in her head. Browbeating her is not going to help. What would help is if you get on the horn to the

Vancouver police. See if they've got a missing persons out on her."

"And if they don't?"

"Get them to check school records, hospital records, anything that'll give us some background."

"I thought you trusted her," Delorme said.

"I do. It's her memory I don't trust."

"You believed that stuff about having a fight? About hitchhiking? You think someone that looks like this woman is going to put her thumb out and accept a ride from a strange man?"

"Maybe. If she was very upset. We don't know her yet."

"I think she was making it up."

"Why would you think that?"

"Her manner. Lack of eye contact. Vague when it suits her."

"Oh, you've worked with a lot of amnesia victims?"

"I think she's hiding something."

Dr. Paley was coming down the hall toward them. "Finished so soon? Why don't we talk in my so-called office?"

They followed him back to the overstuffed closet with its tin desk and stacks of files. Dr. Paley closed the door behind them and excavated a couple of chairs for them to sit on.

"I don't understand," Delorme said. "You told us on the phone Miss Tait was overjoyed to have her memory back. But our red-haired friend seems evasive and nervous and depressed."

"'Depressed' is not the right word," Dr. Paley said. He made a note in a file, set it aside and swivelled to face Delorme. "I think 'overwhelmed' is closer. Miss Tait has been through a hell of a trauma—someone put a bullet in her head—and the implications of that are just beginning to sink in."

"But she doesn't even remember anything about that."

"No, and she never will. But she knows it happened, now. She knows someone tried to kill her. And that knowledge is sticking—she's not forgetting it like she has been for the past week—so this is her first continuous awareness of her predicament. I think anyone would be nervous and upset."

A sparrow landed on the windowsill beside the doctor's desk, eyed Delorme suspiciously and flew away.

"What you're saying sounds right," Cardinal said. "And we don't want to press her too hard . . ."

"That would be counterproductive. Right now she's trying to bear up under a tidal wave of self-knowledge. And frankly, I think she's doing rather well. She may be remembering things she doesn't want to mention. We all have things in our past we're less than proud of. They're not necessarily relevant to her gunshot wound."

"Doctor, it's going to be the negative stuff that leads us to her attacker," Delorme said. "The Partridge Family isn't going to cut it."

"I understand, Detective. I'm sure she'll be more forthcoming as the days go by."

Delorme flipped through the pages of her notebook. "I'm looking at my notes from our first conversation. At that time you were certain that when she got her memory back, she would get it all back at once."

"Yes. Amazingly, that's the way these things work. It's as if a short circuit has been fixed. Suddenly the picture comes clear."

"Not this time," Delorme said. "Miss Tait is remembering some things and not others. She remembers that she was staying in a motel, but not what colour it was. Not whether it was brick or wood. She doesn't remember how many days she was there. She remembers visiting a place on a lake, but not which lake."

"Perhaps she never knew the name. If she was driven somewhere to a tiny lake, she wouldn't necessarily know the name. Some of them don't even have names. Or it could have been a bay of Trout Lake. Someone from out of town isn't likely to know that kind of thing."

"Would she be capable of hiding something at this point?" Cardinal said.

"Oh, yes. She could remember things she doesn't want you to know. She might make something up to cover them. But as to actively misleading you—well, none of us knows her well enough to say whether she's the kind of person who would do that."

—

Cardinal and Delorme were usually pretty much in agreement on how to proceed with a case, how to handle a witness, but the silence in the car was thick. Delorme stopped for a red light, and Cardinal silently counted the seconds.

"Okay," Delorme said. "How come she remembers that a silver car picked her up but she doesn't remember who was driving?"

"Come on. We get that all the time. People remember

what shoes a guy had on but not whether he wore a hat or not. It doesn't mean anything."

"You didn't have the impression she was picking and choosing what to tell us?"

"I have the impression she's recovering from a shock."

"Well, as far as I can see, she already has enough nurses. One more isn't going to help."

"I think she's telling us what she can. I mean, look at her. Does she look like a femme fatale to you?"

Delorme gave him a sidelong glance. "Do you realize you're always easier on women? You never question them as hard as you would a man."

"Not true," Cardinal said. "I've put a few women behind bars in my time. You, on the other hand, seem to cut men a lot more slack."

"It's possible." Delorme shrugged, a gesture that always made her look, to Cardinal's mind at least, very French. "Maybe it's because I resent it more when women behave badly. Or when they don't seem to know what's in their own best interests."

"I don't think Miss Tait falls into either category."

Delorme shook her head. "You're so transparent, Cardinal. You don't even know this woman, but you seem to think—just because she's the same age as your daughter—that you understand her through and through."

"That's so far from being true, I'm not even going to discuss it."

"But it *is* true."

"Really, I'm not even going to talk about it."

"Fine with me."

"You heading to Lakeshore or what?"

Delorme shifted lanes to get around an SUV and stepped on the gas.

—

In the forties and fifties, a lot of motels and cottages sprung up along Lakeshore Drive to take advantage of the beautiful view of Lake Nipissing. Then, in the sixties and seventies, they were followed by boxy apartment buildings. Naturally, the beautiful view no longer exists. On the north side you have the malls and the fast-food joints, and on the south side you have the motels.

Close to town, you find the Phoenix, the Avalon and Kathy's Kute Li'l Kottages, and there's another cluster further along that includes Loon Lodge, the Pines and the ominously named Journey's End. No one has ever satisfactorily explained how the last motel on the road, a plain red-brick bungalow, came to be called the Catalonia.

The Catalonia is on the stretch of Lakeshore that curves up to join Highway 11. It is not right on the lake, but across the road, which is why its sign boasts of such amenities as free local calls, air conditioning and clean rooms. Cardinal and Delorme started at the Catalonia and worked their way back toward town, asking the proprietors if any of their guests had recently disappeared.

Late spring is a slow time of year for these motels. Ice fishing and snowmobiling are long over, but the summer sports have not yet begun. And anyone who has visited Algonquin Bay and experienced the blackflies at this time of year is unlikely to make that mistake a second time. In short, there were very few tourists to go missing and, according to these old hands at the hospitality trade, none had.

Over the next couple of hours, Cardinal and Delorme stopped at every motel on Lakeshore. None of the proprietors reported a missing guest, and none of them recognized Terri Tait's picture.

"Well, that was fun," Delorme said when they were back at the town end of the strip.

"She could have stayed somewhere else," Cardinal said. "Some place we haven't checked yet."

"She said it was by the lake."

"A lake, not *the* lake. There's more than one, if you haven't noticed."

"Okay, but why hasn't anyone reported her missing? Even if only to get the motel bill paid?"

"Motels get stuck a lot. They're not going to call the police every time. And there's always the other possibility..."

"Which is?"

"The people she stayed with are the ones who tried to kill her."

16

MARTIN AMIS SET ASIDE his notepad and took a swig of beer. He was wearing blue jeans that looked just the right degree of lived in, and a cool white shirt with the sleeves rolled up. It had been Kevin's idea to do the interview at the Gladstone Hotel. He wanted the famous novelist to realize that Toronto was just as hip as London or New York. Hipper.

"Tell us about your working habits. Assuming you have some." Martin's tone was easygoing, but the Oxford baritone, not to mention his own literary achievements, gave his every utterance weight. "By which I mean, you make it look easy. One imagines Kevin Tait scribbling lines of verse on airplane napkins and parking tickets."

"Well, there's some truth in that," Kevin said. "I have been known to scribble down an idea or two on a napkin. But you have to have discipline. You have to be willing to put in the time to make something work. I try to be at my desk anywhere from six to eight hours a day."

"That sounds more like a novelist's schedule than a poet's."

"That's the way it is, Martin. I put in the hours like anybody else." A little common touch, there. Never hurt anyone.

"But I heard—and tell me if this is just legend—that you don't even own a desk."

"My desk is wherever I put pen to paper. Doesn't matter if it's a table in Starbucks or a tree stump in a field."

"Sorry, mate. Six hours at a tree stump sounds uncomfortable. Six hours at a tree stump sounds *crippling*."

Kevin took a sip of his single malt. Amis had assured him *Vanity Fair* would be picking up the tab.

"You can write in a hurricane if it's going well. Sometimes, it's like the poem is just flowing in your veins. I'll tell you, one time I made my morning coffee and I sat down at the kitchen table and started to write. I was working on 'Needle'—lots of stanzas—and the words were just flowing. And then the light dimmed and I thought the bulb must have burned out. I got up to change it, and I realized there wasn't any problem with the bulb. It was night."

"You'd worked through the entire day without realizing it? God, I wish that happened to me. I'd like to write for one *minute* and not realize it. One *nanosecond*. You have that sort of experience a lot?"

"Once in a while. Not often enough."

Amis drank some more of his ale, set his glass aside and leaned forward. "Listen to me," he said. This delivered *sotto voce*, a fellow conspirator. "The brutal truth of the matter is you haven't finished a poem in six months, right?"

"Things are a bit slow just now, that's true, but—"

"You've chased off the one person who truly loves you, who really cares about your talent, who really wants you to do well, in a fit of righteous idiocy. And you're rotting in some kind of defunct summer camp with a couple of drug dealers any sane person would flee at warp speed."

Maybe Martin Amis wasn't the best choice for an interviewer. Maybe he should have held out for Larry King. Someone a little less . . . prickly.

"I'll tell you what I think, sunshine," Amis went on. "I think you're in way over your head, looking at a sentence of *eternity* if convicted of trafficking, and by way of medication for the anxiety you've been skin-popping morning, noon and night. It looks to me, Kevin, that you're caught between the mother of all rocks and the daddy of all hard places, because you don't really—not really, deep down in your wholesome colonial heart—want to be a drug dealer at all. But you just can't stand to be parted from your supply. You're a stone junkie, Tait. It's heroin running through your veins, not poetry, and the chances of you ever writing a single line worth reading are receding by the minute."

The reverie popped, and Kevin was once again staring at the rough, grubby wood of his cabin wall. The yellow legal pad under his forearm bore the crossed-out attempts at new verses for his ballad.

Soon the game was over
For the lady and the ghost
She was sleeping on his shoulder
As they came in from the coast.

Well, that moved along all right. It was the next line, *The border guards who killed him*, that really stumped him. The border guards killed him and then what? And how can they kill a ghost? Maybe I'm too literal-minded to write poetry. The impasse had sent him veering off into another interview. And Amis had been getting pretty hostile there.

Okay, Red Bear and Leon were unnerving, to say the least; there was no denying that biker had turned up dead. Red Bear swore he'd had nothing to do with it, that it was some bad blood among the Riders themselves, but Kevin wasn't sure he believed him. In any case, just one or two more serious deals and then he'd be free. Bye-bye, Red Bear. Bye-bye, Leon. Another couple of weeks and he'd fly to Tangiers and write poems that would put poetry back on the map.

In the meantime, he would have to exercise what Keats called negative capability. He had to be able to hold two contradictory ideas in his mind at once: the idea that he was associating with possible killers who scared the shit out of him, and the idea that he was a poet trying to scrape the money together to finance his art.

Certainly, the money was rolling in. Red Bear had some serious connections in western Canada, and now they had the goods to sell them—at a magnificent profit. Red Bear didn't let Kevin or any of the others keep more than tiny amounts—just enough to make a little extra money in town—and he made them account for every ounce. But he paid them well. He kept most of the money himself, of course, but no one had a problem with that. After all, he was the man with the ideas and the contacts.

One day—it was late in the afternoon, and they were just sitting around over coffee at the Rosebud—Red Bear came in and told them all to head back to the camp and get dressed up. "I want you to look like gentlemen," he said.

He drove them to the most expensive restaurant in the area, the Trianon, where they drank fine wine with dinner and finished off with cognac. Kevin would have preferred beer, but he had to admit the steak was the best he had ever tasted.

"We are at the beginning of a long run of good luck," Red Bear told them when the brandies came. "Even the spirits are excited about it and, believe me, they don't get excited about just anything."

The liveried waiters, the white table linens, the gleaming silver spoke of wealth and plenitude, like a crisp, new thousand-dollar bill. We could be a group of successful young businessmen, Kevin thought, except that none of us has ever had anything to do with legitimate business. And one of us dances around dead pigs. And one of us is dumb as a streetcar. What the hell am I doing here?

"My children," Red Bear said.

Children? Kevin nearly snorted into his wineglass. Now we're his *children?*

"I want us to be successful for a very long time. And that is going to require three things." Red Bear gave them that look, reflections of candles and wineglasses sparkling in his strange, pale eyes.

"The first requirement is hard work," he said. "We have to find more contacts, move more product, make more sales. I will be dividing these burdens among you. Possibly there will be some travel involved. In particular, we have to make more inroads into the prairie provinces. B.C. I have locked up, but Alberta and Saskatchewan are still to be conquered.

"The second requirement—and it's so obvious I shouldn't have to talk about it—is discretion. You can never talk about what we do. Never. To no one. Think of it like the Secret Service or whatever you want, but you can never tell anyone—and I mean anyone—what you do for a living."

"Not even family?" Toof said. "I got a bunch of brothers I talk to once in a while."

Red Bear grabbed his wrist, and a shadow of fear crossed Toof's open features.

"We are your family," Red Bear said. "Don't you ever forget that."

"What's the third thing?" Kevin said, trying to take the heat off Toof. "You said success was going to require three things."

Those husky's eyes on him.

"The third thing, my friend, is abstinence. Nobody at this table is ever to touch the product. Ever. You can smoke all the dope you want, I don't care. You can sell your private stashes in town for extra cash, I don't care about that, either. But if I find one of you has used so much as a microgram from our shipments, I will kill you. I am not joking."

"Don't you think that's a little extreme?" Kevin said. "We're living with a lot of temptation here. Human beings are fallible."

"I'm telling you the way it is, Kevin. If you don't like it, you're free to work for someone else. Maybe the Viking Riders would be interested."

Leon laughed, and nearly choked on his brandy.

17

RED BEAR DIDN'T OFTEN DRIVE himself anywhere these days. Leon was always happy to drive for him, and to act as bodyguard. In fact, Leon's progress was a source of great satisfaction to Red Bear. Bring a little magic into someone's life, improve his sex life, and the results were fairly predictable. At this point, Red Bear was confident that Leon would do anything he asked. But today, Red Bear drove himself along Highway 11 to Shanley, a suburb of Algonquin Bay, if a place the size of Algonquin Bay may be said to have suburbs.

Shanley is a picturesque little town, hardly more than a crossroads, really. But there's a lookout halfway up Shanley Hill, and it is not unusual for cars to stop there for a long time as the occupants gaze over the blue expanse of Lake Nipissing. On this particular day, it was a grey expanse. A herd of clouds had gathered over the water and over the hills that morning, and by late afternoon still showed no inclination to move. Whitecaps ruffled the surface of the lake, and even up on the lookout Red Bear could hear the slap of waves hitting the shore.

He had parked his BMW facing the lake and was now sitting in the passenger seat of a Chevy Blazer with windows tinted so dark it made the lake look like a scene of imminent apocalypse. The driver's seat was occupied by Alan Clegg. Clegg was wearing a checked short-sleeve shirt with button-fly Levi's over a pair of brown Timberland boots—not even the tan kind that might still lay some claim to being cool. Really, you couldn't look more like an off-duty cop if you tried.

"Toss 'em again," Clegg said. "I'm in a tricky situation here. I need to know about this stuff."

"It won't do any good to throw again. I told you, I'm tired. I had a late night. Very late."

"Come on, Red Bear. It can't hurt. Toss 'em again."

Red Bear put the multicoloured shells back in their leather pouch and shook them. He tipped the pouch and poured the shells over the Blazer's console.

"Okay. It's a little better," Red Bear said. Sometimes it was like tuning in a picture.

"What do you see?"

"Work. You're going to get a promotion."

Clegg grinned. He had big, thick teeth, too many for the size of his mouth. "Promotion, huh? About time, man. You wouldn't believe the jerks that are making sergeant these days. When's it going to happen?"

"I don't know when. Wait. Someone ahead of you is going to leave or retire or something. When that happens, you'll get your promotion."

"But you don't know when. Let me ask you something, Red Bear: You found Wombat alone, right?"

"He was alone."

"And you found the money, right?"

"We found the money."

"So how come you don't tell the future as good as me?"

"Because I'm not on the RCMP narcotics squad, that's why." Red Bear took off his sunglasses, giving Clegg the look. "I tell you what I see in the shells. If you want a lot of bullshit, get someone else to do your readings."

"Tell me about Mary," Clegg said. "What's going to happen with Mary?"

"I don't see you getting back together. In fact, I'd say she'll likely file for divorce. Now, money. Here's where things are looking bright." Red Bear pointed to a group of three shells that formed a crescent off to one side. "You're going to do very well financially for quite some time. In fact, I do not see anything that will get in the way of your continued good fortune."

"I got something else I wanna talk about."

"In a minute. You ask me to do a reading, have the courtesy to let me finish."

"You're pretty thin-skinned for an Indian. Anyone ever tell you that?"

Red Bear gathered up the shells and sifted them back into the leather pouch.

"What are you doing? You said you weren't finished."

Red Bear strung the bag from his belt with a leather thong. He got out of the Blazer and looked around. There were no other cars in sight. He opened the trunk of the BMW and pulled out a crisp new paper bag. He tossed it through the open door of the Blazer and climbed back in.

Clegg pulled out the three packs of bills. "Seventy-five grand. Not much, considering."

"Considering what? Seventy-five was the deal."

"The deal was I give you the information, you do the rip-off. Rip-off, not murder. Where the hell do you get off pulling something like that? The local force is all over it, in case you didn't know. So help me, if it blows back to me I'm going to come looking for you."

"Don't worry about it. Wombat is working for us, now."

"What the fuck are you talking about? Wombat Guthrie is stone-cold dead. They don't come any deader. And he's short a couple of hands and one head. Is that your idea of concealing his identity? Because it didn't work. This thing is all over the radios. The guy was alone. It was totally unnecessary. Why did you kill him?"

"Who said I killed him? You don't know I killed him. The last time I saw Wombat, we made a deal. From now on, he would be working for us. So if he was murdered, there's no way it's coming back to me. How could it come back to you?"

"Are you telling me you didn't kill this guy?"

"I don't murder people, Alan. It's not my way. The most likely thing is he's been punished by his colleagues for failing the organization so dramatically. I don't see how that's a problem for you."

"All right. Okay. That makes sense." Clegg seemed to relax a little. "How'd your crew react to the takeover? They had to be pretty impressed."

"Yes, I think so. Even Kevin, and he's very skeptical about my magic."

"He's not going to be trouble, is he?"

"Kevin?" Red Bear looked out across the lake, the tiny white pennants of surf. "Kevin won't be a problem."

"Because I'll tell you who *could* be a problem, and that's your little Toofus-Doofus friend."

"Toof is a harmless pothead. How could he be a problem?"

Clegg looked at his watch. "I gotta hit the road. I gotta be back at the detachment by six."

"How would Toof be a problem?"

"I'm not saying he is a problem. I'm saying he might be. Informant of mine gave me a little morsel of info the other day. One Nelson Tyndall. Not the most reliable asshole in the world, but not the worst either—for a junkie. Old Nelson tells me Toof told him that his crew was going to be doing something big in a couple of days. That was before your little trip across the lake."

"'Something big'?" Red Bear said. "'Something big' is not a problem. 'Something big' could be anything."

"How about something big with the Viking Riders?"

"The Viking Riders? Your informant told you this before?"

"No, he told me Toof told *him* before."

"That is not possible. None of them knew we were going near the Riders until we were on the lake and heading for the French River."

"Like I say, Nelson's not the most reliable asshole in the world."

Red Bear cursed. He took off his Wayfarers and rubbed the bridge of his nose.

The sun broke through the clouds above the western shore. Clegg lowered his visor and started the Blazer.

"Keep an eye on the guy," Clegg said. "That's all I'm saying."

18

KEVIN STRETCHED, AND CLOSED his eyes. He had spent the entire morning in Red Bear's cabin under the watchful eye of Red Bear himself, stepping on the dope and packing it into ever-smaller packages. It was torment to be so close to ecstasy and yet forbidden to taste. He thought long and hard about shoving some into his pocket, but Red Bear was never more than a few feet away, talking quietly into the telephone, making deals.

Now Kevin was lying on his bunk, trying to write a poem about Karen, his last girlfriend in Vancouver. So far, he hadn't had any luck with the females of Algonquin Bay, so he thought about Karen quite often. Strictly speaking, Karen had been someone else's girlfriend and, despite her one-night adventure with Kevin, she had chosen to stay that way. Kevin summoned her image in his mind. That mouth, those sweet blue eyes, that silky blond hair. Unfortunately, his thoughts had a tendency to turn lustful, and lust was not conducive to good verse. He had crossed out a dozen opening lines, each one worse than the last.

The door opened, and Leon stepped inside, a dark silhouette against the sunlight.

"Don't you ever, like, go outdoors, man?"

"I'm working."

"Working?"

"Yes, Leon. I'm working. Writing. Some people do actually consider it work, you know."

"Oh, excuse me. What are you, like, William Asshole Shakespeare? Ernest Asshole Hemingway?"

"You're letting the flies in, Leon. I just got rid of the last one, and you're letting them in again."

Leon shut the door behind him. "I hope you're writing a screenplay. That's where the money is."

"Never," Kevin said, and snapped his notebook shut. He felt under the bed for his shoes. "I wanted to ask you something, Leon. The day Terri left, you drove her to the train station, right?"

"What are you going on about that again for? I told you. I'd been back from Toronto, like, thirty seconds and Red Bear says, 'Hey. This is Kevin's sister. She needs a ride to the station.' She was in a hurry."

"Yeah, I know she was pissed off at me. But I called her place in Vancouver and her roommates haven't heard from her."

"I got no answer for that. She didn't give me an itinerary, man. I only just met her. Far as I know, she was catching the train to Toronto. After that, I got no idea."

"I'm getting kind of worried. Normally, she would've called me by now. I don't know where she can be."

"She's probably with friends in Toronto. Why not? Anyways, we got other things to worry about. Red Bear's got a little job for us."

"Shit. What now?"

"What are you talking about, man? We got the easiest gig anybody ever dreamed up. He makes the big contacts, sets up the big scores. All we gotta do is mule the stuff around once in a while."

That was true. Mostly, all Kevin had to do for his money was occasionally meet one of Red Bear's mysterious contacts downtown and put him together with some product at an agreed-upon location. Easy as pie.

"Man, you must be the laziest bastard in the world," Leon went on.

"I just told you, man, I'm working on my poetry. Anyway, what's he want us to do?"

"Toof's been shooting his mouth off to the wrong people. Got to have a little talk with Canada's favourite pothead."

"Nobody listens to Toof. He's a harmless goof." God, Kevin thought, I've been thinking about rhyme too long.

Leon snatched at a fly. "I didn't say we have to beat him to death. We just got to have a talk with him."

Later, when they were in the car, Kevin said, "So what's the deal? Why have we got to talk to him?"

Leon attacked the gearshift and the Trans Am roared onto the dirt road. "Red Bear wants us to convince him to stop blabbing our business to the entire world."

"So why doesn't Red Bear talk to him? He'd be a lot more convincing than you or me."

"It's called delegating responsibility, Kevin. Red Bear actually wants us to do some work, you know what I mean? And he don't mean writing."

"So what are we supposed to do?"

"Just get him to stop, that's all. How we do it is our business. But if Toof doesn't stop, that'll be Red Bear's business, and you know what? I don't want Red Bear mad at me, do you?"

A Toyota Echo cut them off as they turned onto the highway, and Leon leaned on the horn. "Asshole. I oughta run him into a rock cut."

"So who's Toof supposed to have been talking to?"

"Apparently, the little jerk let slip that we had some business with the Viking Riders, and somehow it got back to Red Bear. Is that bad enough for you, or do you need like a detailed transcript? You wanna go back to camp and cross-examine Red Bear on the subject?"

"I don't think so."

"Me either."

They didn't speak the rest of the way into town.

Toof was an easy person to find most afternoons, because Algonquin Bay has only two poolrooms: Duane's Billiard Emporium and the Corner Pocket. He wasn't at Duane's but someone said they'd seen him earlier and he was heading over to the Pocket.

They drove up Sumner and made a left onto O'Riley. The Pocket was a couple of blocks up, handily located near Ojibwa High, which was why Toof liked to hang out there. He'd hustle the after-school crowd of boys and make himself a few bucks.

Unlike Duane's, which was run by a closet thug with a head shaped like an anvil, the Corner Pocket was run by an old couple. They were constantly in a bad mood, and no one knew if that was their normal demeanour or if catering to successive squadrons of teenage boys had soured them.

The old man glared at Kevin and Leon over the cash register as they entered.

They found Toof at the bar, drinking a Cherry Coke and scarfing down a Turkish Delight chocolate bar.

"Hey guys, what's up?" Bits of chocolate clung to his snaggletooth. He pointed to Leon's feet. "You're wearing your fancy hiking boots again. You going mountain climbing?"

"Gotta go for a drive," Leon said.

"Gimme twenty minutes, eh? I wanna take this guy out." He pointed with his Coke at a beanpole of a youth who was clearing a table with one decisive thunk after another.

Leon took Toof's Coke and placed it on the counter. "Now."

19

THE MEMORIES WERE COMING thick and fast now; she couldn't stop them. One moment she was yearning to remember more, the next moment she wanted nothing but oblivion. The nurses would give her Tylenol, but no more of the heavy-duty painkillers. She wanted to sleep, but it was the middle of the day and she was wide awake.

The patients' lounge was noisy. Sophie, one of the suicide wannabes, had three blond witches visiting her and they were all giggling maniacally. Terri huddled in a corner with a *Glamour* magazine, but she couldn't concentrate. The memories dropped into her mind in no order, unbidden, with stomach-flipping changes in intensity and obsessive repetition.

For example, the flies. For the hundredth time she was remembering the flies. Not just the ones that bit her, although she certainly remembered the itch and sting of bites on her forehead and ankles. Those flies were small, silent. But she could also hear the buzzing, thick and multi-layered, of other, fatter flies. Great clouds of them in the sunlight. Where had that been?

Then there was the train station. Kevin had come to meet her. He had been nervous, shifting from foot to foot as if they were strangers. Terri had known instantly that he was using again. She hadn't confronted him about it right away, not there in the station with the crying children, and the drunks wobbling about, and a madwoman yelling incoherently.

Kevin's place. Nothing but a camp bed and a rickety wooden table in a weird little cabin somewhere in the woods by a lake. Sunlight pouring in through the window, making the sweat glisten on Kevin's brow.

"I know you're using again," Terri said. It just came out. She couldn't bear to see him looking so furtive and guilty.

"I'm not mainlining. Whole reason I came back to Algonquin Bay was to get clean. I was happy growing up here. It kinda helped me get some clarity."

"Kevin, I can see it in your face."

"I'm just skin-popping," he told her.

"Uh-huh. And where will that go?"

"It's just something I have to do right now. I'm under a lot of stress."

He'd had a pout on his face as he'd said it, a child who's been chastised. A lot of girls found Kevin's boyishness charming. Terri supposed she could see it. That curly hair—dark, not red like hers. Her brother looked like a guy who was up for a ball game, or for a night of poker, sometimes as if he might pull a frog from his pocket. Unfortunately, along with the boyishness came a lot of immaturity. He'd already done two years in a correctional facility. If he got caught trafficking, or even using, he could get sent away for a long, long time. There was no way she could so much as mention his name to the police, no matter how nice they were to her.

The camp. That's what Kevin had called the place he shared out by the lake. Apparently, the collection of cabins had at one time been a summer camp for handicapped kids. Once upon a time the cabins might have been white, but now they were discoloured, sagging, sorry old huts that barely kept out the flies. He'd dug up a key for the cabin next to his and told Terri she could stay there, but only for a couple of nights. Red Bear didn't like outsiders hanging around, even family.

"Isn't it great?" Kevin said, waving his hand at the view of the lake, the overgrown baseball diamond. "Isn't it fantastic? Look at that lake, Ter, it's huge. We took a boat ride across it last week, and it took, like, an hour, even going really fast. You should see the stars from out there. Incredible."

"You went for a boat ride at night? Why would you do that?"

"I don't know. It was fun. Come on, Terri, you have to admit it's pretty cool to have a whole camp for the summer."

All Terri had discerned in the leaning huts and the rocky beach was the dispirited air of a place long abandoned. It had reminded her of photographs she'd seen of the Great Depression.

And what a collection of people living in it. Kevin and Red Bear and the dim guy with the funny tooth. Supposedly, there was some other character she'd never met. Kevin had never mentioned any of them in his

occasional e-mails, a fact that made her suspicious of his
new friends right from the start.

"Don't you think it's a little much for only four guys to
live in?" she had said. "You could house forty people in all
these cabins."

"Naw," Kevin said. "Most of them are ruined. There's
only maybe six you could live in."

"Still. Four guys."

Kevin walked her over to the biggest cabin, Red Bear's,
the only one with more than one room. It stood in a copse
of birch trees, a miniature house with cedar siding and a
broad window overlooking the lake. Hung from the ceiling were fly strips, where tiny creatures buzzed out their
last moments of existence.

Red Bear had been completely charming. Or rather,
everything he'd done and said certainly *would* have been
charming, if it hadn't also seemed a little too . . . overstated.

"Yes, Kevin has told me a lot about you," he had said.
His smile was like a theatre marquee. Those teeth. "He told
me you were the perfect sister, and now I can see why."

Well, right there, that didn't ring true. It didn't sound
like anything Kevin would say about her, or anyone else
for that matter.

Red Bear's handshake was dry and firm. He was not a big
man, but he was wide in the shoulders and it gave him a look
of strength. His hair was so black it had gleams of blue in it,
like crow feathers, and seemed to flash against his clothes.
His shirt was so white you needed sunglasses to look at him.

"Come, I will read your cards," he said. He offered
them chairs at a large table of country pine, where he pro-
ceeded to set out cards in interesting patterns.

"Ace of diamonds," he said. "This is perfect. A completely sunny outlook for you, Terri."

Remembering someone's name was supposed to be a mark of politeness, but Red Bear's use of it made her uncomfortable.

"Financial outlook is favourable. Health, excellent. No enemies that I can see. You must really be the saint Kevin says you are." This with a sidelong glance at Kevin, who smiled on cue, but Terri knew Kevin was not the sort to call his sister a saint. Why would he?

Snap, snap, snap. One after another, the cards went down. As Red Bear slotted each one into place, he made cheerful comments about Terri's future. Then the jack of clubs slapped down across the king of hearts, and Red Bear's manner changed.

"All right. A cloud on the horizon. A setback. Maybe something worse."

His eyes had some kind of genetic defect, with almost pigmentless irises.

"Tell me," Terri said when he hesitated. Not that she believed in cards, or reading palms or any of that New Age stuff, but she read her horoscope in the paper now and again just to see how far off it was. "Tell me," she said again. "I can take it."

"All right, Terri," Red Bear said. He sat back and folded his arms across his chest. Biceps shifted under white sleeves. He spoke matter-of-factly, a doctor conveying bad news. "Everything I told you just now? Good health, good money, no problems, et cetera? All of that is true. All of that is yours . . ."

"But?"

He tapped the jack of clubs with a manicured finger. "This is a death card."

"Hey, take it easy." Kevin had been leaning on the table, chin on fist, almost asleep, but now he sat up. "You're not supposed to tell people stuff like that."

"Kevin," Red Bear said quietly, "you're overreacting."

"You can't just go round telling people they're going to die. What are you trying to do? Freak her out? She's my sister, man."

"Will you listen to me?"

"It's okay," Terri said. "Relax, Kevin."

Red Bear pointed again at the card. "It's true. This is indeed a death card. But death in the cards does not necessarily mean *death*. It's like death in a dream. It could just mean great change." Red Bear gathered up the cards. "Please, let's not be so solemn. I didn't mean to upset you. I only tell you what I see—the possibilities. We're all in control of our own lives."

"I don't like this card business," Kevin said.

"That's like not liking the weather," Red Bear said. "Not liking it won't improve it. Now, please, let's cheer up. Your sister is here, it's a sunny day, it's no time to be gloomy."

The cabin, the camp and Kevin dissolved, and Terri was back in the present, back in the patients' lounge.

The girls on the other side of the room were collapsing in laughter. Their voices echoed off the tile walls and the plastic furnishings and hurt Terri's ears. She shot them a dirty look, but then another memory flashed before her, obliterating the girls, the lounge, the hospital.

Waking up to sunlight sparkling in cascading water, miniature rainbows arcing in the spray. Waking up to the sound of falling water merging with the buzz of insects. The flies. There weren't even that many of them. Just a handful buzzing around the hideous shape on the floor of the cave. And the smell. That evil smell. Where was that place? How had she got there? The memory was over, but even that split second was enough to send waves of fear and nausea coursing through her body.

"Are you all right?"

Terri looked up into the concerned face of a nurse's aide.

"I need the washroom," she said. "I think I'm going to be sick."

20

"WHY DON'T YOU DRIVE," Leon said. "I'm gonna stretch out in the back. My knee's killing me."

Kevin got behind the wheel, and Toof sat in the passenger seat beside him. His clothes reeked of weed.

"I can't believe it," Toof said. "You're letting someone else drive your Trans Am?"

"My knee's acting up," Leon said. He was lying down in the back. "It's not a big deal."

But it was weird, Kevin knew. Leon was obsessive about his Trans Am. Took it to the car wash every week.

"So, what's Red Bear want to see me about?" Toof said, when they were moving. "Am I in trouble again?"

"Naw," Leon said. "At least, I don't think so."

Kevin didn't say anything. Leon had told him to keep his mouth shut and drive out toward West Rock. Leon would give him more directions once they got off the highway.

"Are you sure?" Toof turned around to face Leon. "Why's he yank me out of a pool game and drag me back to camp if he's not pissed off?"

"I don't know, Toofie-Doof. Have you got something on your conscience?"

"Like what? What are you talking about?"

"I don't know, Toofie-Doof."

"Don't call me that. I hate that. Toof's okay, but Toofie-Doof is stupid."

"Unlike Toof. Fine. I repeat: Have you got something on your conscience? Have you been stealing from the supply, for example? You know Red Bear is going to take a seriously dim view of that."

"I don't use H. You know that. I just smoke dope."

This was true, Kevin knew. And so did Leon, so he wasn't sure why he was playing this game with their less-than-genius colleague.

"Well, if you haven't been dipping into the supply, then maybe you did something else."

Kevin made a left off the bypass onto West Rock Road. After only a couple of hundred yards they were into pretty thick bush on either side of the road. There were some nice houses out here, though.

"Something else, like what?"

"Well, something that doesn't involve the death penalty. I don't know, Toof. Have you been talking to the wrong people?"

"I don't talk to anybody. Not about our business." Toof faced forward again and stared at the emerald green of passing trees. "Except maybe to my family."

"We *are* your family, Toof. That's a quote from the man himself, remember?"

"I remember. I didn't tell nobody nothing."

"Then what are you worrying for? Relax and enjoy the scenery."

They drove a couple of miles in silence. Kevin switched on the radio and they listened to Alanis Morissette yodel about her mistreatment at the hands of some mysterious man. Kevin still didn't know why they were driving out to West Rock.

"Hey, where are we going?" Toof said.

"Shortcut. You've seen it before."

"I have? It doesn't look familiar."

"Well, maybe that's why you're always getting lost."

"Could be, I guess . . ."

Kevin remembered one time he had arranged to meet Toof at the Bull & Bear pub. He'd even drawn him a little map, and Toof had still gotten lost.

"I know why Red Bear wants me," Toof said, and slapped his knee. "I'm so dumb sometimes."

"What is it?" Leon said and sat forward, leaning on the back of the front seat like a friendly dog. "Why's he want you?"

"*You* know," Toof said. "You're just playing dumb to keep me guessing."

"No, I don't know, Toof. Honest."

"Get outta town, man. You know what this is about."

"But I don't, Toof. Kevin, do you know why Red Bear wants to see him?"

"Uh, no. I don't," Kevin said.

"See, neither of us knows, Toof. So if you've seen the light, you're just going to have to let us in on it."

"See, it's 'cause I gave Red Bear my birthday and that, eh? So he could do my chart for me? He knows it's my birthday tomorrow. That's what this is about, I bet. It's like a surprise party—remember, like he threw for you that time?"

It was true; Red Bear had thrown a party on Leon's birthday. He had taken them all out to dinner at Bangkok Gardens. He had tried to order Dom Perignon but the restaurant didn't have anything that good, so they'd had to settle for a Chablis. It had been a good evening; Red Bear had been in an excellent mood.

"It's your birthday tomorrow?"

"Yup. I'll be twenty-seven. No, twenty-eight. No, wait. I'm not sure. Twenty-eight, I think."

"Gee, that's great, Toof. That must be what this is about." Leon touched Kevin's shoulder. "Take the next left."

Kevin made the turn onto a dirt road. It rapidly brought them to the construction site of a new subdivision. None of the houses was finished yet. The road became really rough, then, and they passed bulldozers and backhoes. The construction crews had left for the day.

"Take a right at the end of the road."

The car dipped and swung over deep ruts in the mud. Then Kevin made the turn, and the road got even worse until it wasn't a road at all. They passed a fenced-off equipment yard, and then there was nothing but trees.

"I'll tell ya what I'd really like for my birthday," Toof said. "What I'd really like is a trip to Tahiti. Or, like, maybe Hawaii. Anywhere the girls walk around in grass skirts and no tops."

"I don't think Red Bear would give you anything like that, Toof."

"Oh, no. I know that. Hey, I'd be happy with a new CD or something. A movie and some popcorn. In fact, yeah, that's exactly what I'd like to do. Let's all go to the movies. There's that new thing with The Rock just opened."

"Well, sure. It's your birthday; you can do whatever you want. Stop anywhere up here, Kevin."

"I'm gonna order us a big cake for tomorrow. Dutch chocolate. Three storeys high, man. And maybe after the movies we could go out to the Chinook. I don't need no place fancy. Fact, I like the Chinook better than that Bangkok joint any day. Yeah, let's go there."

Kevin stopped the car. Toof was still going on about the Chinook Tavern when there was a loud bang. He pitched forward so hard he bashed his head on the dashboard. "What the hell was that?" he said. He sat back, eyes rolling. He shook his head. "Did you guys hear something?"

The smell of gunpowder was overwhelming. Leon was sitting forward, the gun resting on the back of the front seat.

Kevin tried to speak, but nothing came out.

Leon fired again.

Toof tipped forward, slower this time. He pressed against the dashboard to raise himself. "Man, my eyes aren't working right," he said. His voice sounded as if he had just woken up from a long nap. "I'm not seeing so good."

Toof got out of the car and stumbled, grabbing on to the fender for support. The back of his head was soaking wet, and blood was running down his jacket in strings.

"Fucking gun," Leon said, and got out of the car.

Kevin wanted to run, he wanted to cry, but found he couldn't do either. It was as if his legs were full of Novocaine.

The trunk opened and slammed shut. Then Leon came round the front behind Toof, with a baseball bat. He smashed him across the head, and Toof went down.

"Happy birthday," Leon said.

21

JOHN CARDINAL WAS A DECENT COOK when he put his mind to it. He was not a man to rely on frozen dinners and pizza deliveries the moment his wife was out of town. Catherine's many hospitalizations had forced him to learn his way around the kitchen. In fact, some of his favourite memories were of Kelly as a little girl "helping" him, chopping apples into uncookable chunks, her hair matted with pie dough.

He made himself a chicken curry and ate it in front of the television, watching the news and then flipping channels for a while. There was nothing on so he went down to the basement and did some woodworking. He was building a set of wide shelves for Catherine's darkroom—nothing difficult, but he had to be careful with the router when he was cutting the grooves. Catherine's darkroom was one of the first things he had built in the house, a long time ago, now; he was running out of projects.

Woodworking was Cardinal's only hobby. He liked the smell of sawdust, the feel of wood in his hands, and he enjoyed the satisfaction that came from completing a project, even a small one like shelves. In law enforcement, satisfaction was an elusive commodity.

Cardinal and Catherine often worked in the basement at the same time, Catherine in her darkroom, Cardinal at his work table. They kept a dusty boom box down there and took turns choosing the music. Other times, Cardinal would be building something and he would hear her footsteps overhead in the kitchen. Alone together. That was how he thought of those times. We're alone together, and sometimes it seemed more intimate than sex.

There were no footsteps overhead now, and Cardinal hadn't bothered to put any music on. He wasn't really enjoying the carpentry, either. With Catherine gone, it wasn't the same.

The phone rang. Cardinal switched off the router, turned off his work light and went upstairs to the kitchen.

"What took you so long?" Catherine said when he picked up. "You had to hustle her out the back door?"

"Hey, sweetheart. I was hoping you'd call me back last night."

"Sorry," Catherine said. "We were out photographing these old grain silos on the waterfront. They look fabulous in the moonlight. And the old Canada Malting factory. It was fun, and I think the class learned a lot. How's work?"

"One murder, one attempted murder."

"Goodness. They must have you working late."

"Pretty late. Kelly called you last night. She said it was just to chat, but I think she needs money. Naturally, she wouldn't accept any from me. Couldn't get off the phone fast enough."

"Oh, John, don't let it get to you. She'll come round. You know she will. Anyway, I can't be thinking about that right now, I've got too much on my mind."

That was not like Catherine. Normally, she was never more concerned and attentive than when they were discussing their daughter.

"I wish you were home," Cardinal said. "Or I wish I was there. It's too quiet here." At least he could say that without being accused of undermining her.

"Well, I can't come home, John. I'm in the middle of some really important stuff here."

"I know that, honey. I'm glad it's going well."

"The thing about these waterfront pictures, we're getting a lot of stars in them, a lot of moon. It's made me reconsider a lot of things. I mean, unless you're an astronomer or something, you pretty much take them for granted, but I'm really thinking about them now. I think I may be beginning to understand them. For the first time."

He could hear the clink and clatter of mania in her tone. A train of thought jumping the tracks of reason.

He said something soothing—"That's good, sweetheart"—but in his mind he was praying. *Please just let her make it through the next couple of days. Please let her make it home.*

"When you photograph stars in relation to the buildings, you can feel their motion. You can sense an *intention* almost. You remember that time we saw the northern lights?"

"You mean in Newfoundland? Yes, of course."

They had seen the northern lights many times in Algonquin Bay, but never the way they had seen them in

Bonavista Bay. Half the sky shimmering with curtains of light—emerald, chartreuse, vermilion. Suddenly, Cardinal had understood the meaning of the word *awe*.

"Well, it's like that. The midnight sky isn't a place at all. It's an unearthly book. We can't read it yet, not really. But you can sense it's readable."

A long time ago, Cardinal and his wife had worked out a code. It was during one of Catherine's best periods. She'd had a couple of years of solid ground, and she was firmly in her sane character, which was many things— smart, funny, generous—but, above all, sweet-natured. She was one of the world's naturally agreeable people.

Cardinal had taken advantage of the opportunity to make a deal with her.

"Cath," he had said, "I hope you won't be upset by the request I'm going to make, but I think it's important."

"Then I won't be upset by it," she said. She had been peering at contact sheets through a loupe. She looked up at him across the table, a little nearsighted from the change in distance.

"I'd like us to work out a phrase. A code. A sentence. I don't know. *Something*. Something I can say to you when it seems clear to me you're on the edge of an episode. I don't mean when you're just excited. Or when it's iffy. I mean when I'm pretty sure you're going to lose it but you don't seem aware of it."

Catherine's eyes clouded and her face sagged a little. Cardinal could read every shade of pain in his wife's features, just as he could read every shade of joy. Nothing hurt him more than to bring her pain. He thought she was going to get angry at him. Here he was spoiling a happy evening.

"I think that's a perfectly reasonable suggestion." Catherine tilted her head back to her contact sheets.

"You're not angry?"

"No. It hurts a little. But it's okay." Her hair cascaded over her face. Her voice was slightly muffled. "What did you have in mind?"

"I don't know. Something normal sounding, but that we both agree on what it means."

And so they had worked it out. Shifting the phone in his grip, Cardinal used it now. "Honey, I think we're looking at some heavy weather, here."

Heavy weather. That was the phrase. A couple of times it had worked. Just as often, it didn't.

"No, we are not looking at heavy weather, John. Everything is perfectly fine."

"I'm telling you what I see. Not what you feel."

"This is not heavy weather, John. *Jesus.* How can you say that to me? Damn it, John. Every time I go away or do anything the least bit independent."

"Please take it easy, hon. Can't you just lie down and relax for a while and take an honest—"

She slammed the phone down.

Cardinal took a shower and got into bed. The true crime book lay unopened on his night table. He couldn't be sure what to do about Catherine just now. If he showed up in Toronto, it would undermine her completely in front of her students. If he did nothing, she could rapidly get worse. Please let her stay sane. Please let her make it home all right.

22

"I'm outta here, Dave. Really, man, I'm into poetry, not violence. Yes, I like dope. Yes, I like free dope even better. But killing people—hey, I'm against it. Totally and unequivocally against it."

Letterman's face broke into the famous gap-toothed grin. Just the guy next door, it said. I would never ask you anything dangerous.

"Come on, Kevin. If you really wanted to go, you could be out of there any time. Why are you still hanging around these two psychos?"

"I need time to think, Dave. These guys are not just gonna let me walk away. I know too much. I have to come up with a way to move on without upsetting them. Easy for you to sit there and ask questions—you haven't been through what I've been through. You didn't see your friend—okay, Toof wasn't a friend exactly. Your associate—you didn't see your associate shot in the head and then beaten to death with a baseball bat. Believe me, you'd need a hit, too, if you'd seen what I saw. Thanks for having me on the show, Dave, but there's things I've got to do, here, so *adios, amigo*."

Kevin suddenly wasn't sure if he'd been imagining the chat with Letterman in silence, or if he'd been speaking aloud. He was standing outside, in the bushes behind Leon's cabin, and the flies were eating him alive. He told himself to keep it together. You can't be talking to yourself when you're pulling a raid on Leon's personal sales stash. Leon is no longer just a business associate; Leon is a fucking evil entity, man. And so is Red Bear.

So why am I doing this? Why take this insane risk? Well, he knew the answer to that: Because I'm a stone junkie, and I need to get high. Need with a capital N, thank you. As in, I'll die if I don't shoot up right now.

The cabin was dark; Kevin took a few steps closer. Leon was over in Red Bear's cabin. Crazy bastards were spending more and more time together. Kevin's plan was to liberate a pinch of Leon's stash and transport it as efficiently as possible to his own pleasure receptors. It was the only way he was going to get through this moment, which was surely the darkest of his life. He wouldn't touch the motherlode.

The motherlode, their main dope supply, was locked up in a tiny, windowless shed made out of cement blocks further along toward the beach. Leon was in charge of security, and he kept the keys with him at all times.

Kevin stood still, listening. No sound from the cabin. Mind you, there was no sound from Red Bear's cabin either, so who knows what they were up to. He remembered the blood streaming down Toof's back, and the grotesque way he had staggered, his body no longer getting coherent messages from his brain.

"Move," Leon had said when he was finished with Toof. "I'm driving."

He tossed the baseball bat into the trunk of the Trans Am and got behind the wheel. Kevin got in on the passenger side. The seat was still warm from Toof's body heat.

Leon took it slow getting away from the construction site. The Trans Am was low-slung; no point taking out the oil pan in some backhoe rut. But excitement made his eyes shine and his cheeks glow, as if he had just won an important race.

"Man, did you see that fucker stagger around? Talk about not knowing when to give up. Two bullets I put in his head, man. Two bullets. And he's still up walking around. Did you see that?"

"Uh, yeah. I saw that."

"Hey, I didn't get any blood on the car, did I? You see any on the dash?"

"Dash looks fine."

"What about the seat? Lean forward a second."

Kevin leaned forward.

"Naw, I think we're good. No muss, no fuss. Fucking gun wasn't much use, way it turned out. Clocked him a good one with the bat, though. Knocked that one into the bleachers, man. Knocked that one out of the park."

As Toof had staggered near the car, the blood had poured from his bullet wounds in red strings, like hair.

"Fucker had it coming, man. He knew the score. You don't talk to anyone about our business. No one. I was clear on that point, Kevin. What about you? Have you been talking to anyone? Telling people we ripped off the Viking fucking Riders?"

"Uh, no. I haven't been talking to anyone."

"Exactly, man. Me neither. That's the problem with Toof. There's no talking to that guy. He's too fucking dumb. Toofus-Doofus."

"Yeah," Kevin said. "Toofus-Doofus."

Leon looked over at him. Eyes bright.

"Scared ya, I bet."

"You definitely caught me by surprise there, Leon."

"Yeah, you were scared shitless, man. Admit it."

"I was scared shitless. You're right." I still am, I still am, I still am.

"Don't worry, Kev. You get used to it. Just listen to Red Bear, man. That guy knows what he's talking about. You get used to things. And it's okay. You do what you have to do. Toof knew the score, Kev. He made his bet and he lost."

"Lost big."

"Only justice," Leon said. "Mouth like that could get us all killed." He turned onto Highway 11, and then it was blast-off, dual exhausts roaring and the Trans Am hurtling south.

"Justice," Leon said again. "Way it should be."

Addicts learn early on to keep all their options open. That was why Kevin knew that Leon kept his private inventory under a floorboard in his cabin. It was also why, one time when Leon had stepped out for something, Kevin had unlatched his window from the inside. It was still too cool at night, out here by the lake, to sleep with the windows open. And they didn't have screens. An open window was an invitation to the flies that were buzzing around Kevin's head and neck.

The unlatched window was at the back; he wouldn't be

seen from Red Bear's cabin. Kevin forced the window up eight or ten inches. He pulled himself through and lowered himself, hands first, to the floor.

He went straight to the floorboard under Leon's bed and pried it up. There were enough glassine envelopes full of dope to knock out an army of elephants, but Kevin took only one. He replaced it with another he had prepared that contained nothing more lethal·than icing sugar. Some junkie would be in for a disappointment.

Toof's face. The rolling, bewildered eyes. The sound of his skull yielding to wood. Kevin would never forget that sound. The memory made his legs quake so bad he had trouble climbing out the window. He dropped to the ground outside and nearly broke his ankle.

He moved quickly through the bush, back toward his own cabin. He did not want to run into Leon—the new Leon. He knew there was violence in Leon's past. Leon had hinted at it a couple of times. And Kevin had seen him beat the hell out of that guy in the pub. But now it was as if Red Bear had roused some black-hearted creature previously dormant within Leon. The entity.

Kevin outran the flies back to his own cabin and shut the door. Got to get out of here. Definitely. But first, let's get myself a little calm, a little clarity.

He pulled out the spoon he had hidden in the wall and cooked up the smack with his Ronson. He drew the milky stuff into his syringe, and this time there was no question where it was going. He cinched his belt around his bicep, pumped up a fat vein and plunged the needle in. When he loosened the belt, the dope hit his brain like a fifty-megaton orgasm.

After a few minutes, he hid his paraphernalia and climbed into bed. He curled up, clasping his hands between his knees. Bliss rode every nerve in his body. His belly felt awash in opium and molten chocolate.

"Kevin, will you come back with me?" Terri's voice sang in his ear, and Kevin wished for the hundredth time that his sister would get married and leave him alone.

"Kevin, will you come back with me?" Her green, green eyes imploring him. He could feel himself bathed in her love and concern.

"Oh, Terri," he moaned. "Leave me alone, will ya?" But the dope was making him giggle.

Waves of pleasure rolled through his body in languid swells. His mind was the translucent blue of a Bahamian sea. Guilt and fear could not survive in this heaven.

Almost lost against that blue ocean was a tiny, dark figure, like an insect crawling across a TV screen. But it was a man, a tiny man, waving to Kevin as if from the wrong end of a telescope.

Kevin smiled. Good news, the guy was giving him. Even though he couldn't quite make out the words, he knew it was good news.

The tiny man was calling. Waving and calling in the blue. It was as if the tiny man was a castaway, and Kevin was a passing jet. He couldn't make out the face, but he knew it was Toof.

Toof was calling to him from that blue immensity. Toof was telling him not to worry. It wasn't so bad being dead. In fact, it was okay. No need to be afraid, Kevin. No need to be upset. Old Toof was fine, man. Everything was fine.

23

"YOU'RE CERTAIN HE'S DEAD?" Red Bear said. "I don't want any surprises down the road."

"He's dead all right." Leon turned the stereo up a notch, a top-of-the-line Marantz. And R.E.M., man, experience counts for a lot. You couldn't beat those old bands. "Had to finish him off with a baseball bat, though."

"Are you all right with it?"

"Yeah, I'm okay." Leon shrugged. "The girl was a little tougher. I'm getting more used to it."

"And this time you did it somewhere else, I hope. You didn't go back to the falls again."

"Naw. We drove way out near West Rock."

The two of them were lying fully clothed on the huge bed Red Bear had had trucked up from Toronto. Teak or something, a four-poster with tons of fancy carving. He had a way with physical objects, Red Bear. Lamps with silky scarlet shades bathed the room in red light, giving the place a certain atmosphere, like a movie set.

There was a massive oak dresser by the window, with

crystal candlesticks and a set of silver hairbrushes that Red Bear used to make his hair shine.

They had smoked a couple of joints. For some reason, Red Bear didn't have any problem with weed. It was just the hard stuff he didn't want them using. Good smoke, too. The music twisted and stretched and drooped in the air like taffy.

Red Bear turned on his side and gripped Leon's bicep. "Thank you for being so loyal, Leon. I think you know loyalty means a lot to me."

"Yeah. Me too."

Red Bear stared into his eyes. Leon couldn't take it for very long; he had to look away.

"I got a question," Leon said. "About the girl, and now with Toof."

"Ask me."

Leon had never before let a man touch him. Somehow, with Red Bear, there was nothing queer about it, nothing effeminate.

"How come you didn't do them the way you did Wombat? You didn't make them suffer. Didn't cut them apart."

"You sound disappointed."

"Maybe."

Red Bear pointed to the ceiling. "The moon. The moon is not waxing just now. It's waning. A sacrifice must always be done when the moon is waxing."

"How come?"

"If you kill them when the moon is waning, their spirit will have power over you. That is the opposite of what you want."

"Great. So now their spirits have power over me? I'm gonna be haunted?"

"Not at all. You didn't sacrifice them. You didn't invoke the spirits. And you did what you did with my blessing. My protection. And now I'm going to increase that protection one-hundredfold. Take your shirt off."

Leon sat up and pulled his shirt off over his head. Red Bear went to the dresser and came back to the bed with an intricately carved wooden box. He opened it and pulled out a chain with a gold amulet hanging from it.

"Classy," Leon said. "What do the symbols mean?"

"I have blessed this with the power of Oggun."

Red Bear hung the chain around Leon's neck. The amulet was cold against his chest.

"Oggun's the one in charge of iron, right?"

Red Bear smiled. "Not just iron. All metals. Lead, for example. From this you will gain the powers of gold: its purity, its strength, its flexibility. Wear this, and bullets cannot harm you. They will pass right through your body without leaving a mark."

"Wow. That's amazing." Leon could feel the gold warming against his skin. He took a deep breath and concentrated, trying to absorb the purity, the strength, the flexibility.

"Now you are bulletproof," Red Bear said. "You have nothing to fear, my friend."

They lay silent for a while. The music had changed to some woman crooning about finding peace. The song set up a sharp ache in Leon's heart. Red Bear was saying something to him.

"What? What did you say?"

"I asked you if it bothered you. Killing a woman."

Leon thought a moment. Something about Red Bear made you want to tell him the truth. Those strange eyes of his made you feel he already knew the truth.

"Yes. I was shaking after. And scared. Maybe because she was a woman, I don't know. That's why I done her the same place you done Wombat. Woman. Man. Don't see why it should make no difference. There's nothing special about women. They've never done anything for me except make me feel like a loser, give me a lot of grief. Kinda feel bad for Kevin, though. He's an okay guy. I don't want him to know about it."

Red Bear tapped Leon's chest, gently. It felt like someone banging on a castle door, loud and echoey, fate come calling.

"There's your loyalty again," Red Bear said. "I admire that so much."

"Kevin better not find out. Him and his sister were close."

"He'll get over it. How was he about Toof?"

"Scared. Same as I was first time."

"I'll calm him down. But now I want you to just lie still. I'm going to give you another little reward."

Red Bear got up and pulled off his sweater. He was well muscled but not much bigger than Leon. Down his back, two long scars formed a V from his shoulders to his tailbone.

"How'd you get those scars?" Leon said. "They don't look accidental."

"Never mind about that now."

"I told you about mine."

Red Bear smiled and stepped out of his drawstring pants. "Maybe I'll tell you about them sometime. But for now, we have other things to do."

Red Bear went to the door and called out to the other room. A moment later, a small blond woman stepped into the bedroom, naked. She had small breasts, a wonderful smile. She looked Russian, with deep-set eyes, wide cheekbones.

"This is Mira," Red Bear said.

Mira sat on the bed. She took hold of Leon's belt and undid the buckle.

"And this is Katya."

A second woman came in, this one darker, bigger in the chest and, like her colleague, naked.

"Somehow," Red Bear said, "I don't think these ladies are going to make you feel like a loser."

24

RED BEAR REMEMBERED RECEIVING those scars to the day, hour and minute. It had been his twenty-first birthday. Uncle Victor had taken him to the tool shed. To this day, no one but the two of them knew the goings-on in that little concrete shed, a miniature outbuilding surrounded by brute high-rises. Who could have suspected the magical power emanating from the backyard of a housing project in Toronto, that least magical of cities?

Victor led him to the tool shed, blindfolded him and steered him in darkness beyond the back wall and into his temple. The stench no longer bothered Red Bear—or Raymond, as he was then known. Far from nauseating him, the stench set his pulses pounding. Uncle Victor had been preparing him for this day; through years of training, had brought him ever closer to the black beating heart of Palo Mayombe. Raymond could feel it pulsing around him, the heart of magic.

"Today is the most important day of your life, Raymond." Uncle Victor's wheezy, disembodied voice was like a speaking kazoo. "Today you will become a full priest of Palo Mayombe. You do not have to take this step, remember. There is still time to change your mind."

"I know. I want it, Uncle."

"You are sure?"

"I am sure. There is nothing I want more." Red Bear/Raymond inhaled deeply the smells of candle wax, cinquefoil and wormwood, and, above all, rotting meat.

"Very well. Two things will happen today. First, you will give up your soul. And second, you will be rayed out. You know what these things mean?"

"Yes, Uncle. My soul will die. And so for me there will be no chance of eternal happiness and no chance of eternal damnation. But I will be freer than any other man alive: free to take other souls."

"And to be rayed out?"

"To be rayed out means that I will accept the pain of the scars in return for the light and the power of Palo Mayombe."

"And you choose to do these things of your own free will?"

"I do."

"Has anyone forced you in any way to do these things?"

"No."

"And you recognize that once done they cannot be undone?"

"I do."

"Very well then, we will proceed."

Raymond heard his uncle draw the ceremonial knife from its sheath. This was followed by the sound of steel against whetstone. Then his uncle secured Raymond's wrists in the leather cuffs hanging from the ceiling. His mouth dried. Tremors shook his body.

That wheezy voice, dry as paper, chanting now in the language of his chosen religion, Palo Mayombe. Then the first searing touch of the blade.

———

Who can number all the ingredients that go into the creation of a monster? A dead body, the brain of a murderer, a bolt of lightning—the mad scientist throws a switch, life courses through dead veins and evil walks the earth. The case of Red Bear is more prosaic.

Long before Red Bear was Red Bear, he was Raymond Beltran, son of a teenaged prostitute named Gloria Beltran, who was shipped out of Cuba in the Mariel boat lift of 1980. Little Raymond had been eight years old then, and if his life in Havana had been unstable, it was nothing compared to the journey he was about to undergo.

Gloria's first stop was Miami, along with the other hundred thousand–plus Cubans of that exodus. She moved in with a cousin who threw her out when she came home to find Gloria plying her trade on the living-room couch, young Raymond not more than ten feet away in the next room. Her next stop was with an uncle, a much older and apparently more tolerant man. Unfortunately, Gloria had to quit that place on a matter of principle when the uncle insisted that she pay her rent in kind. The list of addresses that followed was long: two weeks here, three months there, each basement apartment more unpleasant than the last.

Then Gloria and Raymond caught what seemed like a break when they took up with Inigo Martinez, a drug dealer who had tired of the murderous competition in Miami and set his sights on the wide open market of Canada. Which was how Raymond Beltran came to grow up in a housing project called Regent Park on the east side of downtown Toronto.

Whenever the government does a census, Regent Park comes out as the poorest neighbourhood in Toronto. Most of its inhabitants are recent immigrants trying to realize some tiny approximation of their dreams. Many are single parents living on welfare; almost all are law-abiding. Inigo Martinez was not. Nor was he a successful businessman. His vision of Canada as a vast, undersupplied market for his product turned out to be incorrect. So incorrect that a disgruntled competitor had him thrown from the top of a high-rise.

Gloria managed to evade deportation by persuading a Canadian of Cuban heritage to marry her. For a small financial consideration, he agreed to appear at several immigration interviews, have photographs taken of their "honeymoon" and so on. After her status was legalized, Gloria tried to coerce him into providing "child-support" payments, but he disappeared from her life as people with any sense were wont to do.

That left Gloria to raise Raymond on the income she received from Social Services and the proceeds from selling her body. Neighbours complained, of course, and the police were frequent visitors. The Catholic Children's Aid

Society repeatedly hauled her before the provincial court at 311 Jarvis Street on charges of child neglect. Having left school forever at the age of fourteen, Gloria saw no reason why her son should attend; she liked having him around the apartment.

In addition to his mother, the other major influence on Raymond Beltran's character—the bolt of lightning that zapped the latent murderer's brain to life—was witchcraft.

Witchcraft, or more properly *brujeria*, came to Raymond in the person of Victor Vega, a fellow Cuban who looked to young Raymond to be about a hundred years old. Vega was bony, twisted and stooped. One leg dragged behind the other, the legacy of a long-ago car accident. His brown face was a cartoon exaggeration of brows and cheeks. All in all, an unprepossessing exterior for a man who commanded the respect—even fear—of those who knew what he was.

Vega was a witch, a *padrone* in the religion of Palo Mayombe. Palo Mayombe, like the better-known Voodoo and Santeria, is an African belief system whose gods wear the guise of Christian saints. Like its two sister religions, it concerns itself with magic, but in Victor Vega's hands it was magic of the blackest kind.

He lived down the hall from Gloria and Raymond; they saw each other often in the elevators. They greeted each other in Spanish, exchanged comments about the weather, but not much more than that. But the old man always looked at them with curiosity, as if he recognized them from somewhere. One day, when they were waiting for the elevator to arrive, Victor said, "I see you are a follower of Santeria." He was pointing with a sinewy finger at a huge carved bracelet on Gloria's wrist.

"I light my candles," Gloria said. "I ask now and again for guidance."

"Do you know about Mayombe?"

"Yes. I have a cousin who is a *padrone*. My father and mother did not believe, however, so I did not learn much about it."

"Still, I could see it is in your family."

"Oh, yes?"

"Your son's eyes. He has the kind of eyes that can see the future."

"Well, it's true he sometimes knows things he should not know." She turned to Raymond. "Even as a little boy, Raymond. Even as a child, many of the things you said had a habit of coming true. There was the time—long ago, this was back in Havana—you pointed to the *mulata* Lena Lindo and said, 'But she is dead, that woman.' And the next day she was indeed dead."

"I saw it in a dream," Raymond said. "I thought it was real."

"Yes, of course," the old man said. "Of course you did. But I will tell you something right now, something that is true: One day you are going to be a *padrone*."

"I don't think so," Gloria said. "Raymond is not a religious person."

"Oh, yes he is. He may not know it yet, but it is obvious from those eyes. One day he is going to be the most powerful *padrone* we have ever seen."

After that day, the three of them became more friendly. Vega took a kindly interest in the boy, taking him to Blue

Jays games and teaching him how to fix cars and all kinds
of motors. It was the most sustained attention Raymond
had ever had from an adult, and he thrived under it. He
got along better with the old man than he did with boys
his own age, and Gloria was happy to see him spend time
with someone from the old country. The three of them
became very close.

Victor often paid Raymond to help him with his work.
For, in addition to being a witch, the old man was in
charge of grounds maintenance at the housing project.
From the outside, his tool shed seemed nothing more
than a cramped, concrete structure with a metal door and
a roof of corrugated tin. It was heavily padlocked at all
times unless Victor was inside; no one else had a key. If
any of the local teenagers had decided to break in, they
would have found the usual assortment of clippers, lawn
mowers, weed whackers, shears, gloves and hoses.

But no one ever did break in, and it is unlikely that
anyone would ever attempt it, because the place smelled
so bad. Bags of sheep and cow manure were stacked
against the entire back wall of the shed, and in summer it
stank to high heaven.

That was Raymond's first sense of the place, how the
smell hit you in the face like a wall of cement. The lungs
closed off in self-defence and the gorge rose in the throat.
The first few times he stepped inside, he was consumed
with fear, fear strong enough to set his stomach tumbling
even before Victor opened up the back room, the secret
room, the place he referred to as his "temple."

Whenever Raymond and Victor were together, the old
man talked to him about magic. He taught him that you

could affect the events of this world with help from the creatures of the next. All that was required was a knowledge of how to control them. This knowledge, Victor hinted strongly, was something that was his to convey. Raymond began pestering Victor to teach him. Eventually, Victor agreed to show him his temple.

That first day—Raymond was not yet twelve—Victor squatted beside him and gripped his shoulder hard. His breath smelled of onions, but it was nothing compared to the stench in that shed.

"Little Raymond," he said. "What I am about to show you is a great secret. You have told me you wish to learn about magic. To learn how to command the spirits. To employ them in bringing good things to the people you love, to your mama and to me. To learn how to protect yourself from enemies. To see the future. Are you still interested in these things?"

"Yes, Uncle." Victor had told him to call him uncle and, by now, it came naturally. "Uncle, why does it smell so bad?"

"When you understand magic, you will know that that is a good smell, not bad at all. But now will you listen to what I am telling you?"

"Yes."

"Because it is the most important thing you will ever hear me say. I repeat: What I am about to show you is a great secret. So secret that if you ever tell anyone what you see in here, or what I do in here, or what you do in here, I will kill you. Do you understand me? I will kill you, Raymond."

Uncle Victor's face, seamed and brown as a walnut, drew closer. His black eyes looked into Raymond's, and Raymond knew he could see his fear.

"I won't tell, Uncle."

"I love you, my child, but if you tell, I will kill you with no more hesitation than a butcher kills a pig. You will die, you will be buried, and your mother will weep endless tears for you and she will never be happy again in her life. You don't want that, do you?"

"No, Uncle."

"So, if someone says to you, 'Hey, that Victor is a strange old bird. What does he get up to in that shed of his?' what do you say to this person?"

"I don't say anything."

"They may force you to say something. What will you tell them if they twist your arm and hurt you to make you talk?"

"I will tell them I don't know what you do in here?"

"No, you will tell them this: 'Uncle Victor keeps his gardening tools in there.' That's all. Not a word more. It is the truth, after all. No one can call you a liar. So what do you say?"

"'Uncle Victor keeps his gardening tools in there.'"

The bony fingers gripped his shoulder; it was like being squeezed by a hawk. "Good, Raymond. You are a good boy. You are worthy to learn about magic. Now I will show you my temple."

Victor slipped a foot under a rack of manure bags and pressed on a pedal. Something clicked, and the back wall shifted on a pivot. The smell became ten times worse, and Raymond gagged.

"It's all right," Victor said. "You will get used to the smell. In time, you will come to love the smell. It is the smell of power."

The room was tiny, and pitch dark except for the single red bulb that glowed overhead. As Raymond's eyes adjusted, he saw there was very little in the room: one large table, a hatchet and an array of knives fixed to the wall. The wall itself was painted with symbols he didn't understand. In the middle of the table was a large iron pot. From this, a quiver of long sticks protruded, so straight they might have been arrows.

There was a chicken tied to a bolt in the table, black eyes glistening with fear.

Victor gestured toward the iron pot. "The source of my power. It doesn't look like much, does it?"

Raymond sensed that no answer was required. Victor reached for him to lift him up, and Raymond shrank back.

Victor leaned down and spoke gently.

"You have nothing to fear, my child. Nothing. I am in control here. You will learn to ignore these feelings of fear. Eventually you will feel nothing and, believe me, to feel nothing is a great advantage in this world. For now, know that I will protect you. I will let nothing harm you. Nothing."

"I want to go home, Uncle."

"It is too late, Raymond. Stay by my side and nothing bad will happen to you."

He hoisted Raymond up and stood him on an apple crate so the boy could see into the pot. There was a foul, congealed liquid with solids of indistinct shape adrift in it.

"*Nganga*," Victor said. "This is called the *nganga*. In here we place the things we give to the gods. If we want a favour from Oggun, the god of iron, for example, we might put in a railway spike, or some large nails. If we want a favour from Ochosi, god of hunters, we might put in an arrowhead."

"But there's only one God, isn't there?"

The brown face waggled at him.

"That is a different religion altogether. I'm teaching you a much older, much more powerful religion. In the Christian religions, yes, there is only one God. In Palo Mayombe, there are many. Into this *nganga* we also put the things we need in order to control the spirits. Spirit beings, you see, have no power over human beings unless it is given to them. They are vessels, drifting this way and that, until we give them power. We—that is to say, the wizards—give them life. We give them breath and we give them the power to see, the power to hear, to go places, to grasp things." Victor flexed a claw open and shut before Raymond's eyes.

"Where do spirits come from?"

"From living creatures. Animals. Sometimes from human beings. We take them from this world in such a way that we control them in the next. Then they do our bidding. They work for us, you see. Only wizards have this right, this power. Now be silent. Clear your mind of all fear, and just watch what I do. We will do something nice for your mother. We will ask Oggun to bring her something nice."

Victor turned to the *nganga* and spread his hands like a Catholic priest over the altar. He began to speak in a language Raymond did not recognize. He knew it was not Spanish or English or French.

"*Bahalo! Semtekne bakuneray pentol!*" Victor turned to Raymond and spoke in an aside. "Always you must speak firmly to them. We do not beg on bended knee like the Christians and the Muslims. We *tell* them. We *command.*"

Victor raised his arms over the cauldron once more.

"*Bahalo! Seeno temtem bakuneray pentol!*"

Victor took the hatchet from the wall, grabbed the chicken and removed its head with a single stroke. He tossed the head into the pot. The headless chicken strained at its leash, running this way and that, unaware that it was dead.

Raymond started to cry. He tried to stop himself, but he couldn't; his entire body shook with sobs.

Victor took hold of the chicken by the feet and unclipped the leash. He held the still-struggling bird upside down over the *nganga* so that the hot blood squirted into the pot. He started to say more words, then turned on Raymond, gripping his shoulders: "Stop crying now, Raymond. You hear me? Stop crying." The bony hands shook him. "If you show fear, you allow the spirits to control you. This must never happen. Stop crying now. Take a deep breath and show them you are in command."

Raymond tried to do it, but he was hopeless that first day.

Later that week, when he came home from school, Gloria was entertaining a customer. Raymond went straight to his bedroom and tried not to hear the noises the man made, his mother's elaborate cries of ecstasy. When the man was gone, Gloria came to her son's room.

"Come with me," she said. "I have a surprise for you."

They rode the battered elevator down to the lobby. Gloria took Raymond out to the parking lot and sat him in a brand new Honda Prelude. It had a leather interior and a wonderful radio and it smelled powerfully of new car. Sunlight glittered off every surface. "How do you like Mommy's Honda?"

Raymond touched the steering wheel.

"Isn't it fantastic?" she said. "Uncle Victor got it for me from a friend of his."

"Who?" Raymond asked.

"A friend. I don't know who. It doesn't matter who."

She started it up and pulled onto Gerrard Street. Five minutes later they were cruising along the Gardiner Expressway. Lake Ontario flashed brilliant blue and silver in the sun. The few clouds were absurdly white. Gloria opened all the windows and the sunroof, and their hair whipped about their ears. Raymond didn't have to ask who had given her the car. It had been Oggun. Oggun had given them this car, just as Victor had told him to.

As time went by, Raymond got braver and braver in his uncle's temple. Over the following months and years, Victor instructed him in the art of controlling the spirits. He taught him that when you took a soul, you had to do so with the utmost pain. Really, the sacrifice had to be screaming as it died, otherwise you could not command its soul. And if you showed the slightest fear, then the spirit would end up controlling *you*.

He showed Raymond how you remove the claws or feet, toe by toe, so the spirit would be able to grasp, how you cut off the feet and throw them into the *nganga* so the spirit would be able to move about and, finally, how you look into the sacrifice's eyes in its final agony and tell it you would come for it in hell. Then you took the brain and transferred it to the *nganga*, so the spirit would be able to understand your commands, would be able to think.

Raymond threw up the first few times. But eventually it was just as Uncle Victor had said; he got used to it. The fear diminished, and by the time he was fourteen he felt no fear whatsoever. Chickens, goats, dogs, cats—in the end, it made no difference. Raymond learned to master the screaming animals and to stare into their eyes as they died.

Then his uncle taught him how to summon the spirit of the creature you had sacrificed, how to make him work for you.

—

Time, the twenty-one-year-old Raymond learned, took on a whole new meaning when you were on the receiving end of the blade. The hot blood turned sticky on his back, and his head ached monstrously from gritting his teeth against the pain.

His uncle removed the blindfold, and Raymond had to close his eyes against the candles that blazed in rows and rows. Then Victor released the leather cuffs and sat Raymond down.

"Don't worry," Uncle Victor said. "The wounds will soon heal."

Cool water splashed over his back. His uncle dabbed at him gently. "You have nothing to fear, you know. From the moment I first noticed you—that time in the hall—I looked into your eyes and I said to Gloria, 'Your son is going to be a priest. A very powerful priest.'"

Raymond remembered, but the old man often repeated the story.

Uncle Victor rubbed ointment on the long lines he had cut into Raymond's back. The pain began to attenuate, to become bearable.

"You will have nothing to fear, Raymond. Believe me. You are going to be the most powerful priest walking the earth. A true collector of souls." And then Victor did an amazing thing. He knelt down and bowed his head.

25

STEPHEN P. RUSSELL HAD COME prepared—floppy straw sun hat, bright white bug shirt, Off Deep Woods insect repellent—he was ready for anything. As Algonquin Bay's best-selling watercolourist, Stephen P. Russell prided himself on being an all-weather, all-terrain sort of man. His ancient Volvo wagon was crammed with boots, umbrella, slicker, sandals, sunblock, coffee Thermos, as well as the painterly paraphernalia of the amateur artist: easel, brushes, colours and a none-too-steady folding stool.

Stands of birches were his bread and butter, preferably birches adorned with clumps of snow or dripping with rain. He sold two or three of these works every weekend at the farmers' market. You couldn't live on the money it brought in, but it was a nice supplement to a pension from the Nipissing Separate School Board. He prided himself particularly on his ability to render the platinum sheen on the leaves of the silver birch, the very effect he was creating at this moment.

A steady breeze was riffling the leaves and blowing them back like the fur on a cat. A languid chorus line of Scotch pines swayed beside the birches, but the painter ignored them. These he would do with a green wash later, blurry as you please. That was the great thing about watercolours—it was easy to blur everything you didn't want the viewer to see. Pines were not Stephen P. Russell's strong suit.

The brushwork on the birch leaves took a lot of doing, a lot of concentration. And for some time, the painter had noticed that his concentration was flickering. Normally he could work for hours, thinking of nothing but his subject and his technique, but today he had finished his Thermos of coffee early, and now nature had to take its course.

He turned from his easel and looked behind him toward the nasty construction site. No, he would have to head the other way. He got up with difficulty from his stool—oh, the aches and agues of the so-called golden years!—and tottered stiffly toward the bushes.

At first he didn't realize what it was. The thing was only in his peripheral vision, and he was seeing it through anti-bug mesh. It made him jump because he thought somebody had caught him relieving himself outdoors. It was only after he had zipped up, his face burning with embarrassment, that he turned and realized that this person had not seen anything at all.

26

THERE WAS ALREADY A SMALL CROWD of cops at the scene by the time Cardinal arrived. A pale, reedy man separated himself from the knot of people and began filling out a form that kept curling from his clipboard in the breeze. Once again, Cardinal was in luck; this time the coroner was Dr. Miles Kennan. He tore off the flimsy top sheet of the form and handed it to Cardinal.

"We've got an obvious victim of foul play here, Detective." Kennan had a gentle, breathy voice. "I do hope you'll give my regards to the forensic centre."

"'Cause of death,'" Cardinal read from the form, "'gunshot and/or blunt trauma'?"

"You'll see what I mean when you take a look," Kennan breathed. "Either would have killed him eventually, but you'll need a pathologist to tell you which one actually did him in." The doctor swatted at his neck. "God, I hate blackflies."

"Time of death?"

"You'll have to ask the centre that one. I'd guess he's

been dead between twelve and twenty-four hours. But
even that's a very rough guess."

"All right. Thanks, Doctor."

Cardinal stepped under the crime scene tape.
Arsenault and Collingwood were down on hands and
knees, evidence bags ready. Delorme was on her cellphone, apparently on hold.

"Forensic?" Cardinal asked.

She nodded.

"Who called us?"

"Local artist. He doesn't know anything."

Delorme spoke into the phone. "All right, Len.
Thanks." She hung up. "I asked Weisman if someone from
ballistics could stay late."

"It's already late."

"Yeah, that's what Weisman said." Delorme shrugged.
"I charmed him to death."

"No, you didn't. Len doesn't charm. Do we know who
we've got here?"

"Unfortunately, no. There's no wallet, no ID, no nothing. He appears to be mid to late twenties, five-five, about
a hundred and fifty pounds. Other than that, there's not
much to go by."

"There was nothing at all in his pockets?"

"A ten-dollar bill, some change and a pack of matches
from Duane's Billiard Emporium."

Cardinal stood back and looked over the scene as a
whole. The brush was thick where the dirt road came to
an end. Even Cardinal, no forensic expert, could see
recently broken twigs and branches. And there was a lot
of blood near the victim's head. Droplets had sprayed

upward against the white trunks of the birches. Definitely killed here, not just dumped.

"I can't figure out how this went down," Delorme said. "It's unlikely the killer was just sitting here in a car waiting for a victim to pass by. The two of them—or maybe there were more, I guess we don't know—but the two of them come out here for something. Then for some reason they get into an argument and the one guy kills the other."

"A bullet in the back of the head doesn't read like a spur-of-the-moment thing to me," Cardinal said.

"That's true. It's more like an execution."

"Tire," Collingwood said, restricting himself as usual to a single syllable. He sat back on his haunches so they could see the white patch he was working on. Then he lifted the plaster and turned it over, revealing perfectly formed tread marks.

"Nice work," Cardinal said. "Let's hope it belongs to the killer's car and not to some construction foreman."

Arsenault was a few yards away, just getting to his feet, exclaiming dramatically at his creaking knees. He was holding up a tiny plastic vial, waggling it at Cardinal the way one waggles a stick at a dog.

"Okay, Sherlock," Cardinal said. "What have you got?"

"Take a look, man. I don't have words to tell you how good I am."

Cardinal peered at the vial. It contained a tiny, papery white pocket, like a shred of popcorn hull.

"Is that a maggot casing?" Cardinal said. "Why is this a big deal?"

"Distance from the flesh," Arsenault said. "Maggots will eventually fall off a dead body. Cheese skippers even spring off a corpse and land maybe a couple of feet away. But this little guy is eight feet away, right inside a footprint."

"I hope you're not telling me one of us stepped in maggots and carried them back here."

"Nope. Footprint's got deep treads, probably from a hiking boot. None of us is wearing hiking boots, and none of us has been up to the body and back this way. The tape'll verify that." He waved toward a video camera perched on a tripod, its red light throbbing.

Cardinal took in the scene again. "You're right. And going by the tire marks, this would have been where the back of the car was. The trunk. Whoever killed him must've come back this way, around the back of the car and then into the driver's seat. But why would he have a maggot casing on his shoe?"

"My question exactly," Arsenault said. "Which is why I'm taking this little fellow to Dr. Chin in his own private limo."

"The other day you didn't even want to hear about Chin."

"Obviously I'm learning under your guidance and inspiration. The guy impressed me, okay?"

Cardinal took one more look at the scene as a whole, then stepped closer to the body. He must have let out a gasp or a curse or something, because Delorme said, "Yeah. Pretty bad, isn't it."

The trauma to the face and head was brutal. Half the cranial vault was collapsed.

"I wonder which they did first," Cardinal said. "Shoot him or bash his head in?"

"Does it make that much difference?" Delorme's background was in white-collar crime; Cardinal reminded himself he had to make allowances.

"If you knock him out and then shoot him," he said, "that's one type of person. If you shoot him first, then bash his head in, what does that make you?"

"Either extremely vicious . . ." Delorme looked at him, brown eyes questioning, "or maybe the owner of a defective gun?"

"I'm betting on both."

27

MURDER IS SO RARE IN Algonquin Bay that, when it happens, the detectives tend to stay close to the victim. Yes, they could simply ship the body down to Toronto. Yes, they could get the autopsy results by phone. Same with ballistics and other expert evidence. The problem with that approach is that it tends to take even longer than the eight hours of driving involved in a trip to Toronto and back. From her long years of work in Special Investigations, Delorme had learned that nothing counts in an investigation like face-to-face contact. Which was why she and Cardinal drove all the way to Toronto, 450 kilometres south. If Cardinal was upset about having to make the trip again so soon, he didn't let on.

They were buzzed into the Centre of Forensic Sciences by Len Weisman himself; pretty much everyone else had left for the day, and Weisman always liked to be the first guy to look at a body.

Last time she had worked a homicide, Delorme and Arsenault had taken bets on how Weisman would react. It had been a homosexual affair turned ugly, one man killing his lover in a jealous frenzy. It was so bad they'd found footprints *inside* the body.

Arsenault bet that Weisman wouldn't blink an eye.

Delorme didn't see how any human being could look at a thing like that and not react.

When they got to the delivery dock, Weisman had unzipped the bag. He looked at the footprints in the chest cavity, put his hands on his hips and said, "What do you think? Nine-and-a-halfs?"

I hope I never get like that, Delorme thought now as she shook Weisman's hand.

"Come in, come in. You're late. Patient got here an hour ago." Weisman always referred to the bodies as patients.

"I see you're already dressed for the beach," Cardinal said.

Along with his tweed jacket and his tie and his denim jeans, Weisman wore biblical-looking sandals.

"I get hot feet," Weisman said. "It's a circulation problem."

He led them back to his miniature office. His desk was stacked with reports, textbooks, a tape recorder and several oranges that were fragrantly past their prime. On his desk, a computer was lit up with a toxicology website. Weisman grabbed a lab coat and shrugged himself into it as they followed him down a tiled corridor.

He held open the door for them and they entered the morgue proper, where a bearded man in a white coat was bending over the body.

"Dr. Srinigar, this is Detective Lise Delorme and Detective John Cardinal from the Algonquin Bay Police."

Dr. Srinigar dipped forward in a slight bow. "Forgive me if I don't shake hands. Such a long journey you've taken, you must be even more tired than I." His accent was pleasantly Indian or Pakistani, Delorme wasn't sure which. Straying out from his surgical cap, black hair streaked with grey.

"Thanks for working late, Doctor," Cardinal said. "What can you tell us?"

"Our young patient has met with a most unfortunate end. Only twenty-seven or twenty-eight and this is his brain, here in the scale. Quite a bit heavier than the normal human brain, but only until such time as I removed a significant amount of lead. Two bullets' worth, to be exact."

"Do you have those bullets?"

"No, no. I sent them straight over to ballistics. I trust that was proper."

"Extremely," Delorme said. What a pleasure to run into good manners; it didn't happen a lot in this line of work.

Above his mask, the doctor's eyes were dark brown, bovine and sincere.

"At first I thought there was only one bullet wound in the antero-occipital region, but that was because there was such severe destruction via blunt force trauma. Bits of wood removed from the scalp indicate a club of some sort. Possibly a baseball bat."

"Which happened first?" Delorme asked. "The bullets or the bat?"

"Oh, he was shot first. About this there can be no question. Cranial bone has been crushed into the entry wounds."

"Was he dead when they went at him with the bat?"

"Well, one could happily argue one side or the other of that particular question. There are plenty of factors to back either opinion. But at the end of the day, I must tell you honestly that I do not know. Myself, I would venture to say that the assailant shot his victim first. The first bullet barely entered the brain. The second crashed into the right optic nerve. Balance, vision, hearing—all would have been immediately affected. Indeed, the damage is catastrophic, but with these apparently low-powered bullets, not necessarily immediate. Angle of impact indicates the victim was still standing for at least one blow of the baseball bat."

"So maybe in frustration," Delorme said. "When he doesn't fall down, the guy goes at him with the bat."

"That would be consistent with what I see here. Eminently so, Detective."

"Thank you, Doctor."

Cardinal turned to Weisman. "Who've you got over in ballistics?"

"Fellow named Cornelius Venn. He's very good. Have you worked with him before?"

"You'll love this guy," Cardinal said to Delorme. "I'll let you ask the questions."

Christian good guy, Delorme thought when she first saw Cornelius Venn, with his yellow bow tie and his sincere-looking glasses. One of those characters who appear on your front step with a bible and a grin the size of Lake Nipissing. Sort of guy who'd stop to help you fix a flat and would know the cheapest place to buy hot dogs for the cookout.

Cardinal introduced Delorme.

"Your bullets are extremely mashed up," Venn said. "There's only so much you can expect."

"I'm not expecting anything," Delorme said, "except that you'll give it your best shot. I'm hearing good things about you."

"Really? They're just being pleasant, I'm sure," Venn said. He was bent over his comparison microscope, adjusting the focus. "Everybody's always so pleasant. What are they going to say? 'Here's Cornelius Venn, our worst firearms examiner'?"

Delorme wondered what Venn did in his spare time. She had a feeling it would involve machines, not people.

She glanced at Cardinal, but he just rolled his eyes.

"Ahem." Venn coughed primly into a handkerchief, as if he were tubercular. "You have two .32-calibre bullets here. One is mashed beyond recognition and no use at all for anything." His tone suggested they shouldn't have bothered bringing such shoddy goods to his attention, even if they did transport them in a dead body.

"The second one is only partially destroyed, and I'm just now attempting to see if I can get something worthwhile out of it." He adjusted a knob, turning the bullet under his lens.

"Yes, it's not completely useless. I'll just adjust my magnification a little to cut out some of the clutter. Later, I'll give you a printout in a form you can understand."

As if it's astrophysics, Delorme thought. Guy thinks he's working for NASA.

Venn spoke into his microscope, his voice tinny. "Six left-hand grooves."

"Do you have enough bullet to measure them?" Delorme said.

"Your impatience will do nothing to enhance my performance, Detective."

"It was just a question, Mr. Venn."

He glanced up at her, the microscope's light forming twin reflections in his glasses. "It was a question designed to put me on the defensive."

"Actually, it was a request for information."

"Yes, it was. Implying that I'm not intelligent enough to realize that information is what you are here for."

Delorme glanced at Cardinal, but he gave her no help.

Venn returned to his microscope. "I'm getting a land-to-groove ratio of one-to-one-plus. Grooves are zero point five-six; lands are zero point six-oh."

He gave no sign that any of this information was familiar.

"Colt Police Positive, right?" Cardinal said.

Venn swivelled around in his chair as if noticing Cardinal for the first time. "Among other possibilities."

"Well, why don't we cut to the chase and just compare it to the bullet they took out of our Jane Doe last week. Can you do that?"

"Did you bring the case number?"

Cardinal opened his briefcase and pulled out a form. He read the number and Venn went over to a shelf full of little plastic drawers, the kind home handymen use to store doodads. He pulled one out, extracted the bullet that had been taken from Terri Tait's skull and stuck it under the left-hand lens of his microscope with a bit of beeswax.

"As you know, Detective, it could also be from a J.C. Higgins model 80."

"Thank you for informing me," Delorme said. "What I really want to know, though, whenever you're ready to tell us—and don't let me rush you or anything—is whether it's the same gun. The lands and grooves and even the twist aren't going to tell you that on their own, right?".

"Oh, my. Go to the top of the class," Venn said. He adjusted the left bullet, then the right. After a moment, he said, "The thing about the Colts is, they have distinctive skid marks, the marks made when the round is chambered. In any case, I can tell you right now it's the same gun. Take a look for yourself."

He rolled his chair aside and Delorme bent over the eyepiece.

"Focus," he said. His damp fingers pressed her hand on the knob. Delorme tweaked it and the image went from soft to crystal clear. The incisions and scallops in both pieces of lead lined up perfectly.

"Nice," Delorme said. "Very nice. Thank you, Mr. Venn."

"Is there anything else I can help you with?"

"No thanks," Delorme said. She couldn't help smiling, even if he was a jerk. "I think that's it."

"Then thank you for using the Centre of Forensic Sciences and you have a wonderful evening."

Later, when they were back on Highway 400 heading north, Delorme said, "What's with that Venn guy? It's like he studied all his life to be a dork."

"I don't know what it is that happens to ballistics guys," Cardinal said. "But it sure happens fast."

People claim to do the long drive back to Algonquin Bay in under three and a half hours, but they're lying. To get from downtown Toronto to Algonquin Bay takes four hours minimum. By the time Cardinal was heading up Trout Lake Road toward home, he was thinking he would allow himself exactly one beer before bed; he didn't like to have more than that when Catherine was away, as it tended to depress him.

When he and Delorme had finished with ballistics, he had badly wanted to drop over to Catherine's hotel; the Delta Chelsea was not far from the forensic centre. But he had been faced with a conundrum. If Catherine were at her best, of course, it would be no problem for him to show up. But she was treading rocky terrain, just now, feeling his protectiveness as persecution, and his showing up unannounced might be exactly the wrong move. In the end, he had decided against it, but now he wondered where she was and what she was doing. In her hotel room, he hoped, watching TV. Or on-line with her laptop, trolling eBay for bargain lenses.

His cellphone rang, and it was Larry Burke; he was on guard duty at the hospital. His voice was tight, full of nerves.

"I think you'd better get up here," he said. "Seems our redhead friend has disappeared."

28

Burke was waiting at the front door of the hospital, looking glum, when Cardinal arrived.

"How did this happen, Burke? For God's sake, this girl is in danger."

"I know that. But nobody told me she was a flight risk. I was supposed to be careful about who I let in, not worried about her getting out. It's not like she's being held here on a charge or anything."

"Tell me what happened."

"Nothing happened. She's had the run of the ward since she got here. Everybody loves her. She comes and goes as she pleases. The first couple of times I was a little nervous, but she always told me where she was going and she always came right back."

"Where did she say she was going this time?"

"She said she was going to visit one of the other girls on the ward. She's done that before. Girl named Cindy in 348."

"And you didn't go with her?"

"She didn't want me to. Bad enough she has to be in here when she's not really sick, I figured give her some privacy. Like I say, nobody told me she was a flight risk. There was no reason to worry about her taking off."

"If she has taken off. How do we know she hasn't been kidnapped by whoever tried to kill her?"

"Nobody saw zip. If she was taken against her will, there would have been a commotion."

"Did she have any visitors?"

"Nope. Not one."

"Let me borrow your radio."

Burke handed it over. Cardinal buzzed the station and told the dispatcher to put out an all-points on Terri Tait. He gave a description and switched off.

"Did you ask everyone on duty? You're sure no one saw her leave?"

"I asked everyone. Nobody saw her."

"At least she'll be easy to spot with that flaming red hair. Did you talk to the girl in 348?"

"Yeah. Name's Cindy Peele. Didn't get much."

"I'll talk to her again. Why don't you book off now."

"You blame me she's gone AWOL?"

"I blame myself. I should have warned everyone to stay close."

Cardinal went up to Terri's room. The bed was rumpled, but didn't look slept in. He opened the closet. Her few clothes were missing.

Cardinal went down the hall to room 348. A girl wearing headphones sat listlessly propped against her pillows, watching TV. Her dirty blond hair needed washing, and there was a small white cuff of bandage on her left wrist.

She didn't look away from the TV when Cardinal entered; he walked in front of the screen and pointed to her headphones.

"What!" She snapped at him as if he had been plaguing her for weeks.

"Would you take the headphones off, please, Cindy?"

She pulled the headphones down so that they hung around her neck. Her face was an exaggerated sketch of annoyance.

Cardinal introduced himself.

"This is so bogus. Why can't people just leave me alone?"

"This isn't about you. I just have a few questions concerning the young woman down the hall."

"Like I'm her twin sister or something."

"She visited you a few times, didn't she?"

"So what? Are you going to arrest me?"

Anger radiated from the girl in hot waves. Cardinal was reminded of Kelly's teenage years. Catherine had been in hospital for most of them, and he had had to suffer his daughter's virtuoso command of the negative emotions on his own.

"Why did she visit you?"

"Hello-o. She was probably like totally bored. Who wouldn't be?"

"What did you talk about with her?"

"Nothing. Life. She was trying to cheer me up. As if."

So much rage in one so small. Cardinal estimated Cindy's height at about five-four. Slight build. Very similar to Terri Tait, maybe a little bigger.

"Did she tell you anything about herself? Where she was from? Where she was going?"

"She said she was from like B.C. or Vancouver. Whatever. She was studying acting. Totally wants to be famous—like who doesn't. Mostly she asked questions."

"What sort of questions?"

"She's like, Where do you live? How many brothers and sisters do you have? What do your parents do? And I am so not into it. She's like, Do you have a boyfriend? And I'm like, As if."

"Did she tell you why she's here in Algonquin Bay?"

"No."

"Did she tell you what happened to her?"

"No."

"You didn't ask about the bandage on her head?"

"Bandage?"

Of course not, Cardinal thought. You didn't even see it. No one else exists in your world.

"She did ask to use my cellphone. And I let her. Said she didn't have one, and the hospital phone wasn't working."

"When was that?"

"Last night. Around seven."

"Do you know who she called?"

"No way. Some Vancouver number. She asked first if that would be okay. I didn't care."

"Was it a man or woman, do you know?"

"I'm not a snoop. Soon as she started dialling, I put the headphones on."

"Did she say anything about planning to leave here? Where she might go?"

"Nope. Why are you so, like, after her? What is she, like a total criminal mastermind or something?"

"We're not after her. We're trying to protect her."

"I hate being protected," the girl said, as if people were constantly forcing their protective services on her.

"When did you see her last?"

"Couple of hours ago."

"What was she wearing?"

"Hospital nightgown thing."

She could have hidden her other clothes underneath that, then gone and changed somewhere else.

"What happened?"

"What do you mean, what happened? She came in, made a little chit-chat. And left. I didn't know she was going anywhere. Why would I care?"

"We need to know who she called. May I look at your cellphone?"

"It's right there. Knock yourself out."

Cardinal picked up the phone from her night table. It was seashell pink with a tiny sticker that said *Do Not Enter*. He pressed the memory button and a list of numbers appeared on the tiny screen. There was only one with the Vancouver area code.

"Is this the one she dialled?"

Big shrug. Bored eyes. "Search me. I fell asleep."

Cardinal made a note of the number.

"You fell asleep while she was here?"

"There's not like a whole lot else to do in this place."

"Have you checked your things? Are you missing anything?"

"No, I'm not missing anything."

Cardinal opened the closet. There was a denim jacket, bell-bottoms, cargo pants and a couple of T-shirts on the shelf.

"My hoodie," she said. "Bitch took my hoodie."

"Hoodie?"

"Long-sleeved T-shirt with a hood. Dark blue. That total bitch. That thing was expensive. I'm gonna kill her."

"You may have to get in line."

"That total LOSER." The pale hands slammed down on the bed.

"Listen, Cindy," Cardinal said. "I'm sorry about your clothes, and I want to thank you for your help. I hope you feel better soon."

"As if."

The girl clamped the headphones over her ears, banishing him.

In the corridor, Cardinal pulled out his own cellphone and dialled the Vancouver number. A snippy, synthetic voice informed him that service at the number had been suspended.

"Excuse me," he said to the nurse on duty. "How many women's washrooms are there on this floor?"

"The patients' rooms all have their own washrooms," she said. She looked scarcely older than Cindy, minus the incandescence of rage. "Or did you mean public washrooms?"

"Public, yes."

"There's two. One right there." She pointed to a door across the corridor. "And another one by the elevator."

Cardinal showed her his ID. "I'm looking for your patient Terri Tait. I need to check both those washrooms. Will you come with me?"

The nurse went to the closest washroom and knocked loudly on the door. She pushed it. "There's no one in here."

Cardinal went with her into the white glare of tile and porcelain.

"What are you looking for?"

"I'm not sure." There were only two stalls. He checked both of them. "Will you show me the other one, please?"

He followed her down the hall to the elevator area. Once again the nurse knocked loudly on the door before pushing it open.

Cardinal opened the first stall. Nothing. Then the second. A patient's nightgown and robe hung from the hook on the back of the door.

The nurse bent down and picked up a narrow strip of paper, a patient's ID band. "I guess they never changed her tag," she said.

Cardinal took it from her. It still read *Jane Doe*.

———

Back in the car, Cardinal called Delorme at home. There was a clatter on the other end of the line and then Delorme's sleep-husky voice saying hello.

"I woke you. I'm sorry."

"You don't sound sorry."

"I'm not. Terri Tait has disappeared from hospital."

Delorme's voice cleared. "Abducted, you think?"

"Looks like she just borrowed some clothes and snuck out. Of course, it's possible someone picked her up in the parking lot. Did we ever hear anything back from the Vancouver police?"

"Nothing. But I got a social insurance number. I'm waiting for employment records."

"So we still don't know if she has relatives in this area."

"'Fraid not."

"I'm thinking it's possible she's spent time here before. That she has someplace to go, people who will take her in. If we do the footwork, we'll find the place, find the people."

"What do we do in the meantime?"

"I've got a phone number to follow up on. Someone she called from the hospital."

"Local?"

"Vancouver area code, but it could be a cellphone. I've already put out an all-points. That red hair of hers, somebody's bound to spot her sooner or later. In the meantime, I'm going to bed."

"Where are you now?"

"Trout Lake Road. Coming back from the hospital."

"Do you ever wish you did something else entirely? Something unrelated to police work?"

"I fantasize about running a carpentry business. But then if I did woodworking full time, I'd probably get sick of that, too."

"Me, sometimes I wish I'd just gone into business. I wasn't too far from an MBA when I got sidetracked."

Cardinal realized after he hung up that that was the most personal conversation they'd had in six months.

29

THE BLINDS WERE ALL SHUT; the house was in the dim, lightless grey of limbo. Terri was sitting on her jacket, but even folded up it couldn't soften the hardwood floor. *Run, run, run.* The words reverberated in her head as if they had become the soundtrack for her life.

She stared at the red-brick fireplace and its sooty interior. Whoever had last lived in this house had certainly cleaned the place up before shutting the door for the last time. She wondered who they were, and if they had been happy. There was nothing special about the house itself. There were a hundred just like it in the neighbourhood, but Terri had been happy here.

How odd that she should be so unhappy now, because as a child she had been completely sunny. She had got along fine with her parents, got along fine with Kevin, her kid brother. But then disaster had struck, and Terri and Kevin had had to go out to Vancouver to live with an aunt and uncle whom she didn't much like. She remembered the stink of her uncle's pipe, and how her aunt had always thought everything was just "precious" or "darling," words that set Terri's teeth on edge. That was her mother's sister, but she couldn't have been more different. Her aunt and uncle hadn't been bad people, but they couldn't replace her parents, and that made Terri resent them.

This house had been the last place she had been truly happy—carefree, the way a kid should be. She remembered how the fireplace had glowed on cold winter nights. It used to have a glass screen, and she and Kevin used to fight for the patch of carpet just in front of it, lying on their bellies to watch television. The TV had been in the corner—except at Christmas, when they moved it to make room for the long-needled tree they always got.

Terri got up and walked again through the dining area. Her parents' dining set, Swedish modern, had been too big, and if you sat at the end of the table opposite her father you were actually sitting in the living room. In the kitchen, a peculiar memory assailed her: She had been drying the dishes, and fainted clean away while drying the carving knife. It had stuck in the floor where it had fallen and was still there when she woke up moments later with her parents' worried faces looming over her. A touch of anemia, the doctor had told them.

Her bedroom was much bigger than she remembered. Of course, back then, it had been crowded with bed and dresser and desk, with clothes and CDs and a computer and a skateboard and a huge stuffed tiger that her father had bought for her once when she had been sick. Now it was just an empty box with a cheap window and gouges in the floorboards. She lifted a corner of the blind. Some years, the snowbanks had come right up to the bottom of the glass. There was a swing in the backyard that hadn't been there when she'd lived here, one of those black-strap swings that look like instruments of torture.

She let the blind fall. It sent up a cloud of dust that made her sneeze.

Down in the basement she had no trouble finding the main water valve. When she had been about twelve, a pipe had burst and her father had had to shut off the water. She had been down there at his side in Wellington boots, the little tomboy helping Dad, while Kevin, five years younger, floated a toy destroyer on the flood waters, making bombing noises. Upstairs, she turned on the cold water tap. It gasped and clattered before water, brown and disgusting, jetted into the sink. She sat down on the floor and let it run.

One good thing about coming to this abandoned house and its swamp of nostalgia: It kept her thoughts— for a few minutes, anyway—off the more recent memories, which ran through her mind like movie trailers.

Trailer number one: Sunlight beating down on the camp, so fierce Terri thinks she is going to be sick. She is taking a stroll on the pebbly beach, past what seems to be the edge of the camp property. But as she cuts through the woods on the way back, blackflies swarming around her, she comes across another cabin. This one is smaller than the others, and someone has bricked up the single window. On the front door, a heavy brass padlock gleams. There is a terrible smell, and she veers back toward the water.

Trailer number two: She and Kevin are in town together. It's the one day they have any fun, strolling down Main Street and then walking along the lakefront. Hanging out at the public wharf, and then a visit to the farmers' market. A diamond of a day, bright and clear, and Kevin behaves like the old Kevin—funny, mischievous—the nonaddicted Kevin she grew up with. He drives her around in the old, beat-up Nissan he calls a car, and they take a spin along the lake, then back to the highway. The happiness pierces the armour Terri has lately been wearing in order to deal with Kevin's drug problems. She can't remain silent.

"Why don't we just leave?" she says. "Why not just take off and go back to Vancouver? You say you're having a good time here, but I can tell you're not."

"Aw, Terri, don't start." Kevin gives her that wounded little-boy look. "We were having such a great time."

"I know. And I want you to keep having good times, Kevin. I don't want to wake up some morning and find myself going to my little brother's funeral."

"Lay off, will ya? I'm not little any more, all right? I realize, after Mom and Dad died, you kinda looked after me. Moving to a new family, new city, you were really great. But I'm not a kid any more."

"You're still my brother. I still care about you, even if you don't."

"Terri, I'm not doing that much dope."

"You haven't got a job, so I assume you're dealing to pay for it. Think about what's going to happen when you get caught. Do you know how many years you'll get this time?"

"I just want to stay with this till I have enough money for a couple of years. Then I'm going to get clean for good and go somewhere—Greece or somewhere—and do nothing but write and get sunburned."

Sometimes it's Tangiers. Sometimes Marrakesh. He got the Greece idea from Leonard Cohen, she knows. He's been carrying around a Cohen biography for ages.

"Can you honestly say you're not frightened of Red Bear? You don't think he's dangerous?"

"I don't want to talk about it. He's not that bad."

"I think he's crazy."

"I know how to handle him."

"Red Bear is not a person anybody *handles*, Kevin. Haven't you noticed his eyes? Those eyes are dead, Kevin. There's nothing behind them—no heart, anyway. Nothing real. That's why he wears sunglasses all the time. He doesn't want people to see his eyes."

Kevin looks over at her, slowing a little for a Wal-Mart truck.

"Look, Terri. You're my sister. You're not my mother. You can't be doing this. You can't be telling me what I should do. How I should run my life."

"I want you to *have* a life, Kevin. Do you think I enjoy chasing after you? Do you think I want to be like your chaperone or your maiden aunt or something? I'm missing work, I'm missing acting class, I've got two auditions coming up—believe me, Kevin, I have better things to do than follow you across the bloody country trying to pull a needle out of your arm."

"So, do them! Terri, please! Go back to Vancouver and do them! Just leave me the fuck alone!"

"I can't leave you alone. You're killing yourself—whether by accidental overdose or by getting caught up in some idiotic turf war with Red Bear and his friends—you're killing yourself. And I'm not going to stand by and watch it happen. Why are you pulling over?"

There they are on the highway and he's pulling over onto the gravel shoulder. Several cars shoot by, horns blaring.

"Kevin, what are you doing?"

"Take the fucking car. I'm going back into town where people don't fucking tell me what to do."

"Oh, don't do that. Kevin, wait!"

She jumps out of the car and follows him a little ways, highway grit stinging her eyes. Kevin is walking fast, stalking away from her, back stiff, shoulders raised. Talk about armour. When he gets like that there's no talking to him.

Trailer number three: She isn't sure if this was later that same day or a couple of days after. She's in the "guest" cabin stuffing things into her backpack. Her heart is pounding, and all she wants to do is run. Kevin has gone somewhere and she knows she has to get out of this cabin, out of the camp, instantly. Her hands are shaking so bad she can't make the backpack zipper work. The door opens, no knock or anything, and she lets out a scream.

Red Bear is standing there, a black silhouette against a rectangle of light. She drops the backpack, stoops to pick it up, drops it again.

"It's time for you to leave," Red Bear says, his tone not unpleasant.

"I know. I know. I'm packing right now."

She takes a step behind her bunk, instinctively wanting something between her and Red Bear. "I'll get a ride into town with Kevin."

"Kevin is not here. Kevin is not going to be back for some time."

"I'll catch a bus, then."

"There are no buses for miles. I will have someone drive you."

"No, that's okay. I'll just hitchhike."

"I can't allow that." Red Bear doesn't take his sunglasses off, but she knows he is looking her up and down. "You might get raped. Have you ever been raped, Terri?"

Terri has nothing to say to that. The answer is negative, but an answer is not required.

Red Bear remains a motionless darkness in the doorway.

"I didn't see anything," she says. "I have no intention of talking to anyone."

"Of course not. That would be bad for Kevin. And neither of us wants to hurt your brother, right?"

Then he is gone from the door.

But what had she seen? And who had driven her away from the camp? Terri could not recall. Her last memory of the place was that empty doorway. Now, she got up from the floor. The water was running cold and clear in the sink. There was no hot water, and no electricity to heat this with. But it still felt good to splash it on her face, almost as if she could wash away the fear that Red Bear had stirred in her. How was she going to get Kevin away from him? The first few threads of a plan were beginning to form in her mind, and she stood for a few moments in front of the sink, letting the water run, hoping they would soon become something she could hold on to.

She would get this plan together, and then it would be run, run, run, all right. Only this time it would be the two of them.

30

"EXPLAIN SOMETHING TO ME, CARDINAL."

Detective Sergeant Chouinard didn't ask Cardinal to sit down. Even if he had, there would have been no place in his office to sit. Every chair in the room served as part of Chouinard's idiosyncratic filing system, if it could be called a system. But even if his own routines were haphazard, Chouinard was a man who prized precision and reliability in the men under his command, which was why he was looking a little flushed just now. The detective sergeant suffered from high blood pressure, and when he was angry his face got very red, very fast.

"Explain to me, if you can, how we manage to misplace an attractive young woman with red hair and a bandage on her head. How is that possible, and who was guarding her when it happened?"

"Larry Burke was on duty, but it's my fault. I should have briefed him better."

Chouinard shook his head, his face getting redder. "Spare me the street-cop solidarity. Burke fucked up, is what you're saying."

Cardinal explained as best he could. Luckily for Burke, as a uniformed officer he wasn't directly under the detective sergeant's command.

"You've put out an all-points on this young woman, I trust."

"Yeah, I did that right away."

"Bloody Burke. I'll kick his ass."

Chouinard's phone buzzed; he picked up the handset. "I'll tell him," he said, and hung up. "Bob Brackett's here for you. You're saved by the shark."

—

Bob Brackett was a roly-poly little man with a plain gold hoop in one ear. You wouldn't have known to look at him that this pudgeball was Algonquin Bay's most lethal defence attorney. Naturally, this gave him a reputation around the Algonquin Bay Police Department as an irredeemable pain in the ass, a champion of the criminal classes, a cowboy of the courtroom who'd never seen a technicality he didn't like or a cop he did. Bob Brackett, Q.C., was so mild-mannered that many an unsuspecting policeman or -woman (Brackett was all for equality when it came to dishing out legal mayhem) had had his or her testimony rendered worthless, if not outright ridiculous, before he or she even knew what had happened.

"Please note for the record, Detective Cardinal: My client did not have to come in." Brackett was seated at the interview table, almost hidden behind his open briefcase and a panama hat. "In the first place you have no warrant, and in the second place he resides outside your jurisdiction."

"I realize that, Mr. Brackett. That's why I called you. I could have called the OPP. I'm sure the provincial police would have been happy to round up a few bikers for us."

"Then why didn't you call them?"

"I wanted this meeting to be as friction-free as possible. We're only trying to weed out obvious suspects at this point."

"Fine. Please note that Mr. Lasalle is only here out of a sense of civic duty and loyalty to a fallen comrade."

"We're talking about bikers, Mr. Brackett, let's not make them sound like war vets."

"I merely point out that—"

"Noted, Mr. Brackett. Let's move on."

"So tough," Steve Lasalle said. "Maybe you could have made something of your life if you hadn't become a cop."

Brackett silenced his client with a raised forefinger. Lasalle sat back and propped a foot on one knee, smiling at Cardinal as if they were old buddies. He was wearing an expensive sports coat with an open-necked shirt and pressed jeans. His loafers gleamed, making him look more like the head of a small Internet concern than president of the Viking Riders.

"When did you last see Wombat Guthrie?" Cardinal said.

"Exactly twenty-one days ago. Around four in the afternoon."

"And what were the circumstances?"

"Wombat was on sentry duty. He was supposed to be guarding a certain property of ours. When we came back next day, Wombat was gone and so was the property."

"He ripped you off, in other words."

"Your words, Detective. Not mine."

"This is what you said a couple of days ago . . ." Cardinal flipped back through his notes. "'Last time I remember seeing him we had a few people round, we watched a video, Wombat passed out on the couch. Not unusual for him. I expected to find him here next morning but I didn't.' Your story's changed since then."

Lasalle conferred with his counsel.

"I don't think my client should say any more."

"You also said . . ." Cardinal consulted his notes again. "'Let's just say old Wombat has some 'splaining to do.'"

"Yeah, well, it never occurred to me back then that Wombat was gone for good."

"Oh, I think you can count on that."

Cardinal pulled a forensic photo from his file and tossed it across the table.

Lasalle looked at it for a moment. He tried to maintain his cool posture, but his neck turned pale where it joined the jaw.

"My, my," he said. "That looks nasty."

Brackett took the photo from him, glanced at it and tossed it back on the table with a snort.

"Really, Detective. My client is already cooperating. Shock tactics are beside the point."

"Your client has admitted having a reason for revenge, Mr. Brackett."

"No, he has admitted he believes his colleague is the victim of foul play. That's why he's here. To help find out who has committed this extravagant act of violence upon his colleague. His lifestyle differs from yours; it doesn't make him a liar."

"How did you know Wombat was a victim until I told you?"

"You think you told me?" Lasalle said. "Get real. Believe it or not, I don't rely on cops for my information. I've known Wombat was dead pretty much from the moment he was gone."

"Like I say, how would you know that?"

"His bike. His hog is still right where he left it last time I saw him."

"Hardly conclusive evidence of murder, Mr. Lasalle."

"We're talking about a bike that's worth forty thousand dollars. Not something you leave unattended for long."

"Where, exactly, did he leave it unattended?"

"I can't tell you that."

Cardinal looked at Brackett. "So much for cooperation."

Brackett whispered in his client's ear.

Lasalle looked at Cardinal. "It's not in your jurisdiction, I can tell you that much," he said. He picked up the photograph again, looked at the headless, handless corpse and shook his head.

"That's not very helpful," Cardinal said. "You're telling me you know where Guthrie was last seen. That his bike is still there. That in all probability he was abducted from this site and then tortured and killed. But you won't tell us where that is. This must be the biker loyalty we hear so much about. That famous code of honour."

"He runs the Viking Riders," Brackett said into his double chin. "Be reasonable."

"Suppose we call in the OPP or the RCMP to take a look at your clubhouse. How long do you think it would take them to do a really thorough job?"

"It's got nothing to do with the clubhouse," Lasalle said. "Give me some credit. Assume I'm not an idiot."

"At the moment, Mr. Lasalle, all I see is one dead Viking Rider and another one who had a motive to make him that way."

"I didn't kill him," Lasalle said. "None of the Riders did."

"How do I know that?"

"Because if we had, you'd never have found him."

———

Lately, Lise Delorme found herself spending a lot of time thinking about what she would have done had she not become a cop. After finishing her B.A. in Ottawa with a major in economics, she had thought seriously about getting involved in business. But then she had taken a course in business ethics and that had done two things for her: It took the shine right off private enterprise, and it provoked an interest in white-collar crime. It was that interest that led Delorme to the police college at Aylmer and eventually to her six-year stint in Special Investigations, where she dealt not only with internal police matters but also with crimes deemed to be "sensitive"—which is to say crimes committed by sectors of the population that normally consider themselves law-abiding. Bankers, lawyers, politicians and so on.

Working Special had had its moments—arresting a former mayor was a highlight—but it was also a lonely endeavour. Other cops had never quite trusted her. Besides, the people in CID had looked like they were having a lot more fun, and eventually she had asked for a transfer.

Today was one of those days she was regretting that decision. First, she had reread the pathologist's report on Wombat Guthrie. Histamine tests had confirmed that the horrendous injuries had indeed been inflicted before death. The body had also been virtually drained of blood.

The second reason Delorme felt a pang of nostalgia for white-collar criminals was that she was sitting face to face with Harlan "Haystack" Calhoun, and Harlan "Haystack" Calhoun was a biker through and through. He looked as if he had never seen a white collar, let alone worn one. He was slouched on a plastic chair in the interview room, his snakeskin boots propped on the table.

"Do you not have a lawyer, Mr. Calhoun?"

"I haven't done nothing. Why would I need a lawyer?"

"If you wish to call the legal aid office, we can put this matter off until you've had time to discuss it with counsel."

"Just ask your questions, and let's get on with it."

Delorme pointed out the video camera high in one corner, and the other one off to one side. "We are taping this conversation, and although you are not facing any charges at the moment, I must tell you that anything you say can and will be used against you should any charges be laid at a later time."

"Big deal."

The plastic chair emitted a shriek as Calhoun shifted his weight. He sat forward and propped his chin on his two fists.

"When was the last time you saw Walter, also known as Wombat, Guthrie alive?"

"Three weeks ago. Next question."

"What were the circumstances?"

"The circumstances were I saw him for the last time."

"Where were you?"

"Clubhouse."

"The clubhouse off Highway 11? The one where I saw you the other day?"

"How many clubhouses do you think we got?"

"Just answer the question, please."

"Yes, the one where you saw me the other day. Next question."

"What day was this, exactly? Take your time."

"It was Tuesday, May 12th, at three o'clock in the afternoon. Is that exact enough for you?"

"What were the two of you doing?"

"Splashing this little biker freak."

"Splashing?"

"He was doing her one end, and I was doing the other. If you want, we can set up a demonstration."

"What was her name?"

"Ginger Ale."

"What was her real name?"

"That's what was on her ID. She carried it around to prove she was old enough to drink. If that ain't her real name—guess what?—I don't care. Wombat called her Ginger."

"Where can I find her?"

"Fucked if I know. Try Who's Ho."

"And what day was this?"

"Tuesday, May 13th, at 3 p.m."

"You just changed the date. That's not usually an indication of sincerity, Mr. Calhoun."

"May 12th, then. People don't call the Viking Riders when they want sincerity."

"We want to find out who killed Wombat Guthrie. Are you saying you don't care? You just told me he was your sex partner."

Calhoun made a slight movement of the head, and his right eyebrow lifted a little. Although there were several feet between them, Delorme suddenly had the sense that he was sniffing her.

"You're not answering."

"How'd you get that cut over your eye?" Calhoun said. "Looks recent."

"The person who killed Wombat first cut his fingers and toes and genitals off and tried to skin him alive. Do you really have no interest in catching this person?"

Calhoun leaned forward. Leather wept; plastic cried. "I'll tell you what I'd be interested in. I'd be interested in bending you over and fucking you up the ass a few times."

He leaned back and smiled.

"Someone said exactly the same thing to me just the other day," Delorme said.

"Oh, yeah?"

"It was at the Penetang hospital for the criminally insane."

Delorme snapped her notebook shut.

"Note for the record that Mr. Calhoun is not cooperating with the investigation. This interview is over, subject to resumption at a later date. Good day, Mr. Calhoun."

"That Cardinal prick around?"

"Good day, Mr. Calhoun."

Delorme was holding the door open.

Calhoun got up. Delorme felt like honey, seeing the bear approach. She stepped back at the last moment, so that he couldn't brush against her.

Now that he was out in the CID area, Calhoun shouted. "You tell Cardinal I'm looking forward to seeing him again."

A couple of heads popped up over acoustic dividers: Szelagy, McLeod.

"Are you threatening a police officer, Mr. Calhoun?"

Calhoun winked at her.

"Catch you later, puss."

31

RED BEAR OPENED THE BRASS PADLOCK and stepped into his temple. The smell that would have sickened the most hardened cop had a very different effect on him. He inhaled deeply, like a camper savouring the brisk morning air, and felt the familiar quickening in his belly and a tingling all along his nerves. It was a thrill that never disappointed. He was too excited even to notice the flies.

The moon had begun to wane, so he would not be making any sacrifices for a while, but still it was exciting to step into this temple. Kevin and Leon had gone into town; he had the entire camp to himself. He would join his disciples later in the afternoon, but for now it was necessary to consult the *nganga*.

He lit some charcoal in a censer and sprinkled pinches of wormwood and angelica root over it. Even the best Wicca shops in Toronto were always running out of his ingredients; he often had to order from an occult shop in New York. There were no windows in this cabin; he lit three rows of candles above the *nganga* and the room dimly took shape. He closed the door and locked it.

The *nganga* bristled with sticks. Twenty-eight of these sacred *palos* were used to control the spirit, to shape the nature of your prayer. You had to poke and prod the spirit like an ox; it was the only way to get results.

"*Bahalo!*" His shout rang against the concrete walls of the cabin. "*Bahalo! Semtekne bakuneray pentol!*"

Never kneel, never beg, just as his uncle had instructed.

"*Bahalo! Seeno temtem bakuneray pentol!*"

He spread his hands over the *nganga* in the manner of a Catholic priest and meditated for a few moments on exactly what he desired. Focus was essential for success. He wanted the spirit to travel for him.

"*Seeno temtem naka nova valdor.*"

He stirred the foul liquid with the sticks. A pale, toeless foot swam into view; he braced it against one side of the cauldron with a couple of palos. He probed the depths again until another foot appeared.

"*Sendekere mam koko, pantibi.*" Walk for me, spirit. I who have given you feet to travel, tell you to walk for me, travel for me, discover for me.

He pushed the feet under and now probed for hands. There were no hands, as such, just fingerless palms, severed at the wrist, and the fingers themselves that he had removed one by one for the *nganga*. The memory of his victim's terror and agony made his heart pound. Terror and agony were the portals through which mortal flesh entered the immortal world of the spirit. Terror and agony formed the gateway through which he, Red Bear, could command the spirits of the dead. Terror and agony were his friends.

Several of the sticks were flattened at the ends into spoonlike shapes. He used a couple of these to dredge fingers to the surface. They were white and wrinkled; one still bore a ring with a skull and crossbones on it.

"*Kandopay varonaway d'kran. Bentak po bentak mam tinpay. Naktak po naktak mam kennetay.*" Reach for me, my spirit. Pull close my allies. Push hard against my foes.

Red Bear swirled the dark fluid again; the smells engulfed him. The largest object in the nganga now swam into view. Emerging like a diver fresh from hell, the head bobbed to the surface and twirled in slow motion. Blood and water streamed from the eyes and nostrils. The eyes were half open and stared beyond Red Bear's shoulder.

Red Bear chanted in the magic language. *Spirit, travel for me, learn for me, give me knowledge. Spirit, use the brain with which I have blessed you to tell me what I need to know. Go, spirit, go, and do this work for me.*

32

CARDINAL WAS SITTING AT THE COUNTER in D'Anunzio's, a combination fruit store and soda fountain that had been an Algonquin Bay landmark since before he was born. D'Anunzio's made the best sandwiches in town, which was why he was there. He had finished his chicken salad bagel in no time, but he remained at the old wooden counter making notes.

Cardinal had long ago ceased to believe in inspiration. He had even ceased to believe in his own cleverness. He did not acknowledge in himself any particular investigative talent. A successful investigation, he had come to believe, was simply a matter of putting in the time. You weren't a genius, you weren't Sherlock Holmes, you were a more or less effective part of an organization that devoted itself to covering all the angles of a crime until it was cleared.

So when he first had this whatever-you-called-inspiration-when-you-didn't-believe-in-inspiration, he tossed it aside as an unproductive notion. Too easy, he figured. Too unlikely.

He was making notes on how they should pursue the biker angle. He still had nothing solid to hang Wombat's murder on them. *Call Musgrave*, he had written. *Get more background on VR*. And *Call Jerry Commanda*. He crossed out *Check reverse directory*.

That was one task he had completed. The CID kept reverse telephone directories for all major Canadian cities, not just Algonquin Bay. Cardinal had looked up the Vancouver number Terri had dialled from the hospital, but it wasn't listed. Then he'd called Vancouver directory assistance, which also had no listing. The young man on the other end of the line had informed him that it was a cellphone number.

Next, he'd called Bell Security and told them it was an emergency, explaining that a young woman had been shot and he was trying to notify next of kin. All Bell would tell him was that the number belonged to one Kevin Tait. They had no address for him because he paid for service using prepaid cards and, no, they could not tell him why the number was currently not in service. Most likely, the customer had run out of minutes on his card. Any further information would require a warrant.

A warrant would take a couple of hours, and Cardinal had not wanted to spend a couple of hours on that particular angle just then. So what had he learned? Terri Tait had called her brother's cellphone. Not exactly earthshaking stuff. There was no reason to suppose Kevin Tait was anywhere other than Vancouver. Then again, it was a cellphone; he could be anywhere.

Cardinal's next move had been a computer check of national criminal records. It turned out that Kevin Tait, twenty-two, had been convicted of possession of heroin with intent to traffic three years previously, for which he had been sentenced to two years less a day.

A call to the Vancouver police came up empty; the arresting officer had transferred to another jurisdiction, and no one was able or willing to help Cardinal right then. He'd left his name and number with a detective on their drug squad who promised to get back to him.

All right, Kevin Tait, where are you? Cardinal added several question marks in his notebook. Another thought was pushing its way to the forefront of his mind. What if Terri Tait is not a stranger here? What if she was not coming to Algonquin Bay for the first time? What if she was *returning* here? This was the inspiration he was trying to resist. Was such a scenario even likely? If Terri Tait grew up here, someone surely would have reported her missing by now. But maybe she hadn't lived here for very long.

Back in the squad room, Cardinal put in a call to the Nipissing School Board. School records are confidential; strictly speaking, a warrant is required. But it's different from dealing with a huge corporation like Bell. Sometimes a certain flexibility can soften these situations; it depends who you get on the other end of the line. In this case, it was a young woman—a young woman with a lot of sandpaper in her voice, as if she'd recently left off screaming. Cardinal's first question met with a raspy but firm no.

"I understand your reluctance," Cardinal said. "In fact, I admire it. We need people like you to make sure information doesn't fall into the wrong hands."

"So why don't you get a warrant and try again later?" the woman said.

"Well, of course I could do that. But it would take a lot of time and I don't want to go to all that trouble only to find out that you don't *have* any information. So—without giving me anything personal—I wonder if you could just confirm whether or not a Miss Terri Tait ever attended school here."

"Just confirmation. You don't want grades or anything?"

"No, no. I would never ask for anything like that without a warrant." Thinking, I'm such a liar, I should have gone into acting. "If you could just tell me if Terri Tait ever attended school here or not, I'd really appreciate it."

There was a pause on the Nipissing School Board's end of the line. Even in that vacant line tone, Cardinal thought he detected a distinct rasp.

"How are you spelling that name again?"

"Terri Tait," Cardinal said, and spelled it out. Luckily the spellings were slightly unusual.

He was put on hold. Cardinal twirled through his Rolodex, looking for the number for the separate school board. He would call them next.

The young woman came back on the line.

"Yes, a Terri Tait attended Ojibwa High School back in the early nineties. She was with them for two years, grades nine and ten."

Bingo, Cardinal thought. We're on a roll.

"And her parents?"

"Wing Commander Kenneth Tait. Spouse, Marilyn. Oh, my. There's a note on the file that says they were killed in a plane crash—a private plane—in 1993. The kids went to live with relatives out west."

"I'm wondering about their Algonquin Bay address,"
Cardinal said. "You said the father was in the air force.
Can you tell me, did they live on the base or off?"

"I wouldn't know. Last address we have is 145
Deloraine Drive."

On the base.

"How'd Terri do in math and chemistry?" He wanted
to leave this young woman feeling she'd done a good job.

"Really, Detective, you can't expect me to give you
information like that without a warrant. You'll have to get
a court order."

"Of course," Cardinal said. "I'll do that right now."

He hung up and grabbed his jacket. His phone was
ringing but he ignored it and headed straight out the door.

—

The residents of Algonquin Bay don't like to think so, but
it's all too probable that the city's best years are behind it.
At their peak in the middle of the last century, there were
three railway lines running through town; now there is
one. The CNR station burned down a few years back, a
shame because it was one of the few buildings in this
four-square town with real character. And the former
CPR station, a classic limestone structure on Oak Street,
is being transformed into a railway museum. Only the
former ONR station is still in operation—but as offices,
not as a terminal.

The Cold War had also been very good to Algonquin
Bay. Canada had beefed up its armed forces and joined the

United States in NORAD, a system of linked radar installa-
tions and air force bases designed to intercept any threat
coming in over the ice cap from Russia. By the mid-sixties,
the local air force base boasted three thousand personnel
and an arsenal of nuclear-tipped Bomarc missiles. The
defence department hollowed out a mountain next to Trout
Lake and installed a three-storey radar outfit inside it, a Dr.
Strangelove set that at one time had been cutting edge.

But the Cold War had ended. The missiles were dis-
armed and then dismantled. The armed forces were down-
sized, and one by one the squadrons mothballed. That left
only about 150 military personnel in Algonquin Bay, and
no one seemed to know how much longer they'd be there.

Cardinal drove up to the base checkpoint. Sometimes
the checkpoint was manned, sometimes not; it depended
on the current level of threat. Today it was unmanned,
and Cardinal drove through without even slowing. It
made him wonder about his country's state of readiness.

Cardinal was acting on one little-considered result of
the vanished squadrons: empty houses. No one talked
much about the empty houses, and the military wasn't
about to publicize them. To put them on the market
would destroy the value of all the other homes in town.
So, unbeknownst to most of its population, Algonquin
Bay contains enough empty houses to fill a subdivision,
which is exactly what the air base looks like.

The only difference between the air base and other
sixties-era subdivisions is that all its houses are not just
similar but identical: ranch-style split-levels with two-car
garages and sunken living rooms. The streets look the
same, too—all drives, lanes, circles and courts with

spurious curves and dead ends apparently designed to frustrate the Soviet invader.

Cardinal had thought he knew where Deloraine Drive was, but it turned out he didn't. After he passed the same crooked stop sign for the third time, he pulled over onto the shoulder. There was a solitary man coming up the road on the other side, dressed in the Canada Post summer outfit of white short-sleeved shirt and blue shorts. The man was engaged in an idiosyncratic form of locomotion. He stopped every three or four steps and reared back in a rocking motion, left hand fingering the invisible fretboard of an invisible guitar.

If anyone had earned the right to play air guitar, Cardinal figured, it was Spike Willis. Spike had been a little ahead of him in school, and since the age of sixteen had always been in the best rock bands Algonquin Bay had produced. He had done his stint in Toronto in the seventies, changed bands every year, released a lot of recordings and pretty quickly developed a reputation for making his battered Telecaster *talk*. Then he threw it all over to come back to Algonquin Bay and raise a family. Why, Cardinal never knew. Nor did he know Spike well enough to ask. All he knew was that Spike Willis played the kind of blues guitar that can make grown men cry.

He called him over.

"Oh, shit. I surrender, Officer." Spike threw his hands up with a big grin. He had always struck Cardinal as one of nature's few truly happy men.

"You know, I grew up in this town," Cardinal said. "And I've been back now for about twelve years. So how the hell is it possible that I'm lost?"

"Oh, hell, everyone gets lost up here," Spike said. He hitched his mail sack higher and waved away a blackfly, his good nature apparently insect-proof. "I grew up right here on the base and I'll tell you something. True story. One night after I'd had a few—well, more than a few, really—I came home, opened the door, went inside and suddenly realized my entire family had moved out of town. Mom, Dad, Sis: all gone. Some other family had moved into my house and changed all the furniture. Even the aquarium was gone. It was like I was the victim of a magic trick. I couldn't believe my eyes."

"You'd staggered into the wrong house?"

"I had the wrong house. And I *lived* here, man. Isn't that too much? What are you looking for?"

Cardinal told him, and Spike gave him the directions.

"How many of these houses are actually empty?"

"Oh, geez. Tons of 'em. I don't even need the mail cart up here any more."

"They don't look empty."

"No, the military keeps 'em looking sharp. They figure once they start to go, the whole place'll cave in. Probably right, too."

"What about Deloraine, is it a ghost town?"

"Not really. They haven't let any one street get completely empty. They rent the houses out, you know. Pretty low rents, from what I hear."

"You notice anything unusual on Deloraine?"

"Nope. Same old, same old."

"Okay, thanks. Where you playing next?" Cardinal said.

"Toad Hall, two Saturdays from now."

"I'll try to be there."

"Do that. Got a guest vocalist. Black babe can really wail."

Spike headed off down the road, rocking and tilting, sending another blistering—if silent—solo up to the wide blue sky.

Deloraine Drive proved to be a cul-de-sac. Cardinal parked in a cramped turning circle and walked over to number 145, the last split-level in a row of three. The grass was trimmed and the porch swept, everything ship-shape as Spike had said. The blinds were lowered, but there was no other indication that the house was vacant.

Cardinal walked up to the front door. It was still on the latch and did not appear to have been tampered with. The sliding sections of the front picture window were also unmarked. He stepped down onto the lawn and checked the front window of what would be the master bedroom. The dust was thick along the ledge, and undisturbed.

He went around to the back and saw that one of the basement windows had been broken, just enough to reach inside and slide it open. Cardinal knelt on the grass and a blackfly bit his ear. He slapped at it and cursed. He slid the window open, turned around and backed into it, lowering himself to the basement floor.

It was only a half-basement; just big enough for the washer and dryer, which were still there. He lifted the lid of the washer. Empty. In fact, the entire basement was empty and smelled of nothing except concrete.

He went up the stairs and pushed open the door; it opened onto the kitchen. The fridge and stove were still there, but the kitchen was otherwise empty. He stood there for a minute and absorbed the emptiness of the

place. Not the emptiness of a house between rentals but
the desolation of a place that had once been home to
many and was now nothing more than bricks and wood
and stale air. He could almost hear the voices of children,
the adult voices of old arguments, ancient apologies. He
could almost smell the thousands of dinners that had
been cooked on that Kenmore stove.

The sink was wet. Someone had turned the water on
and used it quite recently. Cardinal opened the cupboard
underneath it and found a paper bag with nothing in it
except an apple core and a banana peel not yet black.

He walked quickly into the living/dining area. There
were places where the dust had obviously been disturbed.
He went up the half-flight of stairs. Nothing in the bathroom, nothing in the master bedroom. But in the smaller
bedroom he found fingermarks on the blinds where
someone had lifted them. He opened the folding doors of
the closet, but there were just a couple of hangers, bearing
the ghostly shapes of dry cleaning plastic.

He stepped into the hallway and looked up at the
square in the ceiling that led to the attic. He knew the
attics in these places. They were tiny, airless spaces full of
fibreglass insulation and not much else, big enough to
store a few suitcases. You needed a ladder or a high stool
to reach them, and the square looked undisturbed.

He went downstairs again and opened the front closet.
Empty. He stood in the tiny vestibule, wondering what to
do next. All units were on the lookout for an AWOL patient
with red hair, but the blue hooded T-shirt would hide
that. Then he noticed the cupboard under the stairs and
for a moment was flooded with memories.

When he was about nine years old, he had been best friends with a boy named Tommy Brown who lived up here at the base. His house had been identical to this one, and the two of them had had great fun hiding in that crawl space, telling Twilight Zone stories and in general trying to scare the hell out of each other. Tommy used to bring his collie, Tango, in there with them, and the space would reek of dog breath.

. Cardinal stepped up to the little door. The bolt was open. He pulled on the handle and the door swung outward. He got down on one knee and looked inside. In the shadows of the back corner, he could just make out the frightened, pale features of Terri Tait.

33

"Terri," Cardinal said. "Are you all right?"

She looked away from him, and her face vanished in shadow. "Please go away."

"Come on out, Terri. No one's going to hurt you."

Cardinal thought he had never seen anything as sad as this young woman huddled in a crawl space hiding from—as far as he knew—the only person who was trying to help her.

She sniffed wetly; tears glistened on her cheeks.

"Terri, come on out and let's see if I can help you with whatever it is you want to do. All right? Let's work together on this."

Cardinal wished Delorme was with him. Mind you, Delorme would probably just drag Terri out of there and ask what the hell was on her mind. Delorme could be a little short on sympathy when it came to attractive young women.

Terri crawled out of the cupboard and stood up, hugging herself although it was not cold.

Cardinal pointed to the stairs.

"Why don't you sit there."

"I think I'll just stand."

"Sit, for God's sake. You look like you're going to faint."

He took her by the shoulders and gently lowered her to the stairs.

"Why were you so frightened?" he asked. "Who did you think I was?"

Terri shrugged. She was wearing the blue hoodie. The sleeves hung over her wrists and made her look like an orphan, which of course she was.

"Did you think I was whoever might've shot you?"

"No. I don't even know who that would be."

"Come back to the hospital with me. You won't have to hide in any cupboards there."

"I don't need a hospital. I'm not sick."

"Someone tried to kill you, Terri. Until we find that person, you're still in danger. Come back with me."

"I don't want to. Believe it or not, I do have a life, and if you don't mind I'd like to get back to it."

"In an empty house? Where you haven't lived for, what, ten or twelve years?"

Terri looked at him. The green eyes, informed now by memory and who knew what personal history, no longer looked so innocent.

"Tell me about your brother Kevin."

"I don't want to talk about Kevin."

"You called him last night. His number's not in service."

"Kevin's away right now."

"Away where?"

"How should I know?"

"Terri, I'm just trying to help you. Your brother has been involved in narcotics in the past. He could have some connection with whoever tried to kill you."

"I told you, I don't remember anything about that. Are you going to arrest me for trespassing or something?"

"I don't want to arrest you. I'm trying to protect you."

"Why? What do you care? You don't even know me."

"I know that. I need to know you better. I can't help you if I don't. Tell me why you're still here. You said your brother is away. Does that mean he's here? Look, I can find out from the phone company where he's dialling from, so you may as well tell me. Is that why you came to Algonquin Bay? To find your brother? If he's not here, why are you still here?"

Terri folded her arms across her chest and looked away from him.

"Look at me, Terri. Is your brother here in town? Is that why you're here?"

"It's really none of your business."

"I think he's here. I think he's what drew you back here. And I think you know where he is."

"I don't."

"I need to talk to him, Terri. He's involved in the heroin trade—it can be a violent line of work. He could even be the one who tried to kill you."

"He isn't."

"You don't know that. You don't know who shot you."

"I know it wasn't Kevin."

"Tell me something. You said you were staying in a motel by the lake. I don't suppose you remember the name of that place yet, do you?"

"No, I don't, as a matter of fact."

"Reason I ask, we don't seem to be able to locate that motel."

"This is northern Ontario, right? There's lots of motels by lakes."

"Here in Algonquin Bay there are exactly twelve. We've talked to all of them and none of them remember any red-haired young woman who suddenly disappeared."

"So, it was a different motel. A different lake. What do I know? I haven't lived here for a long time."

"There are no motels on the other lakes. See, here's what I think's going on—you tell me if I'm wrong: I think you came back here to find your brother. I think he's still here and you intend to find him. I think you remember exactly where he was. You don't want to tell me, and I can only assume that's because he's involved in criminal activity. I don't care about that, you understand? That isn't what I'm interested in right now. I just want to get whoever tried to kill you off the streets."

"Detective, last week I got shot in the head. My memory is not what it should be. Why can't you accept that?"

"Dr. Paley says it's unheard of for a person with your injuries to remember some things and not others. It all comes back at once, not in these convenient little packages you're offering up."

"Dr. Paley doesn't know what I think or what I remember."

"And that's very useful when you want to hide something, isn't it?"

"You should know. You're the detective."

"Well, here's something you should know, Terri. Whoever put a bullet in your head just did the same to someone else.

Only this young man wasn't as lucky as you. He got two in the head from the same gun and he's dead, Terri."

Cardinal was not at all sure it was the right move to make just then, but he turned from her and went to the front door. He snapped open the locks and went outside.

Follow me, he silently urged her. *You must be desperate to know. Follow me.*

He opened his car door, but before he could get in, she called after him.

"Wait!"

She came running down the front steps in bare feet.

"Detective, wait!"

Cardinal got in the car and started the engine.

Terri threw open the passenger door and got in beside him.

"Who was it?" Her pale skin had turned even paler. "The guy who was killed. Who was it?"

"We don't know that yet."

The green eyes were bright with panic.

"Oh, God, you have to tell me! How old was he? What did he look like? Was he thin and sort of gangly?"

Cardinal opened his briefcase and pulled out a forensic photo. The smashed head, the pool of blood.

Terri covered her mouth.

"Is it your brother?"

She shook her head, still covering her mouth. Cardinal hoped she wasn't going to vomit in his car.

"This guy was mid to late twenties. About five-foot-five. Light brown hair."

She let go of the breath she had been holding. "It wasn't Kevin. Kevin's younger. And he's nearly six feet tall."

"It could've been you or your brother," Cardinal said gently. "Whoever did this made absolutely certain with this guy. The gun they're using is malfunctioning and it looks like they finally figured that out. When the bullets didn't kill him they busted him over the head with a baseball bat. The next time I get called to a scene like that, I don't want it to be your brother, and I especially don't want it to be you."

Terri was sitting back against the seat now. She looked exhausted.

"You don't want me to ask any more questions, I won't ask any. But get your shoes and I'll take you someplace safe."

Terri stared straight ahead.

It's now or never, Cardinal thought. She'll either come with me now or I've truly lost her.

"Not the hospital?" Her voice was barely audible.

"Not the hospital."

34

"WHERE HAVE YOU BEEN?" Delorme said, the moment Cardinal got back to the station. "We've been buzzing you."

"I've been over at the Crisis Centre," he said. "I found Terri Tait."

"You found Terri Tait." Delorme raised one eyebrow. The little check-mark injury was fading. "How did you find her?"

"School records. I also looked up her brother, Kevin Tait. Turns out he did two years for intent to traffic in heroin, and I think he's here in town."

"That's why she's been holding back on us. She doesn't want her brother to end up doing serious time."

"Why were you buzzing me?"

"We got an ID back from Forensics. They got a match on the teeth. Have you ever run into a character named Morris Tilley? Also known as 'Toof'—which is why odontology was able to identify him so fast. He had an extra incisor."

"Don't know him."

"Of course not. You, you don't work the small stuff. Seems we've pulled Morris Tilley in at least three times, maybe more, mostly for theft under. He's also been known to sell dope, mostly grass. Morris Tilley's problem is he's a hundred-percent weed junkie. We haven't heard from him for nearly a year, though."

"Maybe he decided to go straight."

"Hah, hah. He didn't have any means of support other than dope or pool hustling."

"Have you notified the parents yet?"

Delorme gave him her sweetest smile; that always meant something unpleasant was coming.

"Parent," she corrected him. "I was hoping you'd come with me."

—

The Tilley home was located on Main West behind the Country Style parking lot. Owing to the national obsession with donuts, this parking lot was the fastest-expanding piece of real estate in town, devouring in its quest a limestone convent, several small stores and a brace of Edwardian houses. The Tilley address was fifty yards west, amid a block of red-brick houses that had recently sprouted ugly storefronts: Deirdre's Beauty Shoppe, Polar Air Conditioning and Prent & Pilaggi Attorneys at Law.

It sometimes happens that a violent crime will lead police to a good address, a household of well-mannered people with degrees from the best universities; Cardinal had been to one or two such scenes himself. But they're rare. Morris Tilley's household was the more common variety.

His mother let them into the front hall. It was a dark, close space and the air had the slightly mouldy, old-fabric smell of the lowest-end thrift shops. Mrs. Tilley herself was a small, sparrowlike woman in faded flowerprint who squinted at them behind pointy glasses.

Cardinal introduced himself and Delorme.

"Mrs. Tilley, are you the mother of Morris Tilley?"

"Yes. Is Morris in trouble again? He doesn't mean to get into trouble. He just doesn't think, you know? He gets excited about something and then he just gets carried away. And that marijuana never did anything good for him. Other mothers complain that their kids are addicted to video games or their computers, and I would give anything if Morris would take up an interest like that. I mean, he discovered marijuana when he was twelve and he's been in a fog ever since. But he doesn't mean any harm. Really, he doesn't. He's a good boy. *Man*, I mean. Though he's still a boy in lots of ways. What's he done now? Nothing serious, I hope."

"I'm afraid we have some much worse news, Mrs. Tilley. Perhaps you'd better sit down."

"Yes, of course. Let's go in the living room."

The thrift-store smell was even stronger in the living room. A brown vinyl rocker listed to one side, and the overstuffed couch appeared to have been savaged at both ends by a Bengal tiger.

"Would you like some tea? Some coffee?"

"No, thank you. Please sit down, Mrs. Tilley."

Mrs. Tilley wobbled a little, and the colour drained from her face as if someone had pulled a plug in her feet. She lowered herself to the torn sofa and folded her hands neatly on her lap.

"I'm afraid Morris is dead, Mrs. Tilley." Cardinal's heart was pounding. He would never get used to this. "Someone killed him."

"Killed him?" A hand rose slowly to Mrs. Tilley's mouth.

"I'm very sorry."

Mrs. Tilley turned to Delorme, as if a woman might talk more sense.

"Why would anyone kill Morris? Morris is—Morris gets along with—Morris wouldn't hurt a fly. He smokes too much marijuana, that's true. And he doesn't seem able to hold a job, but the economy hasn't been good, you know. And Morris is very picky; he won't take just anything. But he doesn't get into fights. It can't be Morris. There's a mix-up somewhere, you'll see. You've got the wrong person."

"His identity was confirmed through dental records," Delorme said. "His teeth. Your son had an extra incisor, I believe?"

The pause that followed was brief, the silence deep. Somewhere a clock was ticking: one second, two seconds, three. And then Mrs. Tilley's howl split the air. It was loud, long, and from a distance might have been canine. She gulped for air, almost choked, and let out another howl that hurt Cardinal's ears not so much because of the volume, which was intense, but because the long, unearthly wail seemed to carry with it all the suffering of all human hearts.

Delorme came back from the kitchen with a glass of water; Cardinal hadn't even noticed her get up. It took a while, but Delorme eventually managed to get the woman calmed down. The howls subsided into sobs, the sobs into soundless tears, and finally she was able to speak.

"I'll need to see him," she said. "I won't fully believe it, otherwise."

"Yes, of course," Delorme said. "We can arrange it with the forensic centre in Toronto, if you like. Or they can make arrangements with whichever funeral home you prefer and you can see him here."

This brought on a fresh round of tears. It was Cardinal's experience that allowing grief to take too full a hold could make getting information impossible. At the risk of seeming callous, he broke in with his first question.

"Mrs. Tilley, when did you last see your son?"

"Quite recently. Two or three months ago."

"Two or three months?"

"Well, two months. Morris gets very involved in things. In his projects and so on, and then I don't see him for a few months. Then one day I'll come home from Loblaws and there he'll be at the kitchen table, wolfing down a sandwich, happy as a clam. He's a good son. He'll bring me flowers sometimes. Tulips it was, last time. He knows I love tulips. His brothers never bring flowers."

"The last address we have for him is Marsden Road," Delorme said. "Up in Greenwood?"

"Yes, that's right. He shares a place with some friends."

"How did he seem when you last saw him?"

"Oh, the usual. Morris doesn't change. He's been the same since he was twelve. Happy go lucky. A little

thoughtless. A bit . . . lost, sometimes. I blame the marijuana for that. He told me he was making some good
money."

"Good money doing what?"

"Working for a trucking firm. Loading and unloading.
Nothing fancy, but it was a paycheque."

"Did he mention who he was working with?"

"No. No, he just said it was a good outfit. That's the
way he put it. He said, 'Ma, I'm finally with a good outfit.
I'm in on the ground floor.' Not that I believed it would
get him anywhere. He never sticks with anything. But I
was glad he had some money in his pocket. He even
brought me some. Didn't say anything, but after he left I
found a hundred-dollar bill under the cookie tin."

"Did you ever see any of the people he worked with, or
any of his friends?"

"No. Well, only one. A boy named Sam he would bring
round every once in a while. The two of them would sit in
the kitchen and polish off a dozen cookies at a go.
Hermits were his favourite—you know, cinnamon and
raisin and not too sweet? Oh, there was no keeping those
in the house when Morris was around."

"What is Sam's last name, Mrs. Tilley, do you know?"

"No, I'm sorry, I don't. Not a bad-looking boy."

"Can you give us a description?"

"He's pale. Very dark hair and very pale skin. He's
shorter than me, and I'm only five-three in stocking feet."

"That wouldn't be Sami Deans, would it?" Delorme
said. "Stocky and sort of bewildered-looking?"

"Well, you could say that. I never knew his last name,
but Morris certainly called him Sami all the time, as if he

was a little kid. Of course, it was Morris who never grew up. I suppose he never will, now."

Mrs. Tilley covered her eyes and cried into her hands for a few moments. Delorme found a box of Kleenex somewhere.

"Mrs. Tilley, are you absolutely sure you don't remember meeting any of Morris's other friends or co-workers?" Cardinal said. "It's terribly important."

"Morris didn't tend to bring people round, I'm afraid. Never did. He's a sociable boy, but at the end of the day he always tended to come home alone—even when he was quite little."

It didn't take long to establish that Mrs. Tilley knew essentially nothing about her son's activities. A few more questions and then she saw them to the door, bobbing along behind them, dabbing at her eyes, apologizing for not being more helpful and thanking them for being so kind.

―

"The thing I'll never get used to about murder," Delorme said, back in the car, "is how many more victims it has than just the one that ends up dead."

"We're going to find the guy that did it, Lise. That's why we're in this business. Tell me about this Sami Deans you mentioned. Kind of threw me for a loop in there."

"That's because you think all I know is white-collar stuff. But us junior detectives have to deal with low-lifes all the time. Unlike elite investigators like yourself."

"Unlike old has-beens is what you mean."

"Exactly. Sami Deans. Lives in a frat house, so to speak. In Greenwood, like Mrs. Tilley said."

Greenwood was one of the first subdivisions built in Algonquin Bay. At one time it had been an address with some cachet, but Greenwood, like much of Algonquin Bay, had come down a peg or two. Now, Greenwood was mostly a haven for retired people on modest pensions, subcompact cars parked beside brick bungalows with bright green lawns. Unfortunately, some of the streets had taken a less picturesque turn.

One such street was Marsden Road, just beyond the Beckers convenience store. It had only three houses. The first was occupied by a half-mad old coot who wore a Second World War trenchcoat even in the blazing sun. The second had been gutted by a fire two years previously, and for complicated tax reasons had been neither repaired nor torn down.

The last house on the block had once been a two-storey, white-brick affair, but now the brick was grey and black. The lawn, those parts of it that were not utterly bald, was a field of litter. Warped plywood covered missing windows. Weeds sprouted through the asphalt drive, where a seventies-era Malibu appeared to have been dropped from a great height.

"Listen to that," Cardinal said as they rolled up.

"Listen to what?" Delorme said.

"I can hear that car rusting. It's actually audible."

"I didn't know you were a car buff."

"I'm not. I just hate to see machines mistreated."

They went up to the front door and knocked loudly.

"It's only the middle of the afternoon," Cardinal said. "What makes you think they'll be awake?"

Delorme rapped again. "Me, I don't care if they're up yet."

A voice came from inside. "Who is it?"

"Police. Open up."

Cardinal glanced at his watch. "How long you want to give them to flush everything?"

"I figure one minute. They've got the routine fine-tuned by now."

The door opened, and they were addressed by a young man whose clothes looked two sizes too big for him. Oily hair hung in a pointy fringe over one eye.

"You should know I already have an attorney," he said. "So I don't personally plan to answer any questions."

Heroin addicts, Cardinal thought. It's like they're under ten feet of water. They form their words with great concentration, as if they have to be transmitted in bubbles.

"We're not here about you, Sami," Delorme told him. "At least, not at the moment. May we come in?"

"Do you have a warrant?"

"We're not here to search the place," Cardinal said. "We're just here to ask some questions about Morris Tilley."

"Toof? Haven't seen him for days."

"When was the last time?"

Sami flicked the fringe of hair. It didn't move.

"Don't know, man. Eternity. Mists of time."

"Try to be more precise," Cardinal said.

"How come? You guys haul him in again?"

"Somebody shot him twice and bashed his head in with a baseball bat."

"Oh, man. That's egregious. That's, like, seriously traumatic."

"It's a crime, Sami. We're going to put someone away for it—assuming we can get any coherent information."

"Fuck. Sorry, man, I just woke up. I'm just not sure how to react."

How lost can you be? Cardinal wondered. And the answer came unbidden: as lost as you want to be.

"Do you know a guy named Kevin Tait?" Delorme said.

Sami shrugged. "He's a friend of Toof's. Seen him around."

"Is he a dealer?"

"Hey. I said I've seen him. I didn't interview him. I never, like, examined his curriculum vitae or nothing."

Cardinal and Delorme walked by Sami into what had once been a living room. It was now a bedroom with a mattress on the floor, a boom box with a dozen scattered CDs and a Razor scooter. Somewhere upstairs, a toilet flushed.

"Sit down, Sami," Delorme said. "You look like death."

"That's okay. I'd rather stand."

"Sit down, Sami." Delorme pressed on his shoulders and he sank toward the mattress. "Now think back. When was the last time you saw Morris Tilley?"

"I think it was about three weeks ago. Yeah, it was three weeks ago. I saw him at the pool hall. Toof's a pretty sharp pool player."

"Was," Cardinal corrected him.

"Was."

"But he shared the house with you," Delorme said. "Why is it so long since you saw him?"

Sami tugged at his fringe. "I dunno. Toof kinda took up with a new circle of acquaintance."

"Oh?"

"Some Indian guy he met. Out-of-town guy. Toof was all secretive about it, but it was obvious he was, like, seriously impressed with this character."

"This person have a name?" Cardinal said. "An address?"

"No address. Toof didn't say anything like that. But name—I don't know. Black Cloud. Something like that. You know, an Indian name."

"Did you ever meet him? See him?"

Sami shook his head. He was hugging himself even though the room was overheated, and there was a fine sweat on his upper lip.

"You guys wouldn't have a cigarette, would you?"

"Sorry," Delorme said.

"How many other people live here?" Cardinal said.

"Seven or eight."

"Which is it?"

"Seven, I guess. If Toof's not coming back."

"He isn't. And we'd like to catch whoever made it that way. Who's he hang around with, other than you?"

Sami looked shocked. "I don't hang around with Toof, man. He just lives here. Lived."

"So who was he hanging around with?"

"I don't know, man. Give me a break, will you?"

Cardinal rapped on Sami's forehead with a knuckle. "Hello-o. Sami? I'm not asking you who he bought his dope from. I'm asking you who he hung around with."

"I don't know. Some doofus thinks he's really hot shit."

"A name," Delorme said. "We need a name."

Sami shouted up the stairs. "Hey, Paco! Who's that jerk Toof hangs around with, man? Guy drives that butch car."

A small, dark man appeared on the stairs, his face a comic exaggeration of fear. "Shit, man. You talking to the cops?"

"Toof is dead, Paco. Just give me the goddamn name."

Paco came down the last of the stairs, scratching his head. The smell of marijuana wafted from his clothes.

"Guy with the Batmobile? Leon something. I don't know his last name."

"What's he look like?" Cardinal said.

"I don't know, man. Average, you know? Brown hair, sorta dirty. Drives some stupid muscle car. Black. Trans Am or something."

"Oh, hey," Sami said. "I just remembered. He's got like a scar on his forehead. Jagged thing. 'Bout that long." He held thumb and forefinger an inch apart.

"Creep probably bashed his head on the toilet," Paco said, and turned to go back upstairs.

"Whoa, Paco. Hold on there, son." Cardinal stepped in front of him. "We'll need to talk to you and everybody else who lives here. Bring 'em all downstairs. Don't worry—if we were looking for dope, you'd already be in the paddy wagon."

———

Cardinal and Delorme interviewed five other young men who lived in the house, each more forlorn than the last.

That was the thing about heroin addicts, Cardinal had often noticed: They weren't nasty people; they just seemed terminally bewildered. One or two of the young men they interviewed might have made something of themselves if they hadn't fallen in love with the needle. Everybody has their crutch, he figured, but some crutches are more crippling than others.

None of Toof's former housemates added anything useful to the information they already had. Yes, they'd seen a guy named Kevin Tait. No, they didn't really know him.

When they got back to the station, Delorme sat down at the computer. Later, she came over to Cardinal's desk with a printout.

"I ran a search for all the guys named Leon we've arrested in the past three years. Guess how many there are?"

"I don't know. Three?"

"None. Not one. But look what I got from Musgrave."

"Musgrave? Are you talking about Sergeant Malcolm Musgrave of the Royal Canadian Mounted Police? You called him already? Is there something about your relationship I should know?"

"Me and Musgrave? You've got to be kidding."

Cardinal took the printout and looked it over.

"Okay, one Leon Rutkowski got himself pinched for running smack in Sudbury. Eight years in Millhaven. Also has priors for aggravated assault and bodily harm. Seems Leon has a bit of a temper."

"The description matches what they told us at Toof's house," Delorme said.

"Brown hair, blue eyes, scar on forehead."

"Look what he was driving when they arrested him."

"Black Trans Am. Known associates doesn't mention any Black Cloud, though."

"I'll call Musgrave again," Delorme said.

While he was waiting, Cardinal called Catherine at her hotel. The chances of finding her in, he knew, were slim, and once again he wished she carried a cellphone. He left a message saying he was thinking of her. Worried about her would have been more accurate, and after he disconnected he felt a burgeoning resentment that he was worrying about his wife while he should be focusing on a case. Then he felt guilty for the resentment.

Delorme grabbed her car keys and put on her jacket. "Want to come for a ride?"

"Where to?"

"Musgrave gave me a contact."

35

CARDINAL SLID INTO the passenger seat beside Delorme. She backed up, making a sharp two-pointer, then left a little rubber in the driveway. Whenever she was driving, Delorme's eyebrows knit in a frown. She had the most expressive eyebrows Cardinal had ever seen, and the fading check-mark wound only added to their appeal.

"So, who are we going to see?" Cardinal said.

"Alan Clegg. He's Musgrave's man on the drug scene these days, at least as far as our neighbourhood is concerned."

"Get out. They haven't had a detachment here for at least ten years."

"It's not a detachment. They have a temporary post over at the Federal Building. Just two guys, but most days Clegg's here alone."

She parked around back of the post office, under a sign that said *Authorized Vehicles Only*. They took the elevator to the third floor. Cardinal remembered when the RCMP had maintained a permanent detachment in Algonquin

Bay. It had always been a small office, never more than
four men, and they'd mostly kept out of the local cops'
way. Then the age of cutbacks arrived and the detachment
was only one of many that had been forced to close up
shop.

Alan Clegg must have heard them coming, because he
stepped out into the corridor, forming a sudden silhouette against the window at the end of the hall.

"You must be Delorme," he said.

"This is my colleague, John Cardinal," Delorme said.

They shook hands. Clegg had the T-shape of a mid-
dleweight. He looked to be in his late thirties but he hadn't
let himself go. He showed them into a cramped office
with two metal desks for furniture and not much else. It
smelled of stale coffee and chewing gum.

"I understand you want to talk about the drug trade,"
Clegg said. "I'll tell you everything I can, short of jeop-
ardizing sources."

Delorme looked over at Cardinal, who nodded. It was
her lead, she could call the shots.

"You're probably aware of the two murders we've had
recently," she said.

"Wombat Guthrie, sure. I haven't heard a name yet on
your other guy."

"Morris Tilley."

"Morris Tilley?" Clegg shook his head. "Doesn't ring
any bells."

Delorme showed him a photograph they had borrowed from Mrs. Tilley.

"The face is familiar," Clegg said. "I'm sure I've seen him
around. But where and in what context . . . you've got me."

"The two killings are linked," Delorme said. "The gun used on Morris Tilley was recently in the possession of Wombat Guthrie. It was also used in an assault—"

Cardinal laid a hand on her arm. "We can't go into that."

"I wasn't going to," Delorme said. She didn't manage to hide the note of irritation in her voice, perhaps she didn't try.

A half-smile formed on Clegg's face. "I understand."

"What do you know about Wombat Guthrie?"

"Ugly as sin, mean as hell. Lifetime member of the Viking Riders. Drug runner from way back. Not the most popular guy with the Riders' new president is what I hear."

"Tell us more."

"Wombat was left guarding a substantial amount of dope. Exactly how much I wouldn't know, but substantial. Other Riders show up, dope's gone, Wombat's gone."

"Do you think they killed him?"

"It's certainly possible. They're excitable boys."

"Tilley was living in a house full of other junkies up in Greenwood," Delorme said. "Why don't we give you their names, and you tell us if any of them are connected to Wombat Guthrie in any way."

Toof's sad-sack housemates had all resolutely denied ever having met Wombat Guthrie, though a few allowed that, yes, they had heard the name—in what context they couldn't recall just at that moment.

Cardinal and Delorme ran through the six names they had. Clegg was happy to take them down in his notebook with a two-inch stub of pencil. He had heard most of the names before, but did not connect them to Wombat. Then there was Sami Deans.

"Sami Deans we're very much aware of," Clegg said. "We're wondering lately if he hasn't branched out into dealing as well as puncturing his arm."

"I don't think so," Delorme said. "We keep hauling him in for break and enter. What about his friend Paco Fernandez?"

Clegg laughed. "Paco Fernandez? Honestly, I think he studied the Cheech and Chong movies when he was a kid and decided he wanted to be just like them. I'm not even sure he bothers with the harder stuff. He wouldn't be able to find his own vein with a map. But you know, we're not interested in guys like Deans and Fernandez. They're strictly a local problem."

"Leon Rutkowski would be more your type of target," Cardinal said.

"Absolutely," Clegg said. "I arrested him way back when. Caught him with six grams of H in his Trans Am. He's been in and out of Algonquin Bay for some time now, but he's been keeping a pretty low profile." Clegg snapped his fingers. "That's where I've seen your Morris Tilley character! I saw him with Leon one time, coming out of Duane's Billiards. I didn't get the impression they were close, though."

"We wouldn't know," Delorme said. "We just heard they hung out together."

"It's possible. I think when Leon first came to town he thought he was going to set up shop here, maybe get himself a little ice cream truck and sell smack from it, become the local Good Shit man. But two things happened: First, he ran into me. Surprise, surprise. The thought of doing another bit in Millhaven kind of let the air out of his tires.

"The second thing that happened was the Viking Riders. The Riders take their drug business very seriously. You can't just waltz onto their turf and expect them to send out a welcome wagon. Even though they almost never set foot in your fair city, I guarantee they control most of the dope flowing in or out of it—the hard stuff, anyway. If Leon's dealing anything, it's very small amounts."

"Is he a junkie?" Delorme said.

"Nope. Former speed freak."

"He has a couple of serious assaults on his record."

"Yeah, Leon can be nasty when he gets worked up. Hasn't done anything like that for a long time, though. Not as far as I know. I've been keeping an eye out for him, but he's been keeping such a low profile I'm beginning to wonder if maybe old Leon is going straight. On the other hand, that would require getting a job."

"We also heard Morris Tilley—also known as Toof—hung around with a First Nations guy. Indian name like Black Cloud."

"Black Fly?" Clegg laughed. "There's a few of them around these days."

"Black Cloud. Something like that."

"Oh, I know who you're talking about. There was a guy named Red Bear in and out of town last year. Kind of a mystical type. Claimed to read people's cards and all that kind of thing. A shaman—isn't that what they're called? I saw him a couple of months ago in Reed's Falls with a bunch of guys—but not Leon. Anyway, I was just passing through—Reed's Falls is OPP territory. He's from the Red Lake reserve. Does this help at all?"

"Sure," Cardinal said. "We don't know anything about him at this point."

"Sorry I can't be of more use. I'm not really here to keep an eye on these little guys."

"But you've got sources in the Riders, correct?" Cardinal said.

"I have sources who sometimes tell me things about the Riders. I think we should put it that way."

"Well, what can you tell us about them?" Cardinal said. "We've got a dead Viking Rider and a dead civilian connected. We also have reason to believe someone else may soon become a victim."

"Really? Who's next on the hit parade?" Clegg said.

Cardinal silently cursed himself. "I just meant the killer or killers are obviously on a roll, here, and will probably kill someone else."

Clegg thought a moment.

"Anything you can give us," Delorme said. "The Riders aren't talking, the junkies don't know anything and we're really up against it."

"All right. This is going to raise hell a little, but I don't think it'll blow my sources. How about if I tell you the last place Wombat was seen alive?"

36

THEY PUT A WATCH ON the Viking Riders' house by the French River: two fishermen in a small boat much plagued by blackflies. And two repairmen on a telephone pole who got bitten even worse. They watched for four hours and saw nobody enter the house or leave it. There were no motorcycles or cars parked outside.

Still, they took precautions. Four cars, not including ident, and all of them with shotguns and body armour. They sweated like pigs. Upon breaking down the front door, they did a quick survey room-to-room and established that the house was empty. When they finished, they were standing in the kitchen, which looked as if it had been gone over by professional cleaners. Appliances, sinks and countertops gleamed.

"These guys can come over and do my housework any day," Delorme said. "As long as I'm not home."

The house was clearly not a residence, not even a part-time one. There were three bedrooms, minimally and cheaply furnished with cots that looked like something from army surplus. Closets and cupboards were empty, reeking of Windex and Fantastik. The parquet floors bore chips and scuff marks, legacies of serious boots. In the fridge were containers of jam, yogourt and curry paste, and these proved after much probing to contain nothing more than jam, yogourt and curry paste.

Cardinal went down to the basement. He could smell the lake and the river, a sense of their blue- and white-water power, and hovering beneath and above all this, smells of concrete and drainpipe. The floor was enviably level compared to the lunar terrain of his own basement. He looked under the stairs, as well as behind and inside the dusty washer and dryer. A country of mould and dust and spiders' webs.

An Ikea dresser yielded one dark blue T-shirt with NYPD in large letters on the back.

"At least they have a sense of humour," Delorme said.

"You have to ask yourself," Cardinal said. "Why would a group of red-blooded Canadians like the Viking Riders have a nicely situated cottage like this and not be using it?"

"Maybe they don't like blackflies," Delorme said. "Me, I never understood all the fuss about cottages, anyway. You go out to the cottage, it's noisier than Main Street."

"I know," Cardinal said. His own house was mostly a quiet refuge, but it was often plagued by snowmobiles, motorboats, Sea-Doos and every other variation of the internal combustion engine known to man.

"It's so clean here, it's almost like they were expecting a raid."

"Yeah, I had the same thought," Cardinal said. "Or they could just be being careful. One of their brothers was murdered, after all."

He lifted up the corner of a copy of the *Algonquin Lode*. The front page had a weeks-old story about a man who had won an annual contest by guessing what day the ice on Lake Nipissing would break up.

"On the other hand," Cardinal said. "Maybe they just don't use this place because it's too hot. I mean, if they're running dope through this house, none of them is going to want to live in it. Whoever stayed here would take the heat if the place got busted."

Arsenault's voice echoed through the empty house, calling them.

They found him on hands and knees, inspecting a closet. He had removed a baseboard.

"I'm coming up with quite a bit of white powder back here. Enough to analyze anyway. Stuff drifts everywhere no matter how much they try to clean up. My guess is they stored a lot of it in here. At lots of different times."

"So we know for sure they ran dope through here," Delorme said. "I'm shocked. *Shocked.*"

"They left the shipment here with only Wombat in charge. That says what?"

"It was a regular thing. They did it a lot."

"Right. They felt totally confident. Then someone comes along and not only rips them off, but kills Wombat and cuts him apart. So who's likely to do that?"

"A rival gang, maybe?"

"What rival gang, though? There aren't any biker gangs closer than Toronto, and if they'd been in town we'd have known about it. Hey, Szelagy!" Cardinal called out toward the front room. "What did we hear back from ViCLAS on Wombat?"

Szelagy's massy form filled the doorway. "Negative. No links to nothing."

"Not even to any unsolveds?"

"Solved, unsolved, they came up empty."

"Did you have them run it without the hieroglyphics?"

"Yeah, sure I did." Szelagy looked wounded. "I asked them to run it both ways. I put the report in your inbox this morning."

"I can't believe they didn't come up with anything," Delorme said. "An MO that unusual."

"Let's think about the gun," Cardinal said. "We know Wombat stole it over a month ago."

"But he couldn't have attacked Toof after he was killed."

"Right. So probably whoever killed Wombat also took the liberty of removing his gun. He or she then used it to attack Terri Tait and then Toof. All of them were connected to the drug trade in one way or another—Terri through her brother. But other than the bullets, we don't have anything solid linking her with Toof and Wombat."

Delorme's brow was creased in thought.

"What?" Cardinal said. "What are you thinking?"

"Assuming the Riders are telling the truth—that they were ripped off by someone else and they didn't kill Wombat—it would have to be a pretty heavy brand of criminal, don't you think? Not a person someone like Terri Tait or even Toof would be likely to run into in the normal course of events. This guy has killed two people in a very short period of time. And tried to kill three. That's extremely violent, even by drug-dealing standards—almost as if he's looking for opportunities to kill."

"I know. Which would mean he's probably still on the hunt."

37

HIS STUDIES OF DEATH and insects have led Angus Chin to set up a farm of sorts among the piny hills of Northern University. Cardinal and Arsenault found him there, shepherding a flock of students. They were gathered like mourners amid a grove of birches over the sad little carcass of a dead rat. It was housed in a cage, as if it might escape, but the cage was only there to keep larger predators—foxes, dogs and crows—from chowing down on the object of study while allowing flies and beetles to dine as they pleased.

When he saw Cardinal and Arsenault approach, Dr. Chin told his students to examine the rest of the sites and make notes on their own; they would discuss their findings next time. He steered Dr. Filbert toward the detectives by the elbow, as if he were blind.

"Have you ever seen our little farm, Detectives?"

"Um, no," Cardinal said. "I'd be very interested another day, but right now we're kind of pressed for time."

"Not to worry. We'll do a walk and talk. That's what they call it in the movies. About once a year somebody asks me to be an adviser to a movie or a TV show. It's a lot less interesting than you might think."

He waved a hand in the direction of the caged carcass. "See, we have eight of these sites, each with a rat cadaver. The rats are already dead when we get them."

"Psychology department," Filbert said. "Psychology generates a lot of dead rats."

"We put them out at the same time in different conditions and then see who comes to visit at what time and for how long. We have a lot of fun, don't we, Dr. Filbert?"

"Some of us do. The rest of us have things we'd rather be doing."

"Dr. Filbert is feeling holier-than-thou these days because he got another grant for his macabre experiments with DNA. Justice Department, NSERC—they all love him. And why not? I created him."

Filbert pointed to a cage further uphill.

"You see, this one has a southern exposure. That means it gets a lot of sunlight and the process of decay is speeded up."

"Speeded up," Arsenault said. "Looks like it's just about over."

"Dry decay stage," Chin said. "All the liquids have seeped away. Picnic for the hide beetle, though." He squatted beside the cadaver. "Yes, there they are, munching away. Yum yum." He stood up again. "Let's visit his cousin, shall we? Other side of the hill."

"Doc, we need to know your findings on the previous samples we brought you. And we have something new, too."

"Fine, fine. More the merrier."

Chin led them down the other side of the hill toward the campus. Through the trees, Cardinal could see a lacrosse game in progress. Shouts of students echoed among the hills. A blackfly landed on his wrist and he shook it off. It landed on his other wrist and bit him.

"Now look at this. This little rodent was planted the same time as his cousin over the hill. Different side of the tracks, so to speak."

The rat was black, and the flesh looked almost liquid.

"What do we call this stage, Dr. Filbert?"

"Black putrefaction. It's been known to set in during some of your lectures."

"Tsk, tsk. Such bile in one so young. Yes, it is black putrefaction. A completely different stage of decay and yet exactly the same post-mortem interval. Even more important: You could examine this rat all day and you will not see a single hide beetle."

"Not even a married one."

"Oh, Dr. Filbert, you are *très piquant*."

Once again, Chin squatted beside the cage. "Yes, you see, here we have *Calliphoridae* and *Sarcophagidae* still in the pupal stage. Amazing what a difference a few degrees can make. Winter, though. That's a whole different story."

"Before the snow, after the snow," Filbert said. "Above freezing, below freezing. You're entering whole new realms of confusion."

Cardinal had had a few winter cadavers of his own, but he didn't want to get into it with them. Please, can we just get to the lab? Please can we focus on the case?

Chin led them past two more cages, two more dead rats, giving them commentary as if he were a museum curator—which, in a way, he was. Finally, they were in the lab and Chin pulled a binder from a shelf. He flipped through to the end and examined some computer printouts.

"Here we are. You're looking at a minimum post-mortem interval of 312 hours and a maximum of 336."

"Fourteen days," Cardinal said. "But you gave us that much last time."

"Well, now you can actually take it to the courtroom. We know beyond a doubt what the species are because we've allowed them to hatch. I'm sure Dr. Filbert would be happy to appear in court for you. He certainly has nothing else to do."

"Oh, no. Just my long, lonely hours at the thermal cycler," Filbert said. "Why don't you show them the data?"

Chin tilted a computer toward them, and a grid lit up the screen. "Succession data. We keep developmental timetables for all the local arthropods in our database."

"What he means is, *I* do," Filbert said. "*He* just takes credit for it."

"Dr. Filbert is not a scientist at all, Detectives. He is actually an escapee from a locked facility. I'd be grateful if you'd take him with you when you go." Chin typed something on the keyboard, and the grid changed colour. Then a list appeared on the left-hand side and the grid filled up with numbers.

"On the left, we enter the taxa found at the site. *Calliphoridae, Cynomyopsis, Staphylinidae*, et cetera. Each has a different time of oviposition or pupaposition and a different time of development. You feed the computer all the taxa you find at the site, enter their different stages of development and, really, you don't even need a computer. You just look at what number of days accounts for all the different stages. The only PMI that could account for all of these being in the same place at the same time is . . ." Chin hit Enter and the screen flashed a number range.

"Three hundred and twelve hours to 336 hours," Cardinal said. "Very impressive."

"Science at its most basic." Chin looked up at them with a smile. Fluorescent lights formed bright ingots in his glasses. "Even Filbert understands it."

"Not my field, really," Filbert said. "I'm just a capillary sequencer."

Arsenault pulled out a couple of vials and handed them to Dr. Chin.

"Another body," he said. "Can you tell us anything from these?"

"Well, you've got mostly eggs here. Hardly any pupae. Fresh corpse, right?"

"Right."

Dr. Chin tapped out one of the eggs and put it under the microscope. "*Phormia regina* you get everywhere. Boring." He put another egg on another slide. "*Lucilia illustris*," he said, adjusting the focus. "Greenbottle. Likes open, dry areas."

"That would certainly fit," Cardinal said.

Dr. Chin tapped out another egg onto a slide and put it under the scope. He adjusted the focus back and forth. "*Phaenicia sericata*. Also known as the sheep blowfly. This one lives in bright habitats. Early arriver, too. Likes to be first in line. Outdoors, in sunshine, I'd say we're looking at the neighbourhood of twelve to fourteen hours post-mortem."

"That would match the appearance of the corpse," Arsenault said.

"You didn't mention either of those species with our first victim," Cardinal said.

"Heck, no. First victim was behind a waterfall and two weeks old. You're not going to see either of these insects at that site. And vice versa: You're not going to see *Cynomyopsis cadaverina* on a corpse that fresh. But I don't understand why you're coming to me about this second victim. You'll get a reasonable time of death from stomach contents and body temperature."

"We found something else at the second site," Cardinal said. "Arsenault did."

Arsenault produced another vial. Chin held it up to the light.

"A single pupal casing?"

"It wasn't part of any masses. It was by itself eight feet away."

"Eight feet?" Chin opened the vial and slid the tiny casing onto a slide. "Sometimes maggots can jump quite far from the flesh," Chin said, "but this is not a cheese skipper. And your second corpse was nowhere near water, correct?"

"That's right. No lake or stream within at least a mile."

"This is a casing from a third-instar *Cynomyopsis*. There were lots of them on your first corpse. But you've got nothing older than first instar on the second one, and it's not old enough to attract *myopsis*. No way this casing is from your second corpse."

"Yes!" Arsenault jerked his elbow downward in the sports fan's sign of victory.

"Hold on," Cardinal said. "If I understand you correctly, this casing couldn't be from the second victim, right?"

"Correct."

"I don't see how that proves somebody tracked it over from the first victim."

"It doesn't," Chin said. "They could have tracked it from somewhere else. Some other site of decay—a dead animal, say. A hunter, a hiker, who knows?"

"You guys are depressing me," Arsenault said. "Are you telling me this casing doesn't mean anything?"

"It might mean a great deal," Chin said. "I just can't prove it with entomology."

"That is really a pisser," Arsenault said. "I thought this was gonna be important."

"Do you mind if I take a look at it?" Filbert said. "Just for a day or so?"

"What for?" Chin said. "We've already typed the species."

"Let me have it for a day or so. I may be able to help."

"Maybe it hasn't broken the case wide open," Arsenault said, "but this little bugger is still evidence. I'm going to have to ask you to sign a receipt for it, and I'm going to have to see the fridge where you will keep it locked up."

Cardinal and Arsenault left soon after.

On the way to the car, Arsenault said, "What do you figure the chances are that some hiker happened by and deposited that maggot at our crime scene?"

"Slim," Cardinal said. "Possible, but slim."

"Murderers have been known to return to the scene of the crime. Could have gone back to retrieve something—

something he lost or forgot. Hell, in Wombat's case, with all that mutilation, the killer could have gone back for more body parts."

"There's another possibility," Cardinal said.

"Oh?"

"Nishinabe Falls worked for him once. He could've gone back there to kill again."

"But Toof was killed over by West Rock."

"I meant Terri Tait."

38

THE COMMON CONCEPTION of the addict is of a desperate person whose day is consumed with the laying of schemes to procure the next fix. Wild-eyed, hyperventilating and slick with perspiration, he curls up in some desperate corner. Under sweat-soaked sheets, a telephone clamped in hand, the junkie frantically dials the numbers of his connections. And when they won't extend him any credit, he starts dialling friends with whom he's lost touch years ago, to beg for a loan, repayable with interest, of course. Then come the lightning calculations of what to sell—the boom box? the CD collection?—assuming there is anything left to sell. When all the worldly goods are gone, and if the city is big enough and the addict attractive enough, it may come down to selling one's body. Or if one lacks the kind of body for which there is a brisk market, then the addict's fancy turns to theft. And so a spur-of-the-moment, just-happened-to-be-in-the-neighbourhood kind of visit might be bestowed upon a relative, an old friend or even an unlucky acquaintance. Then while the unwitting mark's back is turned, the sudden scooping of a radio, a clock, a watch or some silvery memento into a starving backpack.

Many addicts do indeed find themselves driven to such measures. But the majority spend their time not thinking about how to procure the next fix. They've already worked out how to procure the next fix. Their lives, after all, revolve around the fix. They've worked the fix into their daily routines.

No, what the addict thinks about more than any other single subject is when and how he will quit. Such fantasies often involve mornings. Today, I will smoke that pipe, I will fill that vein, I will drain that bottle, and then tomorrow, first thing in the morning—or no, let's make sure this recovery program is a sensible, workable affair this time, not like all the other attempts—next Monday. I'll allow myself just this one more weekend, then first thing Monday morning I'll head down to the twelve-step and get some of that beautiful, earthy wisdom they traffic in and get my head turned around. It won't be easy, but I should be ready by Monday. Yes, that's right. Shoot for Monday.

Thus the days and weeks go by. The addict sees himself as embarked on a course of moderation, leading to all-out cessation, followed for the rest of his life by the Zenlike clarity of abstinence. The rest of his life will unfold in a sweet—but not boring—desirelessness. There will even come a day when the sight of a little hillock of white powder will provoke no emotional response whatsoever—a needle will leave him unmoved.

So it was with Kevin Tait. His latest course of moderation had taken him from snorting to skin-popping and now back to mainlining as swiftly as if he had set his engines full speed ahead for personal obliteration. That had been the pattern with him pretty much since high school.

He knew where it came from, this hole in his being that only heroin seemed to fill. He had been orphaned at the age of ten and, even though the aunt and uncle who took him and his sister in tried their best, nothing was ever the same. It was as if the world had been pulled out from under his feet and he could never trust anything again.

It was okay for Terri; Terri had been fifteen. She had seemed to fit right in. But Kevin had become more and more unruly, and his new parents were always disciplining him: groundings, TV deprivation, docking his pocket money—it was always something. Terri was always interceding for him, trying to soften their aunt and uncle's responses. And she was always trying to get him to behave better. It seemed like the whole pattern of their lives had been inscribed in some implacable book of fate the moment the plane carrying their parents had dived, nose first, into the ground.

Sometimes Kevin resented his older sister for apparently having come through this loss unscathed; her life looked easy and untroubled compared to his. Terri had made it through college and was gradually making her way in Vancouver's theatre world; Kevin had dropped out, figuring a degree was irrelevant to a career in poetry. Besides, it was pretty hard to concentrate on Shakespeare and John Donne when you were panting after the next high. Shortly after he dropped out, Kevin had been arrested with enough heroin on him for ten people.

So far, he had managed to keep knowledge of his full-blown readdiction from Leon and from Red Bear. He always wore long sleeves, and he only injected himself in the middle of the night. Well, all right, sometimes he had to sneak off to the can and slip in a little booster, just to keep him *compos* for the rest of the day. But, except for the day Toof had been killed, he hadn't allowed himself a full-blown fix until after midnight.

He'd done well, so far, to keep it from them—but then, dissembling is the first skill the addict learns. He knew he could not keep it up, and that meant he would have to vamoose, which he wanted to do anyway. Well, yes, that was his *plan*. Abstinence, not addiction, was the chart he had drawn up for the rest of his life. An abstinence that would bring with it a mental clarity he had not known since he was—what? Fourteen? Fifteen? That was what he was after. Not intoxication. He had no intention of spending the rest of his life hanging out at the Rosebud diner with the likes of Leon. Three or four months from now he'd be living on a Greek island, just like Leonard Cohen had done when he was a young poet. He'd live off souvlaki and goat's milk while he worked on a book of poems that would capture everything he'd ever thought about and everything he knew about poetry.

He couldn't see his way clear to actually breaking free of Red Bear and the camp until Monday. The problem was, just now he was so wired he wouldn't be able to write a couplet, let alone the kind of complex, multi-layered works he had in mind. Come Monday, he'd be out of here. He'd already phoned the Centre for Addiction and Mental

Health in Toronto and booked himself an appointment
for Monday afternoon.

But this called for careful steering. He had the
money—Red Bear's entrepreneurial skills had definitely
put cash in his bank account. But first, he had to get
through the next few days. He had to make sure he had
enough smack to get him safely through the next few
nights and then down to Toronto.

Kevin's personal reserve of heroin had run out. So had
Leon's, he happened to know. And yet, despite the dearth
of competition in the area, he had managed to score himself a few crumbs downtown, just enough to see him
through the afternoon, the effects of which had long
worn off. He was still in good shape—actual withdrawal
symptoms were a good twelve hours away—but it was
definitely time to get proactive.

He had turned his light out an hour ago, and had been
watching out the window ever since. There was nothing
going on at the camp. Activity reached a peak when a
soggy raccoon waddled past the leaning volleyball posts.
Leon's light had gone out over half an hour ago, and Red
Bear's cabin had gone dark soon after. Kevin put his
Adidas on and opened the cabin door.

The rain showed no sign of letting up any time soon.
Just as well, really. It would keep the blackflies away. Now
came the easy part. He dashed round to Leon's cabin,
making a circle around back of the camp in about twenty
seconds. The bush was thick here, but full of trails. A pud-
dle disgorged its contents into his running shoe.

Now came Leon's door. He moved silently round to the
front of the cabin, and here Kevin was in luck, because he

had been the one assigned to putting locks on the cabins, and he had had the foresight to have extra keys made. The only ones he didn't have keys for were the motherlode and the stinking cabin out back where Red Bear killed his goats and chickens and what have you. Red Bear had had Leon take care of those locks, and then he'd put Leon in charge of the dope. Not that they kept all of it at the camp. The main stash was hidden somewhere Kevin didn't know about. "For your own protection," Red Bear had assured him, "it's better you don't know." All they kept on hand were a few ounces, for medium-sized transactions between big shipments.

Kevin knew exactly what he had to do next, knew exactly where he had to go. There's no one more observant than a junkie scoping out his supply. He knew where Leon kept the key. It was on a chain strung from a belt loop near the right front pocket of his jeans, along with all his other keys. He also knew where Leon kept his jeans at night. He always hung them over the back of a chair, and half the time the keys were dangling right out in full view.

Kevin stood for a few minutes, listening. His heart was pounding, and suddenly he very much needed to pee. There was no sound from inside. The rain had already soaked through the hood and shoulders of his sweatshirt. He had thought about wearing his leather, but he was afraid it would make too much noise. Craft, craft, saves the day.

"Your poetic ancestors, it has been suggested, are Coleridge and Baudelaire." Martin Amis was back, his handsome, sarcastic face hovering among the pines. "How often do you suppose those literary giants found themselves pilfering narcotics from their sleeping associates?"

Not now, Martin, not now.

"True, Coleridge owned to a taste for laudanum—he even gave it the credit for 'Kubla Khan.' But one can't quite see him sneaking around the woods of northern Ontario in a desperate search for smack, as you call it."

Well, of course not. Laudanum was perfectly legal.

"Nor can one imagine him associating with known murderers. Can you spell out for your readers exactly how this is necessary for your art?"

Beat it, Martin. Maybe I'm not a poet, okay? Maybe I'm just a stone junkie.

Amis and his sardonic smile faded into the rain and pine.

Kevin prayed that Leon's door would be unlocked. He turned the knob ever so gently, an eighth of an inch every second or so, until it would turn no further. Locked.

Kevin had the key with him. It went into the slot without a sound. Really, there was nothing to worry about if you didn't turn it quite the whole way: far enough that it would clear the door frame, but not so far that it would spring open with a clack. He leaned against the door, and it opened half an inch. So far, so good.

He stepped inside and closed the door behind him without latching it. He pressed his back against the wall. If Leon woke now, Kevin was a dead man. Every muscle in his body tensed as he listened for Leon's breathing. It was hard to hear over the pulse beating in his own ears, but it was there, slow and rhythmic. He could see Leon's outline: curled up, facing the wall.

Leon's jeans were hung, as usual, on the back of a chair, but Kevin had to cross the room to get there. He knew a couple of the floorboards creaked, the one with the large knothole and the one that was directly in line with the bottom corner of the window—but there might be others. That Red Bear would kill him, he had no doubt. The only question was whether he would do it himself or ask Leon to do it for him. See, this is exactly why I'm quitting dope. It gets me into untenable positions.

A floorboard creaked. Leon stirred but didn't roll over. Kevin was one yard from the chair. He wouldn't risk any more floorboards. Instead, he bent from the waist and reached out. It was a painful position, but he could just touch Leon's pocket. Straining to stretch even further, Kevin was now balanced on his toes. Then he had the chain in his hand and tugged it upward to extract the keys from the pocket.

He wasn't even halfway home. He had to silently separate the keys from the chain, get over to the supply cabin, remove some dope and then—even when he had successfully completed all that business—he would have to return the keys to Leon's pocket without waking him up.

Using the chain, Kevin managed to pull the jeans close enough that he could unclip it. Then, he pivoted on one foot and took a giant step toward the door. No creak. Leon's breathing remained slow and steady. One more giant step. No creak. He was at the door and out in a flash. He pressed it closed silently, but didn't lock it.

He jumped down from the stoop and darted around the back of the cabin.

Now, I just have to get myself enough smack to see me through until Monday, and then I'm clean and sober. For the rest of my life. None of this one-day-at-a-time crap. I'm done. I'm through. My mind is so all over this I can feel I'm already recovering.

Where Kevin actually was, a moment later, was on the porch of the supply cabin, inserting Leon's key into the lock. He glanced over at Red Bear's place. Still dark. He had a sudden image of Red Bear leaping out of his front door, carving knife in hand, chanting the way he had done that night of the pig.

The motherlode cabin smelled different from the other cabins. It was constructed of concrete and smelled like a basement. Even the windows had been filled in with concrete blocks. They kept it looking like a tool shed. There was a rake, a lawn mower, a bucket and pail. And over in the far corner there was an open bag of cement. Nothing to excite the interest of the casual break-and-enter artist.

Kevin went straight for the cement bag and reached inside. There was more dope than he had expected. Red Bear must have added to the product without mentioning it, because there were three one-ounce bags of smack—and there was no way Kevin could have forgotten that. It was a golden opportunity. Suppose I take all three bags? Just light out of here now and sell the stuff down in Toronto? Make a little extra, shoot a little extra, get me through the transition period.

Don't go crazy, he told himself. Just cover the weekend. He opened all three bags and took a spoonful from each. Oh, hell, he took one more just for good luck. Then he opened the little container of cornstarch he had brought with him, and added a spoonful to each bag. He resealed the bags, shook them to mix the powders and put them back in the cement bag.

A sound from behind.

Kevin whirled around. Red Bear was standing behind

him, a pitchfork aimed at Kevin's back.

"Oh, Christ," Kevin said. "You scared the shit out of me. I thought I heard someone in the stash and I came to—"

Red Bear smiled.

"Where did you get the key, Kevin?"

"The key? Oh, these are Leon's keys. I went over to wake him up and found them still in his door. He must've gone to bed drunk or something. I couldn't wake him up."

"No, I said good night to him and he was quite sober."

Kevin shrugged. "Well, anyways. Dope's all present and accounted for."

"I could push this pitchfork right through your throat. Watch you drown in your own blood."

"Uh, you don't want to do that."

"No, I do want to do that, Kevin. Very much. But I'm going to control myself."

"Okay, cool," Kevin said. "Maybe I should just move out, huh?"

"The reason I'm going to control myself is that it is time for another sacrifice."

"Oh, no. I don't think we need to go into that, man. I'll just leave now, okay?"

"You are going to be that sacrifice, Kevin. Then I will be sure that you are working for us, not against us. You will be firmly on our side. Just like Wombat Guthrie."

Kevin made a run for it. Red Bear lunged at him with the pitchfork, and Kevin felt a searing pain in his side. He kept running for the door, though. Got outside. And was just about to leap off the stoop when something crashed onto the back of his skull, and then his mouth was full of sand and everything went black as if the world had blown a fuse.

39

THE CRISIS CENTRE WAS BETTER than the hospital, Terri decided. For one thing, it was a house—a grand old house—the people who had lived here long ago must have been wealthy. A railway tycoon, maybe; the place occupied a big corner lot on a street called Station, and Detective Cardinal had driven past a charred, boarded-up terminal on the way here. That tycoon must've had ten kids, to judge by all the rooms, and Terri felt a pang for the Victorian wife who no doubt had worked as the tycoon's slave for her entire life before dying in childbirth bearing number eleven.

The guy who ran the place, Ned Fellowes, wasn't that bad either—a former priest, one of the other inmates had informed her, but nothing pious about him, nothing holier-than-thou. He was just a bony, fortyish man with thinning, sandy hair and a pleasant smile. He had signed her in with a minimum of fuss, entering her information on a computer surrounded by tipsy stacks of psychology journals.

The Crisis Centre, he had told her, was originally intended solely for the protection of battered wives, but they took in people for other reasons, too, if they had room. Certainly, a bullet in the head seemed to qualify.

"We're not a jail, and we're not a hospital," he had told her in his jaunty we-can-all-get-through-this-together voice. "We assume that all of our guests are adults and able to look after themselves. We have very few rules, but we expect them to be followed."

Terri's room was surprisingly large for an institutional place. A double bed with a scarlet coverlet proved to have an acceptable mattress, and the overstuffed armchair by the window was almost comfortable. An ancient rug, just this side of threadbare, covered the floor. The bathroom, located at the far end of the hall, was shared but clean.

A couple of her fellow "guests" seemed like decent people, though Terri didn't for one minute consider that she had anything in common with them. One bore a cast on her arm, another had blackened eyes. Terri didn't tell them about her bullet wound, and people in this place knew better than to ask about injuries.

So, all right, yes, it was better than the hospital. She wasn't confined to a bed or the sunroom. There was a real kitchen instead of a candy machine. But in the end, it still felt like being under house arrest.

She was not supposed to go out, according to Detective Cardinal, and Ned Fellowes absolutely concurred.

"We're not a jail," he repeated. "And we're not your parents. But clearly, until whoever did this to you is behind bars, you're in serious danger and you should not be out on the streets."

She spent almost an entire day in her room. She had tried the communal lounge for a while, but people wanted to talk too much—where are you from? what do you do?—and she didn't feel like answering them. She tried to concentrate on a paperback some previous guest in crisis had left behind, but it couldn't quiet her mind. Finally, she threw the book across the room. She got up and put on the hoodie, checking herself in the mirror. Just the thing.

Once out on the streets, she felt much better. The night air still tasted of spring: scents of new flowers, wet soil. A strong breeze was blowing and she had to hold the drawstrings of her hood.

She found Main Street easily enough. There wasn't much traffic, but there were a lot of cars in front of a place called the Capitol Centre—a concert of some sort. After a couple of wrong turns, she found the bar Kevin had taken her to, the Goat in Boots. It was his unofficial hangout, he had said, when he wanted to get away from Red Bear and the others. Smoke assailed her nostrils the moment she entered, and she coughed. It was a typical English-style pub, and didn't look remotely dangerous. Terri pushed her hood back and went up to the bar.

The bartender was a young blond woman, very pretty. "I'm looking for a guy named Kevin Tait," Terri said. "He's my brother, actually. Long dark hair, about six feet tall, always with a notebook? Comes in here quite often."

"I think I know who you mean," the bartender said. "Kevin, yeah. I never knew his last name. Haven't seen him today, though. Haven't seen him for a while, in fact."

"Can you ask the other bartender?"

"Hey, Dora! You seen Kevin lately? Skinny guy with the long hair, always carries a notebook?"

The other bartender looked up from the draught tap and shook her head.

"He's staying at this old wreck of a camp. Bunch of old cabins by a lake. I don't suppose you happen to know where that would be?" Terri said. "It's kind of urgent."

"Haven't a clue."

"Do you see anybody here who might know him? I'm from out of town. I don't know who his friends are here."

"Friends. I don't know about friends . . ."

The bartender narrowed her gaze against the smoke. "There's a guy I've seen him talking to a few times. But I don't know if they're actual friends." She pointed to a small, bearded man at the far end of the bar. He wore wire-rim spectacles and clutched a paperback in his fist as if squeezing the juice out of it.

"Thanks."

Terri moved to the other end of the bar.

"You always read in pubs?" she said to the guy.

He looked up from his book.

"Sometimes," he said. "It beats small talk. Or staring at the TV screen. The only reason I come to this bar is it's the only one that keeps the sound turned off."

"You're a friend of Kevin Tait's, right?"

"Yeah. Well, I mean, I know him. I only see him when he comes in here. Which isn't too often, lately. We talk about poetry."

Thank God, Terri said to herself. Not a dope associate.

"Well, here's the thing," she said. "I'm Kevin's sister. My name's Terri."

"I'm Roger." He stuck out a damp hand to shake. "Kevin mentioned you to me."

"He did?"

"Yeah. We were talking about Yeats. You know W.B. Yeats?"

"I'm not sure."

"He has this great poem. *Heaven has put away the stroke of her doom,/ So great her portion in that peace you make/ By merely walking in a room.* Do you know it?"

"I don't think so."

"Kevin said it always reminded him of you. He also said you had the most amazing red hair. And that you were a really good actress. What happened to your head? Somebody shoot you?"

Terri was stymied for a second, until she realized he was just joking.

"I was in a car accident. A bad one. I was lucky to get off with just a concussion. The result is, I can't remember Kevin's address and my address book got lost in all the turmoil. I need to find him."

"Gee, I don't know what to tell you. I haven't got a clue where he lives. All we ever talk about is poetry. Did you try the police?"

"Yeah. They can't help me. It's not like he's a missing person."

"Well, I don't know. He sure reads a lot. You might try the library or the bookstores."

Terri wanted to hug him for saying that. Here was someone who knew only Kevin's good side.

"Thanks, maybe I'll do that."

He showed her the cover of the book he was reading.

"Baudelaire. You ever read him?"

Terri shook her head.

"He's nifty. They've got the French on one side and the English on the other. I know enough French to know it sounds really good. Makes me want to learn it for real, though. Listen, why don't you sit down and wait for him? He comes in quite late sometimes."

"No, thank you. I've got to find him. It's urgent. If he comes in, would you give him this?"

She copied down the number of the Crisis Centre on a cocktail napkin.

"Tell him I need to speak to him right away."

"I will. Sure."

"One last question."

"Okay."

"Where would I go if I wanted to buy some dope?"

Roger's smile disappeared into his beard. Disapproval rode his brows. "I'm not into drugs," he said.

"Me either. But if you were . . ."

"Try Oak Street. The World Tavern. Not in the tavern itself. There's a parking lot across the street. Here, I'll draw you a map."

Outside, the breeze had picked up. It started to rain as Terri crossed the street. Okay, so I'm not a detective and I'm not a spy. I don't know how to get information without just coming out and asking for it. Let me just do it fast, find Kevin, and haul him back to Vancouver and the rehab centre. I don't care if I have to drag him by the hair.

Oak Street was uncomfortably dark. And the entire block on the far side seemed to be a vast parking lot. Terri found herself looking over her shoulder. The World

Tavern wasn't far. Had Kevin taken her there, too? It didn't look familiar. She saw a group of shadows in the parking lot across the street, and the smell of marijuana reached her, mixed with the smells of the lake and wet pavement.

She crossed the street toward the shadows. There were two young men—boys, really—in nylon jackets, and a girl whose low-rise jeans exposed a good two inches of butt cleavage. They were standing in the lee of a billboard. Their laughter died down, and they eyed Terri silently. One of them stomped out a smoke, but it did nothing to disperse the rich cloud of grass and rain.

"Excuse me," Terri said. "I wonder if you can help me."

"Depends what you want," the larger boy said. His jacket hung down to his knees. Trying to look cool, giving her the narrowed eyes.

"I'm looking for a friend of mine named Kevin Tait. You wouldn't happen to know him, would you?"

The trio looked at each other, then back at Terri.

"Nope," the one in the knee-length jacket said. "Guess not."

"Well, maybe you've seen him. Dark curly hair? Carries a notebook?"

The smaller kid and the girl shook their heads. The oldest one shrugged. "Sounds familiar. But I couldn't say for sure."

"I'm not a cop. I'm his sister."

"Still can't help you."

"Well, let me ask you this. Where would you go if you wanted to score some heroin?"

"Whoa, dude. You wanna know where you can score

smack?" He took a step back, all but vanishing into his jacket.

"Not for me. It's just a way to find Kevin."

"I wouldn't know where to look for smack. Not my kind of thing." The kid had adopted a superior look, no longer interested in her. Snobbery runs rife even in drug circles.

Terri looked at the girl. "Help me. He's in trouble."

"Sorry. I don't know anything."

She looked at the smaller guy.

"Hell, no. Me either. Smack, man. Not for me."

"All right. Thanks, anyway."

She started to walk away.

The big one called after her. "Now, if you wanted something to smoke, that might be a different story."

Terri gathered her hood against the wind and kept walking.

Cars were starting up all along Main Street; the theatre was letting out. Terri walked down Worth Street, heading back toward the Crisis Centre. She cut through a park where a bronze soldier glistened in the rain.

When she emerged on the far side of the park, she had to wait for the light. The line of gleaming cars stretched back to Main Street, wipers flapping. The wind tore at her hood and she gave up trying to hold it; it was soaked through, anyhow.

———

Leon was already through the light by the time he registered who it was he had just seen. The red hair, the turned-up nose, it had to be her. Not possible. Maybe she's got a cousin or there's someone else who just looks an awful lot like her. But what clinched it was the bandage on the side of her head.

The scene came back to him: the falls, the flies, the trembling girl. He had urged her forward through the woods, the gun at her back, taking her to the same place he and Red Bear had slaughtered the biker. It had to be done at the same place; he had never killed a woman before, and he knew he wouldn't be able to do it anywhere else. But when they got to the falls, she made a break for it. Leon's hiking boot slipped on a rock, and she just took off. He had to run behind the falls and out the other side to cut her off. Man, the smell.

On the corner, the wind blew her hood back and she clutched at it. It was the sudden motion that had caught his eye, stuck in this bloody traffic. Then she let go of the hood and folded her arms across her chest, and there it was on the right side of her head: a small white patch.

Leon hit the brakes on the far side of the intersection and the cars behind him leaned on their horns. Worth Street was one-way; he couldn't turn around. He rolled down his window and jerked the side mirror so he could see her. Yeah, she was still on the corner. The light was about to change, damn it.

At the next corner he swung a right and zoomed up the block, scaring the hell out of a couple of pedestrians. Then another right at the first stop sign and back down to Macintosh. The traffic wasn't so bad here, though he could still see the line of wet lights stretching back to Main. Right again and then he was back to Worth Street.

No sign of her.

Leon crossed the intersection and drove slowly for half a block. She'd been heading this way. She must have gone into one of these houses. Either that, or she could have crossed north again once she got across Worth. He got out of the car, not even bothering to lock it, and ran. He stopped at the corner of Station Street, already out of breath. He turned in one direction, then another, squinting into the rain.

40

"WE GOT TO FIND OUT where she's staying," Leon said. "That bitch cannot be alive. She's gonna finger me and they'll put me away for, like, ever, man. I can't do jail, man. I couldn't take that again."

Red Bear was brushing his hair before the mirror. He spent a long time doing that each morning, like he was Snow White or something.

"We got to deal with this," Leon said. He heard the whine in his voice, but he couldn't help it. "We got to do something. We got to lay plans, man."

Red Bear glanced at him in the mirror.

"I will consult the spirits."

"Consult the spirits, hell. Don't you get it? She talks to the cops, I go away to Millhaven again. You know how long they stuck me in solitary, man?"

"Forty-eight days. You told me already."

"Yeah, well, you try doing forty-eight days in that fucking hellhole. See how long you keep your cool, then. I want to plug that bitch. Put her away, man. She cannot be walking the earth."

"I will consult the spirits, Leon."

"We already got Kevin locked up. We could do a sacrifice, man. A double sacrifice. That's what we should do. Make sure we get this right."

"We will do a sacrifice, when the time is right."

"So let's do it, man. Get those spirits working for us big time. Let's get it done."

Red Bear put aside his brush and picked up a pump bottle. He sprayed something into his palm and rubbed his hands together. Then he patted them over his hair. He picked up the brush again.

"I have already explained to you. I cannot perform a sacrifice until the moon is waxing. Right now it is still waning. Do a sacrifice while the moon is waning and the entity will control *you*. That is not what we want."

"What I want is one dead redhead."

Red Bear turned to him. Those eyes of his. Sometimes they caught the light in a certain way and it was like being stared at by a corpse.

"Whose fault is it she's alive?"

"That's not my fault. It's that fucking gun, man. I told you. I pumped two of those motherfucking bullets into Toof's head and he wouldn't even lie down. Guy's still up and around and yakkin' away. Had to go at him with my Louisville Slugger. If I'd a known, I'd a put five in her head, stedda one, man. It's not my fault. I mean, where in the fuck have I sinned?"

Red Bear turned back to the mirror.

"Try not to panic, Leon. I will consult the spirits."

41

LISE ĐELORME HAD BEEN spending an awful lot of time chasing down a lead that seemed certain to propel her face-first into a dead end. According to Jerry Commanda, the strange hieroglyphics on the walls of the cave behind Nishinabe Falls had nothing to do with Ojibwa Indians. So Delorme had followed his advice and called Frank Izzard at the OPP's behavioural sciences unit, then faxed him a photograph of the markings.

Delorme had googled Izzard on the Internet before calling him. Izzard was a cop with an advanced degree in psychology and a particular interest in Satanism and other esoteric practices that have attracted serial killers over the past few decades. His papers on the subject had appeared in the *Annals of Forensic Psychology* and he had written a widely respected book-length study of Richard Ramirez, the so-called Night Stalker who had terrorized Los Angeles twenty years previously. Just from her reading on the Internet, Delorme had discovered that Satanism was far more widespread among serial killers than she had supposed.

"Most of them don't get into it in any organized way," Izzard told her on the phone. "They dabble. They go into it with about as much devotion as the average housewife gives her yoga philosophy."

"I guess it makes sense they'd be interested in anything that appears to condone the evil things they do."

"Oh, their interest isn't ethical. Even with Ramirez. They're not looking for permission from a supernatural being. When a person seething with rage and lust starts playing with Satanic rituals—that is to say, rituals designed to bring Satan or his helpers into your apartment—what happens is they invoke not some supernatural being but an embodiment of their own blackest desires. Imagine a being composed of pure lust and rage—no conscience, no morals, no restraints . . ."

"Pretty hideous," Delorme said.

"And it's going to be *powerful*. For a loser who is otherwise close to nonfunctioning, it's going to be the most powerful experience of his life. With Ramirez—and maybe with your guy, too—what can happen is a borderline personality topples over the edge and becomes an outright psychopath."

"Which brings us to our hieroglyphics."

"You said you may be looking for an Indian? A Native?"

"It's possible. A couple of witnesses have mentioned an Indian named Red Bear."

"Well, these markings have nothing to do with Native Canadians or Americans. Unless you happen to have an Indian who's interested in Voodoo."

"Voodoo? In Canada?"

"Oh, sure. You get all kinds of it in Toronto. Even more in Montreal. Comes up by way of the Caribbean countries, and it's completely harmless in most cases. But these markings you faxed to me, I've never seen anything like them. All those arrows bundled together, and so many repetitions, each one slightly different. I frankly don't know what to make of them."

"But you're sure they're not Indian."

"Let me put it this way. If they are Indian, it's a completely new type of glyph. There's been nothing like it in North America as far as I'm aware. No, I'm thinking maybe some personal variation on Voodoo or Santeria. But that's all I know."

"So what are we going to do? Can you point me in some likely direction?"

"You have to talk to Helen Wasserstein."

"Who's she? RCMP?"

"Try ROM."

⸺

The Royal Ontario Museum is perhaps the closest Canada gets to the Smithsonian or the British Museum. It is on a much smaller scale than either of those two august institutions, but what it does, it tends to do excellently. Virtually every high-school student in Ontario will at some point or other be bused to Toronto to view the museum's dinosaurs, its Roman collection or its totem poles.

Helen Wasserstein was the ROM's curator of Native Canadian artifacts, but luckily Delorme did not have to travel to Toronto in order to talk to her. As it turned out, Dr. Wasserstein was on a dig in the northern end of Algonquin Park, which put her a little more than an hour south of Algonquin Bay.

Delorme liked to drive, and she particularly liked driving into the forest. But the last part of the trip was over a dirt road that could hardly be called a road at all. More than once her head made contact with the roof of the car, and she wished for the first time in her life that she drove a Jeep or an SUV. She came, finally, to a barrier constructed of several strips of red tape.

A sign proclaimed the archaeological dig, and invited those not connected with the project to turn back. There were two Jeeps and a pickup truck parked among the trees. Delorme left her unmarked Caprice facing the tape and headed down the slope.

Smells of pine and loam were thick in the air. So were blackflies. Delorme swatted the air before her face like a neurotic fighting off intrusive thoughts. At the bottom of the hill lay a wide clearing, almost perfectly circular, from which the top layer of pine needles and soil had been scraped away. Three figures on hands and knees probed and sifted the dirt. All three, Delorme noted with envy, were wearing bug shirts.

One of the figures stood upright and stared at her. It was like being observed by an astronaut; Delorme wasn't sure if the figure was male or female.

"I'm looking for Dr. Wasserstein," Delorme said. "I understand she's—"

The hooded figure raised a little spade and pointed to the other side of the dig. Dr. Wasserstein was crouched over a sieve that she was shirring back and forth as if she were a prospector.

"Dr. Wasserstein?"

The hood of netting turned to face her.

"My name is Lise Delorme. I'm a detective with the Algonquin Bay police. I wonder if you could spare me a few minutes of your time."

"Police? I'm very busy just now. But as you've come all this way, I assume it's something that can't wait?"

"I'm afraid not."

"All right. Let's go in the trailer. You're getting eaten alive."

The trailer was an office on wheels. The table inside was covered with maps, notebooks, cameras and survey equipment. A large Thermos sat beside a super-sized can of bug spray.

"Coffee?"

"Sure. That would be nice."

Dr. Wasserstein removed her bug protection and shook out her bobbed dark hair. Delorme had been expecting grey hair and spectacles, but the curator was no older than Delorme, possibly a year or two younger, with dark eyes and perfect skin. Underneath the bug shirt she wore a striped T-shirt of the type favoured by French fishermen.

Coffee was poured, and Delorme explained why she was there.

"You have two murders? And you think they are connected to Native Canadians in some way?"

"There's some possible involvement of a First Nations person. But Frank Izzard at OPP thinks these symbols are connected to Voodoo."

"I know Frank. That's all he told you?"

"He said you'd be the one to narrow it down."

Dr. Wasserstein looked out the trailer window. Outside, her colleagues went about their work, still figures in the tranquil light. Delorme envied them, and felt a twinge of sadness at bringing thoughts of murder into this place of quiet study. Dr. Wasserstein turned back to face her, dark eyes intense.

"You know, people are always labouring under the misconception that Voodoo is a violent religion. It isn't. I mean, yes, they kill goats and chickens and so on, and use the blood in their rituals, but the animals are not treated any worse than the ones we eat every day. Probably a good deal better. Did you find animal bones near the bodies?"

"I'd rather not tell you anything about the bodies until you look at something else. I don't want to prejudice your opinion." Delorme pulled out the photographs of the hieroglyphics. "Can you tell me anything about these?"

Dr. Wasserstein took the photos and examined them in the window light.

"Oh, these are *interesting*. I haven't seen any of these, except in the journals. You found these in Algonquin Bay?"

"In the woods just outside town. We know they're not old."

"No, they wouldn't be. Not in this hemisphere."

"What can you tell us about them?"

"Well, they're not Native, I can tell you that right off. I'm sure Frank Izzard told you the same thing."

"He did."

"Did you find any shells near these markings? Tiny shells? Multicoloured?"

"Yes, we did. What makes you say that?"

"They're not hieroglyphics at all, these markings. What they are is a record of divining the future. Fortune-telling. A witch or priest or shaman—whatever term you prefer—tells the future by tossing cowrie shells and reading their patterns. These marks, the arrows pointing in different directions and so on, are a recording of particular throws of the shells. Different coloured shells get different representations—the hammer for the green ones, for example, the hatchet for the red. They look a little sinister, especially if they're connected to a crime, but in themselves they're actually quite harmless. They answer all the usual questions, you know—is there money coming? Romance? A promotion? They're no worse than astrology. But tell me something else: Did you find any longish sticks nearby? Sticks that look like they had been cut to one length?"

"Yes, we found a few. They were all discoloured at one end. We're still waiting to hear back from forensics on what they were discoloured with."

"Probably blood. *Palos*, they're called."

"Are you telling me it's Voodoo, after all?"

"It's Palo Mayombe."

"What did you call it?"

"Palo Mayombe." Dr. Wasserstein spelled it for her. "It's a relative of Santeria and Voodoo. Much more mysterious, maybe more frightening. We don't actually know too much about it. Like Voodoo, it is used primarily to read the future, and then to adjust the future by invoking the help of particular *orishas*—these are conflations of African spirits with Christian saints. They have different spheres of influence. Ellegua for crossroads, Oggun for iron or metal, that sort of thing."

"How do you invoke them?"

"You make offerings. Offerings related to their jurisdiction. Ellegua likes sweet things, for example. Oggun wants iron, metal."

"Would a railway spike fit the bill?"

"Definitely. Railway spike, horseshoe . . . anything like that."

"Who practises this stuff?"

"In Canada? No one. This is the first I've heard of it here. It comes originally from the Ibo, the Bantu and the Kikongo, tribes primarily found in Nigeria and Congo. We know that it was widely practised in the nineteenth century. Many members of those tribes were brought over to the western hemisphere as slaves, and they brought their religion with them."

"Where in the western hemisphere?"

"Cuba, almost entirely. So, if I were looking for someone deep into Palo Mayombe, I'd be looking for someone from Cuba—or maybe Miami, for obvious reasons. You might find traces of it in Mexico, but really Cuba's the current cauldron for this stuff."

"Cuba. And you're certain this has nothing to do with Native Canadians."

"Nothing whatsoever."

There was a silence. Dr. Wasserstein said, "What? You're looking perplexed."

"You said this Palo Mayombe is more mysterious than Voodoo. Maybe more frightening. Why did you say that?"

"Well, like Voodoo, it involves the usual animal sacrifices. But when it comes to Palo Mayombe, there are many references to human sacrifice. Tales of people mutilated before they were killed."

"One of our murder victims had his hands and feet cut off. And we haven't found his head, either."

"Oh, dear God." Dr. Wasserstein placed a palm on her chest. "How terrifying."

"Yeah. We want to stop him before he does this to anyone else."

"Well, for the sake of accuracy, I should tell you that these days, when it comes to Palo Mayombe, there is a lot of discussion about what is the truth. Defenders of Mayombe make a number of points: First, all of the references to human sacrifice come from missionaries. People whose sole motivation for being in Africa was to convert the populace to Christianity. Historically, the method of choice was to frighten people—thus, you get the pagan gods of old being transformed into devils, figures of pure evil.

"Second point. There's nothing wrong with human sacrifice per se. Jesus Christ was a human sacrifice, sanctioned by God himself. Also, we honour soldiers who give their lives in the cause of defending their country. What are they, if not human sacrifices?

"Three. They say if there was human sacrifice, it was—as in the cases I've just cited—completely voluntary."

Delorme regarded the curator. Despite the bobbed hair and the hip T-shirt, the discussion of violence seemed to have aged her.

"You're very pale," Delorme said. "Are you all right?"

"Yes. Yes, I'm fine. Just a bit—well, what you told me . . ." Dr. Wasserstein shook her head as if she could fling the brutal images away.

"What I was saying—it's all very well for defenders of Mayombe to say the witnesses of such things were prejudiced, or had something to gain by making it up. That's true, as far as it goes. But these were Jesuits, most of them, and their references are not in tracts or the texts of sermons. They occur in their relations of events they sent back to their superiors in the order—in other words, there was no need to frighten anyone. They were just reporting to head office what they were up against.

"Also, they made similar reports about North America. We know that the Iroquois tortured Father Brébeuf horribly and cut his heart out. The Hurons performed similar atrocities on their enemies. And we know these accounts are true."

"And the mutilation?"

"Oh, it's ghastly. There are two elements involved. First, there is the desire to inflict as much pain as possible. The reason being, that if you have your victim screaming and begging for his life, then you can control his spirit in the afterworld. You can command him to go here and there for you, learn things for you, do things for you. It's a belief common to many pagan religions.

"The mutilation follows from this. In order for the spirit to get around and do these things for you, he needs feet to travel, fingers to feel or grasp, perhaps even a brain to understand. So the shaman cuts these off and tosses them into a cauldron. In the case of Palo Mayombe, the cauldron is stirred with a number of sticks or *palos* in order to keep control of the spirit. After you have created it, it then needs fresh blood to keep working for you."

"That's not good news," Delorme said. "You're telling me there'll likely be more sacrifices."

"Unfortunately, yes."

"And yet a lot of people don't see it as anything other than a harmless variant of Voodoo?"

"That's right. Personally, I happen to think they are wrong. I believe the Jesuits on this one. And anyway, you have a mutilated body on your hands, you have the *palos* and you have the cowrie shells. So either you are dealing with a priest of Palo Mayombe who is following the ancient beliefs, or you're dealing with someone who has hideously perverted those beliefs. Either way, you've got a monster on your hands."

42

THE OFFICE WAS GETTING to Cardinal. McLeod was yelling at some lawyer on the phone. Across the room, Szelagy was whistling again, although he had been told twice already to can it. And someone else was pounding a fist on the photocopy machine as if that would encourage it to perform.

No wonder I like working with Delorme, Cardinal thought. She's the only person in this room who is actually pleasant to be around. Except that Delorme wasn't in the room just then; her desk was empty. She was chasing the hieroglyphics.

Cardinal had signed out a large crate of material from the evidence room, and was going through it piece by piece, pulling things out and setting them on his desk. Some were items found at the scene of Wombat Guthrie's murder, which was also, he was beginning to suspect, the place where Terri Tait had been shot. There was the odd collection of straight sticks, now returned from the forensic centre, which had confirmed that the discoloured ends had been dipped in blood, both animal and human. DNA results were still incomplete. Then there was the plaster cast of the tire track from the Tilley scene. Collingwood had determined that it was from a Bridgestone RE 71, the kind of tire you'd put on a muscle car, possibly a Trans Am.

He reached into the box and pulled out the silver locket. He sprung the clasp and looked at the tiny photo inside. Handsome couple in their mid-forties, the man in uniform. Definitely military, but it was impossible to tell in this miniature black and white whether he was air force or not. Cardinal found a magnifying glass and held the photo under his desk lamp. He was pretty sure he could see a resemblance between the woman and Terri Tait.

"Cardinal!"

It was Detective Sergeant Chouinard at the door in his fedora.

"Someone out front to see you! Tell the duty sergeant when he gets back I'm not the damn doorman around here."

Cardinal went out to the front desk, where the pale, boneless features of Dr. Filbert broke into a smile.

"I took a chance coming over without phoning. I figured homicide, someone has to be working late. I tried Detective Arsenault but he's not around."

"What can I do for you?"

"I have some DNA results for you." He held up a sheaf of papers; they looked like a computer printout.

"DNA results? We didn't leave you any DNA."

"If you have a minute, I'll explain."

Cardinal led him into the squad room. He pulled over Delorme's chair for Dr. Filbert to sit in.

Dr. Filbert perched on the edge of it, hands clasped on his lap.

"I believe I can now definitely link your second body to your first body."

"With the maggot casing we left you? But it could have been tracked there from the site of a dead fox, a dead dog. A dead anything."

"That is no longer true, Detective." Filbert waved the printout. "We've now got the same DNA at both sites."

"I don't understand. Whose DNA?"

"The fly's."

Cardinal knew he was tired, but could he really be missing some obvious logic here? He restrained himself from banging on his temples. Instead, he just said, "You did a DNA analysis on the maggot casing we gave you? You can get DNA just from the casing?"

"Sure. You can get DNA from pretty much anything these days."

"But why did you? We already have the *species*. We know it couldn't have come from the second site. Why bother to determine the species all over again with DNA, when you've already done it with the—"

"No, no. I'm not talking about the *species*. I'm talking about the individual *fly*. The individual DNA from this casing matches the individual DNA from the first site. The maggot that came out of this casing has the same mother as dozens of other eggs at the first site."

"You matched the DNA of individual flies?"

Dr. Filbert nodded vigorously, a motion that blurred his rubbery face. "It was easy. Well, it would have been a lot easier with an egg rather than a casing, but I managed to make do. I use a machine called an MJ Research Engine. Takes about twenty-four hours."

"How can you do it that fast? We give DNA samples to forensics in Toronto, it takes them ten days minimum. We're waiting for some right now."

"I have a distinct advantage. I've spent the last six months doing nothing but building up a gigantic background dataset. I know the statistical variations for this area inside out. So my search is already narrowed down. Instead of looking for a needle in a haystack, I'm looking for a needle in, I don't know, a file drawer."

"This is terrific work," Cardinal said. "I had no idea you could do this."

"Anyone could. Well, you know. A lot of people."

"I doubt that very much, Dr. Filbert. Thank you so much for putting in the time."

"Oh, it was my pleasure. It was fun."

When Filbert was gone, Cardinal logged the vial into the evidence room and left the printout on Arsenault's desk. If they ever brought in a suspect, this evidence would be courtroom gold.

He sat down at his desk and wrote a few lines about Filbert in his notebook, looking up at the clock to note the time. Nearly eight, and he still hadn't had dinner. He wondered what Catherine had done about dinner, where she had gone. One of her favourite things about Toronto was the great variety of restaurants; she had a far more adventurous palate than Cardinal. He hadn't managed to speak to her the last time he'd called. He hoped she had just been in the shower or out taking some night shots, but there was a small ache in his chest that always lodged there when he began to worry about his wife.

His phone rang, and for a split second he was sure it was Catherine, but then he saw the call was not on his direct-dial line.

"Cardinal, CID."

"Oh. Hello. Um, I'm not sure how to proceed with this . . ." A woman's voice, maybe forties, vaguely familiar.

"My name is Christine Nadeau. Your wife's student? We met the other morning."

"Oh, yes, sure. I remember." Cardinal kept his voice even, but his heart was sinking. After more than twenty-five years of marriage to Catherine, he had lost count of how many phone calls like this there had been. The first chemicals of fear entered his bloodstream. From somewhere in his lapsed-Catholic heart, the old prayer started up: Please, God, let her be all right.

"Well, um, I really don't know how to put this. And I hope you won't think badly of me for calling. I want to assure you it's only out of concern for Catherine. I mean, she's a wonderful photographer and a great teacher. This is the third course I've taken with her."

"Okay. Why don't you just tell me what's going on?" Please, God, don't let it be too awful. "Is she all right?"

"Well, no. Not exactly. I mean, I don't think so. I talked to two of the other students and one of them thought I shouldn't call and the other one thought I should, so anyway . . .

"She's been acting a little strange the last day and a half or so. The way it's set up, we all meet at a particular place in the morning, spend a couple of hours shooting, then get together for lunch. Well, the other day we met at an old cement factory, and usually Catherine's just all nuts-and-bolts, you know: What are the challenges the setting presents, what are the opportunities, and how should we go about it?

"But yesterday morning she started getting really worked up about provincial politics and energy policy and nuclear power and all this stuff, and it was like she was running for office or something—she just went off on this tirade. I'm sorry if that sounds mean . . ."

"Did anyone try to get her back on topic?" Cardinal said. "To focus?"

"Well, I did. The sun was still very low behind the factory towers and I asked her a question about backlighting and silhouettes. She just skipped right over it and started going on and on about Queen's Park and how reality had to be spelled out to them. I realize this doesn't sound so drastic—I mean, people do have passionate opinions."

"But it was inappropriate, you're saying."

"Completely. And totally out of character. I'm sure Catherine has her politics, but it's never come up before in the classes I've done with her. I've spent time in the darkroom with her, and it's always about the work. That's one of the reasons she's great. She's absolutely committed to the work. And so dependable."

That's Catherine, Cardinal thought. When she's well.

"Is she eating?"

"I was getting to that. The day after we got here, she seemed to start living on milkshakes. I mean, literally. She's calling them breakfast of champions. I don't think she's eating anything except those and some vitamin pills."

"Has she had any alcohol, do you know?"

"Not much. Not that I've seen. A couple of glasses of wine the other night, and boy, did that get her going. Not like she was drunk. Quite the reverse. She got very serious and very high energy. I mean, I was dead on my feet, but not Catherine. She wanted to go out and shoot more pictures, and I believe she did. I don't think she's sleeping very much, if at all. I have to tell you, some of the students are going to complain to Northern. I wouldn't dream of doing that, but they are paying for this trip, and she's supposed to be teaching, not—"

"Do you know where she is right now?"

"I don't, I'm afraid. That's why I'm calling. She was supposed to have dinner with us—a quiet dinner with just a couple of us—but she didn't show and she didn't answer in her hotel room."

"All right. Let me give you my cellphone number. Do you have a pen?" He gave her the number, and also his home number. "If you see her, please ask her to call me right away. I'm going to come down there."

"Really? To Toronto? You think it's that serious? I didn't mean to cause a major upset, I just—"

"No, no. I'm very grateful you called. If you see her, please try to keep her in one place. Or if she takes off again, if you could stay with her and let me know where you are. I should be there in less than four hours. Can you stay up till midnight?"

"Yes, of course. I'm in room 1016 at the Chelsea. It's right next to hers, so I should hear when she comes in."

—

How many times, he asked himself, how many times will I be doing this before we die? Rain hammered at the windshield with such force that, even flapping at full speed, the wipers couldn't keep it clear. How many times have I done this? The call out of nowhere, the sudden rush into the night and the panic—the sheer panic of not knowing where Catherine is or what she's doing.

Cardinal had grabbed some takeout at a Burger King and now the car stank of hamburger. The heat of the food had fogged up the windshield. He turned the blower up, and switched on the radio. The choice of rock songs, country music or an interview with a Gaelic poet (courtesy of the CBC) was worse than the sounds of wind and rain, and he switched it off again.

The first forty miles down to South River were torment. The highway was only a single lane and the weather made passing too dangerous. Once he got to Bracebridge, the road was better and he kept the speedometer pegged at thirty over the limit. He didn't figure the OPP were going to be out in force on a night like this.

He put in a call to the Clarke Institute. Catherine had been treated there many times during their ten years in Toronto. Cardinal prayed that Dr. Jonas was still there. The emergency room told him that Dr. Jonas was indeed still on staff, but was not expected in until the next afternoon. Cardinal explained the situation and that with any luck he would be bringing Catherine in. The woman on the other end said she would call Dr. Jonas and let him know. She sounded the right notes, both professional and sympathetic, but she also sounded terribly young.

Cardinal tried to control his thoughts, tried not to worry too much. But when she was manic, Catherine was capable of terrifying things. One time, back when they were still living in Toronto and Kelly was a little girl, Catherine had set out to hitchhike to an international economic conference at Lake Couchiching. Luckily, a truck driver who had picked her up outside of Barrie realized the state she was in and had had the kindness and good sense to call the local police, who had managed to track Cardinal down in Toronto.

Another time, she had been working for nearly two years on a photographic study of homeless people. At first, she only visited them during the day, and they allowed her to photograph themselves and their makeshift homes. She had won a provincial prize for that series, and was even a finalist in a national competition. But she could not let the subject go, and embarked on a second series of photographs. That time she had disguised herself as a homeless person, and one day left home to go live with them. Other journalists had done the same at different times, but Catherine had been at the peak of a manic phase just then, only to crash when she was living under a bridge near Casa Loma. Cardinal would never forget what the sight of her did to him when he came to find her in Toronto Western's emergency ward. His Catherine—normally fastidious and glowing—hair stiff with grime, fingernails filthy and an ugly abrasion on her forehead.

In the years since, Catherine had been doing better. Sometimes she went as long as two years without having to be hospitalized. Her manic phases were much shorter, and so were her depressive phases. But they were also deeper—black, suffocating weeks during which she would hardly speak or even move. Those were the times that frightened Cardinal the most. If she ever killed herself, it wouldn't be during mania—unless by misadventure—it would be as her final release from an airless hell.

Cardinal passed the Sundial Restaurant on his left. Not much longer now. As he changed lanes to get around a semi, he could not rid himself of the thought that it was now almost exactly two years since Catherine's last stay in hospital.

—

Even near midnight, the traffic surrounding Toronto was frenetic. Highway 401 formed a permanent asteroid belt above the city. Cardinal took the Allen Road exit, and after he turned south on Bathurst his cellphone rang. Let it be Catherine. Let this horrible, familiar drama pass. Let her be calling to say everything is all right, she'll be home tomorrow night on schedule.

It was Christine Nadeau.

"I don't feel good about this," she said in a low voice. "I feel like a spy."

"What's happening?"

"I'm just coming out of the subway. The University line. Catherine came back to the hotel about an hour ago. I was hoping she'd stay in and you could just find her there when you arrived, but unfortunately—"

"Where are you now? What station?"

"Queen's Park. I'm not sure what street this is."

"College Street. What's Catherine doing?"

"She's got two cameras, one slung on either shoulder, and she's walking really fast. I don't know if I can keep up with her."

Cardinal heard her huffing and puffing into the phone.

"Stay with her. I'm south of Eglinton now, and the traffic's not bad. I should be there in ten minutes. Fifteen, tops. Can you stay with her?"

"I'll try. You know, she's not doing anything particularly weird at the moment."

"I realize that. And I hope she's fine. I'll be there soon."

"Oh, geez."

"What? What's going on?"

A screech of tires tore over the line.

"Oh, my God."

"Tell me what's happening."

"She just walked right out into traffic. Just walked straight out in front of this SUV. Thank God the guy swerved in time. Catherine didn't even slow down. I don't think she even saw him."

"Stay with her. I'll be right there."

Bathurst was relatively clear. Cardinal passed St. Clair and then Dupont without much trouble.

The cellphone rang again.

"She's gone into some construction site. I don't know how she did it. She got a little ahead of me and there's all these hoardings. I think she may have squeezed between a couple of boards somewhere."

"You can't follow her?"

"Um, no. I'm not sure where she—"

"Where are you, exactly?"

"Um, the corner of Queen and University."

"Two minutes."

Cardinal tossed the phone aside. He took Harbord over to Queen's Park Crescent. He crossed College, and then he was on University. He had a red light at Dundas, and then there was Queen.

He spotted Christine Nadeau—a tall woman in a long raincoat—on the southwest corner. She was at the opening of a pedestrian walkway beneath a vast wall of scaffolding. Cardinal pulled over and left his hazard lights flashing.

"She has to be in there," she said, and gestured toward the construction site with her thumb. "I wasn't more than twenty yards behind her. But I can't figure out how she got inside."

"If there's a way in, Catherine will find it."

"Is there anything else I can do? I mean, I think maybe I shouldn't be here when you bring her out. I'm feeling pretty guilty about following her like this."

"Don't worry. You did the right thing. I really appreciate it."

"All right, then. Good luck." She turned away and headed toward the subway.

Cardinal approached the pedestrian walkway. A series of rectangular holes had been cut into the hoardings, windows onto the construction site for the curious. Cardinal peered through the highest one.

The site was gigantic, though at this point it was little more than a concrete pit with girders rising into the sky.

A shadow moved on one of the girders, and then there was a sudden gleam: light catching on a lens.

Cardinal hurried along the walkway, his footsteps echoing down the wooden corridor. A little further along there was a chain-link fence, and Cardinal saw at once the spot where Catherine had found entry. There was barbed wire along the top of the chain-link, but it stopped at the edge of the hoardings. It took Cardinal about thirty seconds to scale the fence and pull himself on top of the walkway.

Catherine had moved. He couldn't see her anywhere. There were only a few lights on the site, and the moon had slipped behind heavy cloud. His greatest fear was that Catherine would find some way to get the construction platforms moving—a generator with the keys still in it—and end up on top of this massive steel skeleton.

He ran to the end of the platform and jumped down onto the back of a parked flatbed. There was a ledge about the width of a country road surrounding the pit, and from this there were several bridges to the floors under construction.

Cardinal stepped onto the closest bridge. The sink and sway of the planking unmoored his stomach. The pit was deeper than it had looked from outside; there were at least six underground storeys for future parking. A cement truck at the bottom looked like a Dinky Toy.

"Hello, John."

Her voice was soft. You could never predict how she'd be at any given time on one of her highs. Now she spoke so gently it was like hearing from a benevolent figure in a dream.

Cardinal looked up.

Catherine was a silhouette two storeys above him, the night breeze whipping her hair round her face. Before he could speak, the moon reappeared, and Catherine's face was ghostly white. She was standing on the promontory of a single I-beam above an eight-storey drop.

"Isn't it extraordinary?"

"Catherine, would you move back onto the floor, please?"

"There's something so perfect about a building under construction. You get to see the skull beneath the skin, as it were. That's just the engineering angle, of course. Then there's the human aspect: You know how when you look at an old arrowhead, or a piece of Roman wall, and you have the sense that a man's hands made that? Thousands of years ago, a man who sweated and bled and breathed just like you and me, for some time focused his attention on this brick, this stone, this little piece of rock—or in the case at hand—this girder."

She stamped her foot on the I-beam for emphasis and tottered a little.

"Catherine, please. Move back to the floor."

Cardinal found the temporary wooden staircase and began climbing up. As he reached the next level, Catherine spun around on the beam and put one foot in front of the other in a kind of flamenco move.

"Catherine, please. Try to focus on the here and now. It's a long way to the ground, and despite how good you may feel—"

"I feel fucking great!" She threw her head back and laughed. "I want to feel like this all the time—tiptoe on the bones of something tremendous, an about-to-be skyscraper. The power of this place!"

"Catherine, the reason you feel so great is that your medication is off balance. Try and remember, sweetheart.

This always comes just before a terrible down. So let's not wait for that, let's get you to the doctor now, and try to get you in for a smooth landing."

"Oh, John. John." Her tone was pitying. "If only you could hear yourself, you would never say anything like that to me."

Cardinal climbed the last of the steps; he was on her level, now. He moved toward her slowly, tamping down the fear in his chest.

"As I was saying," she went on, "before I was so rudely interrupted: An unfinished building is a testament of hope. It's optimism set in concrete and steel. Two thousand years from now, some man, some woman—some android, maybe—will look at this beam (no doubt by then collapsed in a heap of dust) and wonder about the man who slotted it into place. What will they think? This beam, this hunk of plain old steel, will form a bridge across time. Will they wonder if a woman—perhaps a woman slightly crazy (a little off her meds, according to her oh-so-prosaic husband)—balanced on it with a couple of cameras on her shoulder and thought of them, two thousand years in the future? We're riding a time machine. Hold on tight and it'll zap us into the year 5000."

"Honey, come over here to me."

"Why? It's thrilling out here. You have no idea of the creative rush I'm feeling."

"Catherine, listen. Your medication is out of whack and you're high. It's the same as if someone stuck a needle in your arm. It's making you do dangerous things."

"Risky things. Risk isn't always bad, John. Where would we be if no one ever risked anything? The fireman rushing into the burning building, the surgeon going after the tumour, Van Gogh painting with his brush of fire?"

"Come to me, honey. You're frightening me."

"John Cardinal admits to fear. Who would have thought? Well, I'm not afraid." Catherine spun again on the beam, and threw her hands wide like Liza Minnelli belting out a song. She shouted so that the words echoed off steel and concrete and, for all Cardinal knew, down the surrounding city blocks. "Let it hereby be known by those here present and all those who fall within my assizes and demesnes that I, Catherine Eleanor Cardinal, do hereby banish and expel from my kingdom—make that queen-dom—all species of fear, trepidation, timidity, anxiety and hesitation, of whatsoever kind or designation, henceforth and forever. Let no man—nay, nor woman—import, carry or otherwise transport any speck of fear to the merest angstrom unit, on pain of a bloody good spanking."

"Catherine."

She spun around again, almost fell. Cardinal cried out, but Catherine righted herself and scowled at him.

"Listen to me, John. I'm not a child. I'm not your ward, I'm your wife. I am a sentient human being. I am a creature of volition. I do what I want, when I want. I don't need a keeper and I don't need a fucking leash. So if you can't enjoy my company the way it is, why don't you get the fuck out of here and head right straight back to Algonquin fucking Bay."

Cardinal sat on the edge of the concrete flooring, though it sent a trembling into his thighs to do so.

"Come and sit beside me, sweetheart. I'm here because I love you. No other reason."

"Love doesn't mean *own*. You want to snap your fingers and have me at your heel."

This was the worst of it. Cardinal could almost take the life-threatening behaviour. He could almost take the sudden disappearances, the wild claims, the theatrical gestures. But what crushed his spirit was how, when she was like this, Catherine could turn on him and throw his love back in his face.

"Will you come and sit by me?" he said. "It's a request, not a command, not a demand." He held up his empty hands. "No leash."

"You're just afraid I'll fall off."

"No, honey. I'm terrified. Come and sit down."

Catherine looked around, taking in the sky, the moon, the pit below. She wobbled a little.

"Jesus," she said. "It's true, what they say about looking down."

"Look at me," Cardinal said. "Just keep your eyes on me and come this way."

Catherine raised a camera to eye level. "Oh, you look so handsome sitting there. Yes, a little tighter shot, I think. And a tripod would help. *Man on a Ledge*. Although I have to say that man is looking pretty tired of me just about now."

She clicked the shutter. Then she slung the camera back on her shoulder and walked toward him, but didn't sit down. She went straight to the wooden steps and climbed down. Cardinal followed her, down the steps, down the second set, and back across the wooden platform. Thinking, Who's the puppy dog here? Who's the one on the leash?

She got into the car without further protest, but only those who have lived with mental illness can know the anguish of what followed: the accusations and recriminations, the insults hurled and retracted, the endless negotiations—argument and counter-argument—and, above all, the tears. Catherine's cheeks were slick and shining with them—tears of frustration, tears of rage, tears of sorrow and regret and humiliation.

Cardinal, already tired from a full day's work and facing a long drive home, was utterly exhausted by it. Catherine, high on adrenalin and a powerful cocktail of brain chemicals known and unknown, seemed almost to thrive, despite the tears. As a policeman, of course, Cardinal had had to deal with all sorts of characters in varying degrees of mental stability and emotional chaos. In such circumstances, the most reliable weapons in the cop's arsenal were a firm voice and a backup paramedic wielding a needle full of diazepam. But he could not bring himself to use these on the woman he had loved since he was a young man. She had to be able to face him when she came back to earth. And so, the endless negotiations.

Cardinal drove them round and round the central city blocks, presenting himself as the voice of pure reason. He knew from long experience with Catherine that there came a time in her highs, a sort of evening hour shortly before sleep—if she were still able to sleep—when she could be reached. Physical fatigue quieted the stormier edges of her mind, and she could sometimes even hear what he was trying to say.

In the end, after their fifteenth circle around a quiet and bleak Queen's Park, she agreed to go with him to the hospital. He drove back down to College Street and took her to the emergency entrance of the Clarke Institute.

The wait was long, but not nearly as long as at a regular hospital: Half of the cases the Clarke gets are transfers from other institutions, or people brought in by police or social workers, and admissions tend to go smoothly. And Cardinal was lucky in another way: As the triage nurse was leading them to an examining room, he heard a familiar voice sing out: "Catherine?"

Dr. Carl Jonas was coming across the emergency ward toward them, clipboard in hand, grey locks flowing. "Why, Catherine. They told me you might be coming in tonight. What brings you back here?"

Catherine turned toward his pink, kind face and burst into a fresh cascade of tears.

43

KEVIN TAIT, PERHAPS MORE than most men his age, had wide experience with emotional ups and downs—being a junkie, even an intermittent one, will do that to you. First, there is the omnipresent guilt that is the addict's lot, whether his drug be heroin, alcohol, chocolate or sex. Then there's the constant fear of getting caught—caught using, caught buying, caught selling, thieving, lying, betraying. The fear of arrest was such a constant that there seemed no remedy for it other than the next needle. And when dealing, there was the fear of rivals who might take violent exception to his horning in on their territory. Kevin had almost wet his pants one night in Toronto, when a sometime Hells Angel had threatened to kill him. But that was nothing—that was low-grade anxiety—compared to the black drug of terror that now coursed through his veins.

He regained consciousness curled up on a rough wooden floor. There was very little light, but he knew immediately which cabin it was by the smell; it caused him to vomit the moment he woke up. His skull throbbed, and he knew his scalp was split because his face was sticky with blood.

His hands were tied behind his back, his feet tied together. He tried to get to his knees and fell forward in agony. That would be the wound in his side from the pitchfork. That was probably what had bashed him on the head, too. He curled up again on the floor and waited for the pain to subside.

The pain did recede after a while, but what did not attenuate in any degree was the unbelievable smell of this place. Thick and soupy, the air pressed a filthy finger into the back of his throat and held it there, wiggled it every time he moved, as if the air itself were composed of vomit.

When, eventually, he did manage to get to his feet, the cabin swung and tilted under him so that he toppled and fell hard. The wound in his side hurt like hell. It took many tries before he stood more or less upright, leaning against a table. The only light in the room seeped through the cracks between the planks of the floor and walls.

A large iron cauldron, big enough to hold twenty or thirty gallons, sat on the table. Plump flies buzzed around it. Sticks perhaps a yard long bristled out of the top, leaning at all angles. One hop toward the cauldron verified that that was where the horrific stench was coming from. There was no way Kevin was going to look inside.

He wondered how long he had been unconscious. He was not hungry, but that didn't mean anything—the stench would take care of that. Besides, loss of appetite was one of the first signs of heroin withdrawal. Goosebumps were another. He had those, too; he could feel them stippling his arms and the skin over his rib cage. Soon he would be in the full throes of cold turkey.

He turned to face a long table, hoping there would be tools of some kind, something he could use to untie his hands. Filthy newspapers were spread all over it, stained brown with what he figured by the smell had once been blood. He was hoping to God it was not human. He turned his back to the table, leaned forward and clamped his jaws tight against the waves of nausea that roared through him. Then, using his tied hands, he tugged the newspapers away from the table. Please, God, let there be a knife, scissors, a nail file, anything I can use to get the hell out of here. But when he turned around again, there was nothing.

44

THE PINK SHELLS CONGREGATED in a tiny heap off to one side. Others, periwinkle blue, were scattered across the console between the gearshift and the cup holders. In the middle of this, three white shells, evenly spaced, formed a miniature Orion's Belt.

Alan Clegg had been psyching himself up for this meeting with Red Bear, telling himself as he drove to the Shanley lookout that there was no need to panic, he would keep his nerves under control. He had even asked Red Bear to read the shells for him, but now he couldn't sit still. Just having Red Bear in his Chevy Blazer was rubbing his nerves raw.

"We're gonna have to call it quits," he said. "The locals have got two murders on their books and they're not about to let them just sit there."

Red Bear made some notes on a piece of graph paper—arrows pointing this way and that, crossed hammers, a lightning bolt, all in a column. He gathered the shells and shook them again. Apparently he hadn't heard.

"Look," Clegg said, "the dope is one thing. I got nothing against ripping off bikers. And I don't mind making a
dollar off moving some junk that sooner or later is going
to find its way into addicts' arms, anyway. Jerks deserve
whatever they get. But you got two murders on your back,
man, and they're not going anywhere good. Christ, if I'd
have known you were gonna start murdering people right
and left—"

"Shut up, please."

"What did you say to me?"

"I said shut up, please. You are not helping."

Red Bear was bent over the shells, his long hair all but
obscuring them. The pink ones were all together again,
the blue scattered, the white seeming to form an eye and
nose in a pink-and-blue face. Clegg wanted to shake him.

"Red Bear, listen: Wombat Guthrie was chopped into
bits and pieces. That's not something the local force can
ignore. They're going to throw everything they've got at
it. Same with Toof. They're not going to stop until they
put somebody behind bars. What the hell did you kill
them for?"

"Who says I killed them?"

Red Bear made another few notations on his graph
paper. Then he looked over at Clegg, his gaze mildly curious. "Has somebody come forward and said I killed
them?"

"No. But we both know who—"

Red Bear grabbed Clegg's wrist and squeezed.

"We know no such thing. Have you forgotten the readings I've done for you? There is nothing that has tran-
spired here that was not foretold in the shells. Did I not

tell you we were going to do well? Did I not say that the Viking Riders' fortunes were going to fall?"

"Falling fortunes is one thing. Wombat Guthrie had his fucking toes and fingers hacked off."

Red Bear squeezed harder.

"Is your courage failing? Are you backing out on me? I sincerely hope for your sake you're not planning to change your allegiance. Perhaps you are already working for the Viking Riders. Playing both sides at once."

Clegg felt a strong urge to punch him, but he didn't want to end up like Guthrie. He yanked his wrist away.

"You know I'm not working for the Riders. I helped you pull off the biggest rip-off in their history. And don't change the subject. You killed Toof, for Chrissake. You didn't have to do that."

"Really." Red Bear sat back. "This is very interesting, coming from you. In case you've forgotten, you were the one who told me Toof was a problem. 'You have to deal with him,' you said. 'Toof is telling stories around the neighbourhood.' Well, let me tell you something, my friend. Toof is dealt with. End of story."

"No, it's not the end of the story. I'm a Mountie, remember? I cover narcotics and I have a supervisor and I have two Algonquin Bay police officers asking questions about Morris Tilley and Wombat Guthrie. I can't keep pretending I don't know anything. They're tight with my sarge, and if I hold back on them they're going to find out and that's gonna blow this whole thing sky-high."

"What did you tell them?"

Red Bear's voice was barely audible. This would call for careful wording.

"They've been questioning Toof's associates," Clegg said. "They got your name from them. Also Leon's. They know we arrested Leon a few years ago. They asked me mostly about him. I told them exactly what's on his sheet, nothing more."

"And what did you tell them about me?"

"Nothing. I didn't have to because they don't have anything on you. I just said I'd heard your name around. Heard you were from somewhere up north and hadn't been seen for a while."

"I may indeed head up north," Red Bear said. "When I'm ready."

"There's something else."

"Oh?"

"Yeah. The two Algonquin Bay cops I was talking to—Cardinal and Delorme—they were very hot on this gun that killed Toof. They know Guthrie stole it—that links him and Toof to the same killer. But they said the gun was also recently used in an assault."

"What did they tell you about it?"

"Nothing. Delorme—she's female. Good-looking, too, if you want to know the truth. Delorme started to tell me about it, but Cardinal stopped her. That means they're keeping this strictly under wraps for some reason."

"Such as?"

"They said 'assault.' They didn't say 'murder.' That says to me the victim is still alive—a witness, in other words. But they're keeping the identity secret. I know there was nothing in the papers linking the gun to another attack. They're trying to protect him, obviously."

"Her," Red Bear said.

"What?"

"Her. It was a woman who saw something she shouldn't. But don't worry, we are taking care of it."

"Don't for God's sake go killing anybody else. The heat's already way too high on this thing. You got the cops on one side, you got the Viking Riders on the other. The Riders are not going to take this lying down."

"Alan, listen to me." Red Bear took hold of Clegg's bicep and this time gave it a reassuring squeeze. "You worry too much. I will not do anything that would put you in danger. We are on the same side, remember?"

45

"WHAT THE HELL HAPPENED to you?" Delorme wanted to know. "You look like hell."

"I'm fine," Cardinal said. In fact, he hadn't slept. By the time he had driven all the way back to Algonquin Bay it wasn't worth going to bed, so he had taken a shower, made some breakfast and driven straight back to work.

"Really, John. You look like you've got the flu or something."

"Thanks, Lise. You're making my day."

Cardinal's phone rang, and he snatched it up.

"Cardinal. CID."

"It's Terri Tait calling."

"Can you speak up? I can hardly hear you."

"It's Terri Tait. I just . . . I've remembered some things. Last night. I had a nightmare and I got some more memory back. Are you going to be there in the next little while? Can I come and talk to you?"

"No, don't come here. It's not safe for you to go out. We'll come and see you at the Crisis Centre."

"I was really hoping to escape this place for a while."

"I know, but it's just not safe. So hang in there and we'll see you soon."

Cardinal hung up.

"Terri Tait," he said. "She's remembering more. And look at this." He showed Delorme the locket he had signed out of the evidence room. "Terri's father was a wing commander up at the air base. I want to show her this, because I'm betting this is her locket and these are her parents."

Delorme took the locket and sprung the catch. "You mean she was shot in the same place where Wombat was murdered? Why would the guy go back to the same spot?"

"It's not unheard of. Maybe it's part of the ritual. Maybe she showed up where she shouldn't have. Tell me what happened with the cave markings."

Delorme filled him in on her talk with the OPP and her visit with Dr. Wasserstein in Algonquin Park. She told him about Palo Mayombe, its belief in human sacrifice, the macabre ways its followers sought to control the spirits.

"Dr. Wasserstein says it's mostly practised in Cuba. Maybe a little in Miami."

"Presumably it'll travel wherever immigrants take it. You know what I don't get?"

"What?"

"Here we have a guy who's chopping off fingers and toes. Cutting off heads. I think we can be sure this isn't something you just jump right into. You work your way up to it. You start with goats and chickens or whatever and then you try your first human and probably you mess it up, and then you try again, and then maybe it becomes your life."

"You're right. This guy, he should have a history. But we haven't come up with any uncleared murders nationally or provincially that resemble Wombat's."

"Right," Cardinal said. "But if this guy comes from Cuba or Miami, maybe there'll be something in the States."

"We don't have access to their records."

"I made some contacts in New York last year on the Matlock case. Let me give them a call."

"Or I could try Musgrave. The Mounties share information with the States all the time."

"We'll do both. See who gets lucky first. But right now, let's go see Terri."

———

Terri Tait had finished her breakfast at the Crisis Centre— a bowl of oatmeal with the consistency of wallpaper paste. Down the hall, two women were quarrelling over a radio program, and on the second floor a young mother was wailing because her children had been taken away by the Children's Aid Society; she'd been wailing since the previous afternoon.

Terri didn't want to sit in the TV room with the other women. They were always watching the most wretched talk shows. She went back to her room and sat by the window, opening the sketch pad Dr. Paley had given her. She tried to draw, but she was too tense and her hand couldn't control the pencil properly.

Terri couldn't stand it any more; hell with waiting around for the cops. She tossed the sketch pad aside. She would get out into the fresh air for twenty minutes or so. If they showed up while she was gone and had to wait a few minutes, it would serve them right for keeping her cooped up here.

The layout of the city was beginning to feel familiar, but she couldn't remember many individual street names: Main, Macintosh, Oak—that was about it. She followed the smell of water down to the lakefront. She walked along a brick-work path, with the waves crashing noisily a few feet below.

Early summer seemed to have retreated to spring. A massive dark cloud shaped like a rolling pin was lowering over the far shore, and she could see a deep grey cross-hatching of rain advancing over the waves. She had never seen so many whitecaps. She held one hand behind her head, trying to keep her hood on, but it wasn't very effective. When the rain struck her face, it was icy cold. A sea-gull circled overhead and cried long and loud.

A good part of Terri was tempted to head back to Vancouver and just hope that whoever shot her would never see her again. But that would leave her brother at the mercy of his addiction and a madman. She'd struck out trying to find him by questioning dope fiends; they don't respond well to questions. And so she was left with the cops. The trick was how to use them to save Kevin, without Kevin getting thrown in prison for trafficking. With what she was now remembering about Red Bear, Kevin might even get put away for much worse.

During the night there had been a crack of thunder, and she had sat bolt upright in bed with her heart pounding, sweat pouring off her. In the dream, it had been broad daylight, the sun blinding, sweat stinging her eyes. And in her ears, an annoying buzzing.

The noise took her behind the white cabins and into the woods. Close by, the crash of waves (yes, that could mean this very lake; not many lakes get surf like that), and farther off, a constant buzzing. She kept looking behind her; the sensation of someone following was strong, but whenever she turned to look there were only trees.

She came to a clearing and another cabin, white but covered with specks—specks that seemed to shimmer and shift in the sunlight. The windows were boarded up. The buzzing was much louder, and she could see now that the buzzing was from the swarms of flies that formed shifting veils over the cabin.

There was a noise from inside, and she shrank back into the woods. She hid behind a bush, hoping her red hair wouldn't show. Red Bear came out, carrying a small hatchet. He looked around, almost as if sniffing the wind, then turned and closed the door. He crossed the clearing and came right toward Terri. She held her breath as he went by, twigs snapping under his feet.

When she was quite sure he was gone, she went up the cabin steps and opened the door. She choked on the stench and, at that moment, knew that this was not a dream; she knew, even in her sleep, that this was a memory she was reliving. She never could have dreamed a smell like that.

She left the door open for air, and also so she could see. She had no intention of staying longer than thirty seconds, just long enough to find out whatever it was that

Red Bear was up to. Kevin was so hopelessly wired he couldn't see anything wrong with Red Bear, or didn't want to, but she had the sense of something deeply wrong with Red Bear from their first meeting. Those dead eyes. If she could show Kevin proof of what Red Bear was, then he would believe her, he would come home with her. Of course, she didn't know exactly what Red Bear was, nor was she prepared for what she found.

That huge iron pot across the cabin. There were several long branches sticking out of it. Terri forced herself to cross the cabin and peer over the rim, holding her breath. The black, murky liquid looked as foul as a sewer, but she couldn't see anything below the surface. She took hold of one of the sticks and gave it a stir. A hairy object bobbed to the surface and rolled over in a slow twirl, revealing mouth, nose and the place where eyes used to be.

She ran. She tore through the woods behind the cabins, hoping no one would see her.

Then she was in the "guest" cabin, throwing things into her backpack. Praying that Kevin would come back so they could both get the hell out of there.

The zipper on the backpack stuck. She was tearing at it with her fingernails when the door opened and Red Bear was standing there and she let out a scream. It was probably the only time in her life she had actually screamed— a sudden, sharp outburst. It was the scream that had woken her up, not thunder. She was sitting upright in bed, soaked with sweat, the memory of Red Bear and his charnel house playing before her eyes.

She was remembering more, now.

"I didn't see anything," Terri had managed to say. "I swear." She had never heard such fear in anybody's voice, certainly not her own.

"You will not phone anyone, you won't be talking to Kevin, there won't be any goodbyes. You pack your things and you will be driven to the airport or the train station. The driver will wait with you for the train or plane. Consider yourself lucky I don't kill you. You can rest assured it is not a matter of mercy." He pointed to the sky. "It's a matter of the moon."

"I won't tell anyone," she had said. "I swear. I won't tell a soul."

"Of course you won't. That would be very bad for Kevin."

Now the rain and the wind off the lake were beginning to get to her. She had come to a decision. The best way to help Kevin was to tell Detective Cardinal everything she knew; she could describe the camp, the white cabins, the islands in the distance. He would be able to figure out where it was.

She left the brick path and turned back toward town. Three or four kids were hanging out across from the World Tavern, where they had been the other night. She crossed the street toward them.

"You find your brother yet?"

It was the big kid, the one who looked down on heroin users. Well, who didn't? She didn't recognize the other three people.

"I thought I'd try one more time."

"Man, I wish my family was that loyal."

"Your family's totally dysfunctional," a nerdy-looking boy said.

"Exactly," the big one said. "That's my point."

There was an older guy with them. Quieter. He looked at her with mild interest.

"Who you looking for?" he said. "I know everybody."

Terri told him.

"Where'd you see him last?"

"In town here." She thought it might be dangerous to mention the camp.

The guy shrugged. "I know a couple of Kevins. What's he look like?"

Terri looked at him. His bony face showed curiosity, no big deal. He didn't look dangerous. She described Kevin to him.

"Sure, I know him. In fact, I saw him this morning."

"Where!"

"You know where the Chinook Tavern is?"

Terri shook her head. "Is it far?"

"Yeah, it is. You'd have to get over to Front Street and then catch a bus out to Trout Lake. Take you an hour, hour and a half. It's a little complicated, too. Why don't I just drive you there?"

"No, that's okay. I'll find it."

"It's no big deal. I'm heading back that way now." He checked his watch. "In fact, I'm running late. So if you want the ride, you gotta come now."

He turned his back on her and headed across Oak Street toward a sleek, black car.

"Wait up," Terri said. "I'm coming with you."

She ran across the street and climbed in the passenger side. The car had one of those big engines that pushed you back into the seat with every acceleration. It smelled of leather and new carpet. As they drove through the downtown streets, the guy fired questions at her—where was she from, what did she do, had she been in town long? He seemed curious, but not pushy. A little nervous, maybe. Every once in a while, he reached up and rubbed at a small scar on his brow.

46

THEY WERE WAITING FOR the light to change. Normally, Cardinal was a patient driver, but now he was hunched in the driver's seat, cursing under his breath.

"Maybe you should go home," Delorme said. "You look exhausted."

"I'm fine. I'm just a little tired."

Delorme had seen Cardinal tired, but not like this. His face was pale and drawn, the circles under his eyes deep, and there was a bitter edge in his manner that she couldn't place. She didn't think it had anything to do with work.

"Is it Catherine?" she said.

Cardinal let out a deep sigh. All he said was, "Yeah."

"She's in hospital again?"

The light changed, and Cardinal gunned it. Not his style at all.

"You've been through these times before, John. She'll be okay, don't you think?"

"I never know how Catherine's going to be. Nearly two years, now, she's been okay. Somehow I managed to convince myself that this time it was for good."

It was the most he had ever said about his wife's illness. Lines of pain radiated across his face like stress fractures in a pane of glass. Delorme wanted to say something—she'll get better, it won't last long, try not to worry too much—but nothing was adequate, and so she went silent and that didn't seem adequate, either.

At the Crisis Centre, Ned Fellowes left them in the office while he went to get Terri. Leaning against the disused fireplace, Cardinal looked like he was going to fall asleep standing up.

"Wonder what's taking him so long," Delorme said.

Cardinal just closed his eyes.

Fellowes came back a few moments later. "It appears our young friend has gone out," he said. "She's not answering her door, she's not in the TV room, not in the dining room. And nobody's seen her for the past half-hour. I told her explicitly she should not leave the building."

"So did we," Cardinal said. "And she knew we were coming."

"Of course, she wouldn't be the first person to avoid the police."

"No, but she called us. She wanted us to come."

Fellowes pulled a ring of keys out of his desk and led them upstairs. Delorme knew the Crisis Centre well. As the only female in Criminal Investigations, she always got to escort the bruised and frightened victims of domestic quarrels to this place. The familiar smells of the carpeting and the old wood made her stomach tense up.

"As I pointed out when Terri arrived," he said, "we're not a jail. I can't keep people here against their will."

He put a key in the lock and opened the door.

"Her jacket's gone," Fellowes said.

"I think something's happened to her," Cardinal said. "She was very definite about wanting to talk to us. She knew we were coming."

Fellowes started to close the door. Cardinal held it open.

"Not without a warrant," Fellowes said. "I can't allow that."

"Ned," Delorme said, "this young woman is in danger. Somebody tried to kill her and we have every reason to think they'll try again. We can go ask for a warrant, but that's going to take half a day. That's time she may not have."

Fellowes looked at Delorme, then over at Cardinal. Delorme silently urged him to come through.

"Look," he said to Cardinal. "Why don't you and I go downstairs and discuss it. Say, for about five minutes?"

"Sounds reasonable to me," Cardinal said.

He and Fellowes headed back toward the stairs, and Delorme shut the door after them.

There wasn't much of Terri Tait in this room. It was an old-fashioned place, still with much of its oak wainscotting and heavy cornices. The walls looked like they had been papered half a dozen times before being painted their current shade of off-white. There were no clothes hanging in the closet.

Near the window, a large notebook lay on the floor. Delorme opened it and found that it wasn't a notebook; it was a sketch pad. The girl had been drawing something. Doodling bird shapes.

She opened a drawer in a small dresser. A lonely pair of socks rolled in a semicircle. There were several pairs of underwear and a bra in another, newly purchased, probably courtesy of the Crisis Centre.

On top of the dresser were a brush, a package of bandages, a nail file and a small plastic bag containing sundry toiletries, also new.

Delorme got down on her knees and checked under the bed. Nothing.

I'm striking out, Delorme thought. We need to find this girl and I'm coming up empty here. Another minute and Ned Fellowes would be hauling her out of there and she would have nothing to show for her furtive little search.

She checked the wastebasket. An old bandage, a candy bar wrapper, an empty Coke can and a folded piece of paper. Delorme spread it out on the dresser. It was another version of the doodles in the sketch pad. This one was much more detailed. It showed an eagle, with huge talons, about to lift off from a branch. It looked like the sort of thing that might decorate the wall of a hunting lodge. Why had Terri taken so much time with this? The highlighting, the cross-hatching, the detailed beak and feathers. Surely she must have other things on her mind.

Delorme tucked it into her inside pocket and went back downstairs. She shook her head at Cardinal as she entered the office. No need to mention her removal of the drawing to Fellowes.

"A one-time-only occurrence, you two," Fellowes said.

"Last thing I need is to get a reputation for letting the cops snoop through people's rooms."

"It's unusual circumstances," Delorme said. "You have to admit."

"That doesn't make me feel better. Anyway, if she shows up here I'll let you know right away."

—

As he started the car, Cardinal said, "Did you really come up empty?"

"It's not like she had any luggage with her. There were just some things the Crisis Centre must've got for her. But I did find this."

Delorme pulled the drawing from her jacket pocket.

Cardinal frowned at the bird for a few seconds. "Okay, so she can draw a bird. That's all you got?"

"That's it."

"All right. We'll put out an all-points. We could get lucky—she's only been gone a short time."

Cardinal stepped on the gas, and Delorme reached for her seat belt.

47

DAVID LETTERMAN HAD NEVER looked so evil. You couldn't be sure if this was really Letterman or a pod-born version animated by the spirit of some creature fresh from hell. Wisps of smoke curled from the famous gap in the front teeth, and the ears seemed to be capped with tiny tongues of flame. It was hard to tell in the slats of daylight that seeped around the edges of the boarded-up windows.

"You look like you could use a drink, there, Kevin." Letterman flashed his boyish grin, and twin plumes of smoke issued from his nostrils. "How about a shot of Cold Turkey?"

He pulled a bottle and two glasses from a drawer in his desk and flashed the label for the audience. There was laughter and a wry comment from the band leader, Paul What's-His-Name, that Kevin couldn't quite make out.

Letterman poured two shot glasses of whisky. He drank his down in one toss before throwing the glass over his shoulder.

Kevin knew it wasn't real. The stink of this place was
making the withdrawal symptoms worse—the smell of
death and things rotting, the cauldron, those two sturdy
hooks screwed into the beam above it. The buzzing of the
blowflies. Sometimes Kevin was certain they were
demons who had taken the form of flies, but most of the
time he knew they were just flies.

The firmest reality was his own body. It is supremely
difficult to doubt the messages of your own body. The
sweats he could deal with. Sweat poured off him, stinging
his eyes, and he knew—aside from the fact that he had
thrown up more times than he could count—this
accounted for the thirst that claimed the entire territory
of his throat.

The shivers, too, were bearable. The chattering teeth,
the quaking arms, the legs that trembled like horse flesh,
even when he pressed them together to try to calm the
shaking. He wept for heroin. Red Bear had had the presence of mind to pluck it from Kevin's pocket before tying
his hands behind his back and locking the door on him,
and Kevin cried like a child now for heroin—not to ease
the shaking, or the sweats, or the nausea—he could live
with those. Kevin had no idea whether anybody else experienced it this way, but for him the prime symptom of his
addiction was the ache in his chest. It came and went, but
when it came it felt as if it would never leave again. This
ferocious gnawing in his chest felt as if his lungs and
blood vessels had been chewed away, leaving only his
heart to beat out an eternal, abject longing.

"What about bone pain?" Letterman wanted to know.
"How are you handling the bone pain, Kevin?"

Of the physical withdrawal symptoms, bone pain was the worst. It was as if iron rods had been inserted through the marrow of all the hundreds of bones in his body, from the tiniest hinges of fingers and toes to the beams of his spine and legs, chest and arms. And now some demon was banging on them with a hammer so that they hummed and howled like tuning forks.

Nothing helped. Not deep breathing, not trying to imagine beautiful things, not trying to concentrate on one object: that widest crack of light, for example, or that paint drip on the floor not more than a foot from his nose. Kevin was not so sure that brown stain was, in fact, paint. He didn't want to know what it was.

"Say, what do you suppose that brown stain is on the floor there, Kevin?"

"I don't know, Dave."

"No, really. I'm just curious. It's not blood, is it?"

"I don't know, Dave."

"Who do you suppose that came from? I thought Guthrie was killed someplace else."

"I don't know where he was killed, Dave."

"I guess it could be Terri's, then."

"It's not Terri's. Terri went back to Vancouver."

"Hard to say, really, without more to go on. Could be hers, could be Wombat's. I mean, that *is* his head in the pot there, Kevin, so I don't know—draw your own conclusions. Those are probably his fingers as well, I imagine. Say, Kevin, do you suppose you're going to end up in there, too? Weren't you supposed to be a poet at one point?"

Kevin lifted his face from the floor and tried to focus. It was hard with Letterman yammering at him, and the clatter in his bones, the sweat pouring into his eyes. He blinked hard several times and squinted. There was a tiny dark spot in the wall beneath the table, about six inches above the floor. The point of a nail.

48

THE ONTARIO PSYCHIATRIC HOSPITAL—or O.H., as it is familiarly known—sits off to the side of Highway 11 a few kilometres west of Algonquin Bay. It's a beautiful location—long drive, wide field, enveloped in pine forest—that reflects the view of an earlier age that those who suffer from mental or emotional turmoil need more than anything to be ensconced in peaceful surroundings. Asylum.

Advances in drugs—and tightened health care budgets—have emptied many of the O.H.'s beds. But at any given time, it still houses some three to four hundred patients. Most of these, so-called chronic care patients, will not be going home. They include the severely retarded, and those suffering from cruel and irreversible dementia. It's not clear, in most of these cases, whether the patient is even aware of his or her present circumstances, let alone what the future will hold or, more accurately, withhold.

A few of the inmates, such as Catherine Cardinal, stay in the hospital from time to time until the acute phase of their difficulties is over and they can be returned safely to the community. Dr. Jonas had given Catherine a sedative and kept her overnight in Toronto. Then, feeling that the most important thing in her recovery would be proximity to her husband, he put her on a new medication and sent her up to the O.H. by ambulance. He would remain in close touch with her doctor up there.

John Cardinal sat with her now in the sunroom on the third floor. They always sat in the sunroom when he came to visit. Later, when she was better, they would go for a walk, maybe even a trip downtown. But for now it was just this overheated, glassed-in room with its vinyl couches and its view of the highway and the trees. The sun itself was hidden behind heavy cloud, and rain dripped down the windows in thick rivulets.

"They should call it the rainroom," Cardinal said.

Catherine didn't respond. She sat at the far end of the couch, elbows on knees, head sunk low, her face hidden by her hair, an allegory of defeat. Cardinal found his sympathy and concern warring with his frustration at not going all-out for Terri Tait. True, they had all units on alert, and there wasn't much else he could do for her right at this moment, but there were other angles of the case that had to be pursued.

"Do you want a Coke or something?" he said. "I could go down the hall and get you one."

Catherine gave no sign that she heard.

"They don't think you'll need to stay in too long this time. Maybe just a couple of weeks."

Catherine said something.

"What was that? I'm sorry, honey, I didn't hear."

"Bravo, John. I said bravo. Does that do it for you?"

Cardinal stared at the cover of a celebrity magazine, headlines about Rosie O'Donnell and Julia Roberts. What am I doing here? I should be down at the station. I should be talking to ViCLAS.

"Christ," Catherine said after a while.

She was in the hospital of her own volition, but that didn't seem to make the experience any less bitter.

"Catherine, please try and remember this won't last. It will be over sometime soon."

"Sure, John." She turned her dark eyes on him, and Cardinal could read there nothing but devastation. "Sure, it'll be over. And then it's going to come right back again. So how is that 'over'? Tell me that, John. How is that 'over'?"

"You've got people on your side, here, honey. They're trying this Lamotrigine and they have every reason to think it's going to work better than the lithium. It's supposed to be particularly effective for people with your profile. They're very optimistic."

Catherine hung her head again, shaking it gently from side to side, a mute no. If there were any way to summarize this illness, at least in its depressive stage, it would be with that two-letter word, in which all the hopelessness in the universe seemed to gather.

When she was like this, every cheerful note rang hollow, every hopeful remark was suspect, every expression of tenderness a lie. But Cardinal couldn't stop himself. "Catherine, I know it's hard. I know it's overwhelming. But please try and remember the reason you feel like this doesn't have anything to do with reality. It's just a chemical imbalance that makes you feel horrible and makes the world ugly, but it won't last. You will feel better. I promise."

She was crying now. Not the deep-chested sobs of relief, but only the squeezed-out tears of bitterness. With the part of him that still prayed, Cardinal prayed that he could take that pain for her. He would bear it himself for the rest of his life if that would spare her this grief.

—

When he got back to the squad room, Cardinal pulled the ViCLAS report from under a stack of paper and checked the summary page once more. It had come back empty on the MO, negative for links of any kind. Meaning they were dealing with a killer who, for the first time in his life, had cut somebody's head and hands off, and shot two people, and had never done these things before. And probably had Terri Tait at his mercy right now.

He put in a call to Jack Whaley at OPP Behavioural Sciences.

"Jack. John Cardinal, here. I keep coming back to the ViCLAS report you guys gave us."

"Your dead biker. Negative, as I recall. No hits whatsoever."

"That's right. But I have a strong sense that this is not the killer's first time. Removing the victim's extremities while he's still alive. The scene was too prepared. The guy had his magic marks on the walls, he had the knives to cut through bone and ligaments, he had something ready to carry them away in, and something to catch the blood. This was not spur of the moment."

"Okay, I've got your case up on the screen. No runs, no hits."

"And under MO have you got the missing extremities, including the head?"

"We do."

"And you have the hieroglyphics on the walls?"

"We do."

"And that's the report you sent us, right? Totally negative."

"That's right."

"What happened when you ran it without the hieroglyphics?"

"I don't know. Did we run it without the hieroglyphics?"

"Ken Szelagy put in a request that if it came back negative then to run everything the same except without the hieroglyphics."

"Where'd he put this request?"

"Right in the form." Cardinal flipped through the booklet. "In the comments section."

"Oh, yeah. I got it. But there's a problem here, John."

"Tell me."

"It's one of the glitches with ViCLAS. It can't handle 'and/or' searches. Everything is strictly 'and' around here."

"You're kidding me. This *is* a computer we're dealing with, isn't it?"

"Yes, it is. It's also relatively new software. They're still working out the bugs. Everyone knows we need the 'and/or' capability, they just haven't been able to engineer it yet. They promise it'll be here soon. Next generation of the software."

"I can't believe this never got run, Jack. We've got a maniac on the loose up here, and he has at least one person captive. Maybe more." Cardinal sighed. Computers were the twin scourge and saviour of law enforcement. "Can you run the search for me without the markings on the wall?"

"I'm doing it right now. Give me a minute. It's gonna take a few keystrokes. How's Catherine, by the way?"

"Just fine. And Martha?"

"We split up. She finally figured out she didn't like cops. Here we go. It's running now."

"This won't give us any hits from the States, will it?"

"Nope. Strictly Canadian content, provincial and national. It's a huge database we've got now, though. Better than anything south of the border. Down there, a lot of the states haven't signed on, so you get— Oh. Here we go."

"What? Tell me. You got something?"

"Give me a second."

Cardinal could hear Whaley tapping away at a keyboard. Then he came back on the line. "Okay. We're really not supposed to do this, but I just pushed the button. You should have it in your e-mail as an attachment."

Cardinal opened up his e-mail. He clicked on New Mail, and the message popped into his inbox. He called it up and opened the attachment.

"Go to the Linkages and Analysis heading. There won't be any analysis, but you should see—"

"I got 'em," Cardinal said. "Okay. Take away the hieroglyphics and it looks like we've got three hits, all in Toronto. The first one ten years ago. That kid was found on a roof at Regent Park. I remember that—it was just after I left Toronto to move up here. I don't recall anything about missing extremities, though."

"Probably it was a holdback at the time," Whaley said. "To keep out the false confessions. Head, hands and feet missing, and they never cleared it. They must have been going crazy down there. Had a suspect, looks like."

"Raymond Beltran. Twenty-two years old at the time. No priors. But he had a grudge against the victim. He had an alibi, backed up by one Victor Vega."

"Old geezer. Paragon of virtue, no doubt."

"No doubt. Let me look at the other two."

Cardinal scrolled down the attachment to the next entry under Linkages, eight years previous. A body found in a shallow grave in the Rosedale Valley area of Toronto. Unidentified male. Head, hands and feet removed. No suspects.

"I'm surprised they didn't suspect Beltran on this one, too," Cardinal said, "seeing how it came up just two years later. Also, Rosedale Valley Road is not all that far from Regent Park. But it looks like he wasn't even questioned."

"It's a matter of the dates, John. This one was found two years after the kid in Regent Park, but the condition of the body puts the killing eight years before the other one. Beltran wasn't living here then; he was living in the States."

"The States?"

"Florida, I think. Check the background notes."

Cardinal scrolled down to number three under Linkages. This one was from four years previous, also Toronto. A woman, twenty-five years old, goes missing from her Mississauga home and turns up two weeks later near Scarborough Beach minus head, hands and feet.

"Number three is also uncleared," Cardinal said.

"I see that. Sort of thing could make you pessimistic. No shortage of suspects this time, I notice."

"Ex-boyfriend didn't have an alibi, but they had no reason to suspect him other than the ex factor. Neighbour in the basement apartment was a known sexual predator, but not known to use a knife or weapon of any kind. They didn't question Beltran about this one, either. The beach isn't that far from Regent Park. Ten minutes by car."

"I can see why they wouldn't question him. All they had on him was a grudge against victim number one. If they can't make that stick, they have no link to the other two cases."

"You're forgetting geography."

"Well, yeah, but two and a half million people share that geography."

There was a pause. Cardinal could hear Whaley breathing on the other end of the line.

"I have to say, John. Looking at this, I wouldn't link these three cases. Even MO, it's not clear in the second case if the hands and so on were removed before death. That's a big difference. So that leaves you geography plus MO on two cases, max. Not much there, my friend."

Cardinal cursed under his breath.

"Yeah, I know how you feel."

"No, no. This is great stuff. I'm just trying to navigate my way around this gigantic document. I want to look at Beltran's background. How do I get details on the suspects?"

"You have to key in on the case number links. They're underlined near the top of the—"

"I got it. Thanks for all this, Jack."

"Listen, that electronic document you're looking at is unofficial, all right? I'll send you the real thing express mail. Have fun."

Cardinal scrolled through case notes about Raymond Beltran. No angel, this kid. Six charges on his juvenile record, and an aggravated assault had got him two years at a training school in Deep River.

Then there were the Toronto cops' comments about the suspect's alibi, Victor Vega. Called himself Beltran's uncle, but they weren't blood relatives. Investigating officers couldn't link him to the crime, but they noted that he seemed sullen and hostile.

Beltran. Not a common name in Canada. Cardinal checked the ID summary. Mother, unemployed. Father, deceased. Citizenship, Canadian. Cardinal skimmed various contact summaries, and had just about given up on this angle when a comment leaped out at him: *Mother says nothing has gone right for her since she emigrated from Cuba. Went from Havana to Miami in 1980. Toronto two years later. Says she gets no help from relatives in Havana.*

"Hey, Delorme." Cardinal stopped her just as she was heading out. She paused with her hand on the doorknob. "Don't even think about leaving. I think we just caught a break."

49

"WE LIVE AND DIE BY contacts," Chief Kendall liked to say, and Cardinal was now putting that maxim to the test. He had spent ten years on the Toronto force, and he now tapped every source and called in every favour he could think of.

Delorme, on the other hand, had spent as little time in Toronto as possible. But one of the central realities of a cop's life is continuing education—investigative techniques, developments in the collection of evidence, the latest in forensics, criminal psychology, agency liaison—there's no end to the ingenuity of the people who arrange such things, and cops don't mind going because they're a prime source of new contacts.

Between the two of them, Cardinal and Delorme managed to put together a considerable file on a person whose name, just a few hours previously, had been utterly unknown to them.

Tony Glaser, probation officer: "Raymond Beltran? I came across Raymond Beltran fifteen, sixteen years ago.

He was sixteen or seventeen, on probe for bashing some kid over the head with a shovel. In some ways, he was the ideal probation customer. Punctual, neat, followed all the rules. Part of the order was that he had to go back to school full time, and he did. Went every day at nine, left at 3:30 with everyone else. Perfect attendance for two years.

"He was quiet, polite, always told you what you wanted to know. Gave no signs whatsoever of hostility. The only negative was he wouldn't talk. Not *really* talk. He'd answer questions with a single syllable if he could get away with it. A shake of the head, maybe, if he was feeling demonstrative.

"And he behaved himself, at least on my watch. No further incidents. But a couple of things he did gave me pause. One example: We're out for a walk one afternoon and we see this woman walking with a cat on her shoulder. I happen to mention that I have a cat at home. And Raymond asked me, 'Have you ever seen the inside of a cat?' Naturally I said no, and he said, 'I have.' I don't know about you, but I find that remark a little unsettling.

"When I asked him how it came about that he had seen the inside of a cat, he said they'd dissected one in biology class. I didn't believe it. In the first place, they always use frogs or fetal pigs for that. In the second place, he was only in grade eleven. He wasn't taking biology.

"Another time, I was pointing out to him that his two years were nearly up. 'Two years,' he says. 'I don't know why they gave me two years for bashing Bobby Blackmore over the head. I've done way worse things than that, and nobody seemed upset.' 'Like what?' I said. But he clammed up the way he always did and you knew there was just no getting anything more out of him. He was one of those guys you just know on first sight there's something wrong with them. Something missing. You watch your back with Raymond Beltran, that's all I can say. You want more background, try the Catholic Children's Aid. The mother was a nightmare."

Delorme had met a protection worker named Sandra Mayhew when they had both served on a panel at a Women and Criminal Law conference in the nineties. Mayhew had been on the front lines of Toronto social work for ten years and had seen just about everything.

Thus Sandra Mayhew on Gloria Beltran and son: "You can't use any of this, Lise. Not for anything other than background. You can't call me as a witness."

"I know that," Delorme said. "We're working against the clock, here. We're looking for anything we can get."

"Let me tell you about Gloria, first. Cuban immigrant, no skills, only visible means of support a drug dealer who got himself killed shortly after she arrived in the country.

"One day, I pay her a surprise visit the way we're supposed to and she answers the door and there's this guy leaving in a hurry, doing up his pants. It's absolutely clear she's been screwing him, and Raymond is sitting there in the corner of the living room, watching television like there's nothing going on. I mean, Gloria is so out of touch she doesn't even realize that what she's doing is deeply disturbed.

"Raymond didn't seem to think anything of it, either. I talked to him alone the next day and he didn't know what I was concerned about. We already had a supervision order and, believe me, we talked about going for Crown wardship. But the fact was, Raymond was fifteen going on sixteen. There would have been no benefit to bringing him into care for a few months.

"The neighbours complained about both of them. Their apartment was filthy—I mean disgusting, and after ten years in this business, believe me, I don't disgust easily. And Raymond was violent—not like some kids who are out of control, constantly getting into fights and so on. He was a brooder. When he bashed that kid over the head with the shovel, it was over some slight that had happened months previously.

"I tried to talk to him a couple of times, but there was no getting through to that kid. No response whatsoever. Partly, I sensed an extreme hostility to women—not surprising, given that his mother was fucking strangers all the time. But it was more than that. He was only hauled up on charges a couple of times, but that isn't because he wasn't a suspect in a lot of things. This is Regent Park we're talking about. Anyone who wants to find trouble will find it.

"Talk to the Juvie Squad at 51 Division. They'll tell you. They never nailed him for much, but ask them who they suspect for Molly Davis—teenage girl who disappeared from his building. Ask them who they suspect for—just a second, here, let me look it up—for Richard Lee, twenty-year-old guy out walking his dog one night in Allan Gardens.

"The long and short of it, Lise, I didn't have much to do with Raymond Beltran. He was close to being outside my jurisdiction under the Child Welfare Act, and I had an apocalyptic caseload. Only thing I ever managed to do for him was get him into a summer camp—it was his first time outside the big city and he absolutely loved it. But I'll tell you, every other contact I had with him, he scared the hell out of me. Creepy eyes. He could be quite charming when he wanted to be, but it was so obviously an act that you just wanted to get away from him.

"Bottom line, Lise. Raymond Beltran is one of nature's mutants. You ever get close enough to interview him, you don't do it alone."

A few more phone calls, a few more faxes, a lot more e-mail. When Delorme had pretty much exhausted her ingenuity, she went to the lunchroom and brewed up a fresh pot of coffee. She found Cardinal in the boardroom, where he had spread out the results of his own investigations. He was staring at the pages like Napoleon examining his maps, but there was a sag to his shoulders even now, when he was on the chase.

"Thought you could use this," Delorme said, handing him a decaf.

Cardinal turned, and she read grief in his eyes for the split second it took him to tuck it away wherever he kept such things.

Delorme outlined what she had learned. Cardinal listened intently, staring into his coffee, stirring it slowly.

When she was done, he said, "I've been working out a timeline. April 1999, Toronto cops head over to Beltran's apartment to discuss a case of forcible confinement involving a fifteen-year-old girl. Out of the country, his mama says."

"Let me guess," Delorme said. "Cuba."

"Close. Miami. Apparently Mama has relatives there. Anyway, he stays in Miami for the next four years, comes back to Toronto August '03 and gets nicked on a gun charge—which is still outstanding, by the way. Toronto cops believe he's 'up north' somewhere, which could mean here, could mean anywhere. But I just got off the phone with Miami."

Delorme set down her coffee cup. "What does Miami say?"

"Turns out Miami has a string of unsolveds: missing heads, extremities removed while the victim was alive, Palo Mayombe signs nearby. Freaked hell out of the Cuban community down there. Killer became known as El Brujo, which I gather means witch."

"And the dates of the killings?"

"First one is December 2000, last one is August 2003."

"When he comes back to Toronto. He's our guy, John."

"I know it. You know it. Now, all we gotta do is find him."

50

RED BEAR DROVE THE BMW past the eagle sign and into the camp. Leon's Trans Am was gone; he was in town looking for Terri Tait. Red Bear went over to his temple and listened for a few moments. No sounds from within. He took his parcels out of the trunk and went into his cabin.

He took a long hot shower and, afterwards, spent considerable time drying his hair.

Then, still naked, he surveyed his packages, all of which he'd ordered over the Internet to be delivered to a rented postbox. He opened a medium-sized parcel first. Inside was a wooden case, only pine but well carpentered, with neatly fitted brass hinges that worked smoothly. He lifted the lid to reveal a Northern Industrial butcher's handsaw, set in a silk lining. The blade was highly carbonized steel and measured a full twelve inches; the rosewood handle fit his hand as if custom made.

From another package he pulled out a set of Brennan butcher knives, ergonomically designed, according to the accompanying literature, "to reduce fatigue and wrist

strain in your meat department. The upright handle
allows YOU to control the blade."

Then there was the commercial-grade Forschner five-
inch boning knife with the famous Forschner blade—
high carbon, stainless steel, hand-finished in Switzerland.
The rosewood handle was a plus.

There was a five-inch lamb skinner with a cheap-
looking nylon handle that didn't please him at all. And a
six-inch Microban skinning blade, which did. He took
out a ten-inch semi-flexible slicer, a seven-inch fillet knife
with one of those disgusting Fibrox handles, and a Swibo
sticking knife with a stiff blade. Several functions for that
one presented themselves to him in a dreamy way.

In a separate box, he found the Henckels International
Classic Meat Cleaver. Heavy, the way a meat cleaver
should be, "so IT does the work." The steel alloy was lesser
quality than a top-of-the-line item, but the handle had
been specially moulded for small hands like Red Bear's.

He set out his new blades beside his Chef's Choice 3-
Stage Diamond Hone Professional Sharpener. It made a
pleasant hum when empty, and a soothing grinding
sound with a knife in place. He loved the way the grooves
held the blades just so, setting exactly the right edge
whether straight, curved or serrated.

Afterwards, he switched off the lights. In the upper
left quadrant of his window, the last of the old moon
formed a dull, orange crescent. Wisps of cloud drifted
from its lower horn. Tomorrow night, it would be a new
moon. There would be nights and nights to feed the
nganga. He would call forth the most powerful spirit of
his magical career.

The moonlight glistened on his naked arms and legs. He took up the sticking knife, with its thin, needlelike blade, and hefted it in his left hand. In his right, he took hold of the Forschner. He struck poses before the full-length mirror. He began to dance. The blades flashed in the moonlight, his muscles rippled. Colours flowed in his vision, scarlet and crimson and, richest of all—the colour of blood in the moonlight—deep black.

51

KEVIN'S WRISTS WERE BLEEDING. He had been trying now for hours to work the knot loose by hooking it on the point of a nail, but he could not see if he had made the slightest progress. Nor could he tell if the knot was any looser. All he could feel was the ache in his arms, the savage pain in his wrists.

Terri lay slumped over on the floor on the other side of the cabin, unconscious. Leon had injected her with something in the car to keep her quiet. Knowing Leon, he had probably used just about enough to kill her. Her breathing sounded laboured and shallow.

Kevin's head had cleared, now; the withdrawal symptoms had passed. Despite the fearful stench in this place, hunger was gnawing at his belly.

"Terri," he said. "Terri, wake up."

She didn't stir.

Kevin hooked the rope once more on the nail and leaned away. The rope slid off like dental floss. He tried again, to no avail.

"Terri, you have to wake up."

With his feet bound at the ankles, he lurched across the floor to her on his knees. He lay down on his side and nudged her with both knees.

"Terri! For Chrissake, wake up!"

She groaned. It was the first sound she had made since Leon had slung her in here and tied her to the table leg.

"Boy, you fucked up big time," Leon had said as he'd tied the rope.

"Why is Terri here?" Kevin had said. "Let her go, Leon. She hasn't done anything."

"She's too curious, man. That's her problem. Inquisitive." Leon finished tying her hands to the table leg. He gave the rope a couple of sharp tugs. "Tough, though. I'll give her that."

"What's wrong with her? What did you give her?"

"Little Seconal. Keep her peaceful."

"Leon, please. Terri's never hurt anyone in her life. Why do you want to do this?"

"Boss's orders," Leon said. "Unlike you, I know what the fuck I'm doing."

Leon came over and squatted in front of Kevin.

"Jesus, man. Stealing Red Bear's dope. Of all the stupid moves, that's gotta be the stupidest."

"I was wired, Leon. Why the hell else would I do something like that? Listen, help us out of here. Red Bear's gonna kill us."

"That's the least of it, I'd imagine."

"Come on, Leon. How can you go along with him?"

"That's just the way it is, bro. Red Bear and me just clicked. He's shown me a few things. Opened some doors.

He's one powerful witch, and you crossed him. Not smart."

"Leon, I thought we were friends, man."

"Did you?" Leon cocked his head to one side. "You never seemed all that friendly to me. In fact, I got the distinct impression you looked down on me. You, with your fucking poetry and all."

"I didn't. Jesus, man. You know what Red Bear's going to do to us?"

Leon stood up and stretched.

"Gonna work a little of that old Indian magic. Gonna get you working *for* us."

Leon had left, then, deaf to Kevin's begging. Kevin had been shredding his wrists ever since.

He kneed Terri in the shoulder. Harder this time. The wound in his side howled.

She groaned, and her eyelids fluttered.

"Terri, wake up. Terri, you gotta wake up."

52

THE FAXPHOTO CAME IN JUST before noon the next day; it was Delorme who picked it up.

The picture showed a young man, maybe thirty, thirty-one, with a narrow, hawklike face. High cheekbones gave him a slightly Indian look. His stare into the camera gave nothing away. "Guess," it seemed to say, "guess what I might be capable of."

The caption at the bottom of the photo said *Raymond Beltran*. Underneath this, the date of the photograph. It had been taken eighteen months ago when he had been arrested on a weapons charge. He didn't look too worried about the outcome.

Delorme showed it around the squad room. To McLeod, to Szelagy and to the ident guys, Arsenault and Collingwood. None of them recognized Raymond Beltran. She drove over to Corporal Clegg's office in the federal building.

—

"You must like it here," she said, "if you don't even take off for weekends."

Clegg was feeding documents into a shredder. He grinned at her over his shoulder.

"Since me and the wife broke up, I'm not in a big fat rush to get home, you know what I mean? I don't see a ring. You married?"

"No."

"Ever been?"

"No. I have something to show you." Delorme dug in her satchel.

"Maybe you and I could go for dinner sometime. After you wrap up this case, I mean."

"Thanks. But I have a policy against going out with guys from work."

"Makes it kinda tough to meet people, don't you find?"

"Yeah," Delorme said. "It does. Listen, we really need to find this guy." She handed him the photo.

"'Raymond Beltran,'" Clegg read. "Latino, right?"

"He's Cuban. Cuban heritage, anyway. Raised in Toronto. But he's also spent time in Miami. Where, incidentally, he's a suspect in three murders much like Wombat's."

"You're kidding me. He cut them up?"

Delorme nodded. "And he didn't wait till they were dead, either."

"That's not nice. Not nice at all."

"Can you help us out? Have you come across this guy? If he's the one that did Wombat, he's likely deep into the drug trade."

Clegg scanned the caption.

"Taken a while ago," he said. "Of course, people can change their appearance quite a bit when they want to."

"Yeah, but it's a distinctive face—the eyes, the cheekbones. Maybe I could go through your files, look at some mugs?"

"I don't have any mugs here," Clegg said. "That's all in Sudbury."

Delorme looked at the dented file cabinet by the window.

"Just paperwork in there," Clegg said.

"Must be pretty inconvenient."

"The RCMP is a federal organization. Nothing about it is convenient. Did you hear about our fire the other night?"

"You had a fire?"

"Sudbury. Property shed went up in flames. We don't even know how much evidence we've lost."

"Was it arson?"

"They don't know yet, but I doubt it. Plain old incompetence is more likely. Guy in charge of that place is about ninety years old and practically blind." Clegg held up the photo. "Can I hang on to this?"

"Sure. I've got copies."

"I'll take a dive into our incredibly detailed and bureaucratic records and get back to you."

———

Delorme drove up Sumner to the bypass and then out to the OPP detachment. Jerry Commanda was at his desk, on the phone. With the receiver jammed between ear and shoulder, he pulled a chair from another cubicle and motioned for her to sit down.

When he hung up, he swivelled around to face her.

"I bet you've come to talk about the interagency ball game."

"Sorry," Delorme said. She pulled out the photo of Beltran. "You said you'd been working a lot of drug stuff, lately. Have you run across this character?"

Jerry took the photo from her and held it at an angle to catch the window light. "I can't say for sure. What do you want him for?"

"Cutting up Wombat Guthrie, for one."

"Really?" Jerry looked closer at the picture. "Well, there's one guy it might be."

He reached into a desk drawer and pulled out a buff-coloured file folder. There was a stack of eight-by-ten black-and-white photos inside. He fanned them out on the desk like a deck of cards and selected one. It showed a group of young men sitting around outside a diner. Three of them seemed to be watching the fourth man, who had very long hair and was dressed all in white.

"Rosebud Diner," Jerry said. "Reed's Falls. We've been keeping an eye on that place for a few weeks now. We think there's a lot of dope moving through the people that hang out there. We have theories, but we're not a hundred-percent sure where they're getting it from, and we don't know where they stash it. Take a look at the guy with the long hair."

Delorme picked up the photo. "But this guy's an Indian, no?"

"Calls himself Red Bear."

"Yeah, we had a tip from a junkie there was an Indian hanging around with Leon Rutkowski."

"Guy's not from around here, I can tell you that. Rumour is he's from Red Lake, and I've been checking on that."

"I recognize the other guys," Delorme said. "Leon Rutkowski, and Toof Tilley, may he rest in peace. And the guy on the right is Kevin Tait."

"You're kidding. Related to our former Jane Doe?"

"Her brother. He has a prior for intent to traffic out west. We think he's the reason Terri came here in the first place."

"We've been wondering who the hell he was," Jerry said. "I might even think you guys are pretty good, except I got the fax that said Terri Tait is missing again."

"I'll get to that." Delorme was holding the two pictures side by side. "The Indian guy could be Beltran. It's hard to be sure, though."

"I think we've got a better picture in here somewhere." Jerry shuffled through the glossy images. "Here we go."

This one was a two-shot. It showed the long-haired man and Kevin Tait. Tait was laughing, but Beltran—and there was no doubting his identity now—was looking dead serious. The same high cheekbones, the same broad brow. And, most of all, the almost transparent eyes.

"I hope this doesn't disappoint you, Jerry. But it looks like your Indian is actually a Cuban."

"That's interesting . . ."

Jerry swivelled away from her and stared at the ceiling for a few moments. Delorme waited. Finally, Jerry swivelled to face her once more. "As it happens, I called the

chief of the Red Lake band. I didn't tell him I was a cop.
Told him I was a banker checking background for a loan.
And the chief vouched for the guy. Called him Raymond
Red Bear. Said he was born and brought up right there on
the Red Lake reserve."

"Why would he go to all that trouble? I heard status
cards are easy to fake."

"They are. Which is why you might need someone to
vouch for you. Might even *pay* someone to vouch for you.
Sometimes it can be useful to have First Nations status,"
Jerry said. "For purposes of employment, for example."

"Very funny, Jerry. What exactly are you talking
about?"

"Up until fairly recently, the Viking Riders used to get
their dope from Montreal. Then they made the mistake of
disagreeing with the Hells Angels."

"No more dope."

"No more dope from Montreal. But being bikers, and
dedicated entrepreneurs, they worked out a deal with
some Native Americans just across the Michigan border.
Started early last summer. They fly the stuff across Lake
Huron, then up the French River to Lake Nipissing. If you
do it right, you never leave Indian territory."

"A good way to keep it out of everyone's jurisdiction."

"You have a dirty mind, Detective Delorme. That's
what I always liked about you." Jerry held up the photo.
"Nice touch for him to dress up like a Hollywood Indian.
Should set us back a couple of hundred years."

"So Beltran comes on like an Indian, complete with a
status card and a chief in his pocket, and he takes over the
Viking Riders' import business."

"That's our theory."

"And now you're going to tell me where we can find Beltran, right?"

"Sorry. We don't have surveillance on him yet. We've just been watching the Rosebud."

"Well, I'll tell you the other reason we're looking for Beltran. We think he's got Terri Tait and he's going to kill her."

Jerry grabbed the phone and punched the intercom button. "I'm going to get an all-points on him, Lise. Minute we hear anything, you will too."

53

SOONER OR LATER, WHENEVER a case got unwieldy, Cardinal ended up in the boardroom with the files. He was in there now, sorting through the stacks of material the other detectives had assembled. He'd been going over the forensics and scene photos from Arsenault and Collingwood. And now he was weeding through Delorme's supplementary reports. Every fragment of information they had was spread out on the table before him.

They had put out the all-points pretty fast, but so far there had been no sighting of Terri Tait. So here he was sequestered with the files, in the hope that they would provide him with a solid idea of where to look for her.

The eye strain was getting to him.

He slouched back in his chair and looked around the room, at the photos lining the walls. There was one of Chief Kendall being sworn in; his uniform would never fit him that well again. And there was one of Cardinal himself, bundled up like an Inuit at the snowy mine shaft on Windigo Island. Then there was the picture of Jerry

Commanda in front of the gate at Eagle Park. Eagle Park was a charity camp on the south shore of Lake Nipissing that had once served handicapped kids and wards of Children's Aid; Jerry had been out there directing a successful search for a missing twelve-year-old. The camp had closed long ago, after a complicated financial scandal—a *kerfuffle*, as Jerry would call it. On top of the gate, a wrought-iron eagle flexed its iron talons, black wings spread as if about to take off.

Cardinal turned his mind back to the files. His Toronto leads had dried up. Beltran's last known address proved to be a dead end; he had pulled a midnight flit, leaving the landlord holding the bag for six months' rent on a huge apartment in the Manulife Centre. Cardinal had even called Beltran's former neighbours, none of whom had anything useful to add. Beltran had been an unexceptional neighbour—wished you good day in the elevator, kept to himself and didn't cause trouble.

Cardinal opened another of Delorme's files. One of the many pleasures of working with Delorme was that her reports were both coherent and detailed. But even with her copious notes from the hospital, and the anthropologist, and the Crisis Centre, there was nothing he could sink his teeth into. Nothing that told him where Raymond Beltran might be—or Terri Tait, for that matter.

Cardinal sifted through Delorme's reports once more. Even when she came up empty, as she had at the Crisis Centre, she was conscientious about writing it up. She had even filed the drawing she had taken from Terri's room.

Cardinal wasn't sure about Terri Tait's talent as a struggling actress, but she showed considerable aptitude for drawing. The feathers on the bird were all nicely high-lighted, and the arch of the wings, just so, gave the image a certain—

Cardinal looked over at the far wall, at the picture of Jerry Commanda at Eagle Park. He snatched up the drawing and held it next to the photograph.

Two seconds later, he was in Chouinard's office.

The detective sergeant lined up the drawing with the photograph on his desk. Cardinal watched his eyes swing back and forth from one to the other. Chouinard tapped on the desk with his pen as he considered. Finally, he said, "They're the same. I'd say this means she was there. The question then becomes, what do we do about it?"

"Eagle Park had two camps on the lake. One on the south shore and one up by the French River. They both have those gates with the eagle on top."

"We don't have enough people to send to both. Which one do you think is more likely?"

"The south shore is closer to where Tilley and Guthrie were found. On the other hand, the north shore is closer to where they ripped off the Viking Riders. It could be either one."

"And neither is in our jurisdiction." Chouinard paused in thought, his pen beating a *rat-tat-tat* on the desk. "All right. You take the south shore. But you take Alan Clegg with you."

"Delorme should be in on this."

"She's out visiting OPP, closer to the French River. That's their territory, anyway. She can head out there with Jerry Commanda. I'll pull together a swat team here. Whichever one of you calls in first with pay dirt, we'll be ready."

54

ONCE THEY GOT BEYOND THE TRAFFIC in and out of the malls, Cardinal put the pedal to the floor.

"You trying out for Formula One?"

Cardinal looked over at Clegg. He had a friendly smile on his face, not criticizing.

"The guy we're looking for cuts people up for a living. I don't want that to happen to Terri Tait."

"Assuming he's got her."

"It's safer than assuming he hasn't."

Clegg adjusted the passenger seat and sat back. He folded his hands on his lap and watched the scenery shoot by: the rock cuts, the Trianon Hotel, the Ottawa turnoff. After that it was hills and trees.

"So, how long you been a cop?"

Cardinal shrugged. "Let's just say I could retire on full pension if I wanted to."

Clegg laughed. "And you don't want to? Guys like you always make me think of those people who win the lottery—I mean, big time. They have a job changing light bulbs in a high-rise or something and here they win twenty-five million and they're not gonna quit work."

"Your pension's twenty-five million? Must've been some boost in the RCMP budget this year."

"We get by."

Cardinal made the turn onto Nosbonsing Road. It had been paved since the last time he'd been out here. They passed a handful of farms, then the road narrowed and they were bumping through the woods, the flashing wall of trees broken by the odd driveway and mailbox. Flies spattered on the windshield.

"So, how do you want to handle this?" Clegg said.

"We'll play it by ear. First thing is to establish whether or not the place is in use. If yes, then establish whether there's anyone there just at the moment. If it looks like our guy is here, then we radio back and they unleash Armageddon. If he's away, we search the place for Terri Tait. How's that sound?"

"I'm with you a thousand percent," Clegg said. "Sounds like *fun.*"

—

Delorme had been on her way out the OPP's front door when Chouinard had called. Now she was in Jerry Commanda's car, somewhere just outside Sturgeon Falls.

"Jerry, can't this thing go any faster? There may be a life at stake, here."

"I'm pretty sure we're gonna come up empty," Jerry said, pressing the accelerator. "After all that financial kerfuffle, camp got bought by some hotel outfit. Not sure what they've done with it, though. If anything."

"If it's sitting empty, it might make an ideal spot for drug dealers."

Jerry shrugged. "If they like blackflies."

Kerfuffle, Delorme was thinking. Only Jerry could use that word and not sound like a librarian.

"This is pretty close to the house where Wombat got ambushed," she said. "Can't be more than a couple of kilometres."

Jerry made a sharp right, spraying gravel.

"Cardinal's checking out the other camp with a guy from the RCMP," Delorme said.

"Oh, yeah? Who would that be?"

"Corporal named Alan Clegg."

Jerry turned onto an even smaller road. Branches whipped at the roof of the car.

"I've dealt with him a couple of times."

Delorme scanned Jerry's profile, finding nothing legible there. Jerry tended to do that a lot, say something with implications and just leave it hanging, as if you should know what he was thinking.

"And?"

Jerry shrugged again. "He seemed to know an awful lot of nothing about what was going down in your neck of the woods. I don't know why they posted him in Algonquin Bay."

"Because of the Viking Riders being so close, is what Musgrave told me."

Jerry gave a little crooked smile. There was the sound of gravel kicking up against the car. "I sometimes wonder about Musgrave," Jerry said.

"Oh?"

"Musgrave moves in mysterious ways."

"Jerry!"

"What?"

"What are you getting at?"

Jerry looked over at her, impassive. "Clegg never seemed to know as much as he should, that's all. Made me uncomfortable, talking to him. Couldn't fathom why Musgrave thought he was the right stuff."

They rounded a bend, and then the construction site came into view. Some of the cabins were still standing, but the rest of the clearing was the province of bulldozers and graders. A chain-link fence surrounded the site. Delorme counted twenty workers.

Off to the right, a wrought-iron eagle spread its wings over an old wooden gate.

"That's the picture Terri drew," Delorme said. "She drew exactly that eagle, right down to the feathers."

"Well, we can ask the foreman a couple of questions," Jerry said, "but somehow I don't think this was the Eagle Park she was at. Why would the guy be showing up in Reed's Falls if he was staying way the hell out here?"

"This camp is much closer to the reserve than the other one."

They drove over deep ruts toward an office trailer that sat in the shadow of a huge sign that said, in French, *Future Site of Northern Lights Spa Resort*.

The foreman was a chunky rhomboid of a man with a Wild West moustache that didn't suit him at all. No, he told them, there hadn't been any strangers around the place. No, there had been no suspicious activity of any

kind. They had been working the site for two months now
and the only people to set foot on the property other than
construction people were exactly two cops, and he was
looking at them right now.

"This means Cardinal and Clegg are heading to the
right place," Delorme said. "I'm going to call Chouinard."

"Doesn't mean there's anybody out there right now,"
Jerry said. "They could've left by now."

Delorme's cellphone rang in her pocket. When she
answered it, Malcolm Musgrave was on the line. He didn't
bother with preliminaries.

"Listen. Are you and Cardinal still working that murder thing with Alan Clegg?"

"Yeah. Why?"

"Don't work with him. He's no good."

"Jesus, Musgrave. You're telling us this now? Why didn't
you tell us the first time we spoke to you?"

"We've had our eye on Clegg for a while, but we didn't
have anything hard core until now. You hear about our
little fire in the property room?"

"Yeah. From Clegg."

"There was two hundred and fifty grand in seized cash
from a bust of his. Now we've had this fire and the Fire
Department is telling me there's no way that cash could
have just turned to smoke. There would have been
pounds of ashes left, and there's nothing. So we've just
executed a search warrant on his place and we've found
enough cash and drugs to start a personal cartel. This guy
is playing for the other side, Lise. Obviously, this is not for
publication till we haul him in, but I wanted to let you
know right away."

"Me, I appreciate it," Delorme said. "But Cardinal's in a car with Clegg right now."

"Not a good place to be. I'm sorry I couldn't say anything earlier."

"I'll call him right away," Delorme said. She hung up and dialled Cardinal's cellphone number.

55

TERRI HAD WOKEN FOR A WHILE—long enough to take in the full horror of their situation—but the drug Leon had given her had taken hold again and she was mercifully unconscious. Meanwhile, the nail had become the absolute focus of Kevin's universe. It was as if he lived inside the rope, as if he himself were twisted among its fibres, numbering every strand. His wrists were raw and bleeding, but the knot was definitely looser.

He worked at what remained of the knot, fixing it under the nail and then leaning forward, tugging it looser with his weight. The muscles in his arms were in torment, and he hadn't been fed since the moment he'd been thrown into this cell. Lack of food and the lingering effects of withdrawal made his muscles tremble. If he did get a chance to fight Leon or Red Bear, he would be no match for them.

The knot came a little looser. It was getting harder to pull at the rope without it slipping off the nail. Across the darkened cabin, Terri groaned and looked up. "Oh," she said softly. "God help us."

Kevin leaned forward and felt the rope slip out of a loop. It was the second loop he had undone. He was fairly sure there was only one more left to undo.

He adjusted his position and hooked the rope under the nail once more. It was right up against his wrist now. If he couldn't undo the last loop, he might be able to saw his way through it.

"I can't move at all," Terri said. "It's too tight."

"I think I'm getting the rope off," Kevin said. "Just a little longer."

Terri nodded. Her eyes filled and tears ran down her cheeks.

"I'm trying," Kevin said. There was nothing else to say. "I'm trying."

The nail caught this time. He could feel it had a good purchase on the last loop. He strained forward, and the rope seared his wounded wrists as it moved against his flesh.

Voices from outside, then a key in the lock. Red Bear came in, followed by Leon.

"Let us go," Terri said. "Just let us go. We'll get as far away from here as possible and never bother you again."

"Why, little princess? You scared?" Red Bear stood smiling at them, hands on hips.

"Please," Terri said. "We don't care about your dope operations, or anything else you've done. Just let us go."

"You should see the moon tonight. A beautiful crescent. And it's growing. That's the crucial thing. It's growing. That means we have perfect conditions for a sacrifice."

Leon set down a bundle on the work table. Kevin heard the clank of steel.

Red Bear opened a large briefcase and pulled out a gleaming blade, which he showed first to Kevin, then to Terri. Terri started to scream, and Red Bear tossed a roll of duct tape to Leon.

"Shut her up."

Leon tore off a long strip and wrapped it around Terri's face.

"We'll take it off as soon as we begin the sacrifice. Then it will be important to hear the screams."

Red Bear lifted up another knife. "These small blades are good for removing fingers and toes. I will show you how it's done, using the girl. When I finish, you can sacrifice the other one."

"I'm ready to learn, man. I'm psyched," Leon said, rubbing his hands together. His eyes were glittering, and Kevin could see he was cruising the stratosphere. There would be no reaching him.

Red Bear was holding up more tools.

"These medium-sized blades you can use for cutting off whatever else strikes your fancy. All of it goes into the *nganga*. We will create a spirit that is made up of both male and female blood. It will be supremely powerful."

"Fantastic," Leon said. "What's it gonna do for us?"

"Anything we want."

—

Cardinal backed the car up and parked a little way outside the camp.

"Better switch off your cellphone, if you're carrying

one," he said. "Don't want to make any unnecessary noise at this point."

"It's off," Clegg said. "But it doesn't look like there's anything going on here."

Even without getting out of the car, Cardinal could see fresh tire tracks in front of them. "I wouldn't be so quick to say that. There's obviously been people coming and going." He pointed across the dark field. "And there's a light on outside that large cabin there."

"For security only, I'm sure. The cabins are all dark."

"Whose security? Eagle Camps is bankrupt, remember? Why are you in such a rush to bail?"

"Sorry," Clegg said. "Been a long day. And then I got a long drive ahead of me later."

Cardinal got out of the car and led the way around the edge of the camp, keeping behind the cabins. When they had gone about fifty yards, they could see around the end of the biggest cabin. There were two vehicles parked there, one of them a black Trans Am.

Cardinal said, "I'm calling for backup."

He pulled out his cellphone; the readout told him Delorme had tried to call.

Clegg pulled out his service revolver and aimed it at Cardinal's head.

"That's not going to happen," he said. "You make one move, and I'll blow your head off. And don't think I won't, because at this point, believe me, I got nothing to lose."

Clegg reached into Cardinal's holster and removed his Beretta.

"You're dirty," Cardinal said. "And I thought you were just incompetent."

Clegg motioned with the revolver toward the main building. "Walk ahead of me."

Cardinal started across the field.

"Put some thought into this, Corporal. My DS knows I'm out here with you. If I don't come back, every cop north of Toronto is going to be looking for you."

"Keep moving."

"Why'd you get into it, Clegg? Was it just the money, or are you wired to the stuff?"

"Just wanted to expand my horizons a little."

"Look, you can still turn this around. Put the gun away and I'll give you a chance to get out of here. We're going to come looking for you—there's nothing I can do about that—but at least you won't be tangled up in any murder."

This was not remotely true, and they both knew it.

They were at the door of the biggest cabin. A security camera stared down at them. Clegg rapped on the door—three short, two long—and waited. He kept the gun—Cardinal's own Beretta—trained on him.

"You think by shooting me with my own gun it'll somehow go better for you? What, the bad guys got my gun away and shot me when I tried to run?"

"Works for me," Clegg said. "They must be in one of the other cabins. That way."

Cardinal headed toward the row of cabins on the east side of the clearing. He wondered if Delorme had reached the other camp yet, if she had already turned around. If she had, then they would know that this was the place. Possibly, they wouldn't need a call from Cardinal to send out more troops; when they didn't hear from him they'd send in the cavalry. Or was that wishful thinking? His heart was pounding and sweat was pouring off his brow.

The line of cabins all appeared dark.

"Looks like you're out of luck," Cardinal said.

"There's another cabin back there. Keep moving."

Cardinal stumbled over a root and nearly fell. Then a dark cabin appeared in the thickets ahead of them. It was much more rundown than the rest and the windows were boarded up. There were voices from inside.

Clegg called out, "Hey, Red Bear!"

The door opened and a man came out. Shoulder-length hair, held back with a headband. Still, he wasn't hard to recognize.

"Mr. Beltran," Cardinal said. "It's all over. No matter what you do right here, right now. It's all over. There are other cops on the way."

"Why did you bring him here?" Beltran said to Clegg.

"I didn't. He brought me."

Beltran came down the steps. A long blade gleamed in his hand. His eyes were transparent, dead.

"Be smart," Cardinal said. "If I'm here, it means others are going to be here soon. You can turn yourself over to me, or you can hit the road. Anything else is just going to make things worse."

"It would certainly make them worse for you," Beltran said. He took another step closer. The blade flashed. "My little friend here would make sure of that. Suppose we were to—"

"What the fuck is he doing here?"

Cardinal recognized Leon Rutkowski from the scar on

his forehead, but Rutkowski wasn't looking at Cardinal. He was looking at Clegg.

"Hiya, Leon," Clegg said. "Long time, no see."

"Fucker put me away for eight years, man."

"Don't worry about it," Beltran said. "He is a friend of ours. You are protected, remember?"

"Horsemen are no friends of mine."

"They are now."

"Leon," Cardinal said. "You don't know me. I'm with the Algonquin Bay police, not the RCMP. Corporal Clegg may be working with Mr. Beltran, here, but I'm not. And I can tell you this: You have about five minutes before a lot more Algonquin Bay cops show up here, so the next few decisions you make are going to matter. If I were you, I'd leave."

Rutkowski rubbed at the scar on his forehead.

"What did you call him?"

"Raymond Beltran. Originally from Cuba. Now wanted for the torture and murder of several people in Miami. Not to mention the murder of a Viking Rider named Wombat Guthrie, but I imagine you knew about that."

"Beltran doesn't sound very Indian," Leon said.

Beltran shrugged. "I use whatever name is useful at the time. Our suppliers were disposed to trust an Indian. Anyway, what do you care?" Beltran pointed with the tip of his knife at a medallion on Leon's chest. "As long as you are wearing that, you have nothing to worry about. That is a power Indians have never dreamed of."

"What do you want to do with this guy?" Clegg said. "Obviously, he isn't going back to town."

"Oh, bring him inside." Red Bear pointed with the knife at the cabin; stainless steel flashed. "We'll put him to good use."

Cardinal felt the Beretta press against his spine.

There was a thrum of approaching engines through the trees.

"I hate to say I told you so . . ." Cardinal said. Lise Delorme, he thought, I am going to give you a great big kiss.

"Cops, man." Leon's eyes looked a little wild. "Let's get the hell out of here."

"Running will get us nowhere, Leon," Beltran said. "Let me handle this."

"Handle it? There's an army of cops coming, and you're going to handle it?"

Beltran touched his arm. It was a strangely tender gesture, given the circumstances. "You said you trusted me," he said. "Now that trust is being tested."

"I trust you."

"I want you to trust me absolutely. Without end."

"I said I trust you, man."

"Good. We have a cop for a hostage. There is no need to run."

The thrum of engines had become a roar. A cluster of headlights appeared, moving singly, not in pairs, and then came bobbing across the field.

"It's the fucking Viking Riders, man." Leon looked like he was going to burst into tears. It was about as appropriate a reaction as Cardinal could think of at that moment. Within seconds, they were surrounded by blinding headlights. Cardinal counted ten.

The engines subsided to a throb. There was the sound of kickstands, then two men took shape in the glare of light. The rest remained in shadow.

"Cardinal," Steve Lasalle said. "Didn't expect to see you here."

"There are places I'd rather be," Cardinal said.

"Not having a good day, I see. You either," he said to Clegg. "I thought we had a deal."

"We do," Clegg said. "I had nothing to do with Wombat."

"Sadly, I don't believe you."

"Whether you believe me or not, you've got two cops here, so I think you'd better back off."

Lasalle nodded at Clegg's gun, still pointed at Cardinal's back. "Doesn't look like you two are all that close."

"It's only fair to warn you," Cardinal said. "There's a lot more cops on the way."

Lasalle grinned. "Sounds like wishful thinking to me."

Clegg whirled on him with the Beretta. Before he could fire, there was an explosion and Clegg dipped on one knee, a priest genuflecting. "Oh," he said, as if he'd just understood something. He clutched at his chest, tried to get up, and fell over on his side. "Oh," he said again, and this time it sounded final.

Harlan Calhoun, all 250 pounds of him, took a step forward and spat on Clegg. Then he raised his gun toward Beltran.

"You killed Wombat," he said. "Nobody kills a Viking Rider and lives."

"You can't hurt me," Beltran said. "And if you try, every spirit in hell will track you down."

Calhoun pulled the trigger. There was a loud click.

"Righteous, man. The magic's working," Leon said. "We're really protected!"

"Fuck you," Calhoun said, and fired again.

A black dot appeared above Leon's left eye. He grabbed at the cabin door, trying to hold himself up.

"Dipshit," Calhoun said.

Beltran didn't even turn to look at Leon; he kept his eyes fixed on Calhoun. "You killed my friend," he said. "I swear by all the gods, you are going to wish you had died with him."

"Oh, yeah?"

There was a crackle of radio static. Amid the moonlight and clouds of exhaust, Cardinal could make out a headset.

"Steve," a voice said. "Cops."

There was a moment of stillness. Lasalle cocked his head. Ever so faint, the sound of approaching sirens.

"Hit the road," he said. "Everyone. Right now."

Beltran dove into the shadows beside the cabin. Calhoun fired a shot after him, and Cardinal used that moment to melt into the darkness behind the cabin. The sirens were getting closer. Cardinal heard a curse, and then Calhoun's massive frame was silhouetted amid the clouds of exhaust. A ragged thunder of horsepower, and a split second later the bikes became a galaxy of headlights travelling full tilt across the field.

Cardinal stepped out front and retrieved his gun from beside Clegg. The corporal wasn't breathing. Cardinal ran into the cabin and nearly threw up at the smell.

He plucked a knife from an array of them on the table and freed first Terri, then Kevin. They were both crying, unable to speak, and Kevin had a nasty wound in his side.

"Can you walk?" Cardinal said, helping them up. "Go and sit in front of the large cabin in the light. There's more cops coming. Sit where they can see you and keep your hands visible. Do everything they say, and for God's sake, don't run or do anything to get them going. They're going to be armed and jittery. I'll be back."

He steered them past the two dead bodies toward the main building. Then he turned to the blackness of the woods.

The moon was just a sliver, but it cast a lot of light in the clearings.

Moving as quietly as he could, Cardinal climbed the hill behind the cabins and came to the edge of a rock cut among a stand of enormous trees. Behind him, he could hear car doors slamming, voices yelling. Szelagy. Delorme.

I should wait for them, he thought. But the chance of Beltran slipping away, finding a boat or leading them on an endless chase through the woods was too great. He couldn't be far.

The moon was thin, but it cast a cool, metallic light on the rock cut. Cardinal kept to the shadows as he skirted the clearing. He found a trail on the other side and followed it into intermittent darkness. The soil was loamy underfoot; he could move almost silently.

A little further on, another trail branched to the right. If he kept straight, the trail would lead to the water's edge. He doglegged to the right, and the trail grew rapidly narrower. A slight rise in the terrain and then, across a clearing, a rock face reared up before him. The moon had gone behind a cloud. In the deeper dark, it was hard to make out handholds in the granite wall.

Later, Cardinal couldn't be sure what had alerted him. A slight rustle overhead? A glint of moonlight on metal? For whatever reason, he stepped to one side, so that when Beltran dropped from the darkness above, his knife missed Cardinal's neck and only ended up grazing his shoulder and upper arm. Cardinal was thrown off balance and stumbled forward as Beltran crashed to the ground behind him.

Cardinal had his gun half raised when Beltran came at him again, knife flashing. The two of them locked together, Beltran gripping Cardinal's gun hand, Cardinal catching Beltran's wrist just as the knife arced toward his chest. They staggered against the rock face.

Beltran leaned into Cardinal with all his weight, and the two of them tumbled over a boulder. A sharp edge of granite bit into Cardinal's shoulder blade. The knife dropped to the ground, point first, and quivered there. Beltran twisted hard on Cardinal's arm and the gun hit the dirt with a thud.

When they came up again, Beltran had the knife and Cardinal's hands were empty. Beltran was babbling something incoherent, veering in and out of English. He kept crying out something like "Ellegua! Ellegua, protect me," followed by a torrent of some language Cardinal had never heard before. Cardinal was focused on the knife, which Beltran swung at him in wide arcs, forcing him to hop back.

Beltran swung again, and this time Cardinal kicked hard and connected. The knife flew against the rock face, sparking on granite. Beltran fell, then scrabbled after it on all fours. Cardinal hauled him back by the shoulder.

Why was it that everything he had learned at police college about hand-to-hand combat always seemed irrelevant when it came to an actual fight? In the heat and commotion, so-called crippling grips fail to even grip, let alone cripple. Nothing in the courses prepared you for the speed with which a cornered human being can move. Beltran's fists seemed to be everywhere at once; and when Cardinal stepped out of reach, Beltran kicked him so hard in the gut that he went down like a spavined horse.

Cardinal landed hard on his knee, and pain shot up his leg. But it wasn't granite he had landed on, it was gunmetal. He snatched up the Beretta just as Beltran wheeled on him once more with the knife.

He was yelling, shouting out to Ellegua to pound his enemies into dust. He came at Cardinal, knife shining. Cardinal aimed for body mass and fired. The bullet hit with an odd sound—a clang—and Beltran fell to his knees, gasping for breath.

He touched a large medallion that hung around his neck.

"You see," he said. "You cannot kill me. I am protected."

He came forward a step, still on his knees. He raised the knife, and Cardinal fired again, this time emptying the magazine.

Beltran fell forward, and the knife slithered from his grasp. His blood spread beneath him, flowing outward over the rocks in a black pool, in which the white moon shimmered like a blade.

56

Lise Delorme was sitting in her car, in the parking lot of the Ontario Psychiatric Hospital. She had tried waiting outside, but up here, near the forest, the flies were still too bad. They were getting better, though. Another week or so and you might actually be able to enjoy a walk in the woods.

She stared at the massive red-brick building with its many dark windows, some of them barred. Something about mental hospitals makes them haunting in a way that, say, prisons or other grim institutions are not. Even now, in the broad, white light of summer, the place made you want to turn your back and think of other things.

In an arrangement almost certainly peculiar to Algonquin Bay, the local coroner shares office space with the psychiatric hospital. Delorme had come here to speak with Dr. Rayburn and get his written, signed reports. That had taken only a few minutes, but when she had come out she had noticed Cardinal's Camry in the lot and decided to wait for him. The coroner's reports were just a formality, just another batch of pages for a very thick file. They contained the routine but necessary observation that the three deceased—Raymond Beltran, Leon Rutkowski and Alan Clegg—had met their ends by foul play and that the services of a forensic pathologist were required.

Add to that list Toof Tilley, Wombat Guthrie and God knew how many others in Miami and Toronto, and Beltran's body count started to look seriously depressing.

A young woman came out the side door of the hospital, followed by Cardinal.

Delorme got out of her car and met them at the edge of the lot.

"Lise." Cardinal's voice was softer than usual. Delorme had never seen anyone look so exhausted.

"How's the shoulder?"

"Not too bad. Kind of throbs sometimes."

"No bowling for you."

"No left-handed bowling, anyway. I don't think you've met my daughter. Kelly, this is Lise Delorme."

"The famous Sergeant Delorme," Kelly said, and shook hands. She had a beautiful smile that resembled her mother's. But she had her father's eyes. Sad eyes, even when she was smiling. "Dad's told me a lot about you."

"Uh-oh," Delorme said.

"No, no. It's all good. He really admires you."

"That isn't what he tells me," Delorme said, but she felt the heat in her face. Admires? She's got to be joking. She glanced at him, but if Cardinal was embarrassed, she couldn't see it beyond the exhaustion.

"I'll wait in the car," Kelly said to her father, and then she was gone, leaving an impression of youth, alarming honesty and, beyond that, something else. There was a spark of glamour in the way she held her head, in the way she wore those New York clothes. Kelly Cardinal was something special.

"I'm sorry to intrude," Delorme said. "I just thought you'd want to know. We matched a gun we found at the camp with the bullets that killed Tilley."

"Excellent. That's good to hear."

"Rutkowski's prints on it. Not Beltran's."

"Huh," Cardinal said. "Soulmates."

His response was so muted, Delorme wanted to shake him. Or hug him. Something. His pain was so clearly not physical.

"They've also confirmed the head was Wombat Guthrie," Delorme said, wishing she could shut up about it.

"How are Terri and her brother?"

"Both pretty traumatized. I think it may have cured Tait's drug problem, though. That's a start. By the way, you were right about the locket. It's Terri's."

"Great."

"You'll also be glad to know Steve Lasalle and Harlan Calhoun were denied bail."

"Good. Well . . ."

"How's Catherine, John?"

"Oh. You know. Hard to say." Cardinal looked off toward the trees, the sunlight bringing out the crow's feet at the corners of his eyes. "Seems she didn't want visitors."

"I'm sorry," Delorme said. "That's rough."

"Tell Chouinard I'll be in tomorrow."

"Take longer, John. There's no need to come back so soon."

"Yes, there is. Tell him I'll be in tomorrow."

Delorme watched him head across the lot. Kelly was waiting for him by the car.

The young woman suddenly bent forward and covered her face with her hands. Cardinal put his arms around her and held her close. They stood together like that for a long time. They were still standing like that as Delorme drove away, Cardinal's left hand stroking his daughter's hair.

Acknowledgements

I wish to thank Les Couchie of the Union of Ontario Indians for his help with matters pertaining to Northern Ontario's First Nations.

The following experts were generous with their assistance in clarifying issues of emergency medicine, traumatic amnesia or forensic entomology. Needless to say, they are not responsible for any errors that remain. Dr. David Gibo, University of Toronto; Martin Ransom, North Bay Police Services; Dr. Mike Lecky, North Bay General Hospital; Dr. Felix Sperling, University of Alberta; Dr. Michael Persinger, Laurentian University.

Special thanks: Detective Sergeant Rick Sapinski of the North Bay police.

Be sure not to miss

By the Time

You Read This

the new John Cardinal mystery

Turn the page for a sneak preview . . .

1

NOTHING BAD COULD EVER happen on Madonna Road. It curls around the western shore of a small lake just outside Algonquin Bay, Ontario, providing a pine-scented refuge for affluent families with young children, yuppies fond of canoes and kayaks, and an artful population of chipmunks chased by galumphing dogs. It's the kind of spot—tranquil, shady and secluded—that appears to offer an exemption from tragedy and sorrow.

Detective John Cardinal and his wife, Catherine, lived in the smallest house on Madonna Road, but even that tiny place would have been beyond their means were it not for the fact that, being situated across the road from the water, they owned neither an inch of beach nor so much as a millimetre of lake frontage. On weekends Cardinal spent most of his time down in the basement amid smells of sawdust, paint and Minwax, carpentry affording him a sense of creativity and control that did not tend to flourish in the squad room.

But even when he was not woodworking, he loved to be in his tiny house enveloped in the serenity of the lakeshore. It was autumn now, early October, the quietest time of the year. The motorboats and Sea-Doos had been hauled away, and the snowmobiles were not yet blasting their way across the ice and snow.

Autumn in Algonquin Bay was the season that redeemed the other three. Colours of scarlet and rust, ochre and gold swarmed across the hills, the sky turned an alarming blue, and you could almost forget the sweat-drenched summer, the bug festival that was spring, the pitiless razor of winter. Trout Lake was preternaturally still, black onyx amid fire. Even having grown up here (when he took it completely for granted), and now having lived in Algonquin Bay again for the past dozen years, he was never quite prepared for how beautiful it was in the fall. This time of year, he liked to spend every spare minute at home. On this particular evening he had made the fifteen-minute drive from work, even though he had only an hour, affording him exactly thirty minutes at the dinner table before he had to head back.

Catherine tossed a pill into her mouth, washed it down with a few swallows of water and snapped the cap back on the bottle.

"There's more shepherd's pie, if you want," she said.

"No, I'm fine. That was great," Cardinal said. He was trying to corner the last peas on his plate.

"There's no dessert, unless you want cookies."

"I always want cookies. The question is whether I want to be hoisted out of here by a forklift."

Catherine took her plate and glass into the kitchen.

"What time are you heading out?" he called after her.

"Right now. It's dark, the moon is up. Why not?"

Cardinal glanced outside. The full moon, an orange disc riding low above the lake, was quartered by the mullions of their window.

"You're taking pictures of the moon? Don't tell me you're going into the calendar business."

But Catherine wasn't listening. She had disappeared down to the basement, and he could hear her pulling things off the shelves in her darkroom. Cardinal put the leftovers in the fridge and slotted his dishes into the dishwasher.

Catherine came back upstairs, zipped up her camera bag and dumped it beside the door while she put on her coat. It was a golden tan colour with brown leather trim on the cuffs and collar. She pulled a scarf from a hook and wrapped it once, twice, about her neck, then undid it again.

"No," she said to herself. "It'll be in the way."

"How long is this expedition of yours?" Cardinal said, but his wife didn't hear him. They'd been married nearly thirty years, but she still kept him guessing. Sometimes when she was going out to photograph, she would be chatty and excited, telling him every detail of her project until he was cross-eyed with the fine points of focal lengths and f-stops. Other times he wouldn't know what she was planning until she emerged from her darkroom days or weeks later, clutching her prints like trophies from a personal safari. Tonight she was subdued.

"What time do you think you'll get back?" Cardinal said.

Catherine tied a short plaid scarf around her neck and tucked it inside her jacket. "Does it matter? I thought you had to go back to work."

"I do. Just curious."

"Well, I'll be home long before you." She pulled her hair out from under her scarf and shook her head. Cardinal caught a whiff of her shampoo, a faint almondy smell. She sat down on the bench by the front door and opened her camera bag again. "Split-field filter. I knew I forgot something."

She disappeared downstairs for a few moments and came back with the filter, which she dropped into the camera bag. Cardinal had no idea what a split-field filter might be.

"You going to the government dock again?" In the spring Catherine had done a series of photos on the shore of Lake Nipissing when the ice was breaking up. Great white slabs of ice stacking themselves up like geological strata.

"I've done the dock," Catherine said, frowning a little. She strapped a collapsible tripod to the bottom of the camera bag. "Why all these questions?"

"Some people take pictures, other people ask questions."

"I wish you wouldn't. You know I don't like to talk about stuff ahead of time."

"Sometimes you do."

"Not this time." She stood up and slung the camera bag, bulky and heavy, over her shoulder.

"What a gorgeous night," Cardinal said when they were outside. He stood for a moment looking up at the stars, but the glow of the moon washed most of them out. He took a deep breath, inhaling smells of pine and fallen leaves. It was Catherine's favourite time of year too, but she wasn't paying attention just now. She got straight into her car, a maroon PT Cruiser she'd bought used a couple of years earlier, started the engine and pulled out of the drive.

Cardinal followed her in the Camry along the dark, curving highway that took them into town. As they approached the lights at the Highway 11 bypass, Catherine signalled and shifted into the left lane. Cardinal continued on through the intersection, heading down Sumner toward the police station.

Catherine was headed toward the east end of town, and he briefly wondered where she was going. But it was always good to see her involved in her work, and she was taking her medication. If she was a little moody, that was okay. She'd been out of the psychiatric hospital for a year now. Last time she had been out for nearly two years when she suddenly embarked on a manic episode that put her in hospital for three months. But as long as she was taking her medication, Cardinal didn't let himself worry too much.

—

It was a Tuesday night, and not much was going on in the criminal world. Cardinal spent the next couple of hours catching up on paperwork. They'd had the annual carpet cleaning done and the air was rich with flowery chemicals and the smell of wet carpet. The only other detective on duty was Ian McLeod, and even McLeod, the station loudmouth during the day, maintained a comparative solemnity at night.

Cardinal was putting a rubber band round a file he had just closed when McLeod's florid face appeared over the acoustic divider that separated their desks.

"Hey, Cardinal. I have to give you a head's up. It's about the mayor."

"What's he want?"

"Came in last night when you were off. He wanted to put in a missing-person report on his wife. Problem is, she's not really missing. Everybody in town knows where she is except the goddam mayor."

"She's still having the affair with Reg Wilcox?"

"Yeah. In fact she was seen last night with our esteemed director of sanitation. Szelagy's on a stakeout at the Birches motel, keeping an eye on the Porcini brothers. They got out of Kingston six months ago and seem to have the idea they can actually get back into business up here. Anyways, Szelagy's reporting back and happens to mention he sees the mayor's wife coming out of Room 12 with Reggie Wilcox. I was never keen on the jerk myself— I don't know what women see in him."

"He's a good-looking guy."

"Oh, come on. He looks like one of those Sears guys modelling the suits." By way of imitation, McLeod gave him a three-quarter profile with a fake-hearty grin.

"Some people consider that handsome," Cardinal said. "Though not on you."

"Well, some people can kiss my—Anyway, I told His Worship last night, I said, Look, your wife is not missing. She's an adult. She's been seen downtown. If she's not coming home, that's apparently her choice at this particular moment in time."

"What'd he say to that?"

"'Who saw her? Where? What time?' Same questions anybody'd ask. I told him I wasn't at liberty to say. She'd been seen in the vicinity of Worth and MacIntosh, and we could not file a missing-person report at this time. She's at the Birches again with Wilcox. I told Feckworth to come on down, you'd be happy to talk to him."

"What the hell did you do that for?"

"He'll take it better from you. Him and me don't get along so good."

"You don't get along with anyone so good."

"Now, that's just hurtful."

—

While he was waiting for the mayor to arrive, Cardinal made out an expense report for the previous month and wrote up the top sheet on a case he had just closed. He found his thoughts wandering to Catherine. She had been doing well for the past year, and was back teaching at the community college this semester. But she had seemed a little distant at dinner, a little impatient, in a way that might indicate some preoccupation other than her photographic project. Catherine was in her late forties and going through menopause, which played havoc with her moods and necessitated constant tweaking of her medication. If she seemed a little distant, well, there was no shortage of plausible reasons. On the other hand, how well do we really know the people we love? Just look at the mayor.

When His Worship Mayor Lance Feckworth arrived, Cardinal took him to one of the interview rooms so they could talk in private.

"I want to get to the bottom of this," the mayor told him. "A full investigation." Feckworth was a lumpy little man, much given to bow ties, and was perched uncomfortably on the edge of a plastic seat that was usually occupied by suspects. "I know I'm mayor, and that doesn't give me the right to more attention than any other voter, but I don't expect less, either. What if she's had an accident of some kind?"

Feckworth was not much of a mayor. During his tenure, all the city council seemed to do was study problems endlessly and agree to let them drift. But he was usually an affable man, ready with a joke or a slap on the back. It was unsettling to see him in pain, as if a building one had grown used to over the years had suddenly been painted a garish colour.

As gently as possible, Cardinal pointed out that Mrs. Feckworth had been seen in town the previous night, and there had been no major accidents that week.

"Damn it, why is my entire police force telling me she's been seen around town but you won't say where or by who? How would you feel if it was your wife? You'd want to know the truth, right?"

"Yes, I would."

"Then I suggest you explain to me exactly what is going on, Detective. Otherwise, I'll just have to deal directly with Chief Kendall, and you can be sure I won't have anything good to say about you or that lunkhead McLeod."

Which was how Cardinal came to be sitting in his car with the mayor of Algonquin Bay in the courtyard of the Birches motel. Despite its name, the Birches was nowhere near a birch tree. It was not near a tree of any kind, being located in the heart of downtown on MacIntosh Street. In fact, it was no longer even the Birches motel, having been taken over by Sunset Inns at least two years previously, but everybody still called it the Birches.

Cardinal was parked a dozen paces from Room 12. Szelagy was parked across the lot, but they didn't acknowledge one another. Cardinal rolled the window down a little to keep the glass from fogging up. Even here in the middle of downtown, you could smell fallen leaves and from someone's fireplace the comforting smell of woodsmoke.

"You're telling me she's in there?" the mayor said. "My wife's in that room?"

Surely he must know, Cardinal thought. How could it get to this stage—his wife staying out for days at a time and renting motel rooms—without his knowing?

"I don't believe it," Feckworth said. "It's too tawdry." But there was less conviction in his voice now, as if seeing the actual motel room door was beginning to shatter his faith. "Cynthia's a loyal person," he added. "She prides herself on it."

Cynthia Feckworth had in fact been sleeping her way around Algonquin Bay for at least the past four years; the mayor was the only one who didn't know it. And who am I to tear off his blinders? Cardinal asked himself. Who am I to refuse anyone the sweet anaesthetic of denial?

"Oh, she couldn't be screwing someone else. That would be—if she's letting another man . . . that's it. I'll dump her. You watch me. Oh, God, if she's doing those things . . ." Feckworth groaned and hid his face in his hands.

As if summoned by his anguish, the door to Room 12 opened and a man stepped out. He had the perfectly groomed look of a catalogue model: take advantage of our mid-autumn sale on men's windbreakers.

"It's Reg Wilcox," the mayor said. "Sanitation. What would Reg be doing here?"

Wilcox ambled to his Ford Explorer with the slouchy, smug air of the well laid. Then he backed out of his space and drove off.

"Well, at least Cynthia wasn't in there. That's something," Feckworth said. "Maybe I should just head home now and hope for the best."

The door to Room 12 opened again and an attractive woman peered out for a moment before closing the door behind her. She buttoned up her coat against the chill night air and headed toward the exit.

The mayor jumped out of the car and ran to block her path. Cardinal rolled up his window, not wanting to hear. His cellphone buzzed.

"Cardinal, why the hell don't you answer your bloody radio?"

"I'm in my own car, Sergeant Flower. It's too boring to explain."

"All right, listen. We got a caller says there's a dead one behind Gateway condos. You know the new building?"

"The Gateway? Just off the bypass? I didn't even realize it was finished yet. Are we sure it isn't a drunk sleeping it off?"

"We're sure. Patrol on the scene already confirmed."

"All right. I'm just a few blocks away."

The mayor and his wife were quarrelling. Cynthia Feckworth had her arms folded across her chest, head bowed. Her husband faced her, hands extended, palms out, in the classic gesture of the pleading mate. An employee was outlined in the doorway of the motel office, watching.

The mayor didn't even notice as Cardinal drove away.

—

The Gateway building was in the east end of town, one of the few high-rises in an area that was breaking out in new strip malls every day. In fact the ground floor of the building was a mini-mall with a dry cleaner, a convenience store and a large computer-repair concern called CompuClinic that had moved here from Main Street. The businesses had been open for a while, but many of the building's apartments were still unsold. Road crews were working on a new cloverleaf to accommodate traffic to and from the burgeoning neighbourhood, if it could be called a neighbourhood. Cardinal had to drive through a gauntlet of orange witches' hats and then detour by the new Tim Hortons and Home Depot to get there.

He passed a row of newly built "townhomes," most still unoccupied, although lights were on in a few of them. There was a PT Cruiser parked in front of the last one, and Cardinal thought for a second that it was Catherine's. Once or twice a year he had such moments: a sudden worry that Catherine was in trouble—manic and somewhere dangerous, or depressed and suicidal— and then relief to find it was not so.

He pulled into the Gateway's driveway and parked under a sign that said Resident Parking Only; Visitors Park on Street. A uniformed cop was standing beside a ribbon of crime scene tape.

"Oh, hi, Sergeant," he said as Cardinal approached. He looked about eighteen years old, and Cardinal could not for the life of him remember his name. "Got a dead woman back there. Looks like she took a nasty fall. Thought I'd better secure a perimeter till we know what's what."

Cardinal looked beyond him into the area behind the building. All he could see were a Dumpster and a couple of cars.

"Did you touch anything?"

"Um, yeah. I checked the body for a pulse and there wasn't one. And I searched pockets for ID but didn't find any. Could be a resident, I guess, went off one of those balconies."

Cardinal looked around. Usually there was a small crowd at such scenes. "No witnesses? No one heard anything?"

"Building's mostly empty, I think, except for the businesses on the ground floor. There was no one around when I got here."

"Okay. Let me borrow your flashlight."

The kid handed it over and let Cardinal by before attaching the end of the tape to a utility pole.

Cardinal walked in slowly, not wanting to ruin the scene by assuming the kid's idea of a fall was correct. He went by the Dumpster, which seemed to be full of old computers. A keyboard dangled over the side by its cable, and there were a couple of circuit boards that appeared to have exploded on the ground.

The body was just beyond the Dumpster, face down, dressed in a tan fall coat with leather at the cuffs.

Just like Catherine's, Cardinal thought.

"I don't see any of the windows or doors open on any of the balconies up there," the young cop said. "Probably the super'll be able to give us an ID."

"Her ID's in the car," Cardinal said.

The young cop looked around. There were two cars parked along the side of the building.

"I don't get it," the young cop said. "You know which car is hers?"

But Cardinal did not appear to be listening. The young cop watched in astonishment as Sergeant John Cardinal—

star player on the CID team, veteran of the city's highest-profile cases, legendary for his meticulous approach to crime scenes—went down on his knees in the pool of blood and cradled the shattered woman in his arms.